Murder
at Union
Station

Also by Margaret Truman
in Large Print:

Bess W. Truman
Murder at Ford's Theatre
Murder at the FBI
Murder at the Kennedy Center
Murder at the Library of Congress
Murder at the National Gallery
Murder at the Watergate
Murder in Georgetown
Murder in Havana
Murder in the CIA
Murder in the Smithsonian
Murder in the Supreme Court

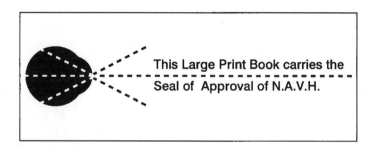

This Large Print Book carries the
Seal of Approval of N.A.V.H.

Murder at Union Station

A Capital Crimes Novel

Margaret Truman

Thorndike Press • Waterville, Maine

Published in 2005 by arrangement with
The Ballantine Publishing Group, a division of
Random House, Inc.

Thorndike Press® Large Print Basic.

The tree indicium is a trademark of Thorndike Press.

The text of this Large Print edition is unabridged.
Other aspects of the book may vary from the original edition.

Set in 16 pt. Plantin by Myrna S. Raven.

Printed in the United States on permanent paper.

Library of Congress Cataloging-in-Publication Data

Truman, Margaret, 1924–
    Murder at Union Station : a capital crimes novel /
Margaret Truman.
      p. cm.
    ISBN 0-7862-7123-X (lg. print : hc : alk. paper)
    1. Union Station (Washington, D.C.) — Fiction.
2. Informers — Crimes against — Fiction.
3. Washington (D.C.) — Fiction.   4. Organized crime —
Fiction.   5. Authors — Fiction.   6. Large type books.
I. Title.
PS3570.R82M7548 2005
   813′.54—dc22   2004059820

In memory of William Wallace Daniel

As the Founder/CEO of NAVH, the only national health agency solely devoted to those who, although not totally blind, have an eye disease which could lead to serious visual impairment, I am pleased to recognize Thorndike Press* as one of the leading publishers in the large print field.

Founded in 1954 in San Francisco to prepare large print textbooks for partially seeing children, NAVH became the pioneer and standard setting agency in the preparation of large type.

Today, those publishers who meet our standards carry the prestigious "Seal of Approval" indicating high quality large print. We are delighted that Thorndike Press is one of the publishers whose titles meet these standards. We are also pleased to recognize the significant contribution Thorndike Press is making in this important and growing field.

Lorraine H. Marchi, L.H.D.
Founder/CEO
NAVH

* Thorndike Press encompasses the following imprints: Thorndike, Wheeler, Walker and Large Print Press.

ONE

A nasty squall had blown across Pitts Bay earlier in the day, the wind tossing sheets of water against the landmark pink facade of the famed Hamilton Princess Hotel. Blue sky and sun followed the storm; the hotel was now bathed in lambent light.

Kathryn Jalick unlatched the sliding glass door of the second-floor suite, slid it open, and stepped out onto the small balcony overlooking the bay. She'd carried a large, fluffy white towel with her from the bathroom, which she used to wipe residual water from the two plastic chairs and glass-topped table. She returned inside to retrieve a glass of white wine she'd poured from a bottle purchased that morning in one of Hamilton's downtown liquor stores, and took a chair.

Below was a pitch-n-putt green on which two men were engaged in conversation between putts. She knew both, one better than the other.

She'd been dating Richard Marienthal

for three years. The anniversary of their first meeting was Tuesday of next week; marking such dates and occasions was important to Kathryn, and she was good at it.

They'd met at Irish Times, a popular place a block east of Union Station, in the northwest corner of the Capitol Hill area. Irish Times was one of three establishments within a block of each other catering to those seeking a wee bit o' Ireland; The Dubliner and Powers Court Restaurant were the other two. A hundred years ago, when nearby Union Station was on the drawing board, its planned location was on the edge of Swampoodle, an infamous Irish slum, which was said to be the ideal place to turn a dishonest dollar. Those days were, of course, gone. A foul swamp had been transformed into a thriving neighborhood anchored by the station. If there were such a thing in Washington as an Irish neighborhood — which there isn't — the area around North Capitol and F Streets would have to do. Although the pubs there were practically interchangeable — same beers, same atmosphere, same spirited conversation — patrons were fiercely loyal, including Marienthal, who wasn't Irish but for whom authenticity was important, and who considered Irish

Times to be, well, more authentic than the others.

He had been at the bar with Winard Jackson, an up-and-coming tenor sax player, when another friend brought Kathryn and a female friend into the room. If there was such a thing as love at first sight, Kathryn experienced it that evening, and try as she might to appear cool and disinterested, her immediate infatuation with him was almost comically obvious. Marienthal's black musician friend, Jackson, eventually whispered in his ear, "I think the lady's smitten with you, man. Time for me to split." Marienthal and Kathryn were soon alone at the bar, where they lingered over fresh, bubbly tap beers.

It became apparent to Kathryn as they drank and talked that this Richard Marienthal was different from other young men she'd met since moving to Washington six years ago to pursue a career as a librarian. First hired by the Daughters of the American Revolution's Library of Genealogy and Local History, she later landed a plum job at the prestigious Library of Congress, where she still worked. The daughter of a plainspoken Kansas pharmacist, Kathryn found most other men with whom she'd worked or dated too slick and sure of themselves, consumed with their appearance, terminally ambitious, and always pretending to know more than they did. Like Geoff Lowe, the young man practicing putting with Rich on the grounds of the Hamilton Princess.

Marienthal was none of those things. He was big and tousled, a teddy bear type. His face was boyish, although she judged him to be in his late twenties or early thirties. His smile, too, was boyish, meaning it looked the way it probably had when he was a little kid, with a hint of mischief in it. Smiles change with age, she knew, but his hadn't. She liked it. This night in Irish Times, he wore a gray-and-red-checked shirt, baggy chino pants, and a tan safari jacket frayed at the neck.

Slightly tipsy, they decided to have dinner together, after which he escorted her home to her apartment on the fringe of Foggy Bottom. She hoped he would kiss her good night, which he did, lightly, like a campaign promise, without commitment. She hoped he would commit to seeing her again, which he also did, saying he would call the next day. He kept his word.

"He's so gentle and kind, and really funny," Kathryn told her sister back in Topeka on the phone that night. "And he's a writer, too. Very handsome in a rugged sort of way, but not macho, if you know what I mean. He's tall. I mean, a lot taller than me. I kidded that we'd have trouble dancing together. Know what he said? He said he'd install a little microphone in one of his shirt buttons and I could talk into it." She giggled. "Know what else he told me? He told me my glasses not only make me look smart, they make me look sexy." Kathryn Jalick had worn big round-shaped glasses since junior high school. She had never been happy about having to wear them — until this night. She and her sister laughed. Kathryn's sudden acceptance of her black-rimmed glasses was symbolic of her acceptance of the large young man.

Three months later, she moved into Marienthal's apartment in the Capitol Hill district, a block from the bustling Eastern Market at Seventh and C Streets, where they'd been living since, discovering more about each other every day and liking what they learned; haunting the market in search of fresh produce and honing their cooking skills for small dinner parties with friends; lazing in front of the small fireplace when the winds blew and ice covered the streets of Washington, D.C.; and strolling the neighborhood on Sunday

11

mornings, buying the papers and going back to bed, where they usually spent the rest of the day under the covers catching up on the news and with each other.

She wrapped the white terrycloth robe tighter around her against a chilled wind off the bay and continued to watch Rich and Geoff Lowe on the putting green. She couldn't hear their words, but she knew what they were discussing. How could she not? That's all Richard had talked about for the past year. He was consumed with it, driven. "I'm a man on a mission," he would often say when she questioned the long hours he worked on the book. She wished Rich hadn't gotten involved with Lowe, a pretentious sort if she'd ever seen one, and she'd seen plenty of them in Washington, D.C., basking in the reflected glory of their powerful political bosses, like secretaries to high-profile physicians who assume their bosses' status and press it upon patients.

Meeting like this in Bermuda was Lowe's idea, silly cloak-and-dagger stuff, Kathryn thought. She didn't like the influence Lowe seemed to have developed over Rich. The man she'd fallen in love with had been changing before her eyes since hooking up with the young Senate staffer, and not for the better.

Marienthal looked up and waved, gave her that boyish grin. She returned the greeting and raised her glass. "Up in a minute," he yelled, and walked off the green with Lowe.

They had dinner that night in the hotel's Harley's Bistro, a large, modern room with huge windows overlooking the pool and Hamilton Harbor beyond, Rich, Kathryn, Lowe, and Ellen Kelly, who worked with Geoff but who was obviously more than that; they shared the same hotel room. Kathryn wished she and Rich could spend a week alone in romantic Bermuda, but that wasn't in the cards. He'd been away for almost three weeks, returning to Washington from Israel only yesterday and announcing they were flying to Bermuda to meet Lowe and Ellen Kelly, who'd already been there a few days enjoying themselves.

Unsurprisingly, Lowe dominated the dinner table conversation, ranting about politics, which, Washington style, he seemed to feel only he had a handle on, and vilifying the current administration and president. Adam Parmele was in his first term and running for a second. Geoff

13

Lowe was a short man, not much taller than Kathryn, who was five feet, four inches tall. He was chunky, with a large face dominated by a broad nose that would not be out of place on a professional prizefighter. Balding prematurely, he had strands of blond hair long at the sides. He was type A personality personified; even when seated he seemed to be in motion.

Rich and Kathryn had heard Lowe's lectures too many times over the past year to react with anything but feigned interest, and she sensed a similar paralysis in Ellen, although Lowe's colleague and girlfriend seemed to exhibit dutiful interest in his words. But the redheaded, green-eyed Kelly also seemed aware of Rich and Kathryn's situation because she would turn the conversation around to them whenever Lowe took a break.

"How was Israel this time, Rich?" Ellen asked.

Marienthal laughed and sipped his wine. "Great place. Same as it's always been," he said. "I've been there so often lately I ought to start wearing a yarmulke."

"Adam Parmele's approach to the Israeli-Palestinian situation, if you can call it an approach, is ridiculous," Lowe said, obviously not interested in learning more from Rich. "His whole foreign policy is a joke. Anybody with half a brain could have seen that when he was running — waffling, saying one thing one day, reversing himself the next." He shook his head and sat back in his armchair. "Another four years with this liberal bumbler and we'll really be down the drain — the economy, crime, foreign policy, all of it."

Again, Ellen changed the subject out of deference to Rich and Kathryn, asking Kathryn a question about her job at the library, which led to a lengthy tale of how she'd only recently been promoted into the rare documents room, which answer carried them through dessert but stopped short of coffee with Sambuca.

They ended the evening in the lobby. At least Kathryn thought it had.

"Flight's at noon," Lowe said. "Airport shuttle leaves at nine-thirty. Come on, I'll buy you a drink."

Marienthal looked at Kathryn, whose face said she wanted to get away from the other couple.

"Thanks, no," Marienthal replied.

"There's something we still have to go over," Lowe said. "Why don't you two gals browse the shops? Some of them are still open."

Kathryn hoped Rich would remain firm in declining a drink with Geoff, but he disappointed her. If there were one thing about him that sometimes bothered her, it was how he always seemed to understand both sides of any debate. On the one hand, it was an appealing trait, often heading off potential arguments. On the other hand, it was waffling, and he was easily led at times, the most persuasive — or the last — voice heard having the most influence on him.

"We'll make it quick, hon," he told her. "Meet you in the room in an hour."

Kathryn and Ellen watched the two men cross the lobby and disappear into the wood-paneled Colony Pub.

"I'm beat," Kathryn said. "Think I'll head up to the room."

"Me, too," Ellen said. "By the way, it's great what Rich is doing, Kathryn."

Kathryn's curt nod did not convey what she really thought. She wished Rich had never agreed to Lowe's proposal. If only he hadn't. If only they could turn back the clock a year. If only she didn't have this nagging feeling of foreboding that kept her awake nights. If only . . .

TWO

He sat in seat 16B, at the window. The seat next to him was empty. He hadn't said much during the flight. When he'd asked for a glass of water or a pillow, the Delta flight attendant had had to lean close to understand him. He spoke in a soft, low, raspy voice, an old man who'd lost the ability to project.

"He's so cute," she said to a colleague as they stood in the galley of the jet. "Have you ever seen such a funny toupee?"

"I've never seen an orange one before."

"It's supposed to be red, I think. It looks like plastic."

"I like men who accept getting bald and don't wear them."

She delivered the tomato juice he'd ordered.

"Thank you. Thank you very much."

"Sure. Anything you need, just ask."

He sipped his juice and pulled his airline tickets from the inside pocket of the jacket of his wrinkled, ill-fitting gray suit, something he'd done dozens of times since

17

taking off from Barcelona. He'd recently acknowledged — to himself, never to others — that he'd become forgetful lately, entering rooms without remembering why he'd gone there, misplacing things, throwing away important receipts.

He'd been afraid of losing his tickets since they had arrived by Federal Express a week ago, delivered to the door of the apartment he shared with Sasha on Basel Street, in the old city. He'd put them in his small, hard-sided suitcase and checked on them every hour, it seemed to Sasha, with whom he'd begun living since shortly after having arrived in Tel Aviv twelve years ago.

"Crazy old man," she'd shouted at him in her native Hebrew when, after looking in the wrong section of the suitcase, he'd failed to find the tickets and panicked. She went to the correct pocket, yanked the tickets from it, and threw them at him. He reacted the way he'd been reacting to her for the past few years. He returned the tickets to the suitcase, locked it, and sat on the small balcony that overlooked the busy street. He'd become adroit at ignoring Sasha and her outbursts, which he knew was the most effective way of annoying her. He sat stoically, deep in thought, thinking of the past, which he did with increasing frequency. Although his memory of recent events had slipped, his long-term memory was still sharp.

She had come to the balcony carrying a glass of Italian wine for him. A large ashtray on a small table overflowed with spent cigarettes, and she added another to the pile.

"*Todah,*" he said, thanking her in Hebrew and taking the glass from her.

"*Prego,*" she answered in his native Italian and patted his hand.

"You should stop smoking," he said. "You smoke all the time, day and night."

"You smoked when I met you," she said.

"Yes, but I quit, huh? Cold turkey. For my health."

Rather than argue, she returned inside, lighted a cigarette, and sat at the kitchen table, on which another full ashtray sat. She knew he was right, but she also knew she couldn't quit. Not in Tel Aviv, where it seemed everyone smoked, maybe to calm the nerves. What was a cigarette compared to a Palestinian suicide bomber?

He continued to sit alone on the balcony, reflecting on better days. Healthier days. "*La vecchiaia!*" he muttered, followed by a string of obscenities in Italian and Hebrew, cursing having become old.

The flight attendant reminded him to buckle his seat belt as the flight approached its final destination, Newark Liberty International Airport. He'd gone to the lavatory half a dozen times during the flight, painfully making his way up the aisle, grasping the backs of seats for support, and thanking the flight attendants profusely when they helped steady him on his way back.

She took the cane from his lap and placed it on the floor beneath his feet.

"Thank you," he said. *"Grazie."*

"Visiting family?" she asked before leaving him to attend to her pre-landing duties.

He looked up at her with cold, wary eyes surrounded by loose skin, yellowed from the chemotherapy. She was taken aback for a moment; his gray eyes testified to having seen things in his life she'd never seen, nor would want to.

"No, no," he said. "It is, ah — it is business."

She wished him well on the rest of his journey, patted his liver-spotted hand, and left. He looked out the window at the clouds through which they descended. He imagined the clouds would support his body and thought it would be nice to be nestled in them. The jet broke free of the overcast and New Jersey was sprawled out below. Louis Russo closed his eyes, picked up the cane, wrapped gnarled fingers around it, and waited for the plane to land.

"Excuse me," he said to a Delta agent directing passengers to connecting flights. "The train to Washington? The Amtrak train?"

"Yes, sir, it's . . . Would you like a cart to take you?"

"Yes, please. That would be good."

An electric-powered cart driven by an airport employee delivered him to the rail link between the airport and Amtrak. He stood stoically on the platform, leaning on his cane, the small carry-on suitcase at his feet, waiting for the Acela Regional train, which had left New York's Penn Station a half hour earlier. He'd used the men's room at the station and considered buying a hot dog and soft drink at a Nathan's stand, but his stomach was unsettled from the bumpy flight and he thought better of it. He stepped into a phone booth, pulled a slip of paper from a pocket, and dialed the number written on it in large letters.

The train pulled smoothly into the station as Russo completed his call. He showed his business class ticket to the female conductor, who pointed to a car toward the rear of the train. He chose one of the comfortable blue seats at the end of the car, close to the restrooms and the café car, wearily settled into it, and sighed. It had been a long, tiring day.

He'd departed from Israel's Ben Gurion Airport at dawn, flying to Barcelona and waiting for the Delta flight to the United States. Sasha had packed his medications in a plastic bag and proudly showed him a red-and-blue-striped tie she'd bought for the trip. "You want to look nice," she'd said. He thanked her and checked that his tickets were safe, swelling the inside pocket of his suit jacket. "Don't forget the yellow pills at lunchtime," she said as he climbed into the taxi in front of the apartment building. "And call the doctor if you don't feel well." His Israeli oncologist had given him the name of a physician at George Washington University's hospital.

He turned as the cab pulled away from the curb, saw her wave, wiggled his fingers in response, and sat back.

Israeli security forces had stopped them twice at checkpoints. Russo was asked to show them his airline tickets, which he did, and they were allowed to proceed.

Now, as the train pulled from the station on its way to Washington, and after he'd presented his ticket to the conductor, he leaned his head back and closed his eyes. There had been a moment while waiting for the train at the Newark station that he considered going in the other direction, to New York City, where he'd been born and raised, and where the happier days of his life had been spent. But that thought came and went. He would go to Washington where he was expected to be, where they would be waiting for him.

THREE

Like most professional bartenders, Bob McIntyre was adept at doing and hearing many things at once — mixing drinks while taking in conversation at his small bar, and listening to the latest news from CNN that played on a plasma screen TV behind the bar. He mixed martinis, stirred not shaken, heard the CNN anchor report on news breaking in the Middle East, and listened to the arguments in progress between members of the Capitol View Restaurant's luncheon club, where congressional staffers and mid-level executives paid fifty dollars a month for the privilege of having lunch at the restaurant, on the roof level of the Hyatt Regency Hotel on Capitol Hill.

McIntyre placed two frosted, stemmed glasses containing gin and vermouth on the bar in front of Geoff Lowe and a portly man named Rex, who managed a branch of the Riggs Bank. They were discussing President Parmele's recent speech in which he opened the door to the possibility of raising taxes to bring a ballooning deficit under control.

"Can you believe it?" Lowe snarled, sipping his drink. "Can you friggin' believe it? He wants to raise taxes so there's more money for the government to spend on Democrat giveaway programs."

The bank manager laughed heartily. "Raisin' taxes when you're runnin' for a second term is pretty damn dumb, even for a politician."

"At least he didn't come up with 'read my lips' BS," a Parmele defender said from the end of the bar. "At least he's honest."

Rex turned to McIntyre, who was pouring red wine into a glass. "What do you think, Bobby?" he asked the veteran barman.

"Well, balancing the budget's a good thing," McIntyre replied. "Wish I could balance my own. On the other hand, nobody wants to pay more taxes."

Smooth. He was good at seeing both sides — or at least sounding as though he did. What he thought privately about Washington's major and sometimes seemingly *only* topic of conversation was another matter, reserved for discussion with regulars later at night who wouldn't comment on his views with the size of their tips. At lunch, there were certain members whose beliefs were so set in stone that a mild challenge, even when their opinions were based upon shaky facts, was akin to spitting in their drinks. Lowe was one of those, his strident viewpoints mirroring those of his graying, crusty, outspoken boss, Karl Widmer, the senior senator from Alaska.

McIntyre glanced at Ellen Kelly, who'd turned from the conversation to speak with a woman, a House staffer from Mississippi, about a less volatile but no less provocative topic — the sexual scandal du jour.

How could a nice, pretty, polite young woman like Ellen put up with Lowe's bellicosity? McIntyre wondered. Did he yap away about politics in bed? Probably.

"Another martooni, Geoff?" McIntyre asked, noting the empty glass.

"No can do, Bobby," Lowe said. "Can't afford to nod off during one of the old man's speeches this afternoon." He laughed. "At least not before he does." His moment of levity was fleeting; he returned to his condemnation of the sitting president and dragged a reluctant Ellen Kelly back into the conversation. McIntyre smiled to himself as he watched the young woman with the curly red hair, the large green eyes, and a splatter of freckles across her nose and upper cheeks enter into the discussions, which by now included others at the bar and one or two nearby tables. It was impossible to know whose political views prevailed on any given day, although the anti-Parmele Republicans tended to talk louder and use more vitriolic language than their Democratic counterparts. If noise levels dictated a winner, Geoff Lowe and his supporters usually carried the day.

Lowe and Kelly brought plates from the buffet to the bar and ate there. McIntyre continued to mix drinks for those at the bar and to fill orders brought by the waitress, Mei, who was as adroit as McIntyre at sidestepping attempts to engage. The lavishly appointed room offered a stunning view of the domed Capitol, but not much of what was new in politics, where not much was ever new. His practiced ears picked up on what his wards were saying, particularly Lowe, who pontificated on why Parmele would fail in his bid for a second term. "I'm telling you," he told a Democratic staffer from the Hill who'd joined the knot of people at the bar, "Parmele's got plenty of skeletons in his closet, and Widmer knows what they are and where they are." To Ellen: "Am I right, Ellen?"

She nodded and finished the Maryland crab cake she'd carried from the buffet.

Ellen Kelly had been working for Senator Widmer for less than a year; Lowe had been with the Alaska pol for seven. While she basically shared Lowe's right-wing views of politics, she would never be, could never be, as strident as he and their boss, Senator Widmer, were in defense of them. Although she'd majored in political science at Georgetown University, for her, politics had never reached the level of passion. She'd sought a job on Capitol Hill following graduation and was recommended to Geoff Lowe by a mutual friend. He hired her almost immediately following a cursory interview, partially because her educational record at Georgetown was solid, more because he loved her looks. Their relationship commenced during her second month on the job. It wasn't as though she'd fallen for him, at least not in the classic way. Physically he wasn't her type, nor was he particularly attentive or loving, although he was capable of performing thoughtful acts from time to time — flowers without an occasion to prompt them, a surprise dinner out, an endearing comment now and then. The attraction was, she eventually decided when allowing retrospective thoughts to intrude upon her busy days and nights, Geoff's dynamism, and the clout he possessed by virtue of his boss's powerful position in the Senate. It wasn't a forever relationship, she knew. It simply had come about and would run its course.

Lowe's cell phone rang. It wasn't always easy to know whose cell phone was ringing, for so many went off throughout lunch. Lowe had programmed his ring to play "Take Me Out to the Ball Game," which created a unique signature tone. Unless, of course, someone else did the same.

"Yeah?" Lowe turned away from the group and placed a finger in the ear opposite the one against which the small phone was pressed. Ellen watched as he squinted, as though that would help him hear better. "Yeah, okay. Thanks, Rich."

He snapped the phone shut and gave Ellen a thumbs-up. "Got to go," he announced to the others at the bar, standing and motioning for Ellen to join him. She looked at him quizzically. "No sweat," he said as they walked to the door. "Everything's on track."

FOUR

"How much longer to Washington?" Russo asked the conductor.

"Should be in Union Station in about forty-five minutes," she said.

He nodded and closed his eyes again, the gentle swaying of the train combining with his natural fatigue to cause drowsiness.

He'd bought a piece of Danish and coffee from the café car, but had to ask another passenger to carry it for him to his seat because he was unsteady on his feet. He silently cursed his increasing feebleness. And cursed the watery, lukewarm coffee.

There was a time — and it didn't seem very long ago — that he was strong and fast, a tough guy who could hold his own in a fight with anyone, including the bigger boys from the New York City neighborhood where he was born and raised. And he could run faster than any of them, which came in handy when boosting merchandise from local stores and having to outrun the owners, or when escaping from the local beat cop.

His father, Nicholas Russo, had come to New York from Italy as a young boy and worked hard to raise and support his growing family. After a series of odd jobs, he was hired by a local bakery to drive its delivery truck and had done that until he dropped dead of a heart attack at forty-eight, leaving his wife, Lillian, and six children without a source of support.

In a sense, his father's death liberated the fifteen-year-old Louis. He'd begun hanging out with local members of the Gambino family, whose social club was two doors down the street from the building in which the Russo family lived. His father had forbidden his son from hanging out with many of his newfound streetwise friends, and had smacked him one day when Louis returned with money earned by running errands for the mobsters. Now, with his father dead and the family really needing money, he felt free to pursue what soon became a full-time criminal career — loan-sharking, numbers collections, running prostitutes, and acting as an enforcer for his second family. It was in that role that he committed his first murder, whacking a Gambino soldier who'd been accused of holding back money, skimming from his loan-sharking operation. The twenty-one-year-old Russo took no particular pleasure from the act, nor did he suffer any particular pain. It was what he'd been paid to do, and he'd done it effectively, including dumping the body in a landfill. The body was eventually found and Louis attended the funeral, where he paid his respects to the victim's widow and children.

Those were good days, he mused, half asleep, dreams and fragments of such memories filtering in and out of his mind. Better days than what the last dozen years had been.

He straightened and looked at his watch. The conductor had said they were forty-five minutes from D.C.'s Union Station. That was fifteen minutes ago. He neatly gathered the paper in which the Danish had been wrapped, put it in the half-empty coffee cup, checked that his return airline tickets were still in his jacket pocket, and gazed out the window as the train neared its destination. Then, sitting up straight, he fell deeply asleep.

FIVE

UNION STATION

Joe Jenks had been shining shoes at Union Station for three years. If you were going to shine shoes for a living, you couldn't pick a better spot than the hundred-year-old beaux arts landmark, created in 1903 by an act signed by President Teddy Roosevelt, falling into disrepair over the ensuing years, but restored in the 1980s to an even greater architectural monument than it had been in its previous splendor. The working philosophy of its original architect, master builder Daniel H. Burnham, was "Make no little plans." Had Roosevelt known that the Wright Brothers would prove man's ability to fly a mere ten months after he'd put into motion the lavish plans for this centerpiece of rail transportation, he might not have called for such a grandiose design.

Working there as a bootblack was a dream come true for Jenks, who'd plied his trade on the street for too many years. It was comfortable working inside the sprawling station, now bright and beautiful, with all its shops and movie theaters, restaurants and services — a pleasant, fancy setting for spit-shining the shoes of important men and women passing through on their way to other cities and other business.

"Back when it opened in nineteen and eight," Jenks's grandfather, who had worked there as a Pullman porter, often told him, "old Union Station had some mighty fancy restaurants, like the old Savarin. My goodness, anybody who was anybody in the city dined there at the Savarin. Barbershop had a dozen chairs and a bootblack and a valet to press your clothes all nice and fine. Back then, Savarin was the only real decent place in all of D.C. where a white man could dine with a black man and nobody seemed to notice. Nobody seemed to care. Way it should be."

Although Jenks was the oldest by far of the three bootblacks at Exclusive Shoe Shine, his was the shortest tenure, so he worked chair 3, alongside the two younger men who didn't demonstrate the same sort of reverence Jenks had for the station. Once he'd started working there, he'd read up on the station's history and enjoyed it when a customer, usually an out-oftowner, climbed into his chair and asked questions about Union Station. That was when Joe Jenks shined, in both senses of the word.

His customer, a tall, slender, light-skinned black man dressed impeccably in a well-tailored tan suit, white shirt, and muted patterned green tie, and carrying a tan trench coat over his arm, had immediately pulled out a pair of half-glasses and opened a newspaper; no historical chitchat with this dude, Jenks knew. The man's shoes were expensive two-toned leather, pointy and with perforations across the toe. Jenks pegged him as an outlander, a visitor to D.C., his judgment helped by the *New York Times* in the man's hands.

The customer looked up occasionally from the newspaper to check the arrivals board.

"Meeting somebody?" Jenks asked as he put the finishing touches on the mirror shine he'd accomplished with his polish and brushes and rags.

"No. What do I owe you?"

Uppity, Jenks thought. *Probably owns a couple of slums.* "Six dollars, sir," he said.

The man stood, reached in his pocket, and pulled out a ten-dollar bill. Jenks went to give him change, but he'd already walked away in the direction of gate A-8, where the Metroliner from New York's Penn Station would be arriving.

"What he give you, man, four bucks?" asked a younger bootblack who'd watched the transaction.

"Yeah. Sometimes you can't figure a man up front, you know? Sometimes the really talky ones stiff you."

"I'd like to catch me about ten or twenty a those today," the younger man said with a laugh.

Jenks ignored him and watched his generous customer saunter toward the arrival gates. What's he all about? he wondered. Then passersby diverted his attention. That was one of the pleasures of shining in Union Station. Seventy thousand people passed through every day, a fascinating parade of humanity, and Joe Jenks had a front-row seat.

"You available?" a casually dressed white man asked.

"Yes, sir, jump right up in the chair."

"Been working here long?"

"Three years," Jenks said, pulling out the appropriate polishes.

"What's the best restaurant?"

"Oh, now, let me see. Lotsa good ones. Got about fifty casual places, you know, and seven or eight places for finer dining. You know, gourmet-type food. Back when it opened, there was the Savarin Restaurant, where . . ."

SIX

As Joe Jenks shined shoes in Union Station, dispensing historical insights to his customers, business as usual was being conducted in the J. Edgar Hoover Building, home to the Federal Bureau of Investigation. President Teddy Roosevelt created the FBI in 1908 to fight political corruption. Fortunately, the federal law enforcement agency eventually went on to focus on more manageable crime.

This day, a meeting took place in a secure room in the rear of the unlovely beige concrete Hoover Building, dedicated in 1975 and immediately branded a prime example of the architectural school known as New Brutalism. Two of the three men in the meeting were FBI special agents. The third, Timothy Stripling, had been a CIA operative, or still was; it was hard to know with such men, who spent their professional lives functioning in the shadows. Chain of command could seldom be applied to people like Stripling. He was one of many who worked for that gray entity known as the government, his various official titles not necessarily indicating his true affiliations.

"Where was he last seen?" Stripling was of medium build, medium height, moderately balding, almost nondescript. He was so average-looking that he didn't stand out in or out of a crowd.

"Tel Aviv," an agent answered.

"So much for the world-renowned crack Israeli Mosad," the other agent said.

"They're certain he's left the city?" Stripling asked.

"They are now. A little late at the switch. When we heard he might be coming here — your people told us that — we set up surveillance through the Mosad. But —"

"My people?" Stripling said, smiling.

"Yeah. Over at the Company."

"My former employer," Stripling said. "You know why I'm here. You know who I'm working this for. *Your* leader."

He'd received a call at home from Mark Roper, his last boss before he had officially retired from the CIA.

"Wake you?" Roper asked.

"No. It's eight-thirty. I've been up for hours."

Roper chuckled. "Now that you're a man of leisure, I figured you might be catching up on all the sleep I caused you to lose over the past year."

"You only thought I lost sleep, Mark. I took more naps on the job than you knew. What's up?"

"I thought you might be interested in some freelance work. Supplement the pension."

Stripling cradled the cordless phone between shoulder and ear, poured fresh coffee into his cup, and resumed his chair at the kitchen table in his Foggy Bottom town house. He was honest when he said he'd been up for hours, only he hadn't bothered getting dressed. He wore a robe over his pajamas, and slippers. The morning paper sat half read on the table.

"What's it pay?" he asked. "Minimum wage?"

"Slightly better. How's your love life?"

Stripling grimaced and looked out the window onto E Street N.W. Unlike those in colder climates who fall into a February depression and hibernate, Washingtonians tend to have the same reaction in summer. Heat and humidity fray tempers and wilt the psyche. This late July day promised to wilt even the heartiest of souls.

Roper's question about Stripling's love life had various meanings, Stripling knew.

Because he'd never married, there was the natural unreasonable speculation. There had been women in his life, plenty of them, but none had stuck. The truth was, he enjoyed female companionship but only in short bursts; he had limited patience with relationships that lingered beyond the initial phase. He knew what was behind Roper's question and ignored it. Under Roper's affable facade was a nasty disposition that he put to good use when wanting to get beneath someone's skin.

"Tell me more about this freelance assignment," Stripling said.

Three hours later, dressed in a light-weight blue suit, white shirt, and gray tie, he sat with a deputy attorney general in the Department of Justice building at Constitution Avenue and Tenth Street N.W. The middle-aged woman, whose dress and hairstyle reminded Stripling of actresses in the Hope-Crosby road movies of the forties, briefed him on what the attorney general expected. Stripling masked his annoyance at her tone. He was Tim, she was Mrs. Klaus; she never referred to her boss by name, always as the attorney general, never as Wayne Garson or Wayne or Mr. Garson or Garson.

"Tim, the attorney general expects you to —"

He noted on her ID tag that her first name was Gertrude, and called her that when they parted. She didn't look pleased. The hell with her, he thought as he walked from Justice to the Hoover Building, where the next meeting was scheduled. By the time he got there, his shirt and pants felt like they were glued to him, and the building's efficient air-conditioning turned everything clammy against his skin. He was not in a good mood.

"So let me ask you something," Stripling said to the two FBI agents in the room. "Why the interest in this guy Russo? What is he, a terrorist?"

A smile crossed one of the agent's faces. "The president might think so," he said.

Stripling started to ask another question but was cut off. "Look, Tim, we're not sure what this is all about. Need to know. What we *do* know is that Garson wants to know where this Mr. Louis Russo is."

"Why the assumption he's headed this way?" Stripling asked.

Shrugs.

"You said Parmele might consider him a terrorist," Stripling said. "Why?"

"Like we said, Tim, it's strictly need to know."

Sure, Stripling thought. You just happened to mention that the president had some interest in Mr. Russo, but you don't know why. Sure.

A knock on the door was followed by the entrance of an aide carrying a sheet of paper, which she handed to one of the agents. He put on his glasses, read it, and handed it to Stripling.

"Barcelona, then to Newark on Delta," Stripling said, reading from the sheet. "Nothing after that. Maybe he has relatives in New Jersey. New Jersey has a few Italians."

"We're convinced he's on his way here," an agent said. "U.S. Air shuttle? Amtrak? Doesn't need a reservation on either one. Look, Tim, we're supposed to not be involved in this. Officially, that is. The attorney general wants it kept outside the Bureau, which is why you're here. We don't know much about you except that you were covert with the Company, and Garson arranged for you to get involved through somebody over there."

"And all I have to do is find this Russo — if he *is* headed for Washington — and keep tabs on him. Right?"

"That's pretty much it. Here."

Stripling was handed a manila file folder. Inside was a black-and-white photograph. A small white label at the bottom of the picture had the name Louis Russo printed on it, and the date 1991.

"How old was he when this was taken?" Stripling asked.

"Not sure" was the reply.

Stripling was handed a slip of paper. Written on it was a phone number with a 212 area code, and the name Courtney Tresh.

"Who's he?" Stripling asked.

"She. NYPD. She can give you some background. Say you're from the Liberty Press."

"Liberty Press?"

"Uh-huh."

"Why don't *you* call her?" Stripling asked.

"Like we said, Garson wants us out of it."

Stripling again consulted the sheet of paper. "According to this, Russo should have landed at Newark hours ago. Hell, if he is coming to Washington, he's probably here by now."

One of the agents pulled a cell phone from a briefcase at his feet and gave it to Stripling.

"No, thanks, I have my own," Stripling said.

"Use this one," he was told. "We've got the number programmed in the computer. We'll get in touch if we come up with anything that might be of help to you. Don't call us. We'll call you. Thanks for coming in."

Stripling was to the door when one of the agents said, "The attorney general won't be happy if you don't find Russo."

"The attorney general. Garson, you mean."

When Stripling was gone, one of the agents asked the other, "Do you know any more than you let on about why the AG is so interested in Russo?"

"No. But you can bet that for Garson to take a personal interest, *his* boss has one, too."

SEVEN

"Damn!"

Rich Marienthal shifted into neutral and slapped the steering wheel with the palm of his hand. "Damn! What the hell is going on?"

"Must be an accident," Kathryn Jalick said from the passenger seat of the Subaru Outback.

Marienthal and Kathryn had been stalled in traffic for twenty minutes on the Lee Highway, halfway between Falls Church, Virginia, and Washington, only a few miles from D.C. They'd driven to Falls Church the previous day to attend the funeral of one of Kathryn's aunts. The post-funeral gathering was held at the home of one of the deceased's sons, a retired FBI agent who lived in the Falls Church area and who urged Rich and Kathryn to stay over. Marienthal balked at the suggestion, but Kathryn, pleased to be with family she seldom saw, prevailed.

Now, after a late start back to D.C. — "I told you we should have left more time," she'd chided cheerfully — they sat in the

traffic jam, Marienthal's frequently consulted wristwatch ticking off the minutes.

He leaned on the horn.

"That won't help anything," Kathryn
said.

He clicked on the radio and tuned to all-
news WTOP in search of a traffic report.

"He told me the train when he called,"
Marienthal growled. "He's due to arrive
any minute, if he's not there already." Another slap on the wheel, harder this time,
shook it, and Kathryn feared it might
break. She placed her hand on his thigh to
calm him, but it was a futile gesture. He
squirmed in his seat, leaned out the
window to look ahead, and blew the horn
again, causing the driver in front to turn
and gesture, not a friendly one.

While Marienthal fumed, Kathryn
thought less cheerfully about the past
twenty-four hours.

Lately she'd been caught between what
the reality of their relationship had become
and what she wanted it to be. The fact was,
things had slid downhill over the past
months, and she wasn't happy about it.
There hadn't been anything tangible to
point to, certainly nothing like physical
abuse or a suspicion that Rich might be

cheating on her. Her sister in Kansas, one of the few people in whom Kathryn confided, had asked whether Kathryn thought Rich might be seeing someone else.

"I'm sure he isn't," she'd replied, with a rueful laugh. "He doesn't have time to see me, let alone somebody else. He's so totally consumed with this book he's working on that —"

"What is the book about?" her sister asked. "You keep saying he's working on a book, but you never say what it's about."

Kathryn hated to lie to her sister. Their adult relationship had been grounded in honesty. But this was different. Rich had sworn her to secrecy, and she was determined to honor her promise to him.

"I'm really not sure," she fibbed. "You never can be sure what a book's about till you've read it. He's very secretive about it. You know how writers are." A nervous laugh.

"No, I don't, Kathy. I mean, I don't know any writers."

"Well, Rich is protective of . . . he's . . . well, he's secretive, that's all. I don't know how else to put it."

Her sister hesitated before asking, "Do you think you guys might break up?"

"I hope not. I know, I know, I've been

complaining a lot lately, and I don't mean to say bad things about Rich. He's really a sweetheart, a terrific guy."

"I'll take your word for it. When do we get to meet him?"

"Soon, I hope. I —"

"You were going to bring him out here over Christmas."

"He was — he was busy with the book."

"The book."

Kathryn laughed. "Yes, *the book*. Got to run. Love you. Later."

She'd cut that conversation short because she realized she'd been sounding like a broken record, complaining to her sister about how Marienthal had become distant from her, perpetually distracted, it seemed. Their lovemaking, which had been frequent and satisfying early in the relationship, had become only an occasional event over the past year. Was it because he'd lost interest in her as a sexual partner? Had he become bored with her? Would he seek a more appealing partner? There were so many attractive, willing women in Washington, although she didn't consider herself unattractive. She'd put a few pounds on since they had met, a little extra flesh on her stomach. But he'd told her he liked that, and enjoyed kissing her belly when they made love. She'd tried new hairdos; she now wore her hair short. It was coal black and rich in color and texture. Her pale skin was flawless, and she applied what little makeup she wore with some skill. Did he no longer love her dimples and what he called her "chipmunk cheeks"? She didn't want to succumb to this self-doubt about her physical appeal. It was so pre-fem lib, so feeding into the *Playboy* image of the ideal woman. But she was human. She loved him and wanted to be perfect for him.

Her need to justify the changes in him trumped more rational explanations.

Maybe it was only natural that after three years, the fire that had characterized that earlier time would simmer down to embers, passion replaced by a more comfortable, less impetuous relationship. Maybe she'd been neglectful of late, taking him for granted and no longer bothering to be sexually provocative.

Like last night. They were in the guest room. She read in bed; he sat at a small desk making notes in a journal he'd started keeping. Kathryn came to him, wrapped her arms around him, and coyly suggested that making love in an ex-FBI agent's house would be fun, something to remember. During the first year together, they'd enjoyed sex in what might be considered unconventional venues — in a bathroom at a friend's house in the midst of a party; on a train; in a public park one night.

"Right under J. Edgar Hoover's nosy nose." She giggled in his ear.

He turned and kissed her on the cheek. "A rain check, huh? I want to get these notes down before I forget them, and get some sleep. Tomorrow's the big day."

Kathryn banked that rain check along with others she'd accumulated recently, read a few more pages, and fell asleep.

They overslept. And now they were planted in traffic on the Lee Highway, halfway between Falls Church and Washington, D.C.

Traffic began to inch forward, but a snail could easily outrun them. At least there was movement. WTOP's traffic reporter said that there had been a multi-vehicle accident with fatalities on the Lee Highway. She felt a pang of guilt.

Marienthal's cell phone rang.

"Yeah? Hey, Geoff. What? We're stuck in goddamn traffic on the Lee Highway. Huh? Yeah, I know, but don't worry about it. I'll be there in time to meet him." He glanced at Kathryn, who raised her eyebrows and looked away.

"Look, Geoff, we're starting to move. Call you later. What? I told you I'd be there. Nothing to worry about. Bye."

A few minutes later they passed the accident, a chaotic scene with ambulances and fire trucks. The burned-out remnants of a car had been pushed to the side of the road.

"How awful," Kathryn said, averting her eyes from the grisly scene. "Nobody survived that one."

Marienthal wasn't listening. He passed a few slow-moving cars whose drivers were still rubbernecking and muttered something under his breath. The accident was indeed a grim scene. But he felt no pang of guilt; he had other scenes on his mind at the moment.

EIGHT

The Amtrak train from New York pulled into its berth at gate A-8 on time. Russo was nauseous and took one of the many pills he carried in a blue plastic case. He was also still weary and wanted to put his head down and sleep. But he couldn't do that. He sat up straight and tried to blink away his fatigue. He debated stopping in the restroom before leaving the train but decided instead to look for a men's room in Union Station.

"Are you all right?" the conductor asked as he slowly walked to the door, his cane leading the way, small suitcase in his other hand.

"Yes, I am fine. Thank you."

"Want help with that?" she asked, indicating the suitcase.

He shook his head. "No, no, thank you."

He stepped from the train and was bumped by another exiting passenger, a young businessman carrying a briefcase and in a hurry. There was no apology.

"*Idiota,*" Russo growled.

There was a time when such an incident might have prompted the old man to strike back. He'd killed over such discourtesy and disrespect. He watched the man disappear in a crowd of people who'd left the train and were rushing to whatever had brought them to Washington: meetings with government officials, business lunches, bullshit, reuniting with family, who knew?

He walked slowly toward where the arrival gates emptied into the station itself, but was stopped by a sharp pain in his side. He drew deep breaths and waited for it to subside before continuing. Immediately to his right was a public men's room. His need to urinate was suddenly intense, as it had been for the past year since the diagnosis. Prostate cancer. There were instances when he couldn't make it in time to a bathroom and suffered the embarrassment of soiling himself.

He paused before entering the facility. Marienthal had said he'd be at the gate to meet him, but he wasn't anywhere to be seen. He took in the people milling about, more than a few of them African-Americans. He didn't like the blacks, didn't trust them. Not that he'd had any bad times with them, but he was brought up to trust only his own, *Italiano*, people of honor. And Sasha.

As he took a few steps in the direction of the entrance to the men's room, he noticed the tall, slender, well-dressed black man leaning against a wall and reading a newspaper. The man lowered the paper and locked eyes for a second with Russo, then raised the paper to cover his face. Did he sense something in the man's eyes? The pain in Russo's side and the need to reach a toilet were momentarily forgotten.

But that was immediately replaced by a sharper pain. He walked as quickly as possible into the men's room.

When he emerged minutes later, the man with the newspaper was gone. Russo looked for Marienthal. Where was he? People passed him in a rush, the staccato rhythm of women's heels on the white marble floor sounding louder to him than it actually was. The whirl of human movement around him became dizzying, and he felt light-headed. He turned and stared into a shop window filled with travel accessories, closing his eyes against his reflection in the glass.

A mild panic set in. He hated the accompanying feeling of hopelessness that had been cropping up frequently of late. Crowds confused him, and he'd avoided Tel Aviv's bustling shops and restaurants for that reason, to Sasha's annoyance.

Where was Marienthal?

He couldn't continue to stand there, he knew. He had to move to avoid passing out.

The sense of confusion and disorientation increased as he walked aimlessly into the train concourse, behind the Amtrak ticket counter and past the Exclusive Shoe Shine's raised platform, where Joe Jenks awaited his next customer.

"Shine, sir?" Jenks said to Russo.

"What?"

"Shoeshine? Best in D.C.," Jenks said, flashing a broad grin at the old man with the red toupee and cane. "Comb your hair in your shoes when I'm done."

Jenks's face went in and out of focus. He looked puzzled.

"Chiacchierone incoerente," Russo snapped at the bootblack, who put up his hands as though to defend himself against the old man's obvious anger.

"Have a nice day, man," Jenks said, shaking his head as Russo continued to glare at him before resuming his path deeper into the mass of humanity that was Union Station at that hour. Marienthal's phone number was in his pocket but Russo didn't look for a phone. He needed to get outside, away from the crowds whose chatter, mixed with music from restaurants, and blaring train announcements, assaulted him.

A woman brushed him.

"I'm sorry," she said, smiling.

For a moment, he thought she was Sasha, and he wondered where he was. Tel Aviv? No, Washington, D.C.

He turned right, in a direction that promised an exit from the huge station to sunlight and fresh air, passing a florist's kiosk and one selling Godiva chocolates, the Main Hall with its soaring 96-foot-high ceilings, modeled after the Baths of Diocletian and the Arch of Constantine in Rome, ahead, its doors leading out.

He tried to walk faster, but pain in his legs and side prevented it. He stopped and took in air, closed his eyes against the blur of movement around him, then opened them.

The light-skinned black man stood between him and the Main Hall. The trench coat he carried over one arm had no right hand showing.

Deterred from continuing into the Main Hall, Russo turned and limped in the direction of a set of swinging yellow doors, next to a tobacco shop whose sign read

PRESIDENT CIGARS. The light coming through small windows on the doors beckoned him. To what? To safety?

The doors opened and a man in kitchen whites pushing a laundry cart came through, allowing the doors to close behind him. Russo looked back. The black man was following — casually, not in a rush it seemed, but following.

Russo's heart tripped as he continued toward the doors. He thought of the handguns he'd never been without years ago, and wished he had one now. He would blast the black bastard into oblivion, he thought, save himself. You don't mess with Louis Russo. But that bit of braggadocio was fleeting, displaced by palpable fear.

He was within ten feet of the doors now, and stopped again. The man had closed the gap, was only a few feet behind. Russo shoved against one of the two doors, causing it to open. The long hallway was brightly illuminated by overhead fluorescent fixtures, which momentarily blinded him. Ahead, men pushed service carts and carried trays to and from restaurants served by this off-limits employee area.

Russo took steps into the hallway and shouted at the men. "Hey, hey! Listen to me. I need —"

His voice was cut off by two shots from behind, the first striking him squarely between the shoulder blades, the second tearing a gaping hole in the back of his head. The force of the shots sent him pitching forward, cane and suitcase flying into the air. One of the workers in the hall who was carrying a large tray heaped with dirty dishes struggled with it. He lost control, the dishes smashing into pieces against the hard floor. Other workers looked at the black man, who'd covered the weapon he'd used with his trench coat but made no move to bolt from the scene.

"What the hell?" a worker yelled.

"Get him," another shouted.

But no one approached Russo's killer, who slowly went through the swinging doors, turned left into the Main Hall, and turned left again into the East Hall Gallery, where kiosks were open for business — a Radio Shack, a handbag shop, a U.S. Mint outlet, clothing and accessories kiosks, and one devoted to miniature replicas of Washington's most famous buildings and monuments. All the kiosks were on wheels and could be rolled away when the East Hall was booked for receptions and other social events.

The man carrying the gun beneath his

trench coat moved smoothly and quickly, but without a sense of urgency that might draw attention to him, past the kiosks and to an auxiliary entrance to the popular B. Smith's restaurant, which led to a small bar area. People at the bar paid him no mind as he passed them and entered the main room.

"Table, sir?" he was asked by one of the restaurant's maître d's.

"No, thank you. Not today."

He left the restaurant through its main entrance and stepped out onto Massachusetts Avenue, in front of Union Station, where taxis waited for and dropped off passengers, and a long line of tourist buses and trolleys stood ready to take visitors on tours of the nation's capital. A large contingent of uniformed police, augmented by National Guard soldiers, patrolled the area. The Homeland Security Agency had recently elevated the colored alert system from yellow to orange; the city was blanketed by security forces.

He waited for a break in the traffic, crossed the wide boulevard, stopping for a second to observe a short, pudgy man playing a trumpet to entertain tourists and hopefully to have them drop money into the hat at his feet, circumvented the 1912

Columbus fountain depicting the Old and New Worlds and the adventurous Italian who'd linked the two, and stepped aboard an Old Town Trolley that was about to transport a dozen sweaty, ebullient tourists around the city.

"Ticket, sir?" he was asked.

"Didn't have time to buy one inside," he said, pulling out his wallet and handing money to the driver.

"Thank you, sir," the driver said. "Welcome aboard. Great day for it."

NINE

Once clear of the accident scene, Rich Marienthal drove as fast as he thought he could get away with. Of the many things Kathryn Jalick liked about him, his patience behind the wheel usually ranked high on the list. Not this day. He weaved in and out through traffic approaching the Key Bridge into Georgetown and on M Street until turning down Massachusetts Avenue.

"What a mess," he said as they approached Union Station.

"Must be the terror alert," she offered, referring to the legion of law enforcement personnel milling about the station. Cars were being prevented from pulling up directly in front, so Rich squeezed into a no-parking zone on First Street, at the side of the station.

"Wait here," he told Kathryn as he bolted from the car and dodged traffic until he'd reached an entrance leading into the West Hall. Although uniformed armed guards patrolled that side of the station, too, no one was stopped from entering and exiting. Marienthal fought the urge to run as he made his way through the throngs of people to the gate area, looking for Russo. Failing to see him, he headed for the information desk in the Main Hall.

"I'm looking for an old Italian man," he breathlessly told the woman at the desk. "I was supposed to meet his train from New York, but I got tied up in traffic — an accident in Virginia — and . . ."

The woman's expression said she didn't know what he expected her to do.

He went back into the train concourse, where a crowd had gathered in the east end of the station, in front of a tobacco shop. He managed to snake through the gathering until he could see activity next to the shop. Yellow crime-scene tape had been strung to create a wide off-limits area near a set of yellow swinging doors. A large contingent of uniformed and plainclothes police came and went through the doors, leading to what appeared to be a hallway.

"What's going on?" Marienthal asked a bystander.

"Somebody died," she said.

"Who?"

"I don't know."

"Somebody got shot," said a man standing next to them.

"Shot?"

"I heard it," yet another person said excitedly. "I was right here."

"I heard it was an old guy with a cane."

A male voice came through a bullhorn: "All right, all right, everybody stand back. There's nothing to see. Please leave the area."

Marienthal's stomach tightened into a painful knot. He backed away until he was clear of the crowd and walked slowly toward the gate area where Russo would have left the Amtrak train. Although his eyes swept the station in search of the old man, he knew deep in his gut that he wouldn't see him. "I heard it was an old guy with a cane," the man in the crowd had said, and his words reverberated through Marienthal's brain. It had to be Louis, he thought — he knew!

"Hey, man, they get the guy?" Joe Jenks asked Marienthal from the shoeshine stand.

"Huh?"

"The shooter. The guy who gunned down the old dude. They find him?"

"No, I . . . I don't know."

Marienthal stood by gate A-8 for what seemed a very long time before going to the Main Hall. He stepped outside and watched the police and military vehicles

64

moving in and out of position. An antenna was extended high above the roof of a TV news remote truck with *WTTG — Channel 5* emblazoned on its side. A reporter and cameraman prepared to beam a report back to the station.

"Any word on the victim's name?" Marienthal asked, his voice weak.

The reporter, an attractive young woman holding a microphone and clipboard, turned to him and shook her head.

"Russo," Marienthal said automatically. "Louis Russo."

The reporter pulled a cell phone from where it was clipped on her belt and said into it, "I've got a witness who sounds like he knows the name of the victim. Russo, Louis Russo." She listened intently for the reply. Once she'd received it, she turned to talk to Marienthal. But he was gone, back inside Union Station and on his way to where Kathryn waited for him in the car.

TEN

If it weren't that a vicious killing had taken place, the multitude of law enforcement officers in Union Station might have been viewed as a fashion show of uniforms. Amtrak's own police force had been the first on the scene of Louis Russo's murder. Simultaneously, a call went out to the Washington PD's First District headquarters, under whose jurisdiction Union Station fell, and men and women from that agency converged quickly on the scene. The Capitol police also responded because of the station's proximity to Capitol Hill, in the event the shooting had political overtones that might herald an attack on members of Congress. Outside, the park police attempted to maintain order, while officers from Washington's underground Metro system took up positions at Metro stops close to Union Station. And because of the elevation of the Technicolor terrorist alert system from yellow to orange, heavily armed members of the area's national guard were being posted to stand grim-faced throughout the station. There were blue, brown, and white shirts;

blue, tan, and black pants; a variety of ties; camouflage outfits; and plenty of tin, brass, and copper badges being flashed.

"Get these people outta here!"

The order came from MPD detective Bret Mullin, a bulky, crusty twenty-nine-year veteran of the department, who'd been parked in an unmarked car around the corner from Union Station's main entrance when the call went out from a police dispatcher. Two recent muggings outside the station had prompted increased police scrutiny, and intelligence sources indicated an increase in small-time drug dealing. Mullin had been assigned to a surveillance detail and wasn't happy about it.

There was a time earlier in his career that long stretches of surveillance didn't bother him. He'd sit in a car and drink coffee and smoke and eat doughnuts and enjoy the parade of humanity. He'd watch men and women pass and wonder where they were going; where they lived; the sort of people they were close to — family, friends; the TV shows they enjoyed watching. Attractive women were mentally undressed as they moved by, and Mullin would speculate on the sort of men allowed to share their beds, starting with himself.

67

But there were times, especially when surveillance had to be conducted on foot and the weather was bad, that the urge to abandon the assigned post for the warmth of a dry and convivial bar and restaurant was too compelling to ignore. That was the beginning of the corpulent Mullin's troubles, succumbing on occasion — on too many occasions, according to his superiors — to the warm ambience of neighborhood bars and fast-food shops, and the pleasures they provided a footsore, bored, and gregarious detective.

"Get 'em outta here," Mullin repeated.

He stood in front of the swinging yellow doors, now propped open by rubber wedges provided by the station's maintenance crew. Beyond the door lay the lifeless body of the victim, a pool of blood surrounding his head. His toupee had been blown off and was against a wall a few feet from the body, looking very much like a dead red rodent. His splintered cane had been blown a dozen feet up the hallway; the small suitcase he carried had split open on impact with the floor, its contents scattered.

The workers who'd been in the hallway at the time of the murder had been corralled at the far end.

"Get their statements," Mullin instructed another detective in plainclothes. He said to other officers: "Fan out through the station and see if anybody saw anything — the victim, maybe the shooter."

Evidence technicians in white lab coats entered the area, followed by a specialist from the medical examiner's office. After conferring briefly with Mullin, they entered the hallway to begin the process of photographing the murder scene and identifying, documenting, collecting, and preserving what physical evidence might be present. Two empty shell casings between the body and the doors had already been noted and marked by small cards with numbers on them.

"I hate scenes like this," Mullin grumbled to Vince Accurso, a detective with whom he'd been paired for the past two years. He looked back at the crowd that was still gathered and shook his head. "Give me a nice, empty dark alley anytime," he said. "What the hell do they expect to see, the victim get up and do a buck-and-wing?"

Accurso laughed without a sound.

Mullin belched and inhaled noisily. His sinuses had been particularly bad the past few weeks.

"He got whacked by a black guy," Accurso commented flatly.

"What evidence?"

"People," Accurso said, nodding.

Witnesses to the shooting in the hall had blurted out their recollections of the shooter's appearance to the first cops on the scene.

"Tall, thin, well dressed, brownish suit, carrying a raincoat," Mullin said, reciting what he learned the workers had told the police. "Consistent."

"How about that? Good, huh? Nobody saw a short, fat white guy in a blue suit."

"Keep things going here, Vinnie. I'm taking a walk."

Mullin hitched up pants that seemed always to be slipping below his belly and pushed through the crowd.

"Who was he?" a woman who'd been there from the beginning asked. "A political big shot? Nobody else worth shooting in Union Station."

"Go get a cup of coffee," Mullin told her. "It's over."

"Are you a detective?" a teenager asked as Mullin gestured for him to get out of the way.

Mullin muttered something profane at the boy and continued walking through the

70

train concourse until he reached Exclusive Shoe Shine, where Joe Jenks had just finished a customer's shoes. Mullin was no stranger to the bootblack station and its employees, especially Jenks. Although never accused of being a fashion plate — sloppy was a more precise description — Mullin liked clean shoes and often stopped in Union Station to have Jenks practice his own special brand of spit-shine magic, minus the spit. At the same time, Jenks was one of dozens of people Mullin had cultivated in the area to lend their eyes and ears to any crime. Joe was at his post in Union Station every day, and on more than one occasion had called in a tip about someone he considered an unsavory character, or a potentially troublesome situation.

"Hey, Mullin, my man," Jenks said. "Caught yourself a big one, huh?"

Mullin climbed up into Jenks's chair.

"What happened, man?" Jenks asked as he pulled cloths and polish from a drawer beneath the chair. "Somebody says an old guy with a cane got it. I think I seen him."

"Is that so, Joe?"

"Yeah. He limps on by and I ask him if he wants a shine. He looks at me like I just called his mother a dirty name, says somethin' in Italian or Greek or somethin',

71

and goes on his way."

"Italian or Greek?"

"He talked foreign, that's all I'm saying. You nab the perp?"

Mullin gave forth what could be considered a laugh. He always found it amusing when people tried to speak cop talk.

"No, we didn't nab the perp, Joe. Maybe you saw him."

A shrug from Jenks as he brushed off Mullin's shoes in preparation for shining. "Maybe I did. You know what he looks like?"

"We had a couple of descriptions. A black guy, skinny, expensive suit, maybe carrying a raincoat. Light, mulatto style they say."

Jenks leaned back and his eyes opened wide. "Oh, I know the dude you're talking about, man," he said. "Four dollars."

"You do?"

"Shined him up. Very cool, like aloof, you know. No field hand or house slave. Uppity is what I thought."

"You gave him a shine?"

"Yup. I didn't much care how he acted 'cause he tipped big."

Mullin pulled a narrow steno pad and a pen from the pocket of his suit jacket. "I'm listening, Joe. Tell me all about this cool one who tips big."

Shoes polished to a mirror finish, and notes made of Joe Jenks's description of his customer — brand of shoes, kind of socks, knife-edge creases, label in the raincoat, *New York Times* — Mullin continued his walk through the station, stopping to ask those in a position to observe whether they'd seen the man now described as Louis Russo's killer.

"I noticed him," a shopkeeper in the travel accessory store near gate A-8 told him. She was in her deep thirties. "He was standing near the gate reading a newspaper."

"How come you noticed him?" Mullin asked. "Was he doing something that caught your eye?"

"He was —" She smiled sheepishly. "I thought he was really good-looking," she said.

"Anything else?" Mullin asked.

There wasn't. But the details checked.

Mullin concluded his walk-through by entering the East Hall, where the rolling kiosks were located. Two detectives were already there asking questions of the kiosk owners.

"This lady says she saw the guy we're looking for," Mullin was told by one of the cops. A conversation with her revealed that the tall, thin man had passed her kiosk and gone into the bar behind B. Smith's restaurant. Mullin and one of the detectives went in and talked to the maître d' at the front door of the restaurant. It featured southern cooking, which attracted a sizable African-American clientele.

"Yeah, I remember him," the maître d' said in response to Mullin's question. "You say he shot somebody inside the station? Boy, he sure didn't look like someone who just shot somebody."

"What do you mean?"

"He was — well, he was very casual, didn't seem in any rush. I asked if he wanted a table and he said he didn't, but he wasn't out of breath or anything. I mean, he didn't run out of here. He just told me he didn't want a table — I think he said 'not today' — and left through those doors." He indicated the restaurant's main entrance leading to Massachusetts Avenue at the front of the station.

After noting what the maître d' said and informing him he'd be asked later for a formal statement, Mullin told the two detectives to work the outside to see if anyone remembered seeing the alleged killer, and returned to the crime scene.

The medical examiner was finishing up his preliminary examination.

"We ID him?" Mullin asked.

He was handed Russo's wallet, as well as an Israeli passport. The wallet contained an Israeli driver's license, a single Visa card, a photo of a woman posing on what appeared to be a beach, and slightly more than a hundred U.S. dollars in cash. Other travel documents included a round-trip airline ticket between Tel Aviv and Newark, with a plane change in Barcelona, Spain, and a one-way Amtrak ticket between New York's Penn Station and Washington's Union Station.

"Louis Russo?" Mullin said aloud. "That's Italian. What's he doing with an Israeli passport?"

Those around him didn't have an answer.

Mullin handed the wallet and travel documents to an evidence technician and left the station, climbed in his car, and drove to First District headquarters on North Capitol Street N.W., where he sat with fellow detectives who'd been at the murder scene. They began to compare notes, speculate, joke, and put together a preliminary report.

"What do you figure the old guy was

doing in D.C.?" someone asked. "Or going to do?"

"Visit family maybe," someone else answered.

"Next of kin?"

"Back in Israel maybe," Accurso said.

"You checked Russos in the D.C. directory?" Mullin said.

Accurso nodded. "You figure the shooter knew Russo?" he asked. "It comes off like a mob hit."

Mullin laughed as he said, "Russo. Italiano. Maybe he's some geriatric godfather nobody ever heard of. Or from some family the New York cops know well. Get New York on the phone."

"Or the computer. It doesn't make sense. Doesn't make sense," the youngest of the detectives said.

"What doesn't?"

"Why some black guy would come up behind an old Italian guy named Russo, who's here from Israel, and do him in public. The witnesses say the shooter was cool, unflustered, in no rush. A pro. So why pick Union Station? Who is Louis Russo, and why would a certified hit man want to whack him? For what? It doesn't make sense."

"You ever see a murder that made

sense?" Mullin offered.

"Yeah, sometimes. You know, some people, well, deserve to get killed," the young detective said. "Sometimes it's justifiable. Justifiable homicide. That's how they get off. Like a guy whose wife is screwing around and gets caught, and he pops her or the boyfriend. In Texas, that's justifiable murder."

"In Texas, that's routine."

Mullin glanced at Accurso, who was putting the finishing touches on their initial report. "See what you can learn by hanging around here, Vinnie?" he said, his voice mirroring his amusement. "Your wife plays around, it's okay to pop her."

"I didn't necessarily mean that," the young detective said defensively.

"You up for a drink?" Mullin asked Accurso.

"Thanks, no, Bret. Got to get home."

"Anybody?" Mullin asked others in the room.

Heads were shaken, excuses made.

"Well, I'm packing it in. After a pop or two. See you tomorrow."

Mullin's apartment was in a four-story town house on California Street, between Dupont Circle and Adams-Morgan. It was too early to suffer the loneliness of the

77

one-bedroom, perpetually untidy place he'd called home for the six years since Rosie, his wife of nineteen years, and he had called it quits, sold the house in Silver Spring, and gone their separate ways. She'd settled in a high-rise up near the National Cathedral and continued to work as a receptionist for a K Street law firm. They seldom talked unless something troublesome arose about their two kids, a son and daughter, who'd flown the coop and were doing pretty well, the girl in Denver where she worked as a personal trainer, the son a cop in a small West Virginia town. He hadn't heard from his daughter in over a year; she blamed his drinking for the breakup of the marriage and had viciously condemned him the last time they spoke. His son kept in touch with an occasional phone call and Christmas and birthday card, but Mullin didn't have any illusions about the depth of that relationship, either.

He was thinking of his dismal family situation when he entered the private entrance to the Jockey Club, in the Westin Fairfax hotel on Massachusetts Avenue. When it came to choosing bars, Mullin was an equal opportunity drinker. He'd been to most of them in D.C. over the years, although he had his favorites, depending upon his mood at the moment. Most nights, he opted for inexpensive neighborhood places near his apartment. But there were times when he felt expansive — or the reverse, particularly depressed, which triggered expansiveness — times when he preferred settings more genteel than the run-of-the-mill. This was one of those nights.

He was treated nicely at this bastion of Washington society — Jackie Kennedy and Nancy Reagan had been regulars; Mrs. Reagan's chicken salad was still on the menu — although he sensed that his arrival wasn't always as welcome as the serving staff made it seem. The arrival of a cop at a fancy spot like the Jockey Club caused a certain unease to set in, even though he wasn't there to hassle or arrest anyone. There were establishments that liked having cops around. They provided color with their stories of life on the streets, and if a customer threatened to act up, there was muscle to handle the situation.

But in posh places, particularly where political movers and shakers tended to gather, sanctity was threatened, especially for those whose reasons for being there weren't exactly aboveboard. Like the old silver-haired guy in a corner booth with his arm around a thirty-odd blonde who laughed too loud and long at anything he said. Or the two men in another booth who spoke in whispers. Mullin chalked them up as a lobbyist and pol cutting a deal that would probably cost the average citizen above-average money, hopefully not worse.

He ordered a bourbon on the rocks on his way to a wine-red leather chair in the bar area, where the AC countered the fireplace glowing on this hot summer evening — form over function. When he drank during the day, it was vodka, always vodka, its relatively odorless quality a necessity. But at night, with no one to smell his breath except his cat, Magnum, it was bourbon, Wild Turkey or single barrel.

He knew the bartender, who came to the table.

"Have a good day, Bret?"

"Good day, bad day, just another day," he said, downing the drink too quickly and holding up the glass for a refill. "How about crab cakes and some slaw?"

"You got it, Bret."

Other customers came and went as Mullin continued to consume bourbons, nursing them more slowly as time passed, and enjoying the crab cakes for which the

Jockey Club was noted. He felt the effects of the drinks and welcomed the feeling. Each drink seemed to shut a door on an unpleasant memory, and he visualized that happening in his brain. Clank! A door shut on the divorce. Clank! His rancorous relationship with his daughter walled off. Clank! The strained relationship with his superiors at MPD locked away.

Sufficiently free of painful thoughts, he paid the tab, left the bar, and got behind the wheel of his six-year-old Taurus. He knew he shouldn't be driving, but he'd never hesitated to drive after drinking. He could handle it, he reminded himself as he pulled from the curb and headed home, where after he fed Magnum, blessed sleep would hopefully come quickly.

But it didn't. In pajamas and slippers, and with a contented Magnum on his lap and a nightcap in hand, Mullin turned on the TV. He considered himself conservative, although his political philosophy was probably better characterized as anti-politician, no matter what the party affiliation. He turned to WTTG, Channel 5, the Fox News channel in Washington, whose right-wing slant usually suited him. He watched the evening newscast through watery eyes, his fingers kneading the cat's fur, and

81

fought to stay awake. Finally, acknowledging it was a hopeless battle, he gently pushed the cat to the floor and reached for the remote to turn off the set.

The TV talker's words stopped him.

"A murder took place today at Union Station, the cold-blooded killing of an elderly visitor to Washington who was shot twice. For more on the story, we go to Joyce Rosenberg, who's standing by at Union Station. Joyce?"

"Yes, Bernie. A murder did take place today inside the station. According to eyewitnesses, the assailant was a well-dressed light-skinned black man who left the scene through B. Smith's restaurant and disappeared into the crowd outside. The police originally intended to withhold the name of the elderly victim until next of kin had been notified. But while getting ready to report earlier today from in front of the station shortly after the murder had taken place, I had a brief conversation with a bystander, a young man who happened to be there. He asked me if I knew the identity of the victim. When I said I didn't, he provided a name and quickly walked away. I reported the name to the police, and they've confirmed he was right. The deceased's name is Louis Russo, who'd evidently traveled here from Israel."

"Any further details, Joyce?"

"Not at the moment, Bernie. Back to you in the studio."

Mullin was more awake now. Some unnamed young guy knew the name of the victim. How? Why? Was he connected with the shooting? Who is he? Where is he?

It took one more nightcap to snap off the final switch in Mullin's mind.

ELEVEN

"I can't believe it's happened," Kathryn Jalick said. "My God, to be shot down like that. It's so . . . so barbaric."

Rich Marienthal didn't respond. He was glued to the news on TV, going from channel to channel to see whether any new tidbits of information about Russo's murder were surfacing. A follow-up report on the Fox News channel now referred to the young man, who had known the name of the victim, as the mystery man. According to the reporter, Joyce Rosenberg, the MPD was interested in finding him and was asking him to come forward.

"That's me," Marienthal muttered to Kathryn during a commercial. "The mystery man."

"Why did you tell that reporter his name?" she asked, joining him on the couch.

"I don't know. I guess I was in shock. I didn't know for sure it was Louis — I mean, I hadn't seen his body and nobody told me it was him. But I knew, you know? I knew it was him. Maybe I was just thinking his name and blurted it out."

"What are you going to do?"

"I don't know. I tried to reach Geoff but got voice mail on his cell. I can't believe he hasn't called me. Hell, he must know by now. He knows everything."

Kathryn fell silent as the news resumed on the screen. Rich leaned intently ahead, his foot tapping on the rug, fingers rolling on his thigh. She'd seen him anxious before, but nothing like this. She understood, of course. The book he'd been writing for the past year caused him to spend a lot of time in Israel. She'd never met any of the people with whom he dealt, and Rich had never invited her on his trips. Nor could she have gone if he'd asked. His visits there were lengthy, too long for her to be away from her job at the library.

He always returned with copious notes, cassette tapes, and transcriptions from his latest interviews. They never made it home. He'd immediately deposit them in two large safety deposit boxes at the local branch of the Riggs Bank. Later, his research secure, he would take her to dinner and was not reticent about details of his travels, including personal encounters and feelings and impressions — but never anything about the book itself. The subject seemed reserved for Geoff Lowe and their frequent meetings.

"That reporter said the police want you to come forward. Will you?" She asked this with some trepidation. Rich was well aware that she disapproved of what he and Lowe had forged, and tended to snap at her whenever she voiced what she felt — that the book was one thing, the plan he spoke of to promote it another.

"What?" he said.

"Will you go to the police and tell them about Russo?"

"No." He turned and looked at her quizzically. "Why would I do that?"

She placed a reassuring hand on his leg. "I'm just worried, that's all," she said. "He's been murdered, Rich, gunned down like some rabid dog. You knew him. You've spent time with him. Doesn't that concern you?"

"Kathryn, I —"

"Who shot him, Rich? *Why* would somebody kill him? Maybe *you're* in danger."

He waved her concerns away and sat back. "That's ridiculous," he said. "I don't know who killed him, but nobody's out to shoot me. So relax, huh? Just relax."

He was anything but relaxed. He stood, crossed the room, and looked down at the street.

"It sure screws things up," he said without turning to her.

She came up behind and wrapped her arms around him. Now the impact of the murder on Rich had sunk in. She knew, of course, that Russo's death had been a shock to the man she loved and that it had shaken him. When he'd returned to the car from Union Station, he'd been frazzled and pale, actually stammering as he told her what had happened inside. She'd sympathized, but simultaneously reasoned that the ramifications wouldn't be dire. He'd already accomplished all the interviews of Russo he'd intended. The book was completed and at the publisher. Yes, he'd lost someone he'd gotten to know, and the cause of the man's death was especially harsh, cruel, and unexpected.

But those were rationalizations. The reality was that there was much more to the story than researching and writing a book. There was Geoff Lowe.

"If I'd only been there," Rich said. "That damned accident on the highway."

Kathryn diplomatically refrained from again suggesting they should have left Falls Church earlier.

"I could have headed it off if I'd been there."

"But you weren't," she said. "Maybe you would have been shot, too."

"I'm going to try Geoff again," Rich said, going to the phone on a small desk in the cluttered living room and starting to dial.

"Rich, why don't you call Mac Smith?"

"What can he do?"

"He helped you with your publishing contract. He's a lawyer, a smart man. Maybe he can give you some —"

"Geoff?" Marienthal said into the phone. "It's Rich."

Lowe took the call at Senator Widmer's desk in his office suite in the Dirksen Senate Office Building, at First and C Streets.

He'd just come from a meeting convened by the crotchety senior senator from Alaska, a white-haired stentorian orator who'd recently celebrated his seventy-sixth birthday. Despite his advanced age, Widmer never failed to impress colleagues and staff with his seemingly boundless energy. A widower for many years, he'd made the Senate his life, his only life. The few friends who had had the privilege of visiting him at his Foggy Bottom home couldn't help but come away surprised at its spartan furnishings and decor. It wasn't a matter of money, they knew. Senator Karl Widmer was a wealthy man. But his lifestyle, which included many nights sleeping in his office and an abhorrence of fancy restaurants, parties, and expensive clothing, indicated something quite different. "Cheap" is what many on the Hill said behind his back. "Mean-spirited," others said among themselves, careful to not trigger the legendary temper in the halls and on the floor of the United States Senate, one that left colleagues and staffers quaking.

Despite these less than sanguine personal traits, Widmer was respected and even well liked by many on the Hill. Of course, sharing his steadfast conservative views went a long way to being on his good side. He was a rock-ribbed old-line right-wing Republican who wore his disdain for liberals and their views on his sleeve. The Democratic administration now occupying the White House, led by President Adam Parmele, represented everything the senator stood against. His determination that Parmele not see a second term was pervasive, some said pathologically obsessive.

The meeting from which Geoff Lowe had just emerged lasted longer than had been allotted for in the daily schedule. Widmer's subcommittee on intelligence had been preparing for weeks to hold a hearing on the current readiness of the Central Intelligence Agency to deal with future terrorist threats. The subcommittee's Democratic ranking minority member and some of her Democratic colleagues had recently waged a public fight with the chairman over the choice of witnesses to appear. The ironfisted Widmer, whose epitaph would never include credit for being a great conciliator, held fast to his rule that the Republican majority would be the sole arbiter of who would be called to appear before the committee.

"A dictatorial tactic," the ranking Democrat said on a meet-the-media Sunday morning TV news show. "Chairman Widmer seems to have forgotten that we function in a democracy."

Widmer, who seldom spoke with reporters, particularly television reporters, issued a written statement through his press secretary: "The Democrats would like to whitewash the inadequacies of the CIA. The truth is, that agency has been weakened by the Democratic administration of President Parmele and his unwillingness to stand up for a strong and effective intelligence effort, even though this nation is faced with continuing and evolving terrorist activities against its citizens. The people my Democratic counterparts on the committee want to parade before us represent nothing other than business as usual, and I will not waste the committee's time, nor that of the American people, with such a transparent ploy."

And so the war of words went.

Widmer's mood was particularly foul this day, and few escaped his wrath during the meeting, with Lowe receiving his share of the senator's anger. When he was finished berating his staff for failing to think things through, Widmer abruptly adjourned the meeting and announced he was going home for the day. That left Lowe to do what he often did in his boss's absence, abandon his own office to sit at the senator's desk in his spacious suite. It was filled with mementos of a long career, dozens of photographs of political bigwigs inscribed to him, his arm about the shoulders of past presidents, plaques and framed citations extolling his contributions to America, family pictures, a glass-front cabinet filled with antique handguns, and other spoils of having been a public figure for so long.

"Did I hear?" Lowe said into his cell phone in answer to Rich Marienthal's first question. "Did I *hear?*" he repeated, his voice louder and angrier. "Yeah, Rich, I heard. Where the hell were you?"

"We got tied up in traffic," Marienthal replied. "There was an accident on the Lee Highway and —"

"I don't give a goddamn about some fender bender, Rich. Do you realize what a spot this puts me in?"

Marienthal started to say something, but Lowe cut him off.

"Do you realize what a spot it puts the senator in, Rich? Do you realize that the senator doesn't care *why* Russo was killed or why he's not here to testify before the committee? Christ, I just came from a meeting with Widmer. For starters, he climbed all over me, reamed me out, nailed me to a cross and left me to bleed to death."

Ellen Kelly came to the doorway to Widmer's office, but Lowe brusquely waved her away.

"Look, Rich, I didn't go along with your goddamn idea to see it get screwed up at the last minute."

Had Lowe been talking with Marienthal face-to-face, he would have seen a quizzical expression cross the writer's countenance. Marienthal didn't say what he was thinking, that the idea had come from Lowe after he'd heard about the book Marienthal was in the process of writing. But maybe that wasn't entirely accurate. The scenario that had unrolled just seemed to develop as they talked, at first an almost whimsical scheme that soon developed into something much more serious and complex. Besides, what did it matter who'd come up with it first? What *did* matter was what to do now that the highlight of the plan had so dramatically and definitely unraveled.

Lowe drew deep breaths to calm himself. He said, "Look, Rich, there may be a way to salvage this. I told the senator I'd come up with something by the morning. Where are you now?"

"Home."

"Meet me in an hour. Downstairs at Kinkead's."

TWELVE

"Public life is a situation of power and energy. He trespasses against his duty who sleeps upon his watch, as well as he who goes over to the enemy."

Chet Fletcher, political adviser to President Adam Parmele, liked to quote Edmund Burke's take on power, loyalty, duty, and their uses. He was fond of such sayings and seemed always to have a dozen of them ready to be dropped into conversation.

Fletcher watched the news on a small, cable-connected TV set while eating breakfast in the kitchen of his Rosslyn, Virginia, home. He'd gotten up at five, his usual hour, and went through what seemed a daily morning routine. "You really should exercise," he told his puffy, blotchy face in the bathroom mirror. A room off the master bedroom held a representative assortment of exercise equipment, which his wife, Gail, used with some regularity. But while Fletcher thought a great deal about exercising, he never seemed to get around to it, as evidenced by his soft girth and weary legs when climbing stairs.

Silently, he rationalized once more on not living an active physical life. He was, after all, an intellectual, with a Ph.D. in political science from the University of Chicago. He'd played some tennis as an undergraduate but wasn't very good at it, and managed to avoid campus softball and volleyball games by proving those few times he did participate that he was even worse at those sports. No one fought to have him on their team.

But Adam Parmele had wanted him on his team when he decided to run for president of the United States. Fletcher had generated a name for himself in political circles through publication of a book that offered a new and radical blueprint for political success in the twenty-first century. Parmele, whose curriculum vitae included elected stints in the House of Representatives and the Senate, a brief ambassadorship, and a three-year tenure as director of the Central Intelligence Agency, brought Fletcher on board for his run at the presidency, and Fletcher soon found himself virtually running the campaign.

His commitment to the Democrat Parmele wasn't based upon a political philosophy on Fletcher's part, who prided himself on not claiming allegiance to any political party or dogma. His fascination was with power and the use of it, no matter the cause. When Parmele emerged victorious and put together his cabinet and team of advisers, Fletcher was invited to join and didn't hesitate to accept. The change in lifestyle for this pudgy Ph.D. was heady and took some getting used to — the easy access to the White House and the Oval Office, the respect afforded him by less influential members of the president's staff, and the mentions in the press. Perhaps most important was the pleasure Gail took in moving to Washington and basking in her husband's newfound importance. She almost immediately joined with other wives of important men and threw herself into the city's social and charitable activities.

All in all, it had been a good move on Fletcher's part to join the Parmele inner circle. At the age of fifty-one, he'd achieved an enviable position of power, and no one questioned any longer his dubious physical shape with the exception of his wife, who consistently failed to entice him into even a walk around the block, and his boss, the president of the United States, Adam Parmele, who seemed to worship physical activity.

By six, an aide had delivered an array of intelligence reports and newspapers to the house, and Fletcher took a fresh cup of coffee and the papers to a bedroom that served as his home office. Two phones sat on the desk. One was a regular home line. The other was a secure line to his office in the West Wing of the White House.

"Good morning," Gail Fletcher said from the doorway. "Sleep well?"

"Yes, I did," he said.

She was a short, slender woman with an easily managed brunette hairdo and a known fondness for simple yet expensive clothing. Her most visible public credential, aside from being the wife of the president's political adviser, was as head of a nonprofit organization whose purpose was to foster political involvement by women in third-world countries, a position that found her frequently away from home. She was as social as her husband was reclusive; they were seldom seen together at the theater or concerts, although they did host occasional small dinner parties at home, where Fletcher donned an apron and chef's hat and produced perfectly cooked meals on the grill.

"What's going on in the world this morning?" she asked, carrying a steaming cup of black coffee into the office and sitting on a small forest-green convertible sofa. She wore a short pink robe over flowered short pajamas and tucked her bare feet beneath her.

Fletcher smiled at the sight of her. That she'd said yes to his proposal twenty years ago never failed to amaze him. This beautiful, trim, and vivacious woman had agreed to be the wife of a dull, introspective college professor. Had she known back then he was destined for something decidedly more visible than teaching the subtleties of politics to college students, and decided to go along for the ride? She claimed she hadn't, said she was pleased to be the wife of a distinguished college professor. But he had to provide himself with some reason for her agreeing to be Mrs. Fletcher. Their only child, a daughter, was away at college in Vermont.

"Nothing especially important," he said, picking up one of the unread papers. "One irresolvable crisis after another. General dire predictions of the nation's future and one question about whether we have a future. What's on your agenda?"

"Meetings at the foundation. Several crises to compound. Lunch with Craig and

Jill. Sure you can't break away, even for an hour?"

He shook his head and gave forth what passed for a smile. "The president has me captive all day, Gail, and probably into the night, too. Won't be home for dinner."

He seldom was home for dinner, so no comment from her was necessary.

She pulled one of the newspapers he'd already read from the desk, and returned to the couch. They read in silence. Then she said, "How bizarre."

He looked up. "What is?"

"This murder at Union Station."

He returned to the paper he was reading.

"An old Italian man named Louis Russo comes here by train. He was from Israel. A black man — they say he was well dressed — comes up behind this old Italian man and shoots him in the head."

"Oh?"

"Why would he do that?"

"Who?"

"This well-dressed man. Why would he —"

"They'll figure it out, I'm sure," he said, standing, stretching, and yawning. "That's what the police are for. I have to get moving. I'm already running late."

He came to the couch, bent, and kissed

her lightly on the hair. "Give my love to Craig and Jill, and my apologies I won't be able to see them while they're visiting. Another time."

"I will," she said.

Minutes later he was in the backseat of the government car dispatched for him each morning. Not long after that, he passed through security at the White House, spent a few minutes in his office gathering notes, and went to the Oval Office, where President Parmele and other members of his staff had gathered.

There were three items on the agenda.

The first two had to do with bills initiated by the White House that were stalled in the Republican House. Walter Brown, Parmele's chief congressional liaison, listed those moderate Republican representatives whose arms he felt might be twisted harder in favor of supporting the bills, and Parmele suggested the twisting begin immediately, singling out three House members who he said would play ball, adding that they probably wouldn't want certain information about them made public. Knowing who was vulnerable in Congress and understanding the right buttons to push were integral parts of Parmele's political arsenal. He was a master at it, as good

100

as Lyndon Johnson had ever been, but decidedly more subtle.

He sat back, clasped his hands behind his head, and launched into a dissertation about how important the passage of those bills would be for his reelection bid.

As he talked, Fletcher observed the man he'd helped put in this position of awesome power. No question about it, this president was a skilled, self-confident politician with an ego necessarily large enough to even consider running for president of the United States. Parmele's monologue this morning on the importance of education was familiar to Fletcher. It was part of a speech he'd helped draft a month ago with some of Parmele's speechwriters. This was typical of the president, taking what someone else had conceived and making it his own, as though it had come to him on the spur of the moment. Rather than resent this, Fletcher welcomed it. It was the sign of a man prepared to seize power and language and to wield them effectively. No shame. No guilt. Just his eye on the prize, in this case a second term.

The third reason for the meeting that morning revolved around Fletcher and his staff. He'd been busy choreographing Parmele's political travel agenda, including fund-raising appearances around the country. Others at the meeting not involved with that issue left the Oval Office, leaving the president and Fletcher alone.

"Well, Chet, give me the bad news," Parmele said.

"Not as bad as we feared, Mr. President," Fletcher said, laying the latest overnight poll numbers on the desk.

Parmele scrutinized them and slid the paper on which they were written back to Fletcher. "Encouraging," said the president.

"Yes, it is, Mr. President. Did Walter brief you on Senator Widmer's hearings?"

Parmele forced a laugh. "Sure he did. Widmer seems determined to go forward with them. You know, Chet, I like Widmer, always have, but I really question his mental health these days. Maybe it's his age. Christ, I hope I don't end up that way."

"I doubt that you will, sir. I'd like to dismiss the senator as just an aging old fool who's on his last legs, political and personal. But we both know he's more dangerous than that, particularly to —"

"Particularly to me," Parmele said, finishing Fletcher's thought.

"Yes."

They spent the next half hour going over the president's plans for the next two weeks, and Fletcher gave a capsule evaluation of what each campaign stop would entail, and his analysis of the issues thought to be of particular importance to citizens in those areas of the country. When he'd finished, he gathered up his papers.

"Anything else, Mr. President?" he asked.

"No," Parmele said. "But I want you to know how much I appreciate the way you've been handling things, Chet."

"Of course, sir."

"You ought to take a few days off, relax a bit. Get some air and exercise. I get the feeling you've almost been living here."

"No, I'm fine, Mr. President. I get plenty of exercise saying no to you."

"Well, say hello to that lovely Gail."

"I certainly will, sir. My best to the first lady."

THIRTEEN

Bret Mullin was up early and at his desk at First District headquarters. He'd slept fitfully, visions of the busy scene at Union Station, the still body, and the many questions they raised interrupting his sleep.

Detective Vinnie Accurso, twenty years with MPD, arrived minutes later.

Accurso was shorter than Mullin, solidly built, and with an outgoing disposition. He liked Mullin. More important, he respected the twenty-six-year veteran. Mullin was a good cop, with solid instincts. He'd broken some big cases over the course of his tenure with MPD, and had put his life on the line more than once.

Those positive traits aside, Accurso had two problems with being paired with the big, caustic detective.

The first had to do with Mullin's reputation for taking the law into his own hands on occasion, resulting in formal complaints filed by citizens. Mullin had what others described as an Old West approach to law enforcement. He'd been known to collar recognized drug dealers and thugs, and rather than arrest them, rough them up, take them to the bus station at 12th Street and New York Avenue, and put them on the first bus out of town, warning that if they returned to D.C., they'd wish they hadn't. Mullin's unconventional handling of such criminals had been brought to the attention of internal affairs by disgruntled previous partners. Ever defiant, Mullin stood firm behind his actions and received no more than a series of official sanctions on paper that were inserted into his personnel file.

The second problem Accurso faced was Mullin's reputation for hard drinking, the subject of MPD rumors, jokes, and concerns. The chief of the detective unit to which Mullin and Accurso belonged had engaged Mullin in heart-to-heart talks, encouraging him to take advantage of counseling available within MPD or to seek help from AA. Mullin, of course, denied that he had a drinking problem, and because no one had ever made the case that drinking interfered with his official duties, no further action was taken beyond those friendly suggestions from superiors.

Accurso carried two coffees from a luncheonette around the corner from headquarters and handed one to Mullin.

"What's up this morning?" he asked.

"The shooter at Union Station, that's what up. Here."

Mullin handed Accurso a composite sketch drawn overnight by an MPD sketch artist, based upon descriptions of the shooter provided by witnesses.

"Good-looking," Accurso said. "It's been distributed?"

"Uh-huh. Chief wants us to hand it out around black sections of town. I told him it was a waste of time. If this guy is from D.C., he's long gone by now. Besides, this was no crackhead from the neighborhood out for some fun. This was a professional hit, Vinnie."

Accurso nodded his agreement and sipped the coffee.

"Look at this," Mullin said, handing a file folder to his partner. "Just came in."

Accurso opened the folder and read a report generated by the FBI's central database. His eyebrows went up as he read, eventually accompanied by a smile and a slow shaking of his head.

"He's an old mobster," he said.

"Yeah. Catch his background. Italian father, Jewish mother."

"Maybe that's how he ended up in Israel."

"No. Read further, buddy."

Accurso went to the second page and frowned. When he'd finished reading, he looked up at Mullin and said, "Witness protection program. Mr. Russo ratted out his buddies."

"Yup. Gambino family. He testified against some of his spaghetti-bender friends and put 'em away."

Accurso, son of an Italian-American family, didn't take offense at his partner's derogatory reference to Italians. Mullin routinely used politically incorrect terms for every ethnic and racial group, but Accurso had learned over time that Mullin was not a prejudiced man, at least no more so than other cops he knew. He used ethnic and racial slang with every member of the force; if there was resentment, no one expressed it, at least not to his face.

"It was a hit, Vinnie, plain and simple. It took the family twenty years to get even, but they did."

"Looks that way."

Accurso read further.

"He spent his first year in the program in Mexico. That's a first."

"Nah. The Bureau's got some sort of agreement with the Mexicans to take in snitches like Russo. Gets 'em outta the country. Harder to find 'em that way. You see where Russo complained about being southa the border, said he didn't like his accommodations. How about that? Maybe it was the spicy food." Mullin snickered.

"So he goes to Israel. We have a deal with them, too?"

A shrug from Mullin. "Why knows? Maybe. You read the last paragraph?"

Accurso again looked at the report. "They lost interest in Russo," he said. "Looks like the FBI had other things to worry about."

"I love the way they describe it," Mullin said, taking the paper from Accurso and reading aloud from it: " 'Operational contact with subject made low priority. Subject firmly settled in Tel Aviv with Jewish female companion. Age and deteriorating health render subject unlikely to leave the country.' "

"They got that wrong," said Accurso.

"Big-time. So, Vinnie, what was Mr. Louis Russo doing here in D.C.?"

"Playing tourist?"

"Look at this list of what he was carrying. Enough pills to stock a pharmacy. A doc's name over at GW hospital. A medical history. Hell, judging from that, he was damn near dead already when he got it."

"They contact this woman he was with in Israel?"

"Yeah. I don't know whether they reached her yet. You watch TV news last night?"

"No, Katie and I watched one of those reality shows."

"This place isn't real enough for you?"

"Stupid show."

"They all are. Sometimes reality is, too. I watched the news. Fox had this gal reporter who was at the station right after the shooting. She says some young guy asked about the victim. When she said she didn't know, he blurts out the name."

"Russo? Louis Russo?"

"That's what she says."

"We talk to her?"

"Eldridge did. She put out on the tube last night we want him to come forward. So how come this young guy knows the victim is Russo? Who the hell is he?"

"She give much of a description?"

"No. Kind of tall, heavyset, she said. Says she only saw him for a second. Excited. But not exactly broken up. I'd love to find this guy."

"Maybe he *will* come forward."

"Depends on what his game is. And mob connection, if there is one."

"The Italian Mafia using black hit men these days?"

"That bothered me, too, except so many of the dago mob are in jail, maybe they have to go outside." He grunted and stood. "Well, let's head over to Northeast and spread the sketch around to some of our more prominent citizens, like the boss wants. That'll kill the morning, and we can grab lunch at that joint we were at last week."

As they walked to the unmarked car assigned them this day, Mullin said, "You know what I think, Vinnie?"

"What?"

"Black, white, mob, no mob, Israel, offing a guy nearly dead anyway — I think this one ain't going to go away any time soon."

FOURTEEN

Mackensie Smith returned to his office after having just taught a morning class at George Washington. He'd intended to take the summer off from teaching, but had been persuaded by his dean to offer a twice-weekly class on changes in criminal law since the imposition of stringent surveillance and detention policies brought about by the tragic events of September 11, 2001, and the ongoing terrorist threat.

The law school class was held on Tuesday and Thursday mornings at nine o'clock and was attended primarily by attorneys already in criminal practice who wanted an updated look at whatever policies the Justice Department had put into place. Teaching working attorneys — there were a few matriculated students in the course, but they were in the minority — posed a challenge for Smith. These weren't wide-eyed young men and women aspiring to careers in the law. Rather, they were seasoned attorneys whose questions were more realistic than those of their younger counterparts.

Aside from teaching this one course, Smith was enjoying a leisurely summer with his wife, Annabel Lee-Smith, the former matrimonial lawyer who now owned a Georgetown art gallery specializing in pre-Columbian art and artifacts.

Smith had been a Washington criminal defense attorney, consistently cited in *Washingtonian* magazine's annual survey of the city's best as one of the top five criminal defense lawyers in town. As discouraging as criminal law — or more particularly, criminal clients — could be, he'd loved what he did and zealously threw himself into his practice.

But that all ended one rainy night when a drunken driver on the Beltway hit a car occupied by his wife and son, killing both. This double tragedy had profound consequences, as might be expected. His enthusiasm for practicing criminal law waned, and although his belief in the justice system remained strong, defending the criminally accused lost priority in his life. He resigned his partnership in the law firm and accepted what had been a long-standing invitation to join the prestigious faculty of George Washington University.

Annabel, too, had found fulfillment from

her law practice and was considered among the first rank of matrimonial attorneys. But a parallel passion going back to her college days had always been pre-Columbian art. It remained that, a pleasant auxiliary interest until she met the handsome, cultured widower, Mackensie Smith, and fell in love with him and he with her. That's when their lives changed forever.

Smith, slightly taller than medium, stocky and strong, and with a slowly receding hairline, had always moved in relatively lofty Washington social and political circles. He predictably had become the object of female pursuit once the requisite amount of time had passed following the deaths of his wife and son, and was occasionally seen on the arm of a woman. But he never considered another serious romantic relationship until he met Annabel.

People said she resembled the actress Rita Hayworth, although Smith wasn't fond of the who-does-she-look-like game. Besides, as far as he was concerned, Annabel Lee was more beautiful than any movie actress, past or present. She was almost his height, even could be as tall as he was depending upon the shoes she wore and how she arranged her mane of auburn hair. Peaches and cream was not a cliché when it came to describing her skin. Her eyes were large, oval, and very green.

They'd met at an embassy party and began seeing each other regularly. He was surprised that she'd never married; it certainly wasn't for a lack of suitors. She'd just never met a man she was willing to commit to.

Mac Smith was that man, and he considered himself fortunate that she'd accepted his proposal and become Annabel Lee-Smith. Over the course of their courtship, they'd discussed their dreams and aspirations, and when they decided to alter their professional lives, their support for each other was mutual and total.

They were married in a small chapel at the National Cathedral and set out on their new life as husband and wife, a handsome couple to be sure, and much in demand. But they'd agreed to be judicious in accepting invitations to preserve as much time as possible for their own use and to enjoy their love. When they were not really together, Annabel worked at making her gallery a success and Mac taught his eager students, as well as lending his considerable legal experience to friends in need of informal counsel.

All in all, though life was not without a

few bumps, Mr. and Mrs. Mackensie Smith were quite contented, thank you, ensconced in their spacious Watergate apartment with its stunning sunset views of the Potomac River, serving as "parents" to their great blue Dane, Rufus, and looking forward to many happy years together.

Mac spent an hour in his campus office sorting through paperwork and catching up on reading or speed-scanning professional journals. At eleven-thirty, he picked up the phone and dialed a local number.

"Kathryn? It's Mac Smith."

"Oh, hi, Mr. Smith," Kathryn Jalick said, surprise at who was calling evident in her voice.

Smith laughed. "It's Mac, remember. 'Mr. Smith' makes me feel ancient."

"I know," she said. "Sorry."

"Is Rich there?"

"No . . . Mac. He's gone to New York."

"Editorial meeting?"

"I guess so. Yes, he has a session with his editor. Be back later tonight."

"And how have you been?"

"Busy as usual. I have the day off from the library and I'm trying to catch up on housework. The place looks like a tornado hit it. And my mind matches the decor these days."

"Well," Smith said, "I just wanted to check in and see how the scribe's book is coming along."

"You're talking to the wrong person, Mac. Rich has been on the go so much lately we never seem to have time to just sit down and catch up with each other."

"I know how that can be, Kathryn. Looking forward to seeing you two tomorrow night."

"Tomorrow night?"

"You haven't forgotten, have you? Dinner at our place. I get to play chef and bartender."

"Oh, no, I haven't forgotten. We're looking forward to it. I have to run, Mac. Thanks for calling. See you tomorrow."

Smith frowned at the dead phone. He didn't know Kathryn Jalick well, having met her only a few times when she'd accompanied Rich to the Smiths' apartment, where Mac went over the publishing contract a New York publisher had tendered for the book Rich was writing. She sounded distracted. But maybe that was her usual telephone style.

He called Annabel at the gallery.

116

"How goes it?" he asked.

"Okay," she replied. "You?"

"Good class. I just spoke with Kathryn Jalick."

"Oh? How is she?"

"Fine. Sounded distracted. I think she and Rich forgot about dinner tomorrow night."

"Good thing you called. They are coming?"

"Yes. He's in New York today meeting with his publisher, back tonight. Up for lunch?"

"Sure."

"Druthers?"

"Whatever restaurant has the best air-conditioning. The unit here at the gallery is on its last legs. It's been groaning all morning."

"Does Zagat rate restaurants on their AC?"

She laughed and said, "Wouldn't be a bad idea here in Washington. Paolo's? An hour?"

"I'll be there. If their AC's down, we'll eat at home, maybe even linger a while."

"I sense a proposition."

"That's one of many things I love about you, Annabel. You're very astute. With any luck, birds have nested in Paolo's air-con-

117

ditioning and it's on the fritz. As a matter of fact, let's assume that. The apartment in an hour?"

"Forty-five minutes, Smith. Don't be late."

FIFTEEN

Tim Stripling, ex-CIA, sat at the desk in his home. On the desk were articles about the Russo murder he'd clipped from newspapers, and a yellow legal pad on which he'd written notes from a call he'd made to New York shortly after leaving his meeting with FBI agents. He'd expected the call to be picked up by a recorded electronic voice. Instead, the ringing stopped when a woman said, "Detective Tresh."

"Hello, Detective. My name is Stripling, Timothy Stripling. Liberty Press. I was told to call you about Louis Russo."

"Hold on."

Detective Tresh came back on the line and read from a prepared script: "Louis Russo. Born 1932 New York City. Father, Nicholas, Italian. Mother, Lillian, Jewish. Five siblings. Joined Gambino family 1947, age fifteen. Loan-sharking, numbers collection, prostitution, enforcement, drug trafficking. Six known murders, first in 1953, age twenty-one. Mid-level soldier in family. Four arrests, three indictments. Arrested on drug charges 1990. Turned informant 1991, age fifty-nine. Testified in RICO trial 1991. Witness protection program 1991. Federal Bureau of Investigation handling. Wife, Anna, deceased 1989. No known children. Year in Mexico under bilateral agreement with Mexican government. Relocated Israel 1993. There since. Cohabitation with Sasha Levine, Jewish, current age fifty-five, residence Tel Aviv. Priority level low."

Stripling heard silence.

"Anything else?" he asked.

"Negative."

"Thanks."

The line went dead.

That conversation took place before Russo was killed at Union Station and before Stripling knew of the murder. Now that the man he was supposed to find was dead, the information he'd received from Detective Tresh was meaningless, albeit interesting. The old mafioso probably had been caught in a drug sting in 1990 and squeezed to cooperate with the feds. Dealing in narcotics after years of forbidding it had brought down more than one mobster. Russo had violated the oath of *omertà,* of silence, and paid the ultimate price thirteen years later. The Mafia's memory was long and unforgiving.

That series of thoughts was interrupted by the phone's ringing.

"Hello?"

"Timothy, my friend. It's Mark."

Stripling's former boss at the CIA, Mark Roper, was fond of referring to people as "my friend" or "old buddy." Stripling learned long ago that when he was on the receiving end of such platitudes, it was reason to be wary.

"Hello, Mark."

"Everything well with you?"

"Yes. You?"

Roper sighed. "Quite well, despite our valiant members of Congress considering themselves experts on intelligence. I've finally come to the conclusion that the House truly represents America — wife beaters, drunks, lawyers, doctors, flimflam artists, born-agains, atheists, pillars of their communities, and absolute rogues. Enough of that. I hear your meeting with our friends went well."

"Didn't amount to much."

"So I read. The fellow you were interested in is no longer."

"If you mean he's dead, you're right."

"But that doesn't mean you're dead."

"Meaning?"

"Meaning they still want you on the case. Two o'clock, same place."

"To do what?"

"They'll explain. Mind a suggestion?"

"I probably will, but go ahead anyway."

"Be cooperative."

Stripling laughed. "I have always been the model of cooperation, Mark."

"A very poor model at times. This is important, Tim."

"To you?"

"To others more important than me."

Stripling resisted correcting his grammar.

"I hate to be crass, Mark," Stripling said, "but you never have told me what I'm being paid."

"Five hundred a day and expenses. It will show up in your checking account."

"Make it seven-fifty."

"Five hundred. Please, Tim, cooperate."

"Thought I'd try."

"I'll be in touch."

"I'm sure you will."

Stripling hung up and again read the information he'd received from the detective in New York and the newspaper clips on the Russo murder. Why the continuing focus on this old guy? Stripling's initial assumption that the murder was a mob hit was now a little shaky. He was to meet with the FBI agents again. Surely, having someone killed who'd been in the witness protection program for thirteen years couldn't be the reason for the Bureau's sustaining interest. And why bring him, Timothy Stripling, into it? The Bureau had plenty of ex-agents looking to free-lance.

He made himself a salad from leftover chicken, did a half hour of light stretching exercises, took the two handguns from where they were secured in a safe inside a bedroom closet and checked them, almost a daily, obsessive ritual, returned the weapons to the safe, and stepped out into the bright, hot sunlight.

Five hundred a day, he thought as he looked for a taxi to take him to FBI head-quarters. It would do, at least for the moment. But money aside, he now had another reason for playing along. He wanted to know who this Louis Russo *really* was and why he was here, and why both the FBI and CIA wanted the answer, too. One thing was certain in his mind. Their interest reflected that of someone high up the chain, *very* high.

SIXTEEN

Marienthal's Delta shuttle flight to New York was delayed by thunderstorms that moved through Reagan National Airport that morning. He arrived at La Guardia almost a full hour later than planned and took a taxi into the city, where he was left off in front of an office building on Park Avenue South. He checked his watch; he still had fifteen minutes before his scheduled meeting and used it to grab a coffee and Danish at a luncheonette next door. Fortified, he entered the lobby, took the first available elevator, and rode to the ninth floor, where the offices of the publishing company, Hobbes, were located.

"I'm Rich Marienthal," he told the young, moonfaced blonde receptionist. "I have an appointment with Sam Greenleaf."

"Have a seat," she said pleasantly. "I'll let him know you're here."

Marienthal browsed a recent issue of *People* until Greenleaf appeared. "Hello, Rich," he said, crossing the reception area and shaking hands. "Come on in."

Greenleaf, Hobbes House's managing editor, was a large man in all ways — head, face, body, and hands. Sporting an unkempt reddish beard, he wore brown corduroy slacks, well-worn space shoes that showed the result of supporting excess weight for too long, and a checked shirt undoubtedly bought through a big-and-tall-man catalogue. He led Marienthal to a sizable office as disorganized as his personal appearance, moved files from a chair in front of a desk overflowing with books and papers, and invited Marienthal to sit. Photographs dangled crookedly on the walls. A window in need of washing reluctantly allowed gray light into the room. The powdery remains of crumb cake were scattered on a piece of foil on the desk.

"Good trip?" he asked.

"Delayed. Weather in D.C. But I'm here."

"Good, good. Coffee?"

"Just had some."

Greenleaf used the phone on his desk to ask someone to fetch him a cup, sat back, and shook his head. "Couldn't believe the news when you called me," he said. "Incredible. Who the hell could ever have forecast such a thing?"

"Not me, Sam. That's for sure."

Greenleaf came forward and rested his chin on a bridge formed by his hands. "What's the latest, Rich? I mean, do you know who did it?"

"I have no idea."

Marienthal adjusted his position in the chair and looked at one of the photographs on the wall, a formally posed portrait of the publishing house's founder and namesake, Wallace Hobbes. The founder, now deceased, claimed to be a distant relation — very distant — to the seventeenth-century English political philosopher Thomas Hobbes. Hobbes had spawned the movement known as Hobbism, whose creed claimed that human beings were so lazy, selfish, and self-aggrandizing that only an absolute monarchy could control them. Why Wallace Hobbes — or anyone for that matter — would want to claim a relationship to a man with such ideas was lost on Marienthal.

Greenleaf returned to a more relaxed posture in his oversized, overstuffed office chair. "What do you figure, Rich, that those former friends of his who ended up behind bars because of his big mouth finally got even? But why now? Didn't you tell me Russo was a sick man?"

"Revenge is the most logical explanation," Marienthal said, reaching into a pocket of his tan safari jacket for a Kleenex. "I think I'm getting a cold," he said, blowing his nose.

"Summer colds are the worst," said Greenleaf. "They tend to hang on forever."

"So I've heard. Look, Sam, the question now is, what does this do to the book?"

Greenleaf held up his hand. "Hard to say. It's all so new. I've already been on the phone with Pamela. She's not happy at this turn of events."

Pamela Warren was Hobbes's publisher, a steely woman who'd come up through the ranks at other publishing houses. Those who knew her and had worked with her agreed that she was a savvy business-woman, a careful publisher, and utterly humorless, especially when it came to the bottom line.

"I'm not happy either," Marienthal said, "about a lot of things. But that's irrelevant. The question is how to get around it." He frowned as a new and unwelcome thought came to him. "She's not considering yanking the book, is she?"

Greenleaf raised his palm against what had been said. "No fear of that, Rich. The story you've so adroitly put together will still have impact, whether Mr. Russo is alive or not." He paused; an unpleasant expression crossed his face. "Of course," he said, "we have lost the timing and the event, the very things we were counting on. How that will impact sales is another question."

Marienthal had expected this issue to be raised and had formulated a response. He started to express it but was interrupted by the arrival of Greenleaf's coffee. The editor tasted it, swiveled in the chair, reached for something on the credenza behind him, and handed Marienthal a color proof of his book's jacket.

"We were supposed to have finished books by now," Marienthal said.

A shrug from Greenleaf. "The wheels of publishing grind slow, Rich. Your book has gone from manuscript to print faster than we've ever done before. It's coming off the presses as we speak. But getting books into the stores is our problem. *Your* problem is what happens now in Washington. Have you spoken with your friend on the Hill?"

"Last night."

"And?"

"And they want to go forward with the hearings, using the book."

"Having a book take the oath isn't nearly as sexy as having your Mr. Russo do it."

"You say that as though I could have done something to prevent his getting killed."

"No, no, no, Rich. I wasn't suggesting that. It's just that . . ."

Marienthal cocked his head. "Just?"

"It's just that when you brought us the proposal, its appeal was — well, let's just say there was a built-in publicity hook that helped in our decision to buy it. It was something that Pamela — that *we* were counting on. Here. Look."

He gave Marienthal mock-ups of ads that had been prepared by an outside agency. Marienthal scanned them quickly and put them on the desk. "What can I say, Sam? They'll have to be redone."

"Provided Pamela is willing to lay out the money to do them over. She runs a tight ship, Rich. I'll be meeting with her this afternoon. I'll see what I can do. In the meantime, we have to go with what we have, minus your inconsiderate Louis Russo."

"Inconsiderate?"

Greenleaf laughed away his words. "Getting himself killed the way he did. Bad timing, if nothing else."

Marienthal resisted commenting on Greenleaf's insensitivity. While his relationship with Louis Russo had initially been solely for the purpose of writing a book, he'd grown to like the old mafioso.

It hadn't been easy convincing Russo to tell his story for the book Marienthal intended to write. He'd had to work at gaining his trust and had been uncomfortable at times with things he'd said and promised to achieve that trust. Russo, if not exactly a gracious host during Marienthal's frequent visits to Tel Aviv, had been unfailingly courteous. So had the woman, Sasha, whose good-natured challenges to Russo seemed exactly what was needed to pick up his spirits when they flagged, and to spur him to believe he might live to see another day.

When Marienthal had started writing his novel about a Mafia hit man, it was inconceivable that he would wind up having Hobbes as his publisher. Hobbes published only nonfiction — right-wing nonfiction at that — reflecting the house's conservative editorial philosophy. It was known as a willing conduit for books generated by the conservative elements in government, and according to some in the publishing industry was handsomely compensated by those elements — a vanity press for special interests whose message matched that of the publisher.

Rich's numerous meetings with Russo in Israel had provided the sort of inside knowledge he needed to give the novel the ring of truthfulness and authenticity. The old man was a good storyteller and seemed to enjoy reliving his days on the streets and in the so-called social clubs of his Mafia family: the women and the rubouts, his brushes with the law, the colorful characters who were his friends and later his enemies. During one of Marienthal's earlier visits to Tel Aviv, Russo had told him a story that shocked the young writer. Was it true? Could it be true? Whether it was or not, it provided Rich with a powerful scene to include in the novel.

Not long after returning from that trip, he was introduced to Geoff Lowe at a party.

"What kind of things do you write?" Lowe asked.

Rich told him about the novel and mentioned the startling story Russo had told him, adding, "Probably apocryphal."

At Lowe's urging, they met for lunch the next day.

After Rich had delivered a more complete version of Russo's story over burgers and beer at Hawk and Dove — Lowe's treat — Lowe asked, "Why the hell are you doing it as a novel?"

"I don't know," Marienthal replied. "I suppose because I'm a novelist."

"Yeah, that's fine," said Lowe, "but how many first novels sell? I mean, Christ, what's the chances of even finding a decent publisher?"

"It won't be easy, Geoff, but I'm confident."

Lowe drained his beer and wiped his mouth. "Listen to me," he said, leaning closer. "What if I can guarantee you a publishing contract?"

Marienthal laughed. "Guarantee me? What are you, a literary agent? I thought you worked for Senator Widmer."

"I do, but I have connections in New York. Look, Rich, I really like you. I don't know, we seem to just hit it off. If you'd be willing to change your book into a nonfiction account of the story the old guy told you, I can get Hobbes to publish it."

"Hobbes? They do what, nonfiction. Right-wing stuff."

"And they're damn good at it. I know they'd love a book like this."

"The story's not enough to support a whole book."

"Don't be silly. You pad it with all the history leading up to it and what came after. I can have one of our researchers help."

Marienthal sat back and slowly shook his head. "I don't think so," he said.

"Suit yourself," said Lowe, slapping his credit card on the check. "But you'll be passing up a big advance and a ton of publicity. Hell, you'll make your name with this book and can go on and write all the novels you want."

They parted on the sidewalk.

"I'll let you know," Marienthal said.

"Okay, but don't wait too long. This book would fit in with some other plans I'm working on. These chances don't come along every day. Ciao!"

Rich called Lowe a week later. "I'd like to discuss the book again," he said.

"Great. Lunch? One?"

"Sure. Lunch at one."

And that's how it started.

Marienthal was well aware of Russo's failing health and admired his gritty determination not to give in to self-pity. The old man was a tough bird, not surprising considering his background, but impressive nonetheless. Marienthal hadn't had time since the murder to allow feelings to intrude upon the shock of Russo's death, but a measure of sadness had begun to surface. He'd lost someone with whom he'd become close. A piece of him was suddenly gone.

"Going to Washington is the best thing for him," Sasha had told Marienthal when he prepared to leave Tel Aviv after his most recent visit. "It will give him a purpose to meet some of your friends there."

"Don't worry, Sasha," Rich had said. "I'll take good care of him."

Guilt, too, had joined sadness.

"Maybe his murder will help sell books," Marienthal offered weakly, and not pleased with the thought.

"Maybe, but nothing compared to having him testify," Greenleaf said.

"Will you have advance copies before the hearings?" Marienthal asked.

"I'll push for it. You'll still testify. Right?"

"That's the plan. It would be better if I had a book in hand."

"You have the galley proofs. That may have to do."

"Do what you can, Sam. Look, I realize what happened yesterday changes things. That was beyond my control. But it doesn't mean the book — the story — isn't as valid. Geoff, Senator Widmer's top aide, thinks what the book has to say will stand on its own."

"But without Russo to confirm it in person, it's liable to be dismissed as nothing more than the fantasies of some old mafioso looking for his fifteen minutes of fame. That's the way reviewers might react."

Marienthal stood. "I'll do everything I can, Sam. You know that."

"Of course you will," Greenleaf said, also standing and coming around the desk. He draped his arm over Marienthal's shoulders and walked him to the reception area. "Look," he said as they waited for the elevator, "I'll work this end. But do me a favor."

"Sure."

"Keep me informed. No surprises. Our publicity people want to coordinate their work with the hearings. Leak some of the juicier stuff just before the hearings start."

The elevator arrived.

"Funny," Greenleaf said.

"What's funny?"

"Your friend, Russo, is going to get his fifteen minutes of fame anyway. Posthumously."

"I'm sure he'll appreciate it," Marienthal said, stepping into the elevator and watching Greenleaf disappear behind the closing doors.

SEVENTEEN

Marienthal left the building and walked slowly up Park Avenue in the direction of Grand Central Station. The day was as gray as his mood. The meeting with his editor had accomplished little, aside from giving him some assurance that Hobbes House and its publisher, Pamela Warren, still intended to go forward with the book. That was comforting. At the same time, he wondered whether he even wanted to see the book, his first and only thus far, published under the circumstances. There was much to think about.

He'd been writing for a living, as tenuous as it might have been, since graduating with a degree in English literature from New York University eight years ago. His first job, writing press releases for a public relations firm in Manhattan, had lasted three years, and he'd hated every minute of it. His dream was to become a successful serious novelist, and he toiled nights and weekends on a novel he'd started while a student.

He completed it just before leaving the PR firm, and on the good days hadn't the slightest doubt it would be gobbled up by a major New York publisher, establishing him as a bright star on the literary horizon.

Publishers to whom he submitted the manuscript were not accommodating. Rejection slip followed rejection slip, eventually eighteen in all, some with encouraging words added to form rejection letters, others lacking even that modicum of encouragement.

Money was tight; he often fell behind on the rent on his tiny fifth-floor walk-up studio apartment in the East Village. Occasional freelance copyediting jobs helped, but only barely. He started a second novel but soon lost interest in it. There were moments — but only moments — when he considered returning home and living in the house in which he'd been raised. That was out of the question. Accepting rejection of his novel was defeat enough; skulking back home would be even worse.

It was at this nadir in his young life that a college friend, who'd moved to Washington following graduation for an entrance-level job with a lobbying firm, called and suggested Marienthal move there, too. "You can bunk with me," his friend offered, "until you get set up."

Rich took him up on the offer and moved south. Within a month, he'd landed another PR job, this with an aerospace manufacturer's D.C. office, where again he ground out press releases lauding the company's achievements, putting a spin on its less-than-successful ventures, and praising the company's management and its contributions to the nation's security. That job lasted two years — until a man named Louis Russo entered his life.

He walked into the splendidly redone Grand Central Station and checked the electronic departure board for Metro North trains to Bedford Hills. The next was scheduled to depart in an hour. He bought a round-trip ticket, had a beer and salad at the bar at Michael Jordan's steakhouse overlooking the vast terminal, then went to gate 29 and boarded.

The hour trip passed quickly, as though it hadn't happened. He'd slipped into a trance state, oblivious to people in the car, sights through the window, and the train's motion itself. His mind was assaulted by images past and present. Although he hadn't seen Louis Russo's lifeless body in Union Station, he could see it as though he were standing over it. That image kept melding into a kaleidoscope of scenes: sipping sweet tea with Russo and Sasha in their Tel Aviv apartment; getting drunk with other students in a jazz joint near NYU; falling off his bike as a kid and opening a gash on his forehead requiring stitches at an emergency ward; Kathryn, naked and enticing him from the computer to the bedroom; Russo's face rimmed with blood; Greenleaf's arm around his shoulder; Pamela Warren's stern, unsmiling face when he first met with her at Hobbes House; the Twin Towers on 9/11; spectacular explosions in Baghdad; scenes from *The Sopranos*; Kathryn cooking spaghetti in their kitchen; his mother comforting him after the stitches; his father lecturing him on what it takes to be a success.

"Bedford Hills," the conductor announced over the train's PA system.

Marienthal looked out the window and saw his father's black Mercedes parked near the entrance to the small, suburban train station. The car's tinted glass shielded a view of the man behind the wheel, but Marienthal didn't need to actually see him to know the expression that would be on his face.

"Hi, Dad," Marienthal said, opening the front passenger door and slipping onto the tan leather seat.

"Hello, son. Glad you could find the time to spend a few hours with us. Been a while."

Marienthal held back from reaching over and offering an awkward embrace of his father, who immediately drove away from where he'd parked and headed for the family home in the prosperous enclave of Bedford.

"How's Mom?" Marienthal asked.

"All right, although I'm worried about her. She seems befuddled from time to time. Not as sharp as she used to be."

Marienthal looked at his father, whose eyes never left the road, his patrician features clearly displayed against the dark window behind. He wore his requisite sharply creased chinos, blue button-down shirt, short, supple brown leather jacket, and perforated driving gloves. He hadn't aged in Rich's eyes; he seemed always to have looked this way.

"How long can you stay?" the father asked as he turned up a long, winding dirt road leading to the house.

"Just a couple of hours. I have to get back to Washington."

A smile crossed his father's thin lips. "You make it sound as though the White House is expecting you," he said, his voice pinched, nasal.

Rich let the comment pass and turned to take in the passing greenery. Two Hispanic gardeners working on the property waved as the car passed; his father returned the greeting with a flip of a finger.

"José still work here?" Rich asked.

"Of course. Why wouldn't he? He's well compensated and loyal."

Is he saying I'm disloyal? Rich wondered. It didn't matter. There undoubtedly would be many such comments to consider.

They pulled into a circular gravel drive and came to a stop. Rich revised his earlier observation that his father never aged. Out of the car, he looked older, slightly stooped; Frank Marienthal had always been proud of his erect posture. As they approached the front door of the 1860s colonial-style home, its white clapboard and antique green shutters and door immaculately painted, the flowering shrubs on either side of the walkway manicured and healthy, he also took note that his father's gait wasn't quite as assured as it had been in past years. Still, he exuded presence and purpose. That hadn't changed.

Rich dropped his knapsack on the granite floor and followed his father into the kitchen, where Rich's mother, Mary Marienthal, a short, slender woman with carefully coiffed white hair and a rosy complexion, worked alongside a black woman in a white uniform.

"Richard, darling!" Mary said, skirting a large stainless steel prep table in the center of the spacious kitchen to hug her son. "Let me see you." She stepped back and took him in from head to toe. "You look wonderful. A little tired. Not getting your rest?"

"Not lately, Mom." He went to the black housekeeper and gave her a hug. "How you doing, Carrie?" he asked.

"Oh, just fine," she said. "Getting older faster."

He joined her laughter. "You don't look a day older than when you first came here," he said.

"Hungry?" his mother asked.

"No, thanks. Had something to eat before I got on the train. A beer, maybe."

He looked through the open door to a long hallway leading to the dining and living rooms. At the end was his father's home office, where he was sure his father had retreated. Small talk in kitchens bored him. Small talk in any room bored noted criminal attorney Frank Marienthal.

A bottle of Killian Red in hand — no glass, thank you — Rich left the kitchen and went to the office. The door was open. The elder Marienthal sat behind his large custom-made, leather-topped curved desk. Floor-to-ceiling windows behind him afforded a restful view of gardens to the rear of the house.

"Come in," his father said.

Rich entered and went to tall bookcases that took up an entire wall. He wasn't looking for anything in particular. Perusing books on the shelves delayed the conversation he knew was about to ensue. Eventually he turned, smiled at his father, whose stern expression didn't change, and took one of a pair of red leather armchairs across the desk. He raised a blue-jean-clad leg and dangled it over an arm, in contrast to his father's stoic, proper posture.

"You wanted to talk to me," Rich said.

"Yes. I've heard about Louis Russo's murder."

"Where did you read it?"

"I didn't read it. I was called about it. I'm surprised I didn't hear it from you."

"I've been busy since it happened. I'm sure you can understand that."

Frank Marienthal paused, his position behind the desk not changing, his eyes focused on his son. "Frankly, Richard, I do not understand it."

"Well, I can't do anything about that. About your not understanding it, I mean."

The father's dark blue eyes bored holes in his son. "Maybe I should educate you a little, Rich. I've tried to do that throughout your life, but you've always resisted, of course. Rebellion and such."

"Dad, I —"

Frank Marienthal's hand slowly came up, fingers widely separated. "Please, hear me out. You do know, Richard, that I was firmly against this book of yours. I tried to dissuade you at every turn for many reasons, not the least of which is the secondary use it might be put to."

Rich removed his leg from the chair's arm and planted both feet on the floor, as though girding himself for war. In a sense, he was.

The elder Marienthal continued. "When you first asked me to intervene with Russo and put you together with him, I initially refused. Remember?"

"Sure I remember."

"But you pressed the issue and I acquiesced. You said you needed to interview him for background material for a *novel* you were writing about the mob. You used privileged information to make your case with me. Frankly, Richard, I resented it then, and I resent it now."

Rich waited a moment before responding. "Look, Dad," he said, "that so-called privileged information wasn't very privileged after twenty years. Besides, it's not information that was important when you represented Louis — when he turned informant and went into witness protection. It was outside lawyer-client privilege."

Frank's eyebrows went up, and he smiled. "Where did I go wrong?" he said through a deep, prolonged sigh. "You're going to lecture *me* about lawyer-client privilege? As I recall, you refused to go to law school as I wanted you to do. Another bit of sophomoric rebellion."

"I didn't want to be a lawyer," Rich said, "any more than I wanted to accept the appointment to Annapolis. I know you meant well in encouraging me in those directions, but they didn't represent what I wanted. Why can't you accept that?"

"How is the writing career coming?"

"You didn't answer my question. You changed the subject, the way you always do. A courtroom technique I would have learned in law school, I suppose."

Rich took a swig of beer, started to place the bottle on the desk, but instead lowered it to the rug next to him. He felt his anger rising, and silently told himself to keep it in check. He'd lost control too often in the past when in such conversations with his father. Each time, his volatility rendered him helpless in contrast to his father's calm, reasoned approach. No matter how right he might have been during those confrontations, losing control quickly became the issue, the only issue. He wouldn't let it happen again.

"Why so combative, Richard?"

"Why is it that whenever I disagree with you, you call me combative?"

"I was asking about your writing career."

"It's going fine. I met with my editor this morning before coming here."

His father slowly shook his head.

"Yeah, I know," Rich said, reaching down for his beer and finishing it. "It's Hobbes House. The fact is . . ."

"The fact is, Richard, that Hobbes House's reputation isn't a secret to anyone, including you."

"They wanted the book!"

"Of course they did."

"Dad —"

"You and your book are being used, Richard. Isn't that evident? You're bright enough to see through that."

"Thanks."

"And you used Louis Russo. The man is dead because you lied to me about the sort of book you were writing. You called it a novel."

"It started out that way. But I changed my mind. Hobbes House is still calling it a novel to keep things under wraps until publication."

"Why did Russo come to Washington?"

"Whoa, hold on," Rich said. "You claim you resented me when I asked to be put in touch with Louis. Well, I resent being accused of using him and being responsible for his murder. He agreed to talk to me — thanks to you — and he went on to tell me his story, the whole story. I really liked Louis."

"I'm sure that's a comfort to him."

"He agreed to come to Washington of his own free will. Sasha — she's the woman he lives with . . . lived with in Tel Aviv for years — told me she thought going to Washington was good for him, gave him a sense of purpose."

"You haven't answered my question.

Why was he in Washington?"

"To meet with me. We were going to talk . . . about the book."

"I thought you finished it."

"I did. I just thought —"

"You believed the story he told you?"

"Yes. Didn't you?"

"No, and I told you that. You entered into this agreement with a sick, delusional old man."

His posture relaxed somewhat as he lapsed into what would pass for reverie. "I remember well his tales of intrigue, Richard. He was like so many of them, looking to enhance his image by inflating his importance. A strange thing about mafiosi. They consider themselves super-patriots, keepers of the flag and flame, appreciating their country more than law-abiding citizens. Crooks? They're desperate for respectability, Richard. They know they're nothing more than common thugs, leg-breakers and murderers. They cost this nation millions in labor union extortion and other illegal activities. Yet they seek approval from politicians and have gotten it on occasion. Louis Russo was no different. He was just a soldier in the Gambino family who got squeezed by authorities and decided to break his oath.

Frankly, Richard, I'm surprised that you would give credence to such a man."

Frank abruptly stood and looked out at the garden. As Rich observed him, he thought back to when, as a teenager, he would be allowed to visit New York City courtrooms where his father defended clients accused of myriad criminal acts — rape, drug dealing, assault, arson, and murder. Some of his highest profile cases involved members of organized crime. He became known in the press as a mob lawyer, although mobsters did not constitute most of his practice. He was an unlikely attorney to be involved with defending members of organized crime, at least from Rich's perspective. Other so-called mob lawyers were New York characters, it seemed to him, Runyonesque types who acted like their clients — brash, irreverent, fast talking, scornful of the judicial system that looked to prosecute them for their crimes. His father was the antithesis of those attorneys — Harvard educated, family money, erudite, soft-spoken, a gentleman.

But he was also a brilliant defense attorney, dedicated to pretrial preparation, skilled at cross-examination (one of three books written by him delved into the art of that subject), and well connected within the community of judges before whom he plied his trade. His success at obtaining not-guilty verdicts was the envy of other lawyers; many sought him out as a co-counsel in particularly difficult cases.

Once, when asked by a TV reporter outside a courthouse, after one of his mob clients had been found not guilty, how he could justify in his own mind defending people who were so obviously guilty, he replied, "The fact that you assume these people are guilty flies in the face of our system of jurisprudence. I certainly wouldn't want someone as close-minded as you on any jury of mine. Excuse me. I have other places to be."

What he didn't add was that he chose his clients based upon their ability to pay his sizable fees. A mafioso's money was as good as anyone else's, and they always had plenty of it to buy the best possible defense.

Mary Marienthal came to the door as Frank turned from the window.

"Not now," he said, waving his hand.

"I just thought Rich might like another beer," she said.

"He's had enough beer," her husband said. "Close the door, please."

She looked at Rich, who'd turned in the chair at her arrival. Her eyebrows went up. He gave her a reassuring smile and she backed away, closing the door behind her.

"You asked how my writing career was going," Rich said after his father had resumed his place behind the desk.

He was met with a noncommittal stare.

"It wasn't going very well for a while, and you know all that. But this book will turn that around. I don't care whether it's Hobbes House or Random House. Geoff, a friend of mine in Washington, knows people at Hobbes House and suggested I submit the book to them. They bit, and with enthusiasm. Sure, I know their reputation. They're a publisher with a conservative bent. Big deal. They've had some best sellers in the past couple of years, and that's what I'm looking for. This is my breakout shot, Dad."

Rich stood and paced the room, coming to a stop in front of the desk. He placed his hands on it and leaned toward his father. "Can't you be supportive of what I'm doing?" He turned to take the chair again and kicked over the empty beer bottle. "Sorry," he said, righting it and sitting.

"It isn't a matter of being supportive, Richard. You certainly can't accuse me of not supporting you. You wouldn't have a book unless I'd put you in touch with Russo."

"You're right, and I appreciate that. Look, I'm as sorry as the next person that Louis was killed. I guess the mob doesn't say let bygones be bygones, exactly."

"*If* it was the mob that killed him."

"Had to be."

His father said nothing.

Rich's cell phone rang. He pulled it from his pocket and answered. It was Kathryn.

"Hi," he said.

"Hi. Where are you?"

"At Mom and Dad's house. What's up?"

"Mac Smith called. He reminded me we're having dinner with them tomorrow night."

"I forgot."

"So did I. With all that's happened I —"

"I'd rather skip it. Mac is a great guy but —"

"I don't see how we can. I told him we'd be there."

"Okay."

"When are you leaving there?"

"A couple of minutes. I'll give you a call from the airport."

"Sorry," he told his father, turning off the phone and returning it to his pocket.

"Have you spoken with Mac Smith lately?"

"No, but Kathryn and I are having dinner with Mac and his wife tomorrow night."

"You'll discuss this with him?"

"Discuss what?"

"Your book. Pulling it in view of what's occurred."

Rich floundered before coming up with a response. "Pull it? That's ridiculous. I wouldn't think of it."

"Maybe it's time you did a little thinking, Richard. Why haven't you given me the book to read?"

Rich made a point of looking at his watch. He stood. "I have to go, Dad. There's a train back into the city in a half hour. Drive me to the station?"

"Your mother will. It will do her good to get out of the house."

Frank Marienthal left the room. It was the last time Rich saw him that day. His mother happily announced that she would take him to the train station. After saying goodbye to Carrie, Rich joined his mother in her green Mercedes and they pulled away from the house.

"Have a nice chat with your father?" she asked, obviously unaware of what father

154

and son had discussed.

"I'm not sure I'd characterize it that way," Rich said.

"He worries about you," she said. "So do I. How is that lovely young lady you've been seeing?"

"Kathryn? She's fine. She said to say hello."

Kathryn had accompanied Rich on a few of his infrequent visits home, and Mary Marienthal had once traveled to Washington to spend a week touring the city with them.

"Well, please say hello back from me," she said, pulling up in front of the station.

Rich kissed her on the cheek and opened the door on his side.

"Richard," she said.

"Yes?"

"Don't be too harsh with your father. He loves you very much."

"I know, I know," he said. "And I love you both. I'd better get inside. The train will be here in a few minutes."

He went to the platform and looked back to where his mother still sat in the car. She waved and blew him a kiss. He returned her wave as the train came into the station and wiped her from view.

EIGHTEEN

Detectives Bret Mullin and Vinnie Accurso spent the morning showing the composite sketch of Louis Russo's killer to people in the predominantly black community of Logan Circle, in the city's northeast quadrant. Once a fashionable neighborhood, Logan Circle had deteriorated into an area known more for its drug dealers, pimps, and prostitutes than for its once stately and genteel four-story Victorian mansions and town houses. For a while, prostitution was less of a problem after the police rounded the prostitutes up and took them to Virginia, to the chagrin of residents of that state. But they eventually drifted back. A few working their shifts on the hot streets of Logan Circle this morning watched warily as Mullin and Accurso passed.

"Good morning, ladies," Mullin said, chuckling.

"You know anybody looks like this?" Accurso asked, showing the prostitutes the composite sketch.

Heads shook.

"You take care," Mullin said as he and

his partner continued down the street. "Don't get mixed up with any wackos."

They showed the sketch to doormen and bellhops at the Vista International Hotel on Thomas Circle, the infamous scene of former mayor Marion Barry's arrest for possession of crack cocaine, and went through Meridian Hill Park, also known as Malcolm X Park. The gardens there, which re-created the splendid formal gardens of seventeenth-century France and Italy, were in stark contrast to the assortment of down-and-out men and women occupying the park's benches. On one was a hefty, brooding black man wearing a hooded blue sweatshirt despite the oppressive heat and humidity.

"Hey, Lucas," Mullin said, sitting on one side of him. Accurso took the other end of the bench.

"What's happening?" Mullin asked, wiping perspiration from his face with a handkerchief.

"Not much," Lucas said. "What are you guys doin' here?"

"Looking for him," Accurso said, holding the composite sketch in front of Lucas, one of a number of informants developed by Mullin.

Lucas swiveled to take in the park.

Mullin and Accurso seldom spoke with him in public, preferring clandestine meetings out of the sight of others.

"Who's he?" Lucas asked.

"Thought you might know," Mullin said. "He's the shooter at Union Station yesterday."

"Oh, yeah. Read about it. Saw it on TV. Never seen him before."

"Sure?"

"Yeah, man, I'm sure. What I read, he's too expensive a stud to be from around here. Least that's what the papers say."

"Anybody around here talking about the shooting?" Accurso asked.

"Nah. Got other things to rap about, you know what I'm sayin'?"

"Yeah, we know," Mullin said, getting to his feet and gesturing for his partner to do the same. "You hear anything, give us a call, Lucas."

"You got something for me?" Lucas asked, again nervously surveying the park.

"We would if you had something for us," Accurso said as he and Mullin walked away.

"Waste a time," Mullin grumbled, loosening his tie.

"How come you always wear a tie?" Accurso asked. He wore an open-neck yellow polo shirt and slacks. A tie wasn't required of detectives unless you were scheduled to attend some official event. Visiting Logan Circle and the northeast quadrant didn't qualify.

"Take it off," Accurso said, referring to Mullin's tie.

"Waste a time," was all Mullin said as they continued to walk through the neighborhood, which, while rundown, exhibited occasional signs of gentrification. As they passed the splendid Basilica of the National Shrine of the Immaculate Conception, the largest Roman Catholic church in the hemisphere, Accurso glanced at Mullin, who surreptitiously blessed himself. He knew Mullin was Catholic, but had never before seen an outward manifestation of his faith.

"You hungry?" Mullin asked.

"Sure."

They went to 12th Street, which passed for an old-fashioned Main Street, and settled at a table by the front window in Murry & Paul's, a southern soul food fixture for years.

"What'd you do last night?" Accurso asked after they'd been served large glasses of ice water.

"Nothing. Had dinner, went home, fed

the cat, and watched a little TV."

"Where'd you have dinner?"

"What are you, keeping a diary of where I go, what I do?"

"Just curious."

"The Jockey Club."

Accurso shook his open hand as he said, "Ooh, fancy, fancy."

Mullin ignored him.

"That's some beautiful church, huh?"

"What is?"

"That Catholic church we passed. You ever been there?"

"No." Mullin looked at the menu. "Ribs," he said, "and slaw. You know that guy they say knew the dead guy's name?"

Accurso looked up from his menu. "Huh?"

"That guy they said told the TV reporter he knew the victim's name. Who the hell is he?"

Accurso shrugged. "Beats me. Ribs, I guess. And slaw."

"I figure this guy, whoever he is, knows more than Russo's name. You know what I mean?"

"Maybe he does. We'll never find him unless he decides to walk in. You want a Coke?" He knew that his big, beefy partner would like a beer or something stronger.

"Yeah, I guess," Mullin said, wishing he were alone in a dark bar.

They'd finished lunch and were on coffee when Mullin's cell phone went off.

"Mullin."

He listened, then flipped the phone's cover closed.

"What's up?" Accurso asked, laying down his half of the bill on the table. Mullin stood and tightened his tie, using his reflection in the window.

"Like I told you, Vinnie," Mullin said, heading for the door, "showing the sketch was a waste of time. They already found the shooter."

NINETEEN

As Mullin and Accurso left Murry & Paul's, Tim Stripling was arriving at the FBI Building for his second meeting with the two agents with whom he'd met the previous day. They huddled in the same secure room at the rear of the building.

"So, it looks like the hunt is off for Mr. Louis Russo," Stripling said. He'd removed his suit jacket and sat at the end of a short conference table, flanked by the agents.

"Yeah," one said. "Somebody found him before you did."

"If I was being paid as a bounty hunter, I'd be unhappy," said Stripling. "Maybe the guy who shot him collected a hefty fee."

When there was no response, he said, "Any word on who did the deed? I read his description in the papers, saw it on TV."

The agent to Stripling's left consulted a paper on the table in front of him, and read from it in a monotone.

"Leon LeClaire. Age forty-three. Residence listed as New York City. Born in Haiti, French passport."

Stripling's eyebrows lifted. "You've nailed him?"

"Somebody did. Literally. They discovered his body down in Kenilworth Gardens. We just got the word."

"A positive ID?"

"That's what we hear. We thought you'd get some info for us."

Stripling chuckled. "Why me?" he asked. "You're the fabled Federal Bureau of Investigation."

His comment was confrontational, but he didn't care. Stripling had always been distrustful of the FBI, having spent a good part of his professional life in the culture of the CIA, where the view of the Bureau was inherently less than positive. Now, as an independent operator, he was free to express what he felt without fear of retribution. But Mark Roper's words came back to him: *Be cooperative.*

The agents ignored his remark. One said, "The case is being handled at MPD by a detective named Mullin. Bret Mullin. They should be at the scene now. Kenilworth Aquatic Gardens, off the Anacostia Freeway, Northeast."

"I've been there," Stripling said. "Nice place. An ex-girlfriend was a plant freak, loved the water lilies at Kenilworth."

"That's nice to hear," an agent said.

The dig wasn't lost on Stripling. "So," he said, "just what is it you want me to find out?"

"Information about how the investigation is going."

"The MPD investigation?"

"That's right."

Stripling shook his head and flashed a smile. "I know I'm going to get the same answer I got last time, but I'm asking anyway. Why have *me* keep tabs on what MPD is doing? Hell, you guys work with them all the time."

"They're not always — well, as cooperative as we'd like them to be."

"Okay," Stripling said. "I'll see what I can do."

"Good. And while you're at it, see what you can find out about this so-called mystery man who blurted out Russo's name to a TV reporter."

"I saw that on TV," Stripling said.

"We'd like to know who he is."

"That won't be easy."

"Which is why they want you to do it."

They. There was no sense asking who *they* were, so Stripling didn't bother. "Anything else?" Stripling asked.

"No. We'll keep in touch on the cell

phone we gave you."

"Okay," Stripling said, standing and slipping on his jacket. He went to the door, turned, and asked, "What do I do if I find this mystery man? Who do I tell?"

"Let your control at the Company know you have something you want to tell us. We'll call and set up a meeting."

Stripling looked at him. A retired CIA agent with a control? The FBI guy was just rubbing it in. He held the man's eyes for a long moment, then left the room and the building and walked to a Hard Rock Café at Tenth and E Streets, relatively quiet at mid-afternoon. He took a table and ordered an iced coffee from the waitress, removed his jacket to allow the AC to reach him, and thought back to the meeting.

It was never easy discerning the true meaning behind what anyone in government said or did. When the agenda said peace, it very often meant war. There were more hidden agendas in official Washington than there were bureaucrats; the challenge was to get beyond the words to figure out what was *really* going on.

Keep tabs on MPD's investigation of the Russo murder and the subsequent killing of Russo's assassin? That wouldn't be difficult. He'd cultivated contacts within the MPD during his stint at the CIA and could call upon them. Of course, no longer being officially connected might make this a little more difficult, but he doubted it. There were always people in every organization who got a vicarious kick out of hobnobbing with spooks, even with men like Stripling, who'd spent most of his career identifying and nurturing moles within America's institutions, as opposed to the more swashbuckling overseas types. He didn't know what use any of the information he developed from these sources was put to, nor did he care. "Don't ask, don't tell" applied to more than the military's policy on homosexuality. Some of the dirt his informants dug up on political bigwigs presumably was passed on to provide other politicians with leverage against them. But again, it was not for him to know. The FBI's *great* godfather, J. Edgar Hoover, exercised power by just *having* information, not necessarily using it.

There was a time not long ago that his working within the United States was against official policy, if not against the law. The CIA's function was limited to foreign shores only. The FBI's mission was restricted to within the borders of the

United States. But that rule went by the wayside as terrorist threats from around the world, among other things, necessitated a blurring of the lines. The FBI began to set up bureaus in other countries, and the CIA practiced its counterespionage role in the States. September 11, 2001, cemented the change in missions. All bets were off after 9/11.

He sipped his coffee and thought of the second job he'd been asked to do, finding the so-called mystery man who was at Union Station either at the time of the shooting or shortly thereafter.

The final mission for the moment was to find out what the real agenda behind the request was.

"Like some dessert with the coffee?" the waitress asked. "Ice cream? Pie? Ice cream *and* pie?"

"Sure. Some vanilla ice cream and chocolate sauce." Everyone had to have a weakness, and ice cream was his. No apologies.

Now cool and his passion satisfied, he pulled from his small briefcase the cell phone given him by the FBI and a telephone book. He had his own cell but figured the FBI could pick up the charges. He found the number he was looking for and dialed it.

"Peck," the man's voice said after the first ring.

"Tim Stripling. How are you?"

"Good. Long time no see."

"My fault. How are things at MPD?"

"Ah, come on. You want to get me started?"

Stripling laughed. "Wouldn't want to do that. Up for a drink?"

"Sure. You buying?"

"Of course. You work with a Detective Mullin?"

Stripling detected a low laugh. "You buying him a drink, too?" the detective asked. "Cost you big-time."

"No."

"So why mention him?"

"No reason. What time do you get off?"

"Six."

"Market Inn at six-thirty?"

"You got it."

"You pick up anything on finding the Union Station shooter this afternoon?"

"There's talk about it."

"Fill me in when I see you. I'm interested."

"How interested?"

"Very. I'll take care of you."

"Six-thirty it is."

His next call was to WTTG-TV's studios.

"Is Joyce Rosenberg there?"

"Hold on."

"Hello. It's Joyce."

"Hello to you. Tim Stripling here."

"Tim Stripling. I haven't heard from you since you fed me that story about the cross-dressing congressman. What's up?"

"I'm following the Union Station murder. You seem on top of it."

"Not really. Nothing much new."

"Tell you what," Stripling said. "I'll show you mine if you show me yours."

"Is this a pitch? I'm engaged."

"Lucky guy. They found the shooter in the Union Station murder."

"What?"

"Yeah. Very dead. Kenilworth Aquatic Gardens, off the Anacostia Freeway, Northeast. Name's Leon LeClaire, forty-three, from New York. He's got a French passport."

"Okay. Thanks!"

He heard her say to someone, "Take this. The Union Station shooter. Down at Kenilworth Gardens. I'll be with you in a second."

"Thanks, Tim."

"Hold on, Joyce. I get to see yours."

"What do you want?"

"I want the big beefy guy who told you the victim's name at the station."

"Don't know it."

"Yeah, but you might have some footage, cutting-room-floor stuff, that could help. When can I come over?"

"Tomorrow. Nine."

"See you then. Thanks."

"Anything else?" the waitress asked.

"Thanks, no," he said with a smile. "You make good ice cream."

He paid his bill and left the table. On his way out, he paused to look at a display of Bo Diddley's first homemade guitar and the bodice worn by Marilyn Monroe in *Gentlemen Prefer Blondes*. Later that night, the place would be packed with people to whom such memorabilia was meaningful. They meant nothing to Stripling. But the ice cream was really good.

TWENTY

Mullin and Accurso drove to Kenilworth Aquatic Gardens, fourteen acres of marshland in the northeastern portion of Anacostia Park. Created by a civil servant in 1882 with a few water lilies from Maine, it grew over decades into a tranquil setting in a marginal neighborhood enjoyed by picnicking tourists, naturalists, and fledgling artists who set up their easels and attempted to capture the beauty of more than a hundred thousand water lilies, other aquatic plants, and water creatures that inhabit the park. Monet would have felt very much at home.

By the time they'd reached the park, it was also filled with uniformed police and plainclothes detectives.

The body of Leon LeClaire lay faceup, his body partially obscured by the five-foot-long platter-shaped leaves of exotic South American *Victoria amazonica* lilies. A small group of onlookers formed a ring about the scene, kept at a respectful distance by uniformed officers who'd been the first responders.

"Hey, Bret. How goes it?" one of the officers asked Mullin as he and his partner approached.

"Okay, okay."

A detective came to Mullin and Accurso.

"Who made the ID on him?" Mullin asked.

"I did," the detective, considerably younger than Mullin, replied. He handed Mullin a wallet and a passport. Mullin examined the wallet's contents and the passport, and handed them to Accurso.

"Who decided he's the Union Station shooter?" Mullin asked.

"I did," said the detective. "And Warner over there. Matches the sketch, same tan suit last seen wearing. Other details fit. It's got to be the guy."

Warner joined them. Opening a brown paper bag, he used a handkerchief to withdraw a 9-millimeter semiautomatic Walther pistol. "Minus two bullets," he said. "Probably match up with the ones that took down the guy at the station."

"Wouldn't that be nice and neat," Accurso said. "Who discovered the body?"

Warner pointed to an elderly couple standing slightly apart from the other gawkers. Mullin went to them.

"I'm Detective Mullin," he said, showing his badge. "I understand you two found the body."

The woman's fist went to her mouth and tears welled up in her eyes.

"My wife is very upset," the husband said, "as I'm sure you can understand."

"Sure," Mullin said. "You were just what? Taking a walk or something?"

"We come here often in the summer," the husband said. "It's cooler than in the city. Very peaceful."

Mullin glanced around and nodded. "You what, just saw him laying there?"

"Yes. At first I thought it was an inanimate object. You don't assume right away that you're looking at a dead body. But then — well, my wife screamed, and I realized it was a person."

"You called 911?"

"No. We got away from here and told somebody else what we saw. He dialed the police for us."

"Who was that?" Mullin asked, looking at others in the area.

"I don't see him," said the husband.

"Yeah, well. Did you see anybody suspicious around here?"

"Suspicious?"

"Yeah. Somebody who maybe was near

where the body was, or somebody running off."

"No."

Mullin looked at the wife. She shook her head.

Mullin took their names and phone number, and rejoined Accurso and Warner.

"How did he get it?" he asked, nodding toward the victim.

"Two slugs in the back of the head — very neat, very professional," Warner said.

That speculation was put on hold by the arrival of the medical examiner's team, who immediately went to the body, joining evidence technicians photographing the deceased from various angles and collecting soil samples.

"Get that weapon over to forensics," Mullin told Warner, "and tell them it's a priority." To Accurso: "Nothing we can do here, Vinnie. Let's head back."

They'd walked halfway to where they'd parked their car when a remote truck from WTTG pulled up, and reporter Joyce Rosenberg and her two-man crew jumped out of the vehicle.

"Hi, Detective," she said. "Joyce Rosenberg, Fox News."

"Yeah, I know who you are," Mullin said.

"Is it true?" she asked. "You've got the Union Station shooter?"

"Could be. Not sure."

"Down there?" she asked, pointing to the crowd congregated by the *Victoria amazonica* lilies.

"Yeah, but it's off-limits."

"Give me a statement," she said, indicating to her crew to focus on her and Mullin.

"No statement," he muttered.

She ignored him and said to the camera, "This is Joyce Rosenberg at the Kenilworth Aquatic Gardens, where police feel they've solved yesterday's Union Station murder. With me is Detective Mullin of the MPD."

Mullin looked at her, smiled, and shook his head.

She consulted notes: "We understand the suspect's name is Leon LeClaire, from Haiti and carrying a French passport."

Mullin's expression changed from bemusement to surprise. He looked quizzically at Accurso, who raised his eyebrows and shrugged.

"Shut that thing off," Mullin ordered, indicating the camera and microphone. She gestured for the crew to comply and followed Mullin out of earshot of the others.

"Where the hell did you get that information?" he growled at her.

"A source," she said.

"What source?"

"Oh, come on, Mullin. You know I can't tell you that."

"Yeah, the press and confidential sources and all that. Shield laws." He leaned close to her face. "Did MPD leak it to you?"

She took a few steps back. "No comment," she said, smiling. "Look, Mullin, you've always been square with me, and I've never screwed you. Level with me. I have it right, don't I? He's from Haiti, name is LeClaire, carries a French passport?"

Mullin nodded.

"So why would this LeClaire shoot an old Italian guy in the back of the head in Union Station?"

"I don't know," Mullin said. "Hey, as long as you're asking all these questions, Ms. Rosenberg, how about answering one of mine?"

"If I can."

"The guy who told you the name of the victim at the station, you know, the guy you mentioned on your newscast."

"What about him?"

"Who is he?"

She laughed. "I'd love to know."

"So would I. You got a good look at him?"

"No. Just a passing glance."

"But you kind of know what he looks like. Right?"

"I suppose so."

"Tell you what. How about giving a description to one of our sketch artists?"

Her laugh turned to a giggle. "Me? Give a description to a sketch artist?"

"Yeah. You see, Ms. Rosenberg, I'd like to know who he is, too. I'd like to find him."

"Why? Why is he important?"

"Once I find him, I'll figure that out. Game?"

"Sure. Now, am I right about the guy down there in the weeds?"

"They're lilies."

"Whatever."

"Yeah, you're right."

"Thanks."

"What time can you come by headquarters tomorrow?"

She started to suggest first thing in the morning, but remembered her nine o'clock date with Tim Stripling. "The afternoon," she said. "Around three?"

"I'll be there."

The medical examiner's people carried the covered body of Leon LeClaire on a stretcher up to the parking lot and slid it into the back of their van. Two uniformed officers remained at the scene, now cordoned off with yellow crime-scene tape. The WTTG crew videotaped the action while Joyce Rosenberg provided commentary. Mullin and Accurso waited until the police vehicles and the TV truck left the parking lot before getting in their own car and driving off.

"What was that about with the reporter?" Accurso asked.

"Her sources are good, Vinnie." He explained his plan to have her meet with an MPD sketch artist the next afternoon.

"You really think it'll help find this guy?"

"Maybe, maybe not. It's worth a shot."

They spent what was left of the day at headquarters filling out their reports.

"Come on, I'll buy you a drink," Mullin said when they were finished.

"A rain check, Bret," Accurso said, gathering his things. "Katie and I have plans this evening."

"Yeah, sure. See you in the morning."

Mullin stayed at headquarters after his partner departed. Aside from arranging for a sketch artist to be available the next afternoon, he accomplished little until leaving at eight, pretending to read files and make notes until it was late enough to face his loneliness. He stopped at Lauriol Plaza, where he downed margaritas on the outdoor terrace and filled up on beef fajitas. He considered swinging by the Market Inn, where an old friend, a jazz pianist, appeared nightly, but thought better of it once he was in the car. He was too tired, aided by the alcohol, to extend the night. He went home, fed Magnum, got out of his clothes — his feet hurt, especially one on which he'd developed a painful hammertoe — and sat in his recliner, fighting to stay awake through the news on TV.

". . . MPD has verified the victim's identity as Leon LeClaire, Haitian-born and carrying a French passport. His last known residence was New York City. Fox News has also learned that LeClaire matches the description of the man accused of being the shooter in the recent Union Station murder. And exclusive sources tell me that MPD interest in the so-called mystery man — who told this reporter at the scene of the Union Station murder the name of the victim before anyone else knew it — has intensified."

The camera pulled back to a wider shot; Mullin and Accurso could be seen in the background.

"I'm Joyce Rosenberg reporting."

TWENTY-ONE

Had Mullin decided to stop in at the Market Inn that evening, he would have crossed paths with a detective colleague, Fred Peck, who sat with Timothy Stripling in one of the bar area's secluded booths.

The restaurant, beneath the freeway at 2nd and E Street, not far from the National Air and Space Museum, had been a fixture there for forty-five years, attracting a wide variety of Washingtonians — seafood lovers, jazz lovers, Supreme Court justices, and other law lovers at lunch, and those looking to extend the evening beyond the city's early-to-bed reputation or their own. The sounds of jazz-tinged show tunes, smoothly played by Mullin's piano-playing friend, accompanied by a bassist, wafted through the smoky bar. The anti-smoking police hadn't invaded Washington yet, but no one doubted it wasn't long before they did.

Peck, a gaunt man with a prominent hooked nose and sizable bags beneath large brown eyes, and whose slightly curved spine caused him to appear to be always going forward, belonged to a small faction of the Washington MPD known as deep throats. Prior to the success of Woodward and Bernstein's account of the Watergate affair, the group had been known as the canaries. No matter what they were called, the view of them by others on the force wasn't benign.

Peck had been a cop for twenty-four years. In the beginning, he'd been a respected and effective officer, with a bright future — in fact a little too bright, according to colleagues who watched him advance through the ranks faster than normal. That's when speculation began to surface about why Fred Peck seemed to be favored over others when it came to promotions.

No one ever developed hard evidence that Peck had become a throat, a conduit of information to MPD hierarchy and Internal Affairs about the activities of colleagues. But suspicion had always been evidence enough in the gossip-driven Washington MPD. Shoulders turned cold, comments were made, and eventually veiled threats began to surface, nothing overt, but pointed enough to send Peck scurrying to handlers up the line in search of cover. He was taken off the street and assigned desk duty in the Missing Persons Unit, his current assignment.

While this took him out of the loop on the street, it didn't interfere with his penchant for ingratiating himself with authorities — and profiting from it — inside the MPD and outside as well. That's how and why Tim Stripling entered the detective's life.

Stripling's primary duty while a full-time employee of the Central Intelligence Agency was to develop relationships with individuals in a wide variety of government agencies and departments, much like his overseas colleagues worked to nurture moles inside foreign governments. His budget to accomplish this was off the books; Congress would not have been happy knowing it was supporting an inherently illegal activity.

The guidelines Stripling used to target potential candidates were the same as those used by overseas agents operating out of embassies — look for individuals with personal problems, particularly those involving money. Through various contacts within law enforcement, augmented by myriad records — credit card usage, credit reports, bank loans, and other personal financial dealings easily accessed — Stripling came up with Peck as one likely candidate.

Peck's wife, Helen, although known to MPD wives as being somewhat pretentious — but within acceptable limits — was a pleasant woman, a doctor's daughter who mixed easily with other spouses. Her relationship with her husband was not as easygoing. She frequently complained to him that his salary as an MPD cop simply wasn't sufficient to maintain the lifestyle she had once had and felt they deserved. Tired of defending himself to her, Peck decided to make an all-out effort to advance himself within the department and deliberately sought out those who could be of help. Like Stripling, with his mission to recruit moles within governmental agencies, the MPD's hierarchy was also on the lookout for officers willing to pass along information on wrongdoing within the force. A ranking officer within Internal Affairs identified Peck as a good candidate. Although no money was paid for information, Peck found himself short-listed for promotion and soon joined the detective ranks.

The increased salary was welcome at the Peck household. But as is often the case, the additional income was soon taken for granted and Helen's complaints resumed. Taking a second job was out of the question for Peck; department regulations prohibited it. So when a friend of his on the Capitol Hill police introduced him to a man named Timothy Stripling, who billed himself as an intelligence officer, Peck willingly listened to what Stripling was offering — a monthly fee for doing nothing more than keeping his eyes and ears open within the MPD and passing along information Stripling might require from time to time.

It didn't take Peck long to agree. The money was easy and steady. He wouldn't be passing on state secrets like some traitorous spy. Whatever information he shared with Stripling would be going from one government agency to another — and in the interest of national security, as Stripling assured. Nothing wrong with being paid for being a patriot. A good deal all the way around. Helen now drove a new car, the living room sported new furniture, and Helen's harping about money had stopped. Life was good, or at least better furnished.

"So, Fred, you're looking, as they say, buff," Stripling remarked after they'd been served drinks and a platter of crisply fried calamari.

"Healthy living," the tall detective said, spearing calamari with a fork.

"How's Mrs. Peck?"

"Fine, just fine."

"That's good to hear. So, my friend, what's new at the great police department in the sky?"

Peck consumed another piece of calamari. "Still heads in the blue. Nothing much new, Tim. How's life outside the Company?"

Stripling sat back in the booth and grinned. When he'd announced to Peck and to others in similar situations that he was leaving the CIA as an employee, there was predictable concern. Did this mean the end of the gravy train? But he'd assured them that he would continue working for an intelligence service as a consultant and would still be the source for supplementary money. Their services were needed more than ever, he told them, because of the continuing terrorist threat to the country.

"Enjoying myself," Stripling said. "There's something to be said for this consulting life. No daily pressures, more time to smell the roses and improve my putting game." He came forward. "So, tell me, for example, what's going on with the Union Station shooting."

Stripling always found it amusing when, after asking Peck such a question, the detective would take in his surroundings, close the gap between his face and Stripling's, and lower his voice. Stripling had learned to widen that gap before Peck started speaking. The detective's breath wasn't sweet.

"Like you said, Bret Mullin's handling the case."

Stripling's expression said *And?*

Another furtive glance around the crowded bar: "He's set up a sketch artist for tomorrow."

"Oh?"

"Yeah. I talked to the artist. He's a faygele, you know? Light in the loafers." He adopted a swishy voice and ran a pinkie over his eyebrow. "An artiste."

Stripling smiled. "So who's this sketch artist sketching? You've already got the Union Station shooter."

"He tells me — the artist tells me — Mullin tells him a reporter from Fox News is coming over to give a description of the guy who knew the name of the victim at the station."

"Really? She knows him?"

Peck shrugged and sat back. "Beats me. I guess she does. You know her?"

"Who?"

"The reporter who's coming over."

"I think so. Why is Mullin so interested in this guy?"

"I don't know. He's a lush, you know. Can't always believe him."

"But you'll find out. And his name. Right?"

"You want me to?"

"Uh-huh."

"How come?"

Stripling signaled for a waitress, who took an order for another round and bowls of clam chowder.

"How come?" Peck repeated.

"What?"

"The guy who knew the victim. I'd like to know why I'm finding out about him. Mullin's interest in him. Like that."

"It's not important, Fred. I'd like a copy of the sketch your artist comes up with. Can do?"

"I suppose so."

"And I want to know everything you guys learn about him."

Stripling observed Peck as he sipped from his second drink. He knew what the detective was thinking. Now that he, Stripling, had indicated considerable interest in the so-called mystery man and was asking Peck to find out all he could, it took on urgency. Might warrant a bonus. *What a whore,* Stripling thought. That was his unstated view of everyone he'd managed to turn into informants. But it was a good thing there were plenty of them working in government agencies. *Without* them, he'd have been out of business a long time ago.

"I think I can wangle a bonus for you on this one, Fred," he said.

"I wouldn't argue," Peck said with a grin.

"I wouldn't expect you to."

It was a two-pound lobster for Peck, red snapper for Stripling, salads, and Key lime pie for the detective's dessert.

"Call me tomorrow, huh?" Stripling said as he placed his American Express card on the check.

"I don't know if I'll know anything by then."

"Call me anyway. By the way, the TV reporter's name is Rosenberg. Joyce Rosenberg. Pull up what you can on her."

"Okay."

"And let me know if you guys come up with any new information, hard information, on the victim, Russo."

"Okay."

Before they parted on the sidewalk in front of the restaurant, Peck laughed and said, "Boy, Tim, this is really going to keep me busy, getting everything you want. I'll really appreciate that bonus."

Stripling slapped Peck on his arm. "Hey, one thing you can never say about me is that I ask you to work cheap."

"It'll be cash, huh? Not deposited in the account."

"Cash it'll be. No sense cutting Uncle Sam in. You say hello to your wife, Fred. Buy her something nice on me."

"Will do."

Stripling watched Peck walk away and turn the corner. He checked his watch; it was still early. An attractive blonde, on the arm of a distinguished-looking older man, came out of the restaurant and passed him. He watched the sway of her hips as the couple went down the street, where the man held open the door of a silver Jag for her. Stripling pulled a small address book from his jacket pocket, found the number he was seeking, and dialed it.

"Hello," a dreamy female voice said.

"Jane? It's Tim Stripling."

"Hello, stranger. Where've you been?"

"Busy. Doing God's work."

"God's work?" She giggled.

"Got some time for me?"

"I always have time for you, lover boy. It's a slow night."

"Yeah, well, we all have to rest some time. I'll be by in a half hour."

"I'll be waiting. Bring some of God's money with you."

"Oh, I will, Jane, I certainly will."

TWENTY-TWO

Lobster and red snapper weren't on the menu that night at the Watergate apartment of Mac and Annabel Smith. But they all ate well. After drinks accompanied by scallops wrapped in bacon, Mac grilled marinated chicken kebabs and vegetables on a hibachi on the terrace, whipped up his signature Caesar salad, and heated bread fresh from the Watergate bakery downstairs.

"Delicious," Kathryn Jalick declared after her first taste of chicken. "What's the secret to the marinade?"

"If I told you that, Kathryn, it wouldn't be a secret any longer," Smith said pleasantly.

"Spoken like a real chef," Marienthal said.

"Mac's a wonderful cook, but only when the spirit strikes him," Annabel said. "I think he secretly always wanted to own a restaurant, but knows what an insane business that can be. I prefer a college professor for a husband." She touched his arm.

"Actually," Smith said, "I've been threatening for years to give up teaching, study cooking in Provence, and get a job in some restaurant kitchen. One of many unrequited fantasies."

"Care to share them with us?" Kathryn asked.

"Not in mixed company," Mac said, laughing. He turned to Marienthal. "So, Rich, we're anxious to hear the latest with your book, and your read on the murder at Union Station. The victim, Russo, served as your inspiration, as I understand it."

Marienthal appeared uncomfortable fielding the question. He sipped from a Belgian-style beer brewed in a Baltimore microbrewery that Smith, knowing Marienthal was a beer drinker, had bought especially for the evening. Rich looked at Kathryn, who avoided his eyes and focused on her plate.

Realizing an answer was expected, he said, "Well, things are going okay with the book. It's at the printer and should be out soon."

"What about Mr. Russo?" Annabel asked. "Had he come to Washington to meet with you?"

"Ah, yeah, he did."

"You must have been in absolute shock," said Annabel, "when you heard the news."

"How *did* you hear?" Mac asked.

"I got a call."

"I thought you might have been that mystery man they mentioned on TV," Mac said with a chuckle. "The one who supposedly blurted out Russo's name to the TV reporter."

"I'd still like your marinade recipe," Kathryn said.

"Sure, I'll write it out after dinner," Mac said. To Marienthal: "Did you get to see your folks when you were up in New York?"

"Yes, I did. Dad said to say hello."

"How's he doing?"

"Pretty good, I guess. He's slowing down. Doesn't practice much anymore."

"I don't blame him," Mac said. "Criminal law can take a lot out of you. It can be, well, almost criminal."

"You should know," Kathryn said.

"Yes, I suppose I should. I'm sure he had some comments about the murder. After all, your dad represented Russo in the plea proceedings and put you in touch with him."

"That's right," said Marienthal. "He wasn't crazy about the idea at first, but I guess he realized how much I needed a book like this under my belt."

"I'm dying to read it," Annabel said.

"So am I," Mac said.

"You'll be among the first to get a copy," said Marienthal. "I have to thank you again, Mac, for going over the publishing contract so thoroughly with me. I really appreciate it."

"The least I could do. As I told you, publishing law isn't my bag, but I was happy to do it." He shook his head and laughed. "I'd never seen a contract like that, Rich. The publisher — what is it, Hobbes House? — really stacked things in their favor. That returns policy is a license to steal."

Marienthal laughed, too. "I know," he said. "The publisher sells books to book-stores on consignment. The store orders, say, ten, sells two, sends the other eight back to the publisher for full credit."

"How does that impact the writer?" Annabel asked. "I looked at the contract, too, but my bag, as Mac puts it anachro-nistically, was matrimonial law."

Mac answered. "From the way I read it, Rich gets paid royalties twice a year, pro-vided he's earned any beyond the advance. But the publisher has the right, according to the contract, to withhold a big portion of what's due him in the event there are returns during the next six-month accounting period. It's a hell of a float for the publisher."

The peculiarities of the publishing industry occupied the conversation through the end of dinner.

"We'll have dessert on the terrace," Annabel announced.

"I'll help clear," Kathryn said.

While the women took dishes to the kitchen, Smith and Marienthal went out on to the terrace. The night air was still hot and heavy. A full moon illuminated ripples on the river. The spires of Georgetown University were lighted in the distance. A peaceful setting. Rufus, the Smiths' great blue Dane, settled down next to Smith's feet.

"What are the plans to publicize the novel, Rich?" Smith asked. "Will you be doing interviews, book signings?"

"I think so," he replied. "I don't think those plans are firmed up yet."

"Getting late, isn't it? You say the book is about to be published."

"Yeah, you're right. They'd better get on the ball."

"I didn't realize Hobbes House did fiction, Rich. I know they publish a lot of conservative nonfiction."

His comment seemed to make Marienthal uncomfortable. After a false start, he said, "They want to branch out and do fiction. I guess I submitted my novel to them at the right time."

"Good for you," Smith said. "The public seems to have an insatiable appetite for novels about organized crime, the Mafia. I'm sure your book will do extremely well."

"I hope so," Marienthal said.

"Did Mr. Russo have a family in Israel?" Smith asked.

"No, not really. He lived with an Israeli woman named Sasha."

Smith fell silent for a moment before saying, "I suppose the prevailing theory is that the mob killed him. You wouldn't think they'd carry a grudge that long, but they evidently do."

"Looks like it," Marienthal said. "Did you represent mobsters when you were practicing law here in D.C.?"

"Not mafiosi. Other gang leaders."

"Any of them go into witness protection?"

"No. Some copped a plea and did less time as a result. What was it that Russo told you that so captured your imagination? As I recall, you said he was a lower level mobster in New York, not a major player."

"Well, he — any chance of another beer, Mac?"

"Coming right up."

Annabel and Kathryn accompanied Mac back to the patio. Annabel carried a platter of fancy cookies bought at the bakery; Kathryn brought a tray holding cups and saucers, cream and sugar, and spoons. Annabel went to the kitchen and returned with a carafe of hot coffee. Once they were all seated, Mac said, "I was talking with Rich about Mr. Russo. It's pretty evident that his former criminal associates got even with him for having turned against them." He said to Kathryn, "You know, of course, that Rich's dad represented Russo during the trial."

"Yes," she said. "Rich has told me all about it."

This led to a discussion of the ethics of cutting deals with members of organized crime in order to put others, usually higher-ups, away.

"I've always had trouble with it," Annabel said. "Some murderer with a dozen killings under his belt cops a plea, turns on his bosses, and gets paid off with a sweet deal, the witness protection program, a new life and identity, money, other perks. I just can't square that in my mind."

"Was Russo a murderer?" Smith asked.

"Yes," Marienthal replied. "Quite a few. Mob stuff, disputes over territory, or matters of discipline — or, as the bosses see it, honor."

Annabel wrapped her arms about herself, as though it had turned cold. "Gives me the shivers, these people who place so little value on life."

Smith said, "I've always found it interesting and ironic the way organized crime has to operate. It's a major industry in this country — at least it was — but it can't resolve business disputes in courts of law as other industries and companies do. So it's got to solve its differences privately."

"By killing competitors," Kathryn said. She'd said little since they'd gathered on the terrace.

"What was Russo's attitude about having killed people?" Smith asked.

"He was — Oh, I don't know. He viewed it as a job, I suppose. He grew up in the streets, saw the wiseguys dressed nice and on the arms of pretty women. I know he was a killer, but he could also be a nice guy. At least he was to me."

"Mellowed with age," Annabel commented.

"I suppose that happens to everyone,"

Marienthal said, "even mob muscle men."

As they were about to call it a night, Annabel mentioned a newscast she'd seen late that afternoon on which the discovery of the body in Kenilworth Aquatic Gardens had been reported.

"I saw only a portion of it," she said, "but the reporter indicated the body might have been of the man who shot your Mr. Russo in Union Station."

Kathryn started to say something, but Marienthal interrupted her. "I didn't hear that," he said.

"I'm sure it'll be repeated," Annabel said.

"Yeah, I hope so," Marienthal said. "This evening was really great. The meal was wonderful."

"That recipe for marinade," Kathryn reminded.

Smith wrote the recipe on a slip of paper and handed it to Kathryn as they said good night at the door.

When they were gone, and after Mac had helped Annabel straighten up the kitchen and they had walked Rufus, they wound down the evening on the terrace with small snifters of Cognac.

"A nice couple," Annabel said.

"Yeah, they are. But there's something strange going on."

"Like what?"

"I don't know. He seems very distracted, reluctant to talk about his book. Ever meet a writer who didn't want to talk about his work? And Kathryn gives me the impression of wanting to say things but not being able to."

"Why would that be?"

"I don't know that either, Annabel. The whole situation is a little bizarre. Rich is put in contact with this former Mafia hit man by his father, who represented the man in his plea deal and entrance into the witness protection program. According to Rich, he interviewed Russo as the basis for his novel, which is being published by Hobbes House."

"And?"

A shrug from Mac. "As far as I know, Hobbes House doesn't publish fiction. It's always been the leading publisher of non-fiction books with a right-wing slant. Rich says they're beginning to publish fiction. He wasn't terribly convincing. At any rate, Russo suddenly leaves his safe haven in Israel and shows up here in Washington. Rich says he came to meet with him, but that's it. No further explanation. I mean, this man who supposedly inspired Rich's novel is gunned down, and Rich has nothing to say about it? By the way, what's this about a body being found in Kenilworth?"

Annabel recounted what she'd heard on TV.

"Did you see Rich's reaction when you mentioned it?"

"He didn't have one."

"That's right. Didn't ask one question or volunteer one comment. Nothing."

"There must be a logical reason."

"There must be a reason. Whether it's logical or not is another matter."

"What I find unusual is that he's never offered to show you the manuscript."

"Oh, I don't think that's significant. He's a writer, probably filled with superstitions about having people see his work. His father certainly isn't happy with his son's decision to become a writer. That came through loud and clear the last time I spoke with him."

"Kids don't always go in the direction parents want them to. My father was thrilled when I became a lawyer. If he were alive, I'm not sure how he'd respond to my having given up all that education and experience to own an art gallery."

"I'm sure the fact that you're happy

would be good enough for him. Ready for bed?"

"Yes."

When they were under the covers and on the verge of sleep, Annabel said, "Maybe you should call Rich's father and ask him what's going on."

"Maybe I should. I owe Frank a call anyway, just to see how he's doing."

"I wonder what *his* reaction to his client's murder is," she said sleepily.

"I'll ask. Good night, Mrs. Smith."

"Good night, Professor. Pleasant dreams."

TWENTY-THREE

A 737, recently acquired to join the fleet of presidential aircraft, had flown into Indianapolis earlier in the day, carrying Democratic President Adam Parmele and his wife, Cathleen, a large contingent of White House and campaign staff, and a small group of reporters traveling with the president on his increasingly frequent campaign trips. Some mistakenly believe that the designation *Air Force One* is applied solely to the huge 747 from which the president of the United States is often seen deplaning during official and not so official trips. In reality, it is the designation given any aircraft on which the president happens to be traveling — a 747, 727, or even a four-seat Cessna.

As with every Parmele campaign appearance, this rally had been choreographed from Washington by White House political adviser Chet Fletcher, whose exquisitely detailed plans had been transmitted to political operatives from the Indiana Democratic National Committee. Judging from Fletcher's seeming obsession with detail, it was assumed that the roly-poly adviser relished putting together such appearances. The truth was that Fletcher did not enjoy the task, beyond deciding where the president would appear and what he would say. The requisite circus atmosphere created by local partisans — the audience of the already convinced and committed; the exuberant high school bands that would play at the drop of a hat for any politician; the balloons and posters and signs placed in the hands of the party faithful; the usual cast of local politicians lined up to praise their leader, make their speeches, and hope they weren't backing a loser; the programmed applause and scripted cheers — was distasteful to this particular political puppeteer. He viewed such events as being akin to the epidemic of unrealistic reality shows on television. But to leave such planning to others would have been unacceptably stressful. Fletcher micromanaged it all.

The black sedan in which he rode was directly behind Parmele's black limousine. With Fletcher was the president's congressional liaison, Walter Brown, and Parmele's lead speechwriter on domestic policy issues, Laura Havran, a Ph.D. and former American history professor. Fletcher had lobbied for her to join the staff once Parmele took office; he was more comfortable around academics than around the veteran political operatives occupying the most important positions in the administration.

"Did you make those changes I wanted?" Fletcher asked Havran as they proceeded from the airport to where the rally would take place.

"Yes," she said. "Of course he might not follow the script."

"As usual," Brown said, laughing.

Fletcher winced and looked out the window. A small crowd had gathered and was strung out along the boulevard to witness the procession of limousines and police vehicles. He didn't understand why anyone would waste time gaping at a bunch of cars passing by. This was no presidential motorcade, with the nation's leader waving to the crowd from an open limousine. That scenario had been considered. But with Indiana designated as a politically hostile state — and with JFK and Dallas always in mind — Fletcher had nixed any notion of open cars. Get to the rally as quickly as possible, put his man at the podium, pump out the requisite messages to the party faithful, bag the checks, and get back to D.C.

"The first lady seemed in good spirits this morning," Brown said.

"She looked lovely," Havran said.

"Yes, she did," Fletcher agreed, his attention still on the onlookers lining the route.

"I thought Robin handled the questions about her nicely yesterday at the briefing," Havran said, referring to the president's press secretary, Robin Whitson, another handpicked Fletcher hire and a former academic with a Ph.D. in communications. The questions had come from a cantankerous wire service reporter known to be a perpetual thorn in the administration's side.

"I'm sure you're aware, Robin, of talk that the president and the first lady have discussed divorce once he wins a second term," the reporter had said. "Will you deny that divorce is being discussed?"

"As I've said before, the president's personal life is very much his own and shouldn't be a subject of questioning at these briefings."

"Oh, come on, Robin," said the reporter. "A president's personal life, especially his relationship with his wife, can have an impact on his performance. The American people have a right to know if things are rocky in the White House bedroom."

Before she could answer, another reporter said, "Where has the first lady been? She's never with him."

Robin smiled, leaned on the podium, and said, "The first lady happens to have a very busy schedule of her own, and the president supports her activities. She'll be traveling to Indianapolis with him tomorrow. Unless you think she's a body double, you might want to reconsider the statement that she's never with him."

Fletcher squared himself in the rear seat of the vehicle and looked at Havran. "You've included the usual material in today's speech about the first lady? His better half? He married up? Most effective first lady in history? Country is blessed to have her in the White House?"

"It's a macro in my computer, Chet. I was surprised she agreed to this trip."

"She's going to have to make a lot more of them if this rumor is ever going to die," Fletcher said.

Reports that Parmele's marriage was shaky and that the nation might end up with a divorced president had surfaced during his initial run for the White House.

Right-wing publications and think tanks, some supported by conservative religious groups, had doggedly pursued anyone claiming to know something about the Parmele marriage, more particularly allegations that Parmele had been unfaithful on more than a few occasions. Cathleen Parmele, too, was the subject of such inquiry; it was alleged she'd had an affair during the time her husband ran the CIA.

Although nothing concrete had ever surfaced — no evidence of marital infidelity, no smoking gun — it didn't matter. Presidential politics wasn't played out in a court of law. Innocent until proved guilty beyond a reasonable doubt wasn't applicable when the world's most powerful position was at stake. Accusations themselves, no matter how baseless, were sufficiently scarring.

But the anti-Parmele forces weren't the only ones conducting investigations into extracurricular lives. Fletcher had quietly sicced private investigators on those Republican members of Congress who claimed moral superiority while leaking the unsubstantiated charges against Parmele and his wife. He had orchestrated a succession of leaks about their dalliances, real or imaginary, to the media. It was a game of mutual deterrence between Democrats and

Republicans, played not with bombs during the cold war, but with revelations ready for release should the other side launch a preemptive strike.

A dirty business to be sure.

And exhilarating to men like Chester Fletcher, who viewed politics as war without the restraints of a Geneva Convention.

The entourage pulled into a fairgrounds festooned with colorful banners and a thousand balloons. Spirited march music blared from huge speakers located throughout the welcoming area.

Getting out of his car, Fletcher looked up into a gray sky, thick with rain that would undoubtedly fall within the hour. Rain was the perpetual curse of such rallies. The speaker's stage would be covered as ordered, but the crowd would be thinner than expected. The threat of getting wet could dampen even the most fervent political zealot.

He watched the president of the United States step from his limo and extend a hand for his wife. Surrounded by Secret Service agents, the first couple was led through hundreds of well-wishers into the fairground itself, where many more men and women, some with children on their shoulders, broke into cheers. Adam and Cathleen Parmele went to the podium and joined a dozen local dignitaries waiting to shake their hands.

Fletcher, Brown, Havran, and press secretary Robin Whitson were herded to a spot at the side of the stage.

"They'd better get on with it," Havran said, glancing skyward.

They did, one local Democratic politician after another addressing the crowd until impatience and a few stray drops of rain forced the issue and moved them on to the main event. After a rousing and flowery introduction by Indianapolis's mayor, Parmele raised his arms, stepped to the microphone, and shouted, "It is good to be here in Indianapolis!"

The anticipated enthusiastic response erupted from the crowd. Parmele smiled broadly, then took in those in the front rows and pointed an index finger at some of them, as though they were old friends receiving special recognition. He spread his arms to quiet the assembled and said, "Receiving a welcome like this is gratifying. But I don't harbor any illusions. The person you really want to greet is Cathleen, the splendid first lady of this land and —"

Applause and whistles interrupted.

"— and I admit it. I married up and got myself more than the most wonderful wife any man has the right to deserve. This great nation of ours has the best first lady in its long history!"

And so it went.

First lady Cathleen Parmele addressed the crowd after her husband. She kept her remarks brief, saying only that it was a privilege and honor to represent the American people in the White House and adding the requisite tagline: "I am looking forward to being at my husband's side as he leads our nation for another four years. God bless you. God bless America!"

One of Parmele's aides, who'd been standing close to the president, looked to where Fletcher stood. The political adviser indicated with a nod of the head to get Parmele and the first lady off the stage and to the limo.

A fat raindrop hit Fletcher's nose, and he absently wiped it away. He was about to leave the area when a *Washington Post* reporter covering the president's trip came to Robin Whitson's side and said something in her ear.

"Let's go," Fletcher said.

Robin held up a hand. "In a minute, Chet."

Fletcher's frown matched the press secretary's. *What's going on?* his expression asked. *We have a schedule to keep.*

The press secretary walked with the reporter to a secluded pocket away from others' hearing.

The first couple passed; Havran and Brown fell in behind them. Fletcher stayed where he was, his attention never leaving the press secretary and the reporter.

"Where's Chet?" Parmele asked when he reached his limo.

"With Robin," Havran said.

Robin Whitson finished her furtive conversation with the *Post* reporter and joined Fletcher.

"What was that about?" he asked as they headed for the waiting cars, heads lowered against a steady rain.

"You tell me, Chet," she replied.

"Meaning?"

"Meaning — what's going on with the Widmer hearings?"

"That's what he wanted to know?"

"Yes."

"Why doesn't he ask Widmer?"

"He tried. Widmer's staff is treating the

hearings as top secret. What's with this book, Chet?"

"Book?"

"About the chief. He even asked me about the man who was killed in Union Station."

"Not now, Robin."

"Not now? Look, Chet, I'm supposed to be kept in the loop. I don't like being blindsided by a reporter."

"Not now!"

Fletcher climbed into his car where Havran and Brown were already seated.

"Went well," Brown commented.

Fletcher said nothing.

"A problem?" Havran asked.

"What? No, no problem."

Later, airborne and halfway back to Washington, Fletcher huddled with the president in his private office at the front of the aircraft. When he emerged and headed down the aisle toward the rear, he came face-to-face with Robin Whitson. Her expression was one large question mark.

"Don't worry about anything, Robin," Fletcher whispered. "Everything is taken care of. There is no problem."

TWENTY-FOUR

Tim Stripling saw the departure from Washington of President Parmele and his entourage on CNN that morning. Why TV and cable networks bothered to cover the president winging off on a fund-raising and campaign trip to Indianapolis puzzled him, as coverage of such nonevents always did. Leaving to attend an international peace conference or to address a conference of mayors or governors might have justified TV time. But a campaign trip on *Air Force One*, financed by the taxpayers? There'd be plenty of those as Parmele's quest for a second term got into gear. Did the public really want to watch every time the president's plane lifted off a runway? Maybe it was the need on the part of news organizations to fill the time, or not to be caught short by competitors. The why didn't matter. As far as Stripling was concerned, the whole thing was dumb.

While Stripling, the former CIA operative, cared little about Parmele's campaign swings, it didn't represent a total lack of interest in this president, or in others, for that matter. His years of developing information on Washington bigwigs — those already in power and those poised to achieve it — had given him privileged insight into aspects of their lives. He sometimes thought of himself as the ultimate voyeur, encouraged to snoop on men and women in the public eye and paid handsomely in the process — a supermarket tabloid reporter with a badge and official government cover.

The use to which his superiors at the CIA put the dirt he'd uncovered wasn't, as noted, for him to know, although it didn't take much imagination. After all, this was Washington, D.C.

After a breakfast of two soft-boiled eggs, an English muffin, juice, and coffee, he dressed and headed for WTTG-TV's studios on Wisconsin Avenue N.W. and his nine o'clock appointment. He was kept waiting for half an hour; Joyce Rosenberg was in an editing room doing a voice-over. He watched a TV monitor in the reception area. The president's departure for Indianapolis was still the lead story; it would play over and over all day. *How many times can you watch a plane's wheels leave the ground?*

"Hi, Tim."

Stripling turned to see the short, slender, dark-haired Rosenberg crossing the room. He stood, they shook hands, and she led him back through one of the studios to a tiny, cramped room that served as her office. There was no place to sit; even the chair behind her desk was piled high with scripts and cans of videotape.

"So," she said, hands on her hips, a crooked smile on her lips, "what's this all about?"

Stripling shrugged and took in some photos of the reporter with political hotshots, the pictures fixed to the wall with pushpins. "You get to rub shoulders with the high and mighty," he said.

"I get to meet, as they say, interesting people. Okay, Tim, I only have a few minutes. Hate to rush you, but —"

"Think nothing of it, Joyce. As I told you, I'd like to get a fix on the guy who gave out the name of the Union Station shooting victim."

"So you said. I had an editor run through file footage we shot that day at the station. He's not in any of it."

"Okay. So, tell me what you remember about him."

She leaned back against the edge of the desk, pushed her glasses up onto the top of her head, screwed up her face, and said, "Let's see. He was pretty tall. I mean, taller than you. Over six feet, that's for sure. Maybe six-two."

"White."

"Yeah, white. Wore a tan jacket if I remember right. Like one of those safari jackets they used to sell at Banana Republic."

"Hair?"

"Sandy, maybe."

"Full head?"

"He was young."

"How young?"

A shrug. "Thirties, maybe."

"Heavy? Skinny?"

"I'd say on the heavy side. Not fat, but big. A big guy."

"And all he said to you was the name of the victim?"

She nodded. "That's it. I have to run."

"I saw your report last night from Kenilworth Gardens. You said MPD was interested in the same guy."

Another nod.

"They've been talking to you about it?"

She shook her head.

You're lying to me, he thought. *You're meeting with a sketch artist this afternoon.*

She went to the door, pushed aside a pile

of books with her foot, and closed it. "Care to fill me in on why you want this mystery man?"

"No. You say you're engaged."

"That's right."

"Who's the lucky man? A TV anchor?"

"A medical student from Baltimore."

"You'll make a good doctor's wife. Used to working all hours, middle-of-the-night emergencies, stuff like that."

"At least he's not from Washington and he's not involved with politics. That's a big plus in his favor."

"Yeah, I know what you mean. Thanks for the time. Invite me to the wedding. I'll bring a present."

"How did I get so lucky?"

She walked him back to the reception area.

"How about my present now?" she said.

"Huh?"

"Look," she said, "I may not be Walter Cronkite or Edward R. Murrow, but I smell a story when I —"

"It's 'you *know* a story when you see it,' " he corrected.

"Something like that. If finding this guy is as important as it seems, I'd like the inside track."

"That can be arranged."

"Promise?"

"Do my promises carry any weight?"

She smiled. "If you give me what I need, they will."

"Count on it."

"I intend to. By the way, there's a rumor floating around —"

He feigned shock, hand to his heart. "A rumor? Here in Washington?"

She laughed. "How about that? Speaking of rumors, which I think we were, what do you know about Senator Widmer's hearings on the CIA?"

"Nothing. What's the rumor?"

"Some sort of bombshell, is what I'm hearing."

"What do his people say?"

"Not a word. All behind closed doors. Clammed up. You'd think they were about to declare war on somebody."

"Maybe they are. I'll ask around."

Stripling left WTTG's studios and ducked into a coffee shop, where he ordered coffee and dialed a number on his cell. It was answered by a man in the Capitol Hill office of a Republican senator from Colorado.

"Jimmy? Tim Stripling here."

There was a pause before Jimmy, a top aide to the senator, responded. "How are you, Tim?"

"Couldn't be better. Well, maybe I could. Up for lunch?"

"Today?"

"Yeah. We haven't gotten together in a while."

"I'm really up to my neck, Tim. Another time?"

This time Stripling paused. When he again spoke, his voice was lower; there was a hint of warning in it. "I really would like to have lunch today, Jimmy."

He waited. Finally Jimmy said, "Sure. Where?"

"You're still a member of that lunch club at the Capitol View in the Hyatt, I assume."

"Yes."

"One o'clock?"

"Not there."

"Where?"

"Tony and Joe's. On the terrace."

"See you then. Just Tony and Joe, you 'n' me."

TWENTY-FIVE

Bret Mullin awoke that same morning with a hangover. He often boasted about never suffering them, no matter how much he'd consumed the night before — no frayed nerves, dry mouth, and pulsating headache. "Something in the Mullin genes," he liked to say.

But like an inveterate gambler who always claims to be ahead in his wagers, Mullin wasn't being entirely truthful. As he'd grown older, his ability to handle the juice had diminished, and hangovers, to a greater or lesser degree, were no longer alien.

He considered calling in sick but didn't. He'd already used up his yearly allotment of sick days, and it was only July. After two glasses of milk to help quell the fire in his stomach and a cup of black coffee to stoke the flames again, he slumped against the tile shower wall and allowed warm water to flow over him, gradually increasing the amount of cold water in the mix until it became uncomfortable. He dried himself and stood before the bathroom mirror. "Jesus," he muttered at his mirror image.

His eyes were red, the flesh around them swollen and puffy. He started to shave but abruptly stopped. His hand was shaking, and he was afraid he'd cut himself. He went to the kitchen and poured what was left in a vodka bottle into a glass, added a splash of orange juice, and downed it. Drinking in the morning was relatively new, and he wasn't pleased that it had come to this, but it was either take a couple of shots to calm his nerves or go to work shaking.

He finished his bathroom ablutions, dressed in yesterday's suit but chose a clean shirt and different tie, and looked out the window. Another nasty hot humid day. Magnum rubbed against his legs, and he bent to ruffle the cat's fur behind its neck. "Hey, baby, you stay here and guard the joint," he said. "Keep the bad guys out." He straightened up painfully, left the apartment, and drove to headquarters, where Vinnie Accurso had already arrived.

"Check this out," Accurso said, handing Mullin a printout of the initial forensic examination of the bullets from the gun found on the body in Kenilworth Gardens. "Perfect match with the ones that took down Russo at Union Station."

Mullin grunted and dropped the report

on his desk. "No surprise, huh?" he said.

"Another case closed by D.C.'s finest," said Accurso.

"The hell it is," Mullin said.

"What?"

"Sure, we've got the shooter cold. But *why* did he shoot the old man? And who shot *him?*"

A young detective sitting nearby chimed in: "A mob hit, Bret. Just that simple. And the shooter gets shot to keep his mouth shut."

Mullin said nothing.

"What are you thinking, Bret, that this so-called mystery man who knew Russo's name before anybody else did might know why it happened?" his partner asked.

"Yeah, of course, that's exactly what I'm thinking."

"What guy are you talking about?" the young detective asked.

"Nothing," Mullin said.

Mullin's phone sounded and he picked up the receiver. "Yeah, all right," he said, hanging up. To Accurso: "We've been summoned."

"God?"

"Yeah."

They were about to leave for the office of the chief of detectives when Fred Peck came to where they sat. "How's it going?" he asked.

"Fine, Fred," Accurso replied.

"You guys caught a break with the station shooter, huh?" Peck said.

Mullin and Accurso looked at him blankly.

"The forensics match on the bullets," Peck said. "Hey, by the way, I see we're trying to locate that guy who knew the victim at the station. You working that?"

"What guy?" Mullin asked.

"The one who said his name right after the shooting. Heard on TV that we're looking for him."

"We wouldn't know about that, Fred," Accurso said. "Excuse us. God wants to give us commendations and a promotion."

"He does? For what?"

Mullin and Accurso walked away, leaving Peck staring after them. When they were gone, he went to an office on another floor where one of the department's sketch artists was interviewing a witness to a shooting the night before, showing her cards on which a variety of facial features were displayed. "A chin like this one?" he asked her.

She shook her head.

The artist noticed Peck in the open

doorway. "Excuse me," he told the woman and followed Peck into the hall.

"Sorry to bother you," Peck said, "but I know you're doing a sketch this afternoon with that TV reporter."

"That's right," said the artist. "Mullin set it up."

"I know, I know. I was just talking to Bret and Vinnie about it. I'll need a copy of what you come up with."

"Sure. No problem. You working that, too?"

Peck patted the artist on the shoulder. "Thanks. Drop it by my office when you're done."

Mullin and Accurso took chairs across the desk from the chief of detectives, Philip Leshin. Leshin was as big as Mullin, but in a different way. While Mullin's body had gone soft, Leshin had kept in shape. He neither drank nor smoked and was a regular at a gym close to headquarters. His shaved head glistened in light from overhead fixtures; a heavy five o'clock shadow was already evident.

"What's up, Phil?" Mullin asked.

"You tell me," Leshin said. He was in shirtsleeves. His tie was wide and colorful, like his suspenders.

"Tell you about what?" Mullin asked. He

realized his hands were trembling and kept his fingers laced together on his lap.

"This TV reporter, Rosenberg. Fox News. She says on the air that we're trying to find the guy from the station shooting."

"Yeah, she's right," Mullin said.

"You know we've got the shooter. Bullets match."

"Right," Accurso said.

Mullin said, "I think this guy we're looking for can fill in the blanks, Phil, maybe tell us why the old guy was gunned down."

"That may be, but how come Fox News knows about it? You been talking to somebody over there?"

"No," Mullin said, motioning with his hands for emphasis, then quickly linking them again.

"You and Vinnie were in the reporter's piece last night. In the background."

"Sure we were," Accurso said. "We were there at the gardens."

"We did the interviews with the couple that found the body. Others, too."

Leshin stared at Mullin, who twisted in his chair.

"That's it, huh?" Leshin said. "You just happened to be standing there when she did her report."

Mullin and Accurso nodded in unison.

Leshin leaned back as far as his chair would allow and placed his hands behind his head. A small, satisfied smile crossed his lips. He said, "If that's true, then why is that TV reporter coming here this afternoon to give a description to a sketch artist?"

Mullin's shrug was exaggerated. He moved his head left and right, changed position again in his chair, and said, "Because I think that's the way to go, Phil."

He didn't express what he was really thinking: *Who told* you *about it?*

"You don't agree?" Accurso asked their boss.

"It's okay with me as long as it doesn't eat up much of your time. What's *not* okay with me is talking to the media — about anything! That's what we have Public Affairs for."

"Yeah, no problem," Mullin said, wiping beads of perspiration from his upper lip.

"You let this reporter give her description, that's it. No comments to her. Got it?"

"Got it."

"Got it."

"Good. By the way, the woman Mr. Russo was living with in Israel is flying here today." He glanced at a paper on his desk. "Sasha Levine."

"She claiming the body?"

"Once the M.E. releases it. Shouldn't need it anymore now that we've got the shooter."

"I'd like to talk to her," said Mullin.

"Go ahead. She's due here at five. But, Bret —"

"What?"

"Don't make this a big deal. Yeah, it would be nice to know why Russo got it, but it's not priority."

Mullin and Accurso stood to leave, but Leshin asked Mullin to stay. The big detective looked at Accurso and raised his eyebrows.

"See you downstairs," Accurso said.

"Close the door, Bret," Leshin said after Accurso was gone.

Mullin did as requested and faced his boss.

"How's the drinking, Bret?" Leshin asked flatly.

"The drinking? What about it?"

"I hear you've been hitting the bottle pretty good lately."

Mullin guffawed.

"True?"

"No, of course not. Who'd say something like that?"

"Sit down, Bret."

When Mullin was seated, Leshin stood over him. "You don't look good, Bret."

"Whatta you mean?"

"You look like hell. Your hands are shaking. I saw it."

"No, I'm —"

"Bret, listen to me. You're a good cop, have been for a long time. But I don't like being squeezed. I get a call from up top about somebody saying they saw you drinking on the job or drunk someplace, and bingo, I'm on the hot seat to do something about it. Understand?"

"Sure, Phil, and I wouldn't do anything to make it tough on you. But I'm telling you, I've got the drinking under control. Last night, I had a couple of margaritas with dinner. That's it. You have a drink before dinner?"

"I don't drink."

"Yeah, I know, but what I'm asking is whether having a drink or two before dinner is such a big deal. It's like — it's like, you know, civilized."

Leshin laughed lightly and returned to his chair. " 'Civilized,' " he said absently, shaking his head.

"I'm fine, Phil," Mullin said, pushing himself up from the chair. "Believe me,

I'm fine. You don't have to worry about a thing with me."

Leshin covered his eyes with one hand and waved Mullin from the office with the other.

I wish I didn't have to worry about you was what Leshin was thinking.

I should have had a second vodka this morning was Mullin's thought as he left the office. *Stops the shaking.*

TWENTY-SIX

Tony and Joe's fish restaurant was in Washington Harbour, on the Potomac at 31st Street, in Georgetown. Formerly the site of a cement factory, it had been developed into a riverfront park in 1986 by Arthur Cotton Moore, who'd created the mixed-use development of shops, restaurants, offices, and apartments. Architectural critics termed the complex hideous; Washingtonians and tourists ignored any architectural shortcomings and enjoyed the open feeling, the boardwalk promenade, the computer-controlled central fountain, and whimsical sculptures scattered throughout the area.

Stripling arrived early and took an outdoor table with an umbrella, on the river side of the terrace. He'd just been served an iced tea when Jimmy Gale, wearing an open-necked white shirt and carrying a blue denim sport jacket over his arm, skirted other tables and took a chair across from the former CIA operative.

"Maybe we should eat inside," Gale said. His face was blotchy; a film of perspiration testified to the heat.

Stripling smiled and took in the terrace with open hands. "It's lovely out here, Jimmy. Liable to catch a cold in the AC."

Gale, who was in his mid-forties, pulled a damp handkerchief from a pants pocket and dabbed at his face. "I don't have much time," he said. "We're busy. Very busy."

Stripling waved a waitress over. Gale had an iced tea, too. Both men ordered shrimp Caesar salads.

"What do you want, Tim?" Gale asked, downing a glass of ice water. "As I said, we're very busy. I shouldn't even be here."

"The Widmer hearings," Stripling said, not looking at him.

"What about them?"

Stripling now faced him. "It's like Los Alamos. What's all the secrecy?"

"I don't know. It's Senator Widmer's hearings. Ask him."

"Your boss is on the committee, Jimmy. Of course you know what's going on."

Gale looked about nervously. His tea came and he eagerly drank it. Stripling sat back, glass in hand, and took a certain quiet pleasure in Gale's overt anxiety. Exerting power over others was something he'd come to enjoy after years of creating the conditions under which such power was possible. There had been so many

Jimmy Gales, each having made a single human misstep in their lives, an isolated indiscretion, a drunken moment, a loss of control over their passions, a mistake in judgment experienced by every person at some point in their lives. The difference was that these very *human* beings worked for the U.S. government.

Stripling had first learned of Gale eight years ago, while still on the payroll of the agency. His success at identifying and turning government employees into informants for the agency had been beyond expectations. The stable of men and women he'd developed, willing to pass on information if asked, had grown to more than a hundred. Of course, there were those who left government service, and by extension lost their usefulness to Stripling and the CIA. But there were always others to take their place. Amazing, Stripling often thought, how vulnerable people were to having their private lives exposed, how willing they were to risk their professional and personal reputations in the pursuit of a vice or secret pleasure.

He'd found Washington's brothels, call girls, and escort services to be a particularly rich source of recruits. Married men who frequented such services were easy targets, although Stripling was judicious in his selection of which ones to pursue. If he'd elected to enlist every married man who visited one of the prostitutes on his payroll — some of whom agreed to install a tiny camera in the bedroom in return for easier money than plying their usual trade — the stable would have been too large and unwieldy to control.

Prostitutes providing other than conventional sexual experiences had been especially good to Stripling over the course of his career. That certainly was the case with Jimmy Gale. Married and with three children, Gale had come from Colorado to Washington with his family a dozen years ago to work for the senator from Colorado, and had quickly established himself as one of the most respected staffers on the Hill, a man fiercely loyal to his boss and mentor and someone whose word could be trusted. His reputation in his community of Rockville, Maryland, was equally positive. Gale was active in civic affairs, Little League, his church, his kids' schools, and the local Republican club.

He was also a man who'd questioned his sexuality since he was a teenager. He'd kept that question under wraps well into his adult years, through his marriage and the birth of his children, submerged, stifled, but always there below the surface.

One night, after a party at a restaurant popular with Senate and House staffers, and after he'd consumed more alcohol than he was accustomed to, he dragged out a number he'd been given for a Capitol Hill brothel that offered male prostitutes. He didn't remember much about the experience, whether it had been pleasurable or not or whether it had validated his questions about his true sexual orientation. All he knew was that it had been wrong to seek sexual gratification outside his marriage. He tore up the phone number and put the event behind him, to be forgotten and never repeated.

Until he was contacted by one Timothy Stripling, who made it known that *he* knew about the visit to the male whorehouse, and who thought Gale would be willing, even anxious, to keep it between them in exchange for occasionally passing along information from the Hill. "After all," Stripling had said, returning the black-and-white photos of Gale at the brothel to their envelope, "I'm not asking for you to divulge state secrets, Jimmy. It's all in the interest of national security. Look at it this way; you'll be doing a service to your country and adding to your bank account. What could be better?"

Gale looked at Stripling across the table and felt what he always did when in Stripling's company. He hated this man who'd intruded into his personal life and who'd used a single, solitary incident to blackmail him into submission.

Although few had expressed such feelings to Stripling over the years, he was well aware that those emotions existed. He waited until the waitress had delivered their salads, slowly buttered a roll, leaned his elbows on the table, and said, "Now, Jimmy, let's start over. The Widmer hearings. I know that you know what they're all about." He took a forkful of shrimp. "Let's eat while we talk. While *you* talk. Shrimp shouldn't sit out in this heat."

TWENTY-SEVEN

Sasha Levine had debated long and hard about flying to Washington to claim Louis's body.

Her initial reaction when called in the evening, Israel time, by someone from the Washington MPD, was resignation. Louis was a sick old man. His death was just a matter of time, and she'd mentally prepared for the day it would come. Still, projecting an acceptance of the inevitable and experiencing it in real time are quite different things, which she would soon discover.

She slowly lowered the receiver into its cradle, went to the small terrace on which they'd spent so many lazy evenings, looked up into a threatening sky, and bellowed a cry of anguish that stopped passersby on the street below. She collapsed into a chair and wept softly and steadily until there were no tears left to shed.

Dry-eyed and carrying a freshly lit cigarette, she returned to the living room and stared at the phone. The caller hadn't said how Louis had died. Had he collapsed on the street? Been rushed to a hospital? She hadn't asked and now wanted to know. The caller had left a twenty-four-hour number in Washington. It was morning there, and she made the call.

"Murder?" she said, incredulous. "He was shot dead?"

"Yes, ma'am."

The end of that second call did not result in any hysterical outburst by Sasha. In a sense, his having been gunned down fit more neatly into who he was. At least what she knew about him.

Russo had been living in Tel Aviv under the witness protection program for almost a year when he met Sasha at the Tango nightclub in the Tel Aviv Sheraton Hotel, on Hayarkon Street. It was 1993; he was sixty-one years old, still physically and mentally fit, virile and self-assured. Although he wasn't tall — five feet, seven inches — he carried himself in such a way that he appeared to be. Shoes with built-up heels contributed to the effect. She noticed that he dressed nicely, although he was overdressed in the informal atmosphere of the club — an Italian-cut double-breasted black suit, a white shirt with a high collar, a black tie, and pointy, polished black shoes.

Sasha was dressed that night in a tight black sweater and slacks, which showcased her full figure and complemented her close-cropped raven-colored hair. Of Jewish-Hungarian parentage, she'd immigrated to Israel from Budapest ten years earlier. Well-schooled, she spoke excellent English and quickly found work as an administrator in an Israeli import-export firm, whose major clients were American companies. Her decision to leave Hungary had been an easy one. Trapped in an abusive marriage, she'd happily walked away from it and looked forward to an exciting, fulfilling new life in that new frontier called Israel.

She accepted a drink from Russo at the nightclub's bar and found him amusing. His New York accent was thick, adding to his colorful stories of life in Manhattan.

"What do you do?" she asked.

"I'm a businessman," he said.

"What sort of business?"

"Construction."

"Oh, you build things."

"Yeah, something like that. Cigarette?"

"Thank you, yes."

She gave him her phone number at the end of the evening, and he promised to call. She forgot about it until a week later when her phone rang. He asked her out to dinner, and she accepted, but not without reservations. Her previous experience with men had not been positive; it had left her gun-shy and distrustful. Still, a harmless dinner with this amusing older American man couldn't hurt, a pleasant evening out, nothing more.

They dined on Dizengoff Street at a Chinese restaurant: "This Jewish food ain't to my liking," he'd announced when he told her where they'd be eating. She wore chino slacks and a white sweater to dinner. He wore a suit and tie, which set him apart from everyone else in the bustling, informal restaurant. It was like a continuation of their conversation at the bar the previous week. Russo was a natural-born storyteller, regaling her with stories of his youth in New York, his life on the streets, his parents, his friends, the wiseguys he knew, cop stories, trips he took to Miami and Los Angeles and Chicago, the celebrities he'd met: "I knew Sinatra pretty good," he'd said. "I used to pal around with Don Rickles and —"

"Who's he?"

"A famous comedian. I always had front row center when Sammy and Dino were in Vegas. One night —"

His life had certainly been an interesting one, colorful and unpredictable, but with a hint of danger, and she wondered whether he'd been involved in some sort of criminal activity. She'd read about the Mafia in America and had seen the *Godfather* movies. Had this funny man seated across from her, fumbling with his chopsticks, dressed so formally and with such exaggerated good manners, been like one of those men she'd seen in the movies and read about in books? She'd wanted to ask but was afraid to, so she accepted his claim of being in construction and had subsequent dinners with him, an occasional movie, a few drives to the seashore on sunny weekends. By this time, she found herself looking forward to seeing him, even missed him between their times together.

She didn't know where he worked in Tel Aviv, or even if he did. When asked about it, he'd reply only that he was exploring business opportunities and hadn't found the right one yet. He lived in a residence hotel, which she'd never visited, and always seemed to have money. And he was unfailingly polite, opening doors for her and standing whenever she approached the table, pulling her chair out for her, lighting her cigarettes, and never failing to introduce her as Miss Sasha Levine.

Loneliness on both their parts eventually closed the gap between them. Unpleasant memories of her failed marriage back in Budapest faded, and after many discussions in Tel Aviv's cafes and restaurants, she agreed that they should begin living together. For Russo, this woman named Sasha Levine offered a refuge of sorts in a strange land in which he didn't speak the language, practice the religion, or like the food. And so they moved into her apartment on Basel Street and had lived there in relative happiness over the ensuing years.

It was shortly after they'd started living together that Sasha learned who Louis Russo really was and why he was in Israel.

They'd been sitting on the balcony at sunset, sipping wine and discussing their respective days. She'd had a stressful experience at the import-export firm and commented that one of the partners had been making suggestive comments to her for the past few weeks. Although she'd witnessed an occasional flash of temper in Louis, his reaction this time was extreme. He stood and paced the terrace, swearing in English and Italian and demanding to know where the partner lived. "I'll take care of the bastard tomorrow," he snarled.

"No, no, Louis," Sasha said, trying to calm him. "Don't make such a tzimmes."

"What the hell is that?"

"A fuss. It's no big deal. He's stupid, an ugly little man."

"I'll kill the bastard, he lays a hand on you."

"Please, Louis, I'm sorry I mentioned it." Her thoughts were on the revolver he'd brought with him when moving in. She'd asked about it: "For protection," he'd explained, placing it on the highest shelf in a clothes closet and covering it with sweaters.

He sat again. "I killed people like him for less," he muttered, his words barely audible.

"You *what?*"

He proceeded to tell her the story of his life — his entry into the gangs of New York, his work for organized crime, the men he'd killed — and of his testimony against his superiors and entrance into the witness protection program. It was as though he'd been wanting since meeting her to explain to her who he was, and he told her these things with a sense of pride, speaking the words flatly, as though reeling off a grocery list, looking out over the street to the buildings across from them, never looking at her. She listened in silence, at once shocked and fascinated.

When he was finished, he slowly turned and asked, "You want me to leave?"

"I don't know," she said. She paused before continuing. "It was good of you to have turned in your criminal friends. An honorable thing to do."

"No," he said emphatically. "Killing the men was honorable. They deserved it because they were not men of honor. There was no honor in betraying my friends."

They barely talked for the next few days. When they finally did, Sasha put her arms around him and said softly, "I don't care what you did before, Louis. I know who you are now. Please, don't leave me."

The subject of Russo's previous life came up only now and then. He would occasionally slip into a reverie fueled by wine, and would reminisce about his early days. Of his five siblings, only three were alive, although he couldn't even be sure about that because he'd had no contact with them for years. A brother had died of cancer, he'd heard; a sister had been killed in an automobile accident.

"What do the others do?" Sasha asked.

He shrugged. "I don't know and I don't

care. They looked down on me because of the life I chose." He placed his fingertips beneath his chin and flipped them into the air. "They don't matter," he said. "The hell with them."

He never mentioned his brothers and sisters again.

Now she sat in a spartan office at a police headquarters in Washington, D.C., with a heavyset detective. It was a few minutes after six. While awaiting her arrival, he'd debated slipping out to a nearby bar for a couple of quick ones, but thought better of it. Now he wished he had. The urge was becoming acute.

"You have a nice trip here?" Mullin asked.

"The flight? Yes. But there is no smoking on the plane. May I smoke here?"

"Afraid not. The rules."

"Yes, the rules. Always the rules. The flight was all right. The reason for it? No."

"Yeah, sure. I can understand that. I'm sorry for your loss."

"Thank you."

"You're, ah — you're Jewish, right? An Israeli, I mean."

She smiled. *You're a good-looking woman,* Mullin thought. *The old mafioso had good* taste. Large breasts pressed against the fabric of a purple silk blouse; her crossed legs were shapely beneath a short tan skirt.

"I'm Hungarian," she said. "My parents were Jewish."

He nodded. "I see," he said. "Well, so you're here to claim Mr. Russo's remains."

"Yes. We were not married, you know."

"Yeah, that's right. I know that. But no other family member has stepped forth to claim him. I guess that means you."

"Is it all right if I ask you something, Detective?"

"The name's Bret. Sure. Go ahead."

"I am told you found the man who shot Louis."

"That's right. I mean, we didn't exactly find him. Alive, that is. Somebody shot him."

She shook her head. "Everybody shooting everybody. It's like in Israel. Bombs, always bombs. People killing people."

"Yeah. I know. Too much a that. I don't want to offend or anything, Ms. Levine — I mean, considering your loss and all — but there's some questions I'd like to ask you."

"About Louis."

"Yeah. About Louis. I don't know how

much you know about him, but —"

"That he was a criminal in the United States before he came to Israel under your witness program? I know that."

Mullin started to say something, but she continued.

"I know that he killed people for the Mafia. I know that he did many bad things here. I wish he hadn't, but that was all before I met him. I knew a good man, not a murderer."

Mullin felt uncomfortable. It was hot in the room despite the air-conditioning. His collar seemed to have shrunk around his neck. And he wanted a drink, a quiet one in a quiet, cool bar.

"Do you know why he came to Washington?" he asked.

"Yes."

"Why?"

"To meet with Richard."

"Who's Richard?"

"Richard Marienthal. It doesn't matter. Louis was working with him on a book about his life. That was all."

"This writer. He's from D.C.?"

Her reply was to take a Kleenex from her purse and blow her nose. "Excuse me," she said.

"That's okay. You see, Sasha, even

though the guy who shot Louis is dead, and we know for certain that it was him who did it, the case is still open. Who is the guy who shot Louis's murderer? How come he did — shoot Louis's murderer? If we know why your, uh — not your husband but your friend — came all the way from Israel to Washington, that might help us get to the bottom of things and wrap it up."

"I understand, Detective, and I would like to help you. You seem very nice. I appreciate your courtesy. When may I take Louis home for burial?"

"That's not up to me. The M.E. makes that decision. And my bosses, the D.A. Pretty soon, though. I mean, there's no reason to keep him anymore." He ran his finger around his collar. "I suppose you're unhappy about the delay. I mean, being Jewish and all, you like to bury the dead right away."

"That's right," she said. "But Louis wasn't Jewish. He was Italian."

"Yeah, I know. I guess that makes a difference. You, ah — you have a place to stay here in D.C.?"

"A hotel." She consulted a slip of paper from her purse. "The Lincoln Suites. On L Street." She smiled and returned the paper to her purse. "You name the streets with letters," she said. "I didn't know that."

"Yeah, well, that's the way they planned it. Nice place, the Lincoln. That's what I hear. I never been there. Not too expensive, either. You checked in yet?"

"No. I came directly here from the airport."

"Tell you what, Miss Levine. I'll drive you over to the hotel. You get checked in, and I'll buy you dinner. How's that sound?"

"I wouldn't want to put you out."

He stood and waved his hand. "No problem. It'll be my pleasure."

They went to Zola, named after the novelist Emile Zola and next to the International Spy Museum, where Mullin knew the bartender. They sat at the bar. Sasha ordered a white Zinfandel, Mullin bourbon on the rocks. She chain-smoked; he chain-drank.

"Here's to meeting you," he said, holding his second glass up to hers but withdrawing it quickly to avoid having her see that his hand shook. "Wish it was under better circumstances."

He sipped his drink slower than he would have had he been alone, but finished it and ordered a third. Fortified, he relaxed and conversation flowed freely — her life in Hungary and Israel, his take on Washington and its problems. "Damn politicians," he said. "Could be a nice place if it wasn't for the politicians. The whole country's screwed up 'cause of them."

They eventually gravitated to a black and red velvet booth in one of the restaurant's small, dark rooms, its walls covered with visuals to carry out the spy theme — shredded CIA documents, Plexiglas cases containing stills and posters from famous espionage movies, photographs of the nation's most infamous spymasters. It was grilled tuna and a salad for her, corn with bacon chowder and roast chicken for him.

"So," he said over coffee, "you know anybody here in D.C.?"

"Yes."

"This writer who was doing a book on Louis's life?"

She nodded and yawned. "I'm sorry, but I am sleepy. The flight was so long and . . ."

"Hey, I understand. I'll get a check." He waved for their waiter, dressed entirely in black.

He pulled up in front of her hotel. "I really enjoyed tonight," she said. "Thank you very much. You're a kind man."

"Yeah, well, not all cops are bad. It isn't

all like you read these days. I appreciate you not smoking in the car."

"It is not a problem."

"You have plans for tomorrow?"

"No. I have to call Richard and —"

"This writer?"

"Yes."

"What's he like, this writer?"

"He's very nice."

"An old guy?"

"Pardon?"

"Just wondered whether he's an old guy. Maybe I know him. Maybe I read stuff he wrote. I read a lot."

"No," she laughed. "He's quite young. I really must go inside. I don't want to fall asleep on you here in the car."

"Sure, I understand."

"Good night, Detective."

"It's Bret, huh? Look, I'll call you tomorrow? Maybe if you're not doing anything tomorrow night, we could have dinner again."

"I — perhaps. Thank you again, Bret."

He watched her enter the hotel, sat for a minute, then went to a bar near his apartment and had a few more drinks before calling it a night. His last act before going to bed — and after feeding Magnum and downing one final drink — was to write down the name she'd mentioned, mis-spelling it Richard Mariontholl. He'd check this guy out in the morning.

And he'd be sure to call her about dinner.

TWENTY-EIGHT

That same evening, Mac and Annabel Smith returned to a phone ringing in their Watergate apartment after having enjoyed dinner out. Annabel picked up the receiver.

"Hello?"

"Annabel? It's Frank Marienthal in New York."

"Hello, Frank. Your timing is good. We just walked in."

"Glad I still have good timing," he said pleasantly. "I seem to be losing other things."

"Join the club," said Annabel. "You're looking for Mac, I assume."

"If he's available."

She held her palm over the mouthpiece.

"I'll take it in my office," Mac said, heading there. "I've been meaning to call you, Frank," he said after settling in his chair and picking up the phone. "How are you?"

"Quite well, Mac, although Mary has been having problems. But that's not why I called. I wanted to talk to you about Richard."

"We had Richard and his lady friend, Kathryn, to dinner recently."

"I know. He was here that afternoon and told me he'd be seeing you. Did he discuss his book with you?"

"Barely. I asked him a lot of questions, but he seemed reluctant to get into it." Smith laughed. "I told Annabel I didn't know many writers who didn't want to talk about their books."

"I'm concerned, Mac. You know about that murder at Union Station."

"Yes, I do."

"And that his killer has also been found dead."

"I heard that, too, just recently. What does Rich say about it?"

"Nothing. I haven't spoken to him since he was here. I've been calling but keep getting his infernal machine. He hasn't returned my calls. That's not surprising. We don't always see eye to eye. But Mary's left a message, too. You'd think he'd at least return a call to his own mother."

Annabel brought Mac a cup of tea; he nodded his appreciation. He was glad for the distraction. Frank Marienthal's anger about Rich's apparent lack of responsiveness was escalating.

Smith said, "Frank, I know that Rich's

book is based upon this Louis Russo's life with the Mafia. The question is, What does Russo's murder mean to Rich, not necessarily in regard to his book, but personally?" He paused before asking, "Do you think Rich's life might be in jeopardy?"

"Don't you?"

"I don't know. It crossed my mind, of course, but I'm afraid I haven't given it much thought. Based upon your call, maybe I should — give it more thought. You obviously have."

"Let me level with you, Mac. You know that Rich's book is being published by Hobbes House."

"Of course. I reviewed the contract."

"I've been doing some research on Hobbes House. It's a conservative publisher, a willing extension of right-wing causes."

"And not reticent about it."

"It doesn't publish novels."

"Rich told us his will be their first."

The elder Marienthal said, "Hobbes House has put Rich's book up on its Web site. I've been checking it every day. It showed up today for the first time."

"And?"

"It doesn't list it as a novel. It doesn't indicate anything about whether it's fiction or nonfiction. All it has is the cover and this descriptive line: 'A startling, explosive exposé of murder in the highest of places.' "

Smith grunted.

"Have you seen the manuscript, Mac?"

"No. I chalked it up to some sort of writer's paranoia. You know, don't let anyone see a work in progress, bad luck, that sort of thing. Have you seen it?"

"No. If Russo was killed because he turned on his fellow mobsters, they made sure anything else he knew about them was dead along with him. But that doesn't mean Rich didn't learn things from Russo. They might want to shut him up, too."

"I'm not sure I agree with you, Frank. Russo spilled what he knew ten or twelve years ago. If the mob did kill him, it was strictly to get even for his having turned on them."

"But what if it wasn't the mob that killed Russo? And there's this murder of Russo's assailant. Who killed him, and why?"

"Look, Frank, I understand your concern. I'd be worried, too. I'll try and get hold of Rich. When and if I do, I'll let you know. Maybe between us we can get him to sit down and think things out."

"I can't ask more than that. I'll come

down at a moment's notice."

"You'll hear from me."

Smith hung up and dialed Rich Marienthal's number. The machine answered.

"This is Mac Smith, Rich. It's important that I speak with you. Please call at your earliest convenience." He left his number and ended the call.

"A problem?" Annabel asked when Mac joined her on their terrace.

He recounted the conversation.

"Rich hasn't returned any of their calls?" she said.

"According to Frank."

"That is worrisome," she said. "Maybe we should go over to their apartment."

"I thought about doing that, but I'm not sure it's appropriate. Rich is an adult. I got the impression from Frank that their relationship might not be all it should be."

"Still," Annabel offered, "something could be terribly wrong."

Mac took a minute to think about it. Chances were that everything was just fine with Richard Marienthal and his good-looking girlfriend, Kathryn Jalick. To go banging on their door might be viewed as an unwarranted intrusion into their lives. Still . . .

"Okay," he said.

They took the car from the Watergate's underground parking garage — their reserved space had added thousands of dollars to the price they paid for their apartment — and drove to Capitol Hill. Annabel waited in the car as Mac went into the foyer and buzzed the apartment shared by Rich and Kathryn Jalick. There was no response. He noted on the intercom board the apartment number for the superintendent and pushed the button. A man with an East Indian accent answered. A TV playing loudly and a crying baby could be heard in the background.

"Sorry to bother you," Smith said, "but my wife and I have been trying to contact two of your tenants, Richard Marienthal and Kathryn Jalick."

"They're not home?" the super said.

"There's no answer from their apartment. Are they away? Have you seen them recently?"

"Today."

"Did they indicate where they might be going?"

"Oh, no, they said nothing. Just hello to me," he yelled over the background din.

"What time was that?"

"This afternoon. At lunchtime. What was your name?"

"Smith. Mackensie Smith. I'll leave a note in their mailbox."

"Very good. I will tell them Mr. Smith was here looking for them."

"I appreciate that. Thanks."

Smith returned to the car, wrote on a piece of paper the same message he'd left on the answering machine, and placed it in the mailbox, noting that the box appeared to be empty.

Back home at the Watergate, he said to Annabel, "Well, at least they're alive, according to the super. I'll call and let Frank know that we tried. Meanwhile, I've got an hour's worth of work to get ready for tomorrow's class."

"And I'm off to bed," Annabel said, kissing his forehead. "Don't be too late."

Mac immersed himself in his classroom preparation and, with the exception of an occasional mental lapse during which he thought of Rich and the call from Rich's father, managed to relegate such thoughts to the back burner.

Rich Marienthal was well aware of the message Mac left on his answering machine. He called from where he and Geoff Lowe had been having dinner at the

260

Capitol Grill to check for messages, and heard Smith's voice, along with those of his father and his editor in New York, Sam Greenleaf. He'd hoped to reach Kathryn and get the messages from her, but wasn't surprised that she was gone. His departure earlier that evening to meet with Lowe had fueled a spirited argument.

"Again?" she'd said when he announced he was going out for dinner with Geoff.

"What do you mean, again? I haven't had dinner with Geoff in a while."

"It has nothing to do with whether it's dinner, Rich. It has to do with my never being with you. You're either holed up listening to your tapes or reading the proofs — God, don't you know what's in the book by now? — or slinking off to meet with your buddy." She said *buddy* as though describing a venomous snake.

His anger was rising and he tried to keep it in check, but failed, the way he always seemed to during confrontations with his father.

"Damn it, Kathryn, you pick the worst times to get on your high horse and criticize me. You know damn well I'm getting close to making all the work pay off, and Geoff Lowe is the reason for it. Now just

261

shut up and leave me alone."

"Shut up? You're telling *me* to shut up? Who the hell do you think you are, Rich? What ever happened to the Rich Marienthal I fell in love with?"

"He's standing right here, Kathryn. He's no different, but you are, and I'm sick and tired of your goddamn harping about Geoff Lowe and what I do for a living. You don't like it, then get the hell out."

She fought back tears as she stomped into the bedroom, threw on a jacket, grabbed her purse, and stormed from the apartment, slamming the door behind her.

He'd wanted to run after her, say he was sorry, patch it up, get her to understand that what he was going through wasn't easy. It would be over soon and they could get back to the way it had been between them in the beginning. He wanted to tell her that he wouldn't be involved with Lowe if he didn't need him at the moment. The truth was — and he couldn't admit this to Kathryn, at least not yet — was that he hated Lowe as much as she did, and couldn't wait for it to be over, when their mutual using of each other would end.

He left the apartment twenty minutes later and walked off his anger — but not his unhappiness — on his way to the Hyatt

Regency Hotel on Capitol Hill. He rode the elevator to the roof level, and entered the virtually empty Capitol View Restaurant, where Geoff Lowe sat alone at the bar, a half-consumed martini in front of him.

"Hey, buddy, how goes it?" Lowe asked as Marienthal took a stool next to him.

"All right," Marienthal replied.

Bob McIntyre, leaning against the back bar watching a baseball game on the plasma TV, greeted Rich.

"A beer," Rich said.

"We'll be over there, Bobby," Lowe said to the bartender, pointing to a leather couch in a corner of the room.

"Mei will bring it over," McIntyre said, indicating the martini.

"So, ready for the big day?" Lowe asked after they'd settled on the couch.

"No," Marienthal said, thinking of Kathryn and wishing he were with her.

"No?" Lowe said, laughing, as the waitress delivered his drink and Marienthal's beer. "What do you mean, no?"

"Nothing," Marienthal said. "Look, Geoff, considering everything that's happened, I —"

"What everything, Rich?"

"Russo getting killed. The guy who did it getting killed. Maybe we should —"

Lowe turned abruptly, his face less than a foot from Rich's. "Am I hearing right, Rich? Am I hearing that you're getting cold feet? If I am —"

"Wait a minute," Marienthal said, pulling back. "Hear me out. That's all I ask, just hear me out."

Lowe leaned back and sipped his drink. "Go ahead," he said. "I'm hearing you out."

Marienthal thought for a moment before saying, "I'm having second thoughts about Louis, Geoff."

"Second thoughts? About what?"

"About maybe he exaggerated. You know, he was getting old and he was sick. I mean, Geoff, you're about to take down a president."

Lowe held up a hand to silence Marienthal. He surveyed the room before saying, "You're wrong, Rich. *We* are about to do that. It doesn't matter how old or sick Russo was. It doesn't matter if he exaggerated. What *does* matter is that he had a story to tell, and he told it — to you. He's gone. That leaves you, Rich, and the tapes of Russo, to tell the tale." Sensing Marienthal was about to say something

264

else, Lowe added, "And you and those tapes will tell the tale, Rich. Senator Widmer will be pleased that he could bring the truth to the American people, and you'll have a best seller on your hands." He indicated to Mei with his hand that he wanted the check. To Marienthal: "Drink your beer, Rich, and we'll grab some dinner. My treat. The Capitol Grill. I'm hungry, in the mood for a porterhouse."

Lowe drove Marienthal home after dinner. Marienthal looked up at his apartment window hoping to see lights on, see Kathryn's shadow moving about the apartment. But it was blank, like his mood.

"Look, Rich," Lowe said as they sat in his car, the engine running. "I understand you're uptight, and I know why. You're a writer, for Christ's sake. What do you know about politics, huh? You sit at your computer and make pretty words that maybe somebody will buy. Politics ain't pretty, my friend. It's the ultimate war — take no prisoners, baby. You don't think our dear president, Mr. Parmele, doesn't shoot to kill? You think Mr. Parmele and his gang of cutthroats, his VP, cabinet, his political guru Chet Fletcher, play by the rules, follow the Geneva Convention?" He slapped Marienthal on the arm. "Yeah,

Rich, it's a war, and the stakes are big. This country either goes down the tubes with another four years of Parmele and the Democrats in control, or we get a straight-thinking Republican, one of *our* Republicans, in there to make things work again."

This time he grabbed Rich's arm. "What we are doing, my friend, is saving the republic. Hell, they might even erect a statue honoring you."

Marienthal again looked up to the apartment window. The subject of what he was about to do hadn't come up during dinner. Instead, Lowe had delivered his usual series of political diatribes, tossing in bits of history that might have been accurate or not, railing against the liberal establishment and the harm it had inflicted on the nation. His words from across the table had faded in and out of Rich's consciousness. Rich was thinking of Kathryn, wondering where she was, what she was doing. He did a lot of nodding during Lowe's speeches, responded with a series of grunts and "Sure" and "Yeah" and "I see what you mean." But it all meant nothing to him. He wanted the evening to end so he could make it better with Kathryn.

"I'm going in," he told Lowe, his hand on the passenger-door handle.

Lowe retained his grip on Marienthal's arm. "I have a suggestion, buddy," he said.

"What's that?"

"I think the reason you're so uptight is that you're sitting on all the notes and tapes you got from Russo."

"Yeah?"

"What I'm suggesting is that you give all that stuff to me. I'll hang on to it, keep it safe until the hearing."

Marienthal shook his head. "I'd rather keep it myself, Geoff, until the hearing."

"You're not listening to me, Rich. Let me have all your source material. You don't need it anymore. Hell, the book is written. It's about to come out."

"I'd really rather not."

Lowe continued as though Marienthal hadn't said anything. "It's better if we have those materials, Rich. That way —"

That way, if something happens to me, the hearing can still go on, Rich thought.

"I'll think about it," he said.

"I'll call you in the morning," Lowe said.

"Yeah, fine."

"Rich."

"Yeah?"

"This is bigger than either of us. We don't count for anything in the scheme of things. We're talking national security, the fate of the country. Got it?"

"Yeah, I've got it."

"First thing in the morning."

Kathryn returned after midnight. Frost permeated the apartment until they eventually sat together at their small kitchen table, cups of coffee in front of them, and talked about what had occurred. They remained there until the sun came up. By that time, a thaw had taken place. They kissed and promised to never allow an argument to progress to the stage it had.

And Rich announced a decision he'd made, with which Kathryn Jalick wholeheartedly agreed.

TWENTY-NINE

"Kathryn? It's Mackensie Smith."

"Oh, good morning, Mr. — Mac."

"There's a lot of people worried about you and Rich."

"Worried about us?"

"Calls not being returned. Did you get my message and the note I left in your mailbox?"

"Yes. I'm sorry, but it's been so hectic here that —"

"I'm sure it has," Smith said, "but Rich's mom and dad are concerned that they haven't heard from him. His father called me last evening and —"

"I told Rich he'd better call his folks, but with all that's going on, I guess it slipped his mind."

"You're both okay?"

"Yes, yes. We're fine."

"Can I speak with Rich?"

"He's not here, Mac. He went out for the day."

"Can you reach him? His cell phone?"

"I'll try, and have him call you."

"Have him call his father first."

269

Smith hung up and pondered the conversation. *What was going on there?*

"Did you reach him?" Annabel asked when she emerged from the shower, her body wrapped in a large blue towel, wet red hair secured beneath a smaller towel.

"I spoke with Kathryn. He wasn't there, out for the day, she says. I can't figure it out, Annie. What's he trying to be, his version of J. D. Salinger? It obviously has to do with his book."

"You asked him to call you?"

"After he calls Frank and Mary." He got up from behind his desk and gave her a damp hug. "You smell good," he said.

"Thank you, sir. Go get your shower in. Your scent will improve, too. I'll make breakfast."

Later that morning, Mac dropped her at the gallery in Georgetown before proceeding to the university, where he was scheduled to meet with the law school's incoming dean. The intense heat spell of the past week had broken. The air was less humid and there was a slight coolness to it, both conditions representing a welcome change.

"What've you got?"

Bret Mullin sat in the central computer

room of the precinct where an officer had done an Internet search for the name *Richard Mariontholl.*

"Nothing under that spelling," he told Mullin. "But there's this."

He handed the detective a printout of entries for Richard Marienthal. There was a bio from the rudimentary Web page Kathryn had created for Rich; a listing of some of his magazine articles from the Washington Independent Writers' Web site; a photo of him atop a piece he'd written for *Washingtonian* magazine; and a page from Hobbes House's Web site announcing the forthcoming publication of a book by Marienthal: "a startling, explosive exposé of murder in the highest of places."

"This the guy you're looking for, Bret?"

"Must be. Got an address and phone for him?"

He was handed it a minute later, again from the computer database.

"Thanks, pal."

"Anytime."

Mullin went to the detective's bullpen and laid the pages on his desk next to the artist's sketch that had been given him earlier that morning. Joyce Rosenberg's description, captured by the police sketch artist, was surprisingly close to the photo taken down from the Internet.

So this is the guy, he thought, leaning back and finishing his coffee, now cold, from a Styrofoam cup. Sasha had said that Richard Marienthal was writing a book based upon Russo's life in the Mafia, and that after many meetings in Israel, Russo had come to Washington to meet with him. Russo gets iced the minute he steps off the train by a slick black guy who's done time in mob school and disappears. Then that guy is found shot dead, floating in the lilies at Kenilworth Gardens. Had the mob ordered both hits, taking Russo down because he'd ratted on them a dozen years ago, then making sure the shooter wouldn't live to finger them?

Possibly.

But something didn't compute for Mullin with this scenario. *Murder in the highest of places?* What did that mean?

Vinnie Accurso entered the area and took the desk across from Mullin, interrupting his partner's series of silent questions. "Whatta you got there?" Accurso asked, pointing to the sketch and the downloaded pages.

"Our man," Mullin said, turning them so Accurso could better see them.

"The guy at Union Station?"

"One and the same. I had dinner last night with Russo's lady."

"How come?"

"She arrived to claim Russo's body. Nice gal. I figured the least I could do after she flies all the way here was to buy her a meal."

"Where'd you go?"

"You wouldn't know it. Zola."

"I know it. By that spy museum."

"Yeah. Well, anyway, she tells me that Russo came here to meet with this writer, Marienthal. The sketch is the one Rosenberg, the Fox reporter, gave our artist. Good, huh?"

"Looks like the picture."

"That's what I mean. What say we pay Mr. Marienthal a visit this morning?"

"Why don't we call him first?"

"I'd rather surprise him," Mullin said, standing and twisting against the pain in his back.

They went to the unmarked car assigned them that day.

"So tell me about dinner last night," Accurso said as Mullin started the engine and pulled out of the lot.

"What's to tell?"

"What's she look like?"

"Nice-looking. Not a kid. A little over-weight, maybe."

"I guess you'd notice that," Accurso said playfully.

"Whatta you mean by that?"

"Nothing. Nothing. I just — I just find it strange you'd take her to dinner. How many women have shown up here over the years to claim a body? Plenty, right? You ever take any of *them* to dinner?"

Mullin ignored his partner and drove in the direction of Marienthal's apartment on Capitol Hill. They were on Seventh Street, approaching Eastern Market, when Accurso asked Mullin to stop.

"What's up?" Mullin asked.

"I want to get some fruit, Bret. I told Katie I'd bring fruit home."

"You crazy, buying it here? They charge a fortune."

"I'm not going inside. There're a couple of nice stands outside, on the other side. Cheap, too."

"Yeah, all right," Mullin said, pulling into a no-parking zone by the market and across from a mini-shopping center.

"You coming?" Accurso asked after he'd exited the car and saw that Mullin hadn't moved.

"Go on, go on. I'll stay here."

Mullin watched the passing parade while waiting for Accurso to return. Ten minutes later, he saw his partner, carrying a plastic shopping bag, round the corner of the building that had housed greengrocers and butchers since 1873. Accurso was within ten feet of the car when he stopped and looked across the street. "Look!" he shouted.

Mullin swiveled his head. A small branch of a local bank was nestled between a video rental store and a dry cleaner. Two men were in front of the bank, by its ATM machine. One of them, an older man, had his back against the machine and had raised his hands. The second man, considerably younger and wearing a T-shirt and jeans, with a red bandanna wrapped around his head, pointed what looked like a gun at the older gentleman.

Accurso didn't hesitate. He dropped the bag of fruit to the ground, pulled his revolver from its shoulder holster, and headed across the heavily trafficked street, holding a hand up in an attempt to stop motorists from hitting him and yelling, "Hey, hey, police! Drop the gun!"

Mullin grabbed their mobile radio from the dash, struggled out the driver's-side door, and also withdrew his weapon.

Accurso had reached the other side of the road as Mullin started across. He was stopped by the sound of a single gunshot snapping through the air. Mullin, who was only a few feet into the road, stared in disbelief. Accurso was on the ground; the ATM bandit had taken off to his right and disappeared around the back of the stores.

"Vinnie!" Mullin shouted as he threaded his way through automobiles that had stopped when their drivers saw what was going on. He reached his partner, fell to his knees, and asked, "Where you hit, buddy?"

"It's okay," Accurso said, trying to get to a sitting position. "My leg. That's all. Just my leg."

Mullin saw a crimson puddle forming around Accurso's knee. He barked into the radio, "Officer down! Officer down!" and gave the location.

"Get the shooter," Accurso said.

"Yeah, later, Vinnie. He's gone. You see him?"

Accurso whimpered against a sharp pain. "Yeah, I saw him."

"Good."

"Let Katie know I'm okay."

"Sure."

"And give her the fruit. She wanted fruit."

"Yeah, I'll give her the fruit, Vinnie. She'll get the fruit."

Detective Fred Peck was in a good mood that morning, which reflected the fact that Helen had awoken in sufficiently good spirits to have gotten up with him and prepared breakfast, as rare an occurrence in the Peck household as candor at a presidential press conference. The reason for her springtime mood was a hand-painted mirror imported from France that she'd wanted for the foyer since spotting it weeks ago in a local antique store. Fred had stopped by the shop on his way home the evening before and bought it for her. After many attempts to hang it precisely where she wanted it, he finally succeeded. The glass in it was wavy, but he didn't mention that flaw to her. She was pleased, which was what counted.

He signed in to the Missing Persons Unit, closed his office door, sat behind his desk, and examined the copy of the police artist's sketch of the man Fox News reporter Joyce Rosenberg had described. It was interesting — the ability of police artists to create a workable composite of men and women based upon descriptions by witnesses always impressed him. But whether this sketch would be of any use to Tim Stripling was conjecture. All Peck could and would do was deliver it to Stripling, as promised. He slipped the sketch into a large manila envelope, wrote *TS* on it, placed it in the wide center drawer of his desk, and left the office.

"Hey, Fred," a detective in the bullpen said when Peck entered.

"Where's Mullin and Accurso?" Peck asked.

"Out. Mullin came up with the name of the guy who was at Union Station when the old Italian got whacked."

"He did? How'd he do that?"

The detective shrugged and pointed to a half-consumed box of Dunkin' Donuts on the desk. "Want one?"

"No, thanks."

"He got some info off the Internet," the detective said, helping himself to a jelly doughnut.

Peck went to the central computer room and asked the officer on duty about Mullin, whether he'd downloaded information about a potential witness to the Union Station shooting.

"Yeah, he did. He had the name spelled

wrong, but it was close enough."

"What did you come up with?"

"You want a copy?"

"I'd appreciate it."

Armed with the same information Mullin had been given, Peck returned to his office, closed the door, and placed a call.

One of the two cell phones Tim Stripling carried rang. He saw that it wasn't the one provided by the FBI and flipped open the cover on his personal phone. "Hello?"

"Tim. It's Fred Peck."

Stripling had just finished breakfast at Patisserie Café Didier, in Georgetown.

"What's up, Fred?" he asked.

Stripling smiled at Peck's lowering of his voice. "I have what you want," said the detective.

"Meaning?"

"The name of the witness at Union Station."

Stripling pulled a pen from his jacket and positioned it over a white paper napkin. "Shoot."

"No," Peck said. "I want to give it to you personally."

"Why? Just give me the name."

"I have a picture, too."

"The sketch?"

"And a photo."

Stripling glanced around the popular patisserie and also lowered his voice. "Now?" he asked.

"I'm tied up this morning," Peck said.

Sounds kinky, Stripling thought. "Lunch?"

"Yes. But, Tim."

"Huh?"

"This will cost you big."

Greedy bastard, Stripling thought. *His wife must be holding out on him in bed unless she gets paid.*

"I'll take care of you," Stripling said.

"I mean, it's got to be a lot more."

"Yeah, yeah, okay."

"South Austin Grill in Alexandria. Noon?"

Tex-Mex food, Stripling thought, wincing. He disliked southwestern food. All beans and mush. "All right," he said.

He'd no sooner closed the cover on his cell phone when the other one rang.

"Stripling."

"We'd like to meet," the FBI agent said.

"Why?"

"To get an update."

"I don't have anything to update you on."

"That's disappointing."

"That may be, but —"

"One o'clock. Usual place."

"No can do. I'll have something for you later this afternoon."

"What time?"

"Four."

The agent hung up.

He used his personal phone to call Mark Roper at CIA headquarters in Langley, Virginia.

"What a pleasant surprise hearing from you," Roper said.

"Always aim to please, Mark. I've got a breakthrough for your friends."

"My friends?"

"You know who I'm talking about. I'm due for a raise."

"Timothy, please, I —"

"Seven-fifty starting today. And a bonus of two thousand."

"For Christ's sake, Tim."

"I'm serious, Mark. It's either that or you get somebody else. My expenses have suddenly gone up."

"What's this breakthrough?"

"We have a deal?"

"All right. But —"

"I'll get back to you. Or maybe your friends will. Ciao."

Marienthal didn't take time for a leisurely breakfast at a trendy Georgetown patisserie that morning. He was at the local branch of his bank when it opened at nine, presenting the keys to his safe deposit box to the by-now-familiar woman on the platform. He'd been in and out of the safe deposit vault on a daily basis for almost a year.

"How's your book going?" she asked as she inserted his keys and the master key into his rented boxes.

"Oh, good. Yeah, pretty good."

"That's great."

She discreetly left as Marienthal emptied the contents of the boxes into a large canvas shoulder bag. He signaled her; she returned and together they locked the boxes.

"Thanks," he said.

"See you this afternoon?" she asked, aware of his habit of returning materials to the boxes just before the bank's closing time each day.

"Not sure," he said.

He walked quickly to his car parked around the corner, opened the trunk, deposited the canvas bag in it alongside a suitcase, slammed the trunk closed, looked around to ensure no one was paying attention to him, got behind the wheel, and eased his way into traffic. A half hour later, he was checked into the River Inn in Foggy Bottom, a small, all-suite hotel within walking distance of the Kennedy Center, a favorite of visitors contemplating a longer stay in Washington. He used his cell phone to call Kathryn Jalick at the Library of Congress.

"For you, Kathryn," a colleague in the rare documents room said.

"Rich?"

"Yeah. I'm here."

"Are you okay?"

"Fine. I'm fine. You?"

"Okay."

"Look, Kathryn, just remember what I told you. Nobody, and I mean nobody, is to know where I am."

"I know."

"Don't write down the number here. Don't write down anything and leave it around the apartment."

"I won't. But, Rich, what about your folks? Mac Smith? What do I tell them?"

"Just say I'm out of town on business. I'll be gone a week, maybe longer."

"All right."

"When will you tell Geoff?"

"I don't know. I'm not sure what I'll tell him. That's what I have to figure out while

I'm here. Don't worry. Just go about your life like normal."

"Normal."

"It'll be over soon. I love you."

She glanced at her colleague, who was busy preparing a rare document for a researcher due to arrive later that morning. "I love you, too," she whispered, hung up, and brushed a tear from the corner of her eye.

THIRTY

"He was fortunate. The bullet didn't do any major structural damage to the knee. Mostly soft tissue trauma."

The young physician delivering good news to Katie Accurso, Bret Mullin, and a contingent of senior police officers led by the commissioner had just come from performing surgery on Vinnie Accurso's leg. He wore OR greens and black clogs; a wilted surgical mask hung loosely around his neck.

"That's wonderful," Katie said, breaking into tears. "Can I see him now?"

"Give him a couple of hours in recovery," the doctor said.

An MPD public information officer conferred briefly with the commissioner before going downstairs to brief press camped at D.C. General's front door. The commissioner and others filed from the room after offering their good wishes to Katie, leaving her alone with Mullin.

"I'm so thankful," she said, dabbing at her eyes with a handkerchief he'd assured her was clean. "He could have been killed," she said.

"The perp was a lousy shot," Mullin said.

"Will you find him?" she asked.

"Our guys are all over the neighborhood," he said. "Oh, I almost forgot." He handed her the plastic bag of fruit from Eastern Market. "Vinnie bought this just before he got shot."

"What is it?"

"Fruit. He said you wanted fruit. That's all the fruitcake thought about. The fruit."

She laughed, and he joined her.

"I have to go," he said. "You need anything, you yell, huh?"

"I will. Thanks, Bret."

Mullin stopped in a small neighborhood bar a block from the hospital and downed two shots of vodka before returning to the precinct, where the buzz was all about Accurso's shooting. Mullin answered questions about how it had happened and what he'd seen, but soon tired of repeating the story. He secluded himself in an empty interrogation room and worked on multiple forms to be filled out regarding the shooting of a police officer. He was engrossed in the task when one of Chief Leshin's lieutenants poked his head in:

"Chief wants you in his office, Mullin."

"Now?"

"No, next week. Yeah, now."

Leshin was wrapping up a meeting when Mullin arrived. He watched through the glass as those in the room nodded at something the chief said, then came through the door. Leshin waved Mullin in.

"Close it, Bret," he said, indicating the door.

"What's up?" Mullin asked, directing his words away from his boss in case the supposedly odorless vodka wasn't odorless.

"The Union Station case. It's closed."

"Yeah, I know."

"I mean *really* closed, the Russo hit and the LeClaire hit."

Mullin's face indicated he didn't understand.

"This guy you've been looking for, the one who knew Louis Russo's name when he was shot."

"What about him?"

"Drop it. Quit looking for him. It's over."

"You said —"

"What I said was that you could try to run him down, provided it didn't take too much of your time. With Vinnie out of commission, you don't have time. Okay?"

"If you say so."

"I say so. Tough about Vinnie."

"Yeah."

"You'll hook up with a new partner tomorrow."

"I have a choice?"

"No."

"Just don't give me one of the young ones, huh? They get dumber every year."

Leshin's silence said it wasn't a debatable issue, and that the meeting was over.

"How's the drinking?" the chief asked as Mullin opened the door.

"How is it?" He laughed. "Better than ever."

"Get out of here, Mullin."

Leshin sat behind his desk and thought of the call he'd received earlier in the day from someone in the commissioner's office instructing him not to pursue the identity of the Union Station witness.

"How come?" Leshin had asked, knowing his question wouldn't be answered. It wasn't.

"Okay," he'd said, understanding without being told that someone in D.C. with clout had called off the hunt. Not that it mattered. As far as he was concerned, the official departmental finding — that

Louis Russo had been killed in retribution for having testified against his Mafia goombahs a dozen years ago, and that his killer, Leon LeClaire, had been murdered by the same people — was good enough for him. Closed cases were good cases. The more you closed, the better it looked for you personally, and for the department. That's what it was all about, wasn't it? Looking good.

His thoughts shifted to Bret Mullin. *He* didn't look good. All that damn booze. He'd given up on trying to lead Mullin into programs promising the chance of sobriety. With any luck, the big, beefy detective would walk with his pension in a year — after putting in thirty — and be out of his hair.

Mullin was thinking the same thing, that it was just another year to the pension. Accurso's shooting was hitting home. Mullin was no different than any other cop who knows from the first day on the job that some creep's bullet might have your name on it. He'd been lucky; he'd never taken a bullet, although one had come too close for comfort a few years back. The memory of that incident prompted him to abruptly leave the precinct, get in his car, and drive in the direction of the apartment he'd called home since the divorce. But going home wasn't an option. Not yet. He parked at a hydrant in front of a restaurant, went inside, sat at the bar, and ordered a double Grey Goose. He was virtually alone in the damp coolness of the bar area. The barmaid, an older woman with sharp features and red hair piled high on her head, delivered his drink. "How about a glass of tomato juice with that?" Mullin said.

He pulled his cell phone from his jacket, dialed the number of the Lincoln Suites, and asked for Sasha Levine, who was on the phone instantly. The sound of her voice startled him. He was sure she wouldn't be there.

"Ms. Levine. Bret Mullin here. The detective. Remember?"

"Of course I do."

"I got tied up today and forgot to call. There was a — my partner got shot and —"

"How terrible."

"Yeah, it was. But he'll be okay. It was his leg. He'll be fine."

"I am glad to hear that."

"I was wondering whether you were available for dinner, like we discussed."

"Yes, I am."

"Good. Did you catch up with that

writer friend of yours, Mr. Marienthal?"

"No. I called, but there was only his machine that answers."

"How long ago did you call?"

"This afternoon. I tried two or three times."

"Tell you what. How about you try again? Maybe he's home by now."

"All right."

"If he's home, bring him to dinner with us. Don't tell him I'll be there. My treat."

"I don't think —"

"I'm serious. Happy to get you two together."

"I will try."

"Good. I'll pick you up at the hotel, say, in about an hour? Hour and a half?"

"An hour and a half would be better."

"You got it. See you then."

The vodka burned his throat and stomach as he downed it in a single swallow.

"Another?" the barmaid asked

"No, thanks, sweetie. Got to run."

He intended as he got in his car to go home, shower, and change clothes. Instead, he drove to the Eastern Market area and pulled up in front of the address he'd been given for Richard Marienthal. He turned off the ignition and pondered whether to see if Marienthal was home. That could be awkward, however. He'd already arranged with Sasha to invite the guy to dinner. Still, he didn't want to wait that long. If Bret Mullin had any virtues, patience wasn't among them.

He was about to leave the car and approach the building when the front door opened. A nondescript middle-aged man wearing a suit and tie stepped through it and stood on the set of six steps leading down to the sidewalk. *Is that you, Marienthal?* Mullin wondered. Too old, he decided. A better look at the man's face confirmed it wasn't the person in the artist's sketch and computer-generated photograph. He took note of a leather catalogue bag dangling from the man's hand. Judging from the way he carried it, it didn't have much in it.

Come on, come on, Mullin silently said. *Move! Get going!*

The man looked left and right before slowly descending the steps. He went to a car parked at the corner, tossed the bag into the backseat, climbed behind the wheel, and drove off — but not before Mullin scribbled down the make, color, and plate number. He waited a few minutes before going to the building, entering the foyer, and checking the names on the intercom board. He pushed the button for the apartment in the name of R. Marienthal and K. Jalick. Nothing. He tried again. And again. He pushed the button for the super's apartment.

"What do you want?" a man answered in an East Indian accent.

"You the super for this building?" Mullin shouted to be heard over the sound of a TV in the background.

"No time now. Go away."

Mullin felt his anger rise. "Hey, I'm the police. I need to talk to you."

"The police?"

"Yeah, the police. Come on, I don't have all day."

The superintendent came through the door separating the foyer from the building interior.

Mullin flashed his badge. "I'm looking for these people, Marienthal and —" He looked at the intercom board again. "And K. Jalick."

"I don't know nothing about them," the super said, making a move to retreat back inside.

"Hey, buddy, hold on a minute. They live here. Right?"

"Yes. I have to go. I am busy."

The super's overt nervousness caused Mullin's antennae to go up. Sure, people got uptight when confronted by a cop, especially foreigners. But this guy looked like he was about to race from the foyer. *What've you got going inside, baby?* Mullin wondered. *Illegal alien? A few bags of crack? Running some broads?*

"Calm down," Mullin said. "I just want to know where these two people are. Marienthal and this K. Jalick."

"I don't know," the super said in his singsong voice. "At work. They work."

"He's a writer. Right? He works at home. Right?"

"She works someplace else. The library. She is a nice lady."

So Marienthal is a heterosexual, Mullin thought.

"What library?"

"I don't know. I swear I don't know."

"You seen them today?"

"No. I have not seen them."

"All right," Mullin said. "Maybe I'll be back. That okay with you?"

"Yes. Yes. Okay with me."

"Good."

He sat in his car another five minutes before deciding to head home in preparation for dinner with Sasha Levine. Had he stayed another five minutes, he would have seen Kathryn Jalick walk up the street and enter the building. And if he'd been there five minutes after that, he would have seen her exit the building, a frantic look on her face, a cell phone to her ear.

Her first thought upon entering the ransacked apartment had been to call the police. But she stopped herself and decided instead to leave the apartment and go outside, where she called Rich at the River Inn.

"Somebody trashed it?" he said.

"No. I mean, nobody damaged anything. But whoever it was went through everything, the dresser drawers, the desk, pulled stuff out of the closet."

"They take anything?"

"I don't think so. I don't know. I saw my jewelry still on the dresser. The TV's there, the radios."

"How'd they get in?"

"The door seems okay. My key worked. I checked the windows. They're locked."

Rich fell silent.

"I don't want to stay here tonight," Kathryn said.

"Yeah, I understand. You want to come here?"

"Yes."

"Okay. Go back upstairs, pack some clothes and a toothbrush, and head over. I'll be here."

"One for dinner?" a hostess asked when Tim Stripling entered McCormick & Schmick's on K Street N.W.

"I'll sit in here," he said, walking along the 65-foot bar already crowded with after-work revelers, and found a small table in that portion of the restaurant. It was still happy hour; for $1.95 he could have ordered a giant hamburger to go with the dry Rob Roy a waitress brought him. But he wasn't in the mood for a burger. He ordered a Crab Louis salad — "Extra Russian dressing on the side," he said — sat back, and took in the noisy scene. Conversations drifted his way along with smoke from the bar. A young man trying to impress a leggy brunette told her how important he was to his employer, the Department of Agriculture. Another man, older and sitting erect on his stool to hold in his developing paunch, told dirty jokes to two women whose laughter was more polite than authentic. *The world's oldest game was on,* Stripling thought, breaking off a piece of bread. An expensive game, all those drinks, and dinner, and maybe tickets to the Kennedy Center or Blues Alley, all in the pursuit of a warm body for the night.

His "game" was also expensive, he mused as he ordered a second drink. It was good Roper had agreed to the raise. Peck had hit him up for seven hundred at lunch, and the superintendent at Marienthal's apartment building haggled until agreeing to accept two hundred to let Stripling into the apartment. A waste of money; there was nothing of interest in the apartment. You couldn't hit a home run every time out. Ask the men at the bar who would empty their pockets and go home alone to lick their wounded egos.

"Dessert?"

"What's on the ice cream menu to-night?"

"Chocolate, vanilla, strawberry."

"Whip me up a hot fudge sundae with vanilla ice cream. Add an extra scoop, huh. My sweet tooth is aching tonight. Oh, and a couple of extra cherries, too."

THIRTY-ONE

President Adam Parmele and his entourage of advisers and aides, accompanied by those members of the press corps privileged to travel with him — and whose boredom at being on yet another campaign trip was evident — sat in the massive 747 waiting for it to touch down in Miami.

The president was not his usual gregarious and available self this day. On previous campaign flights, he'd ingratiated himself with reporters, making frequent forays from his private airborne quarters and office to the press section of the aircraft, joking, replying to questions, playing his practiced ability to schmooze with them to good effect. This day, however, he kept to himself, disappearing inside the president's space with his political adviser, Chet Fletcher, and congressional liaison Walter Brown. His wife, Cathleen, who had been scheduled to accompany her husband, canceled at the last moment: "The first lady regrets that she will be unable to accompany the president to Miami," read the short, bland press release from her office.

The reporters in the rear did what they usually do on these flights, filled up on food served by White House stewards assigned to the plane and swapped the latest political jokes and D.C. rumors. Those who'd covered previous presidents had learned to be circumspect when the jokes involved chiefs of state. Parmele was different. He laughed heartily at humor in which he was the target, and often repeated what late-night talk-show hosts had quipped about him during their opening monologues.

"Must be something heavy-duty going on up front, huh?" a wire service reporter said.

"Maybe he's planning to invade Mississippi, punish them for not voting for him."

"He doesn't want to answer questions about his wife," someone else offered.

"Mississippi, hell. If he's going to use the military to get anybody, it'll be Senator Widmer."

"What've you got on those hearings coming up?"

"Nada. Zip. I've seen a tight clamp on hearings before, but nothing like this. Even the best leaks aren't talking. What are we coming to?"

The press representative from the *Wash-*

ington Post had chosen a seat apart from his colleagues. One called to him: "Hey, Milton, you pick up anything new on the Widmer hearings?"

"No," Milton said, and went back to a magazine he'd been reading.

The reporter who'd asked the question leaned close to the ear of a correspondent from CNN. "Widmer's got some surprise witness," he said.

"Yeah, I heard that, too."

"Got something to do with that murder at Union Station."

"Get outta here! Where'd you hear that?"

"I've got a source who —"

Robin Whitson's sudden entry into the press section from where she'd been sitting midships brought the conversation to a halt.

"Hey, Robin, come sit here," someone suggested.

"In a minute," the press secretary said, plucking a sandwich from a tray being passed by a steward and bantering with reporters nearby. A few minutes later, she slipped into an empty seat next to Milton from the *Post.*

"What've they got, a thing going?" someone whispered to a colleague.

"Milton? Come on." Now he lowered his voice so that it could barely be heard over the jet's four engines. "He's got something on the Widmer story."

"How do you know?"

"I hear things."

Robin sensed the undercurrent of talk and came to the front of the section. "Okay," she announced, "here's the drill in Miami. The president will be talking about his new initiative on education and the escalating tension in North Korea, and he'll float some ideas on strengthening the crime bill currently under discussion in Congress." She motioned for her assistant press secretary to distribute advance copies of the speech Parmele would deliver in Miami.

"What's with his wife canceling, Robin?"

"A scheduling conflict."

"Hours before she's due to make the trip?"

"That's what happened. Hey, get off this nonsense about the president and first lady. Okay? You've got better things to think about."

The first lady and her absence was the last thing on the minds of Parmele, Fletcher, and Brown as they sat in a tight circle of club chairs in the president's office compartment.

Brown, who had just briefed Parmele and Fletcher on new information concerning the pending Widmer hearings, had learned over the months to leave the president and his political adviser alone after delivering sobering news. "Nobody in until the chief says so," he told a uniformed Marine lance corporal, who stood at rigid attention outside the president's flying office.

Parmele swiveled in his leather chair to look through the window at towering cumulus clouds on the eastern horizon.

"See those anvil-shaped formations on top?" Parmele said, his eyes not straying from the vista outside the aircraft.

Fletcher came to another window and crouched. "Yes," he said.

"Thunderstorms," said the president. "Violent thunderstorms inside those clouds. They could tear this aircraft into bits."

"Not a pleasant thought," Fletcher said.

Parmele turned to Fletcher. "Neither is what Walter just told us," he said, grim-faced.

The president left his chair and paced the thickly carpeted area. As usual, he'd removed his shoes immediately after takeoff and was in his stocking feet. The incessant whine of the 747's engines provided white noise to fill the silence between the men.

Fletcher had taken a seat, crossed his legs, and watched his leader — America's leader — walk, as though it would force clarity into his thinking. Fletcher had seen Parmele do this numerous times before. Being in motion seemed to energize the man when he was grappling with particularly thorny problems. The briefing Walter Brown had delivered certainly qualified.

Parmele went behind his desk, sat, leaned forward to prop his elbows on it, and said, "Nobody will believe it, Chet."

Fletcher cleared his throat. "Mr. President, those who wish to believe it will. Those who don't won't. But it isn't that simple, sir. These charges are serious. Widmer will shape it for maximum impact."

"It's all hearsay," Parmele said. He'd been an attorney before entering politics.

"But this isn't a court of law," Fletcher countered. "You aren't considered innocent until proved guilty beyond reasonable doubt. The court of public and political opinion doesn't deal in such niceties."

Parmele leaned back and threw up his

hands. "He doesn't have anything, damn it! You heard Walter. The old Italian who was going to testify is dead. What does Widmer have? The word of someone trying to make a fast buck, that's all."

Fletcher sighed as he added, "And notes and taped interviews with Louis Russo. That's what I'm told."

"Secondhand stuff."

"Mr. President," Fletcher said, "the Widmer hearings will be televised. They will be front page on every paper in America, and overseas, too. If there are tape recordings and they contain Russo's allegations about you, hearing them will be riveting to the American people. They —"

"How do you know? Have you heard the tapes?"

"No, sir, but I assume they contain Russo's charges in his own voice."

"What about this guy's book? What's his name? Marienthal?"

"Richard Marienthal. His book is being published by Hobbes House."

Parmele guffawed. "Hobbes House! Why am I not surprised?"

"I've had the editor and publisher queried, Mr. President. They'll say nothing more than it's a novel."

"A *novel?* Widmer's going to base his

hearings on a goddamn piece of fiction?"

"I don't believe it is a novel, Mr. President. Chances are they're calling it a novel at this juncture to keep its true nature under wraps. It has to be a nonfiction recounting of what Mr. Russo claims happened and his role in it."

Parmele stood again. "This is nothing but a goddamn political hatchet job to derail a second term."

"Of course it is," agreed Fletcher, not adding that it represented considerably more than that. The word *impeachment* never passed his lips.

Congressional liaison Walter Brown's breaking the news about the substance of the Widmer hearings hadn't come as a surprise to Fletcher. Far from it. As tight as security had been surrounding the hearings, tidbits about the genesis of them had begun to ripple around official Washington as early as two weeks ago. Light on specifics, the rumors had been brought to Fletcher's attention by well-placed sources inside Congress, members of Parmele's political party.

This posed a dilemma for the political adviser. He considered going to the president soon after learning of it, but decided

305

against it. It was all too vague at that juncture, too grounded in innuendo and half-truths. Too, there were the sources of the information, those unnamed men and women whose own agendas had to be questioned.

Instead, Fletcher made the decision to pursue it through his own contacts, keeping the president out of the loop, at least in the short run.

His first step had been to confer with the attorney general of the United States, Wayne Garson. That meeting had taken place in the west wing of the White House, a room not much in demand because it was not much bigger than a closet.

Of all Parmele's Cabinet appointments, Wayne Garson had been the most controversial. Before being tapped by the newly elected president to be his attorney general, the tall, rawboned former Louisiana attorney general had the reputation of being a tough prosecutor, an advocate of the death penalty and a champion of the unborn, a deeply religious man who seemed to ride above the rough-and-tumble politics of the Bayou State. Parmele had spoken against the death penalty during his campaign, and was an advocate of a woman's choice when it came to ending a pregnancy.

So, the pundits asked, why choose Wayne Garson as your attorney general?

Although political adviser Chet Fletcher wasn't the one asked publicly for an answer, it had been *his* choice when asked by the president for recommendations. The polls had indicated that Parmele, even though he'd won the election, was perceived by many in the country as being too liberal, too soft, particularly with social issues. Garson would add muscle to the administration. Of course, there was the hurdle of Garson's confirmation hearings, which became more contentious than most other such hearings in recent memory. Garson's gruff personality and impressive knowledge of the law and the Constitution carried the day. It was almost as though senators on the panel were reluctant to challenge Garson's views and experience. He couched responses to questions about his views on abortion and capital punishment, was confirmed, and lost little time in shaping Justice in his own image.

Garson and Fletcher's meeting wasn't on the White House schedule, by design. Each man had been involved in earlier official meetings; their entry into the small office seemed to just happen, accidental and unplanned. Garson arrived first, preceding Fletcher by barely a minute. The AG, his broad shoulders seeming to fill the room — "You forgot to remove the hanger, Mr. Attorney General," was a favored line around Washington — was admiring a painting on the wall when Fletcher entered. Fletcher closed the door and lost his hand in Garson's meaty fist.

"What's on your mind, Chet?" Garson asked, folding himself into a chair and narrowing his eyes.

Fletcher told him what he'd heard, that Alaska Senator Karl Widmer was planning to hold hearings into the period when President Parmele headed the CIA.

"Ancient history," Garson muttered.

"Not so ancient, Wayne," Fletcher countered. "And possibly damaging to the president beyond repair."

Garson grunted. "Go on, tell me more."

"Details are sketchy at best," Fletcher said, taking a chair across from the AG. "I have people trying to come up with more. Private sources, very discreet." If he was looking for a nod of approval at pursuing the matter with discretion, he didn't get it from Garson. He continued: "What we know at this juncture is that Senator

Widmer has made contact with a man named Louis Russo."

"Who's he?"

"Mafia in New York. He lives in Israel now."

"Israel? A former New York mafioso?"

"He was placed in the federal witness protection program a number of years ago."

"He turned?"

"That's what I'm told."

"What the hell does Widmer want from a Mafia turncoat?"

"His testimony about the president."

"When he headed the CIA."

"Yes." Fletcher lowered his voice to a whisper. He leaned close to Garson and said, "The Eliana matter."

Garson's expression said that he either hadn't heard Fletcher or hadn't registered what he had heard. Then his face changed from puzzlement to recognition. "I understand," he said, his whisper more gravelly than Fletcher's.

"This Russo, I'm told, claims to have been hired to kill Eliana."

"By the CIA?"

An affirmative nod from Fletcher.

"Back when —"

"Yes."

"Is he claiming that the president ordered it? When he was at the Company?"

"I'm not sure. I just know that the potential ramifications are immense."

"Are you sure of what you're saying?" Garson asked.

"No. But we must find out, and do it fast."

"How did Widmer end up with this Mafia type?"

"I don't know."

Garson grimaced and hunched his shoulders, running a hand through his thicket of unruly gray hair. "Know what I think?" he said.

"What?"

"I think you're right — *if* this Russo is who you say he is, and *if* he's willing to lie in front of a Senate committee."

Garson's assumption that Russo would be lying if he testified might have provided a modicum of comfort to Fletcher. It didn't. If this thing progressed to the point of a former member of the Mafia testifying that the president of the United States had, while head of the CIA, in fact, ordered the assassination of a Central American leader, one of the many spins put on it would be that he was lying, seeking his day in the sun, his fifteen minutes of fame, demented, ailing and losing his faculties, a criminal, a lifetime liar and cheat, all the usual, the dupe of a vindictive senator out to destroy a presidency.

Better not to have it happen in the first place.

"Can you find out more about Russo and what he intends to say in front of the committee?" Fletcher asked.

"I'll get on it," Garson replied gruffly.

"It has to be kept away from the White House."

"You damn well bet it does," said Garson, standing. "And from Justice, too. Does he know?"

"The president? No."

"Better he doesn't until we have a better handle on it."

"I agree."

"I'll get back to you."

The 747's PA system came to life from the cockpit: "We'll be landing in twenty-two minutes."

Parmele put on his shoes and laced them. Fletcher waited for the president to speak. He'd laid out everything he knew about the Widmer hearings, which was considerably more than Walter Brown had known. Parmele remained silent during Fletcher's briefing. Shoes tied, he turned to his political adviser, smiled, and said, "I think I owe the Mafia a debt of gratitude, Chet."

"Sir?"

"For getting rid of this turncoat. What's his name? Louis Russo? They did me a favor."

"But there are the tapes and notes, sir. And I expect that the writer will be called to testify, too."

"Maybe we'll get lucky with him, too. What do you know about him?"

Fletcher started to respond, but Parmele cut him off. "I'm sure he didn't vote for me," he said with a small chuckle. "Do what you can, Chet. I'll be damned if some hack writer and a lying mafioso are going to deny me a second term."

The president slapped Fletcher on the back, left the office, and went to the press section, where he told reporters, "Sorry I couldn't be with you earlier. I'm sure Robin has taken good care of you."

"Sir, any comment about why Mrs. Parmele decided at the last minute to not make this trip?" he was asked.

Parmele flashed a big smile and said, "She's probably gotten bored of hearing me extol her virtues on the stump. Needed a day off from me — and you. See you on the ground."

THIRTY-TWO

As Adam Parmele, president of the United States, winged south in search of a second term, Alaska Senator Karl Widmer was hard at work in Washington, D.C., doing what he could to deny him another four years.

The mood in the senator's suite was not upbeat that morning. Members of his staff knew what the tenor of the day would be the moment the aging, cantankerous Alaskan stepped through the door. They'd learned to read his walk, posture, and facial expressions, and the tone of his voice when, or if, he bothered to return their greetings.

He'd started the day by attending a morning prayer breakfast with like-minded legislators. The exhibition of kindness to his fellow human beings was quickly left behind. He ignored those saying "Good morning, sir," as he entered his private office, flung his jacket on a couch, and took the chair behind his desk.

Carol, his lead secretary, followed him in carrying a sheaf of phone messages. "Senator," she said, holding up papers, "these

313

two are especially important."

He indicated that she should put them on his desk as he picked up the phone and dialed an office within the Dirksen Building. She did as instructed, careful to keep the two priority ones separate, and quickly left. She'd been with Widmer long enough — since he first came to Congress — to know when to leave him alone. This was one of those times. She was almost to the door when he barked, "Where's Lowe?"

She turned. "Geoff was here earlier, sir, but he left just before you arrived."

"Get holda him. Now!"

"Yes, sir." She'd almost said, "I'll try," which might have prompted something like, "Do better than try." Or worse.

She went to where Ellen Kelly was in her office at the far end of the suite.

"Do you know where Geoff went?" she asked.

"No."

"Try and reach him on his cell, Ellen. The senator is anxious to talk to him. I'd do it, but I'm swamped."

"And I'm not?" Ellen said, not looking up from her computer screen.

Widmer's secretary turned on her heel, a sour expression on her face, and went to her desk, where she dialed Lowe's cell phone number. After six rings, a recorded voice informed the caller that the cell phone user was not available, and suggested leaving a voice mail message.

"Geoff, this is Carol. Senator Widmer is anxious to speak with you. Please call the minute you hear this."

Lowe's cell phone rang in his pocket, but he ignored it. He stood in the foyer of Rich and Kathy's building and held his thumb against the buzzer for their apartment, a string of four-letter words augmenting the metallic sound.

"Son of a bitch," he muttered as he left the foyer and got into his car.

This time he answered the ring of his phone.

"Geoff, it's Ellen." Her voice was muffled, as though she used a hand to keep others from hearing.

"He's not there," Lowe said.

"Geoff, the senator wants to talk to you right away."

"Yeah, I bet he does. I can't find Rich. Not a sign of him at the apartment. No answer on his phone. Damn! Did you try Kathryn at work?"

"She called in sick."

He breathed hard. "What the hell is going on?"

"I don't know, Geoff. But the senator —"

"Look, Ellen, make some calls, huh? You've met some of Kathryn's girlfriends. See if you can find somebody who knows where the hell she is. Knows where *Rich* is."

"The senator —"

"Yeah, yeah, I know. We have to find Rich. I told you I tried to get him to give me the tapes and notes, and I thought he was going to. We need him and those tapes. That's why Widmer wants to see me. He wants to know whether I have them."

"I'll make calls."

"Good. Tell Widmer I'll be back in an hour. Tell him I — I'm pulling together top secret materials for the hearing. Tell him everything is on track."

He ended the call and dialed 411, requesting the number for Mackensie Smith, in the Watergate Apartments.

"Hello?"

"Mr. Smith?"

"Yes."

"This is Geoff Lowe, Mr. Smith. I'm a friend of Rich Marienthal."

"Oh, yes. He's mentioned you."

"And he often speaks of you. I know you handled his book contract."

"I wouldn't say I handled it. Looked it

over. What can I do for you?"

"I've been trying to get hold of Rich, Mr. Smith. I thought you might know how I can reach him."

"Sorry, but I'm no help. You're not the only one looking for him."

Lowe forced a laugh. "The vanishing author. Well, I thought it was worth a try."

"If I do hear from him, I'll mention you're looking for him."

"Thanks, I appreciate that. Have a good day, and sorry to have bothered you."

Another call went to Hobbes House in New York. "This is Geoff Lowe, on Senator Karl Widmer's senior staff," he told the receptionist. "It's important I speak with Sam Greenleaf."

Greenleaf came on the line. "I'm glad you called," he said. "I've left three messages on Rich's machine. You don't know where he is?"

"No. That's why I'm calling."

"Russo's murder was a hell of a shock."

"Tell me about it. Look, not having Russo testify in person at the hearings is a blow. But it's not fatal — as long as we have Rich's taped interviews with him."

"And Rich to validate the recordings."

"That, too. What's the status of the book?"

"Funny you should ask. I have the first copies off the press on my desk. They arrived this morning. They look great. I'm having a courier deliver a dozen to you at the senator's office."

"When will you start promoting?" Lowe asked.

"Immediately. But I don't think we'll have to do much."

"What do you mean?"

"We're already getting calls from media. Fox News seems to know the whole story — or at least the guts of it. Our publicity people got a call this morning from a Fox reporter in Washington. Looks like your dam has developed some leaks — big ones."

"That's okay. If you hear from Marienthal, please call me any time, day or night. Frankly, I'm pretty damned upset with Rich. I sent him and his book to you in the first place, and he pulls this crap on me. Here's my cell number."

"Good luck with your hearings, Geoff. Looks like we might have a best seller on our hands, and you've got an issue to run with."

Lowe considered trying to reach Marienthal's father in New York, but thought better of it. He checked his watch.

No sense in postponing Widmer any longer. He'd have to fudge it with his boss, keep him thinking everything was going smoothly. Widmer had demanded that Lowe get the tapes and notes from Marienthal — which had triggered Lowe's not very subtle suggestion to Marienthal that he turn them over in advance of the hearings.

His stomach knotted as he drove back to Capitol Hill.

"How's Vinnie?" Bret Mullin was asked as he entered the detectives' bullpen.

"Okay. He'll be okay. Gimpy for a while. Any luck in finding the shooter?"

"No, but we've got a description from witnesses. An APB went out this morning."

"Good."

After phone messages — none worth answering, he decided — Mullin went to Phil Leshin's office, where his superior was being briefed on serious crimes that had been committed overnight. Mullin waited outside until the briefing officers left.

"What's up?" Leshin asked.

"I've got the name of the guy from Union Station."

"What guy?"

319

"The one who knew Louis Russo's name."

"Bret, I told you to drop it."

"I did drop it, Phil," Mullin said, taking a chair across the desk. "It was dumped in my lap."

"Is that so?"

"Yeah. The woman who came from Tel Aviv to claim the body — Sasha Levine — she told me who it was. His name's Richard Marienthal. He's a writer who was working on a book with Russo."

"A book? What kind of book?"

Mullin shrugged. "I didn't get into that with her. But I know who he is, where he lives. I think we ought to bring him in as a material witness."

Leshin muttered something under his breath and ran a hand over his shaved head. He said to Mullin, "Do I speak in some foreign tongue, Bret? Did you not understand me when I said to drop it? The Russo case is closed. Officially closed."

"No," Mullin said, "I understood what you said. But let me ask you a question."

"Make it quick."

"Why has it been dropped? On whose orders?"

"On *my* orders."

"Yeah, but who told *you* to drop it?"

Leshin got up from behind the desk, went to the door, and opened it. "I'm pairing you up with Bayliss."

"Thanks," Mullin said, his tone indicating he meant anything but. He left Leshin's office and returned to his desk, where his new partner, a recently promoted detective named Craig Bayliss, waited.

"Looks like you've drawn me," the freckle-faced redhead said, offering a wide smile.

"What'd I do to get so lucky?" Mullin said. To his mind, the younger cop looked like Alfred E. Neuman from the old *Mad* magazine days, right down to the small void between his front teeth. Mullin picked up a folder containing the preliminary report on the shooting of Vinnie Accurso, including the description provided by witnesses. He and Bayliss would join dozens of other detectives that day with one assignment: find the assailant. Cop shot? All hands on deck.

"Want me to drive?" Bayliss asked as they walked to their assigned unmarked car.

"No. I'll drive. And do me a favor."

"Sure, Bret."

"Don't talk a lot, okay?"

★ ★ ★

Actually, Mullin's mood had been good earlier that morning.

After failing to make contact with Rich Marienthal at his apartment building the previous evening, he'd made a fast stop at his apartment to freshen up and to change clothes in anticipation of dinner with Sasha Levine. She was in the hotel lobby when he arrived, the ubiquitous cigarette going from hand to mouth and back again. She greeted him warmly, and entered his car through the door he held open, dropping the partially finished Camel in the gutter.

"I'm really glad you could have dinner with me," he said, joining the flow of traffic.

"It is good of you to ask me," she said.

"You in the mood for anything special?" he asked. "Some kind of ethnic food, maybe? Middle Eastern or something like that?"

"I will be happy wherever we go," she replied, sounding as though she meant it.

He was glad she was open to suggestions. Although he would have taken her to any restaurant that pleased her, he'd never been keen on food from other countries, except occasionally Italian and Mexican now and then. They went to The Prime Rib on K Street, where the bartenders and manager greeted him — and where he knew what would be on his plate.

Once settled in a black leather banquette, Sasha, who wore a black skirt and sweater and a red blazer with gold buttons, took in her surroundings — brass-trimmed black walls and leopard-skin carpeting, the waiters in black tie, and a tuxedoed pianist with flowing white hair playing nostalgic tunes on a glass-topped grand piano.

"I feel like part of the decor," she said.

Mullin laughed. "Yeah, you wore the right thing," he said. "You look great."

"Thank you," she said. "This must be a very expensive restaurant."

He waved her concerns away. "No problem," he said.

"I had upsetting news today," she said.

"Oh? What happened?"

"A friend in Tel Aviv called. Someone broke into my apartment."

"I'm sorry. What'd they do, steal stuff?"

"My friend doesn't think so. Maybe it was things Louis had that they were looking for."

Mullin nodded. "He had important stuff there, papers, money?"

"I don't really know. He didn't discuss his business with me."

"So when are you taking Mr. Russo back with you to Israel?"

"Tomorrow. I have made the arrangements today with the airline and your police doctor. Tomorrow —" She fell silent and her eyes became moist.

Mullin placed his hand on hers. "Must be tough," he said.

She shook her head and smiled. "It is life, that's all. Louis used to say dying was the price you pay for living."

"Sounds like he was a philosopher or something."

"He was a much smarter man than many thought. Because he did not have a formal education and did bad things early in his life, people thought he wasn't intelligent. But he was. I thought such things, too, when I first met him. But I came to know a gentle man who liked to read and who thought deeply about many things."

"I'm glad to hear that, Sasha. I guess you got to know him pretty good, living with him for so many years."

A waiter interrupted to take their drink orders.

"A glass of white Zinfandel," she said.

"I'll have a glass of wine, too," said

Mullin. "Red. A house red." He turned back to her. "Sorry you couldn't get hold of your writer friend, Marienthal," he said.

"I tried many times. He must be away on a trip."

"Yeah, probably."

When the waiter returned with their drinks, they clinked the rims of their glasses.

"Hate to see you leave," Mullin said.

"Thank you. Maybe one day I will come back."

"That'd be good. What was this book Mr. Marienthal was writing with your — with Mr. Russo?"

She sighed deeply, picked up her wine in both hands, and sat back in the banquette.

"You don't have to say if you don't want to," he said.

Another sigh, more prolonged this time. "I really don't know much," she said, taking a tiny sip. "When Louis decided to do the book with Rich, he told me he didn't want me to know anything about what would be in it."

"How come?"

"He said he wanted to protect me."

"From what?"

She came forward and forced a smile. "It is better we don't talk about it. What do you recommend at this restaurant?"

"Well," he said, pleased to be asked, "I usually have the prime rib. They serve real, fresh horseradish with it, you know? Lots of people have the crab. Crab Imperial, they call it, baked in a shell with other stuff."

"That sounds very good."

Mullin was relieved that as the evening progressed, Sasha became more talkative, sparing him from having to carry the conversation. She spoke of her childhood in Budapest, her family and schooling, and her decision to move to Israel. Mullin was sorely tempted to order another drink, something stronger than wine this time, but successfully fought the urge. He wanted very much to impress this lady from Tel Aviv, to have her like and respect him. Getting drunk wouldn't accomplish that.

The restaurant's subdued lighting cast a flattering glow over Sasha, and it crossed Mullin's mind as they ate and talked that she looked a little like his ex-wife, not so much in their features, but their coloring was certainly similar. Mullin had always been attracted to women with dusky skin and dark hair. Maybe it was the contrast with his blotchy, fair skin that appealed. Sasha's eyes were large and almost black, her lips sensually full. She had a way of looking directly at him as she spoke, as though seeing beyond his facade into what he was thinking and feeling.

He was also wondering what had attracted her to an old former mobster, a killer and leg-breaker, living in Israel like a hunted animal, never sure whether the next passing car contained those who would avenge his traitorous act. Did it represent some character flaw in her? Or was it a middle-aged woman's desperation — any man in a storm? He didn't ask.

"Tell me more about this writer," he said. "Maybe I'll get to meet him. He lives here in D.C.?"

"Yes. Would you like his address?"

"No, I — sure. That'd be great. I'll look him up sometime. You must have talked to him after the murder."

"He called once. I said I would see him when I came here to claim the body. I suppose that will have to be another time."

They sat with their own silent musings as the waiter served coffee, no dessert. Carnal thoughts came and went for Mullin, and were troubling. It had been a while since he'd been intimate with a woman, and visions of being naked with Sasha were vivid and stirring. But she was here to take home the body of a man with whom she'd lived for a long time. *Don't make an ass of yourself.*

They declined after-dinner drinks on the house, and he drove her back to the hotel.

"This was lovely," she said as he walked her into the lobby. "I did not expect to be entertained by one of the city's best policemen."

"Strictly unofficial," he said.

"Good night," she said.

"I'll walk you upstairs, make sure you're safe."

"Oh, that isn't necessary. I —"

"No, no, I insist," he said, taking her elbow and moving to the elevators. "There's a lot of crime, you know, especially against women. I'd feel better knowing you're okay."

They rode to her floor. She unlocked the door, opened it, and flipped the light switch. He moved past her and entered the room first, glancing into the bathroom, the light of which had been left on, then moving farther inside. She watched him with admiring amusement. He was checking out the room the way the police did in the movies. Would he pull out his gun and look under the bed?

"All clear?" she asked playfully.

"What?" he said, turning to where she still stood in the empty doorway. He grinned and shrugged. "Too many years a cop," he said. "Just wanted to make sure you'd be all right."

"I will be fine," she said, turning on lamps. "Living in Israel teaches you to not be afraid."

"I guess it does," he said, relieved that a sudden strong urge for a drink passed. "I just figured if somebody broke into your apartment back home, they might —"

"Who is *they?*" she asked.

"Oh, I don't know. See, Sasha, you're here in Washington because your —"

"My boyfriend? My lover? Either is fine."

Boyfriend didn't seem right to him for a middle-aged woman. "Yeah. Your lover comes here and got killed, so that could mean somebody might come after you, too."

"I don't think so."

"Better safe than sorry," he said, sitting on the edge of the bed. "I'll stay awhile," he said.

"That is very kind of you," she said. "You are a very sweet man. I am very tired. I would like to spend more time with you, but —"

"No, no," he said, standing. "You don't have to explain. I'm sure you'll be just

329

fine." He went to the door.

"Thank you for everything," she said, joining him there. "It was a lovely evening."

"Glad you liked it," he said. "Here's my home phone number." He handed her his card. "I'm going straight home. You call any time, any hour, you need something. Got that?"

"Yes. I've got that."

"And don't let anybody in the room."

"Why would I do that?"

"Just keep things locked up, that's all."

She smiled, touched his chest, and kissed him lightly on the lips. "Good night, Detective Mr. Bret Mullin," she said.

"Good night."

He did as promised, went straight home. After feeding Magnum, he opened a kitchen cabinet and pulled down a half-filled bottle of vodka, put ice in a glass, and poured vodka over the cubes. But instead of drinking it, he poured it in the sink, went to the living room, switched on the TV, and turned it off again. *Just a goddamn habit,* he told himself. *Like smoking.* He wished she didn't smoke. *Who needs another drink? Not me!*

He went to bed desperately hanging on to that thought.

THIRTY-THREE

Mullin knew that if he'd stayed up and watched television, he wouldn't have been able to resist the vodka in the kitchen. Had he watched the tube, he would have seen news alerts flashed on every cable news station in town. CNN had the story. So did CNBC and MSNBC. But Fox News had the most to report simply because its on-air reporter, Joyce Rosenberg, knew more than her competitors.

She'd heard from Tim earlier in the evening. Stripling had called from home, sated with Crab Louis and hot fudge.

"I have something wonderful for you," he'd said, "which means you'll owe me one."

"I'll be the judge of that," she said.

"Pad and pencil at the ready?"

"Shoot."

"All right. Here's what's gone down, Joyce, and you can take it to the bank. The old gentleman, Louis Russo, came to our fair city to testify at a hearing being chaired by that charming Alaska senator, Karl Widmer."

"You're sure of that?"

"As sure as I'd propose to you if you didn't have Mr. Right already panting for your body."

"Cute."

"That I am. Okay. Mr. Russo comes to D.C. to testify at the hearing and gets his brains blown out when he gets off the train. Next, his assailant — a gentle term for his murderer — gets chopped down among the lilies."

"I already know this."

"But you don't know what Mr. Russo was testifying about."

He could sense her anxious anticipation. He paused for effect before continuing. "Mr. Russo, who seems to have a penchant for spilling his guts to the wrong people, collaborated on a book with a writer from right here in the nation's capital, a Mr. Richard Marienthal."

"And this Marienthal is the guy who blurted out Russo's name to me at the station?"

"One and the same, according to my sources."

"Which are impeccable."

"Of course. Ready for the bombshell?"

"Stop playing games, Tim. What is it?"

"According to Mr. Russo's account in this book by Marienthal, he — I stress *he* — was the gentleman who assassinated one Constantine Eliana. Ring a bell?"

"Jesus."

"No, the Romans killed *him*. Russo killed Constantine Eliana."

"Some time back. He was going to testify to this at the Widmer hearings?"

"You're quick and bright."

"Thank you."

"Sure you want to marry this medical student? He'll be off delivering babies every night while you sit home wondering what was ever appealing about the jerk."

"The jerk's name is Michael."

"What's his number? I'll straighten him out."

"He's bigger than you are. Come on, Tim. I don't have all summer."

"Know what Russo claims?"

"Tell me."

"That his New York family — the crime side of it — got the contract."

"And Mr. Russo pulled the trigger."

"This future M.D., with an HMO license to steal, doesn't deserve you, Joyce."

"Russo says he pulled the trigger? On whose say-so?"

"On orders from no one other than

Adam Parmele, currently president of the United States, then director of the Central Intelligence Agency."

"Wow!"

"You sound positively orgasmic, Joyce. Then again, getting the big story is always better than sex for you real newshounds, isn't it? Does your intended know that?"

"I'll see if I can go with this tonight without corroboration," she said, deliberately ignoring him as she counted off what she'd need. "Unless I can get a statement from Widmer's people or from the White House."

"Want my advice?" Stripling said.

"Probably not, but go ahead."

"Run with it, Joyce. You wait for statements from Widmer and Parmele, you'll get scooped. I'm giving you this exclusively. Trust me."

He ended the call and reflected on what he'd told her. It wasn't exactly true that he'd given the information only to her. He hadn't spoken to any other members of the press, but he had shared it with the two FBI agents with whom he'd been meeting, laid out for them everything he'd learned from Detective Fred Peck and Senate staffer Jimmy Gale.

His four o'clock meeting with the agents, to whom he'd now mentally assigned the nicknames Curly and Moe, had been like the other meetings he'd suffered through with them. A couple of Bureau losers, he'd decided, who'd pass along what they'd learned to other inept higher-ups who'd analyze it to death and undoubtedly come to the wrong conclusion. That wasn't his problem. He'd earned his money, pulled in markers owed him, and dutifully passed along all the dirt he could find. As far as he was concerned, job over.

Until . . . he received a call early that evening from Mark Roper.

"Good evening, Timothy."

"Hello."

"I understand you've done a very good job, Tim."

"According to who? Nuts and Bolts?"

"Pardon?"

"The two clowns I've been socializing with. We met this afternoon."

"I know, I know. They say you've performed admirably."

"I doubt if they put it that way. So what do I do now, return the cell phone they gave me?"

"No. You're still employed."

"I've been thinking, Mark, that I'd like to be retired."

"Retirement is expensive, Timothy. Get in your car and take a pleasant drive over into Virginia."

"Tonight?"

"Yes. There's a woman who very much would like to spend an hour with you, enjoy a drink together, chat about life in general."

"Are you fixing me up?"

"In a sense. You'll ask for the Klaus reservation in the Grill at Clyde's, Tysons Corner."

"Funny name for a woman."

"Last name."

"Klaus? Klaus? Sounds familiar." He snapped his fingers. "Gertrude!"

"Two hours, Timothy. Call me when you get home."

"This is Joyce Rosenberg with a breaking story from Fox News. We've learned through exclusive sources that the murders of Louis Russo at Union Station and his assailant, Leon LeClaire, whose body was found a few days later in Kenilworth Aquatic Gardens, might be tied in some way to the upcoming Senate hearings into possible CIA complicity in the assassination seventeen years ago of Central American dictator Constantine Eliana. The Chilean strongman was gunned down during a state visit to Washington."

File footage of the crime scene at Union Station, and of the aftermath of the assassination of Constantine Eliana, played behind Rosenberg. She continued.

"Fox has also learned that Russo, the Union Station victim who'd come here from Israel where he'd been living under the federal witness protection program after having turned evidence against Mafia leaders in New York, was to testify in person before the committee about his role in the assassination. Russo had collaborated on a book with Washington writer Richard Marienthal about his involvement in the assassination."

The accompanying visual was of Senator Widmer walking the halls of Congress.

"According to highly placed sources exclusive to Fox News, Russo has claimed in the book that he pulled the trigger on orders from his crime family bosses, and that those same bosses had received the contract to kill Eliana from then CIA director Adam Parmele, now president of the United States."

Parmele's image came on the screen.

"According to our sources, the hearings will be conducted despite the loss of the key witness, Louis Russo, with the writer, Richard Marienthal, introducing taped interviews with the former Mafia boss. Attempts to reach someone at the White House or in Senator Widmer's office were unsuccessful. I'm Joyce Rosenberg. More on this story as Fox News develops further information."

Rich and Kathryn watched the Fox report on the TV in Marienthal's suite at the River Inn.

They'd discussed the ransacking of the apartment — someone obviously after Rich's tapes and notes — and speculated on who might have been behind it. Now there was no need to speculate on what people knew about the Widmer hearings and Louis Russo's connection to those hearings. The whole District knew, thanks to the voracious cable TV channels, and the nation would shortly.

"Oh, my God," Kathryn said, her eyes wide.

"It's started," Marienthal said to no one in particular, getting up from the couch and going to the kitchenette, where he refilled his glass with Coke from the fridge.

Kathryn followed him. "What are we

going to do?" she asked.

"What are *we* going to do?" he said. "You've got to stay out of this, Kathryn."

"How can I stay out of something I'm already knee-deep in?" she asked. "I'm here!"

He returned to the suite's living room, pulled aside drapes on the window, and peered into the darkness. She came up behind and placed her hand on his shoulder. "Rich," she said softly, "this has gotten out of hand. You've got to drop it, get rid of the tapes and notes, tell Geoff you're not testifying, and wash your hands of the whole mess."

He continued looking through the drapes without speaking. Finally he allowed the drapes to close again, turned, and embraced her. They stood that way for a minute before returning to the couch. Kathryn turned off the TV, looked at him, and said, "I love you, Rich. I hope you know that."

He nodded. "What about the book?" he asked.

"You can't stop that," she said, "but you don't have to be used the way Geoff and Senator Widmer are using you. You supported President Parmele when he ran. What Russo claimed will destroy him and his run for a second term."

His jaw was rigid as he said, "You know how I felt about that, Kathryn. I'm a writer. It's not my business to decide who gets second terms. I don't care about politics. All I wanted was a good book, a best-selling book. Let the chips fall where they may."

"I know that," she said, carefully choosing her words to avoid stifling what promised to be a calm, reasoned, and useful conversation, the first they'd had in a while. She shifted on the couch so that she faced him. "Look," she said, "I was a hundred percent behind you when you started the book. *The novel!* How could I not be? It all seemed so logical and right, learning how the Mafia works from an insider to give your novel authenticity. Your father represented him and paved the way for you to meet Russo. I remember how hard you worked to convince him to open up and tell the story. And I know the difficulties it caused with your father." She paused, weighed her next words, and added, "It all made sense until Geoff Lowe came along."

"Want a beer?" he asked.

"No."

He pulled a can of beer from the refrigerator, returned to the living room, and took a club chair across the coffee table from her. He leaned forward, elbows on his knees, chin propped on interlaced hands. On the table was a list of phone messages she'd taken from their answering machine and delivered to him at the hotel.

"Rich," she said.

"What?"

"Get rid of the tapes."

"I can't do that."

"Why?"

"You know why. Russo's dead. The tapes have him saying in his own voice that he assassinated Constantine Eliana and did it for his crime family under orders from Adam Parmele. The tapes are the only things I have to back up what's in the book. Without them and without Russo, the book will be dismissed, debunked, chalked up to a writer's imagination."

"Then turn them over to the White House."

He guffawed. "Tapes in the White House," he said scornfully. "Tapes in the White House get erased or lost or burned."

"And maybe they should be," she said in a flat, judgmental tone.

He glared at her. She expected an outburst. Instead, he drew a deep breath before saying, "And what do I tell Greenleaf

341

at Hobbes House?"

"The hell with him."

"Sure. The hell with him! When I changed the proposal from fiction to non-fiction and sold it to Greenleaf, he bought it based upon my claims that I had access to Russo and that Russo was the real thing. The novel would have brought a small advance, peanuts for a first-time novelist. And that's assuming I could even find a publisher. It's not like there haven't been books about the Mafia before. But when I met Geoff and told him the story — and he got Widmer to plan hearings on it based upon the book — Hobbes House upped the ante big-time. And then I got Russo to agree to testify in person and boom, up went the advance again. This is my shot, Kathryn. I don't care who falls, who takes the rap, who comes out smelling good or bad." He paused and grimaced. "At least I didn't . . . care."

Kathryn smiled. "But you do now," she said.

"Yeah, I do."

She left the couch and fell to her knees in front of him. "Rich, I have an idea."

"What's that?"

"Give the tapes and notes to Mac Smith."

"Why?"

"I trust him. Let's go to him, tell him everything that's happened, and ask his advice."

Marienthal shook his head.

"Then give them to the White House."

"No."

She frowned. "Not to Geoff!"

He got up and paced. "Widmer will subpoena the materials, Kathryn. He can subpoena me to testify."

"Which is why you need legal advice. Mac Smith is terrific. You know that. His reputation is top-notch."

"So's my father's reputation. I'm not about to go to him."

He abruptly stood, went to the window again, and looked through the drapes. Kathryn waited patiently until he turned and said, "Here's what I've decided to do, Kathryn. I'm going to lay low, stay off everybody's radar. Without me and the tapes, Geoff and Widmer just might cancel the hearings. Once they do — and this whole thing blows over — I can surface again." He laughed ruefully. "Maybe going underground will hype the sales of the book, provided Greenleaf goes through with it." He struck a thespian's pose. "Where is Richard Marienthal, and why has he gone into hiding? Where is the handsome mystery man?"

Kathryn didn't find it funny.

"I have to get out of here," he said. "I checked in under my own name."

"Where will you go?" she asked, getting up from the carpet.

"Better you don't know, Kathryn. I want you to go back to the apartment. Get a locksmith in and don't give a new key to the super. I don't trust him."

"Where will you be?"

"With a friend. A *male* friend."

Tears formed in her eyes. He took her by the shoulders, gave forth with a boyish grin, and said, "Hey, no crying. Got that? I'll be fine. It'll just be a few weeks. Just go about your life as though nothing's happened. Anybody calls looking for me, I'm away on a research trip for a new book I'm writing."

"I'm frightened, Rich."

A laugh designed to comfort accompanied his wide grin. "Frightened about what?"

"Two people involved with Widmer's hearings have been murdered. Someone doesn't want Russo's story told. Isn't that obvious?"

In his head he agreed with her. Aloud, he said, "Don't you worry about a thing. I'm going to pack up. I'll tell them I have a family emergency and have to leave the hotel early. You take the car and drive back to the apartment. I'll take a cab."

He didn't wait for a response. He went into the suite's bedroom, repacked his small bag, pulled the large canvas shoulder bag with the interview tapes and notes from the floor of the closet, and returned to the living room, where Kathryn still stood by the window. He stood still, too. While he was in the bedroom, the obvious had occurred to him: if he was in some sort of physical danger, she could be, too. He tried to rationalize that thought away, at least for the moment. Those who might want the tapes and notes wanted him, not her. Someone had already searched the apartment and come up empty-handed; he was certain it was the tapes and notes they were after. No reason to bother her again, except to try and locate him. All she had to do was insist she didn't know where he was.

"Ready?" he asked, scooping up the phone messages she'd brought and shoving them into a pocket of his tan safari jacket.

She opened the door to the suite and led him down the hallway to the elevators. They rode down in silence. He informed the desk clerk that an emergency had come up and that he had to check out. He paid with his credit card, and they went out of the River Inn into the muggy night. He led her to where he'd parked the car, handed her the key, pulled her close, and kissed her long and hard on the mouth. When they disengaged, he said, "Tell you what. When this is over — and we're talking a week, two at the most — we'll take a nice long vacation, just the two of us. Anyplace you say."

"Okay. Not Israel, not D.C."

"Now, go on, go home. I'll keep in touch. I'll call when I can."

"Okay."

He gripped her chin with his thumb and forefinger, tilted her face up to meet his, and said, "Come on now, get rid of that deer-in-the-headlights look and give me a smile."

She obliged.

"There's absolutely nothing to worry about," he said, opening the driver's-side door to allow her to slip behind the wheel. She started the engine, switched on the lights, and turned to him.

"You look so sexy in those glasses," he said, causing her to laugh. He closed the door and watched her drive away, the car's red taillights disappearing in the thick cloud that seemed to have suddenly descended on the area called Foggy Bottom.

THIRTY-FOUR

Timothy Stripling stopped at a supermarket on his way home from Virginia to pick up items for the apartment — orange juice, English muffins, fruit salad, a quart of milk, and a package of Good Humor toasted almond pops, his favorites. He put his purchases away, got out of his suit, and took a fast shower. With a towel draped around his midsection, he went to his bedroom closet, opened the safe, and removed from it his two registered handguns, a 9-millimeter Tanarmi parabellum model with a fifteen-shot magazine, and a customized, snub-nosed Smith & Wesson .44 Magnum, made considerably smaller than its original version and popular with undercover cops. After examining them, he loaded the Smith & Wesson, returned the Tanarmi and ammunition to the safe, took a shoulder holster that hung among his suits, slipped the Smith & Wesson into it, and went to the kitchen. There, with a bowl of Ben & Jerry's on the table next to the holstered weapon, he went through the ice cream and the materials contained in a dog-eared manila file folder.

* * *

Earlier that evening, when Stripling entered the Grill at Clyde's in Tysons Corner, Gertrude Klaus, one of many assistant attorneys general in the Parmele administration, was at the bar sipping a colorful drink with a pink parasol protruding from it. She looked different this night from the first time he'd met her. Her retro hairdo had been replaced with a softer, more natural and modern look; the severe suit she'd worn during their first meeting had been discarded in favor of a multicolored sheath.

"Hello, Gertrude," Stripling said, sidling up next to her. "I almost didn't recognize you."

She turned and said, "Mr. Stripling," as though reading his name from a list.

Stripling said to the bartender, "A perfect Rob Roy, straight up." And to her: "You're buying, I'm told."

She laid cash on the bar, swiveled on her bar stool, and indicated with a nod of her head that they were going to a booth in a secluded end of the Grill. She received her change, left what Stripling considered an inadequate tip, and carried her half-consumed drink to the booth. He followed, admiring the sway of her hips on the way.

She slipped into one side of the booth, he into the other. A waitress delivered his Rob Roy.

"You look different at night," he said, raising his glass.

She didn't return the toast. Instead she sat and stared at him.

"So, Gertrude," he said, "why am I here?"

"Have you had dinner?"

"As a matter of fact, no, but I wouldn't want to put a strain on Justice's budget."

She motioned for the waitress to return with menus. She opened hers and almost immediately closed it. "A Cobb salad, oil and vinegar on the side." She cocked her head at Stripling, who hadn't opened his.

"Might as well make it the same," he said.

"So," he said when the waitress had left them alone, "I'll ask again. Why am I here?"

He noticed her makeup, nicely applied.

"An assignment," she said. "A very sensitive one."

"An assignment," he repeated with exaggerated awe. "Sounds absolutely spooky."

"Mr. Stripling, the attorney general —"

"Wait a minute, Gertrude," Stripling said. "Let me get this straight. What's your job with the AG?" When he received no reply, he continued. "What do they do, keep you in a frumpy suit during working hours, then tell you to drag out your prom dress and mascara and have clandestine meets with people like me? You look good."

Her expression was vacant, nonresponsive.

The waitress brought rolls and butter.

"No offense," he said.

"I took none. If you're finished with your snappy dialogue, Mr. Stripling, I can get to the point."

"I can't wait."

She glanced down at blood-red nails on one of her hands before speaking. "I don't like you, Mr. Stripling. I find you offensive. For the record."

"I take that as a compliment," he said, settling back in the booth and crossing his arms on his chest. "For the record."

She beckoned him closer with her index finger, and he obliged. She, too, leaned forward. Her voice was low but clear. "That said," she said, "I also understand that when certain tasks must be accomplished, we can't always deal with those people we like."

"Go ahead, Gert. I'm listening."

If his pointed use of her first name rankled, she didn't show it.

"You are aware, Mr. Stripling, that we are in the midst of a war against terrorism."

"Yeah, I heard something about it. How's it going?"

She ignored his flippancy. "Significant progress has been made under President Parmele's leadership."

"Is this a pitch for a campaign contribution? Who do I make the check out to?"

Her face reflected her first moment of pique since he'd entered the bar. It caused him to smile. He said, "Let me see, Gertrude, I was told to drive over here to Tysons Corner to receive a personal briefing on the war against terrorism. I really appreciate it, but I had other plans for the evening. You mentioned an assignment. What is it?"

Her answer was delayed by the arrival of their salads. He wished he'd ordered something more substantial, a burger or a rack of ribs. Once the waitress had departed, she said, "I have other plans this evening, too, Mr. Stripling, so I'll get to the point. I'll talk, you eat — and listen. When I'm finished, please leave."

"Good," he said, spearing a forkful of salad. "You're on. You've got until I finish this salad, which should give you about six and a half minutes."

Seven minutes later, he wiped his mouth with his napkin, took a healthy swig of water, and said, "Nice presentation, Gertrude. You must make the attorney general proud. I'll get on it right away."

She started on her salad.

"When I find the stuff you're looking for and the guy, I'll let you know."

"Through your usual channels. We never had this meeting."

He placed a small piece of paper on which he'd been taking notes into the breast pocket of his shirt, laughed, and slid from the booth. "Believe me, Gertrude," he said, looking down at her, "I'll find it easy to forget I ever saw you."

Now, back in his apartment, he finished his ice cream and reviewed the notes he'd taken during his meeting with Assistant Attorney General Gertrude Klaus. He'd written on the paper the names Frank Marienthal (New York mob attorney, father of Richard Marienthal, represented Russo), and Mackensie Smith (family friend, former criminal lawyer in D.C., prof at GW, vetted Marienthal's publishing contract), and took another look at a picture of Richard Marienthal he'd taken from the folder on the kitchen table. He dialed Marienthal's number.

"Hello?" Kathryn Jalick said.

"Is Richard there?" Stripling asked.

"Who's calling?"

"Name's Simmons. I'm with Liberty Media. I've been assigned to interview him about his new book."

"I — I'm afraid he's not here."

"My bad luck. When do you expect him?"

"Not for a while. He's away — researching his next book."

"If you'll give a number, I'll be happy to call him no matter where he is. I'm on deadline."

"I don't have a contact number for him, Mr. —"

"Simmons. Charlie Simmons. I'll try him again another time."

"If you give me a number at which you can be reached, I'll —"

The line went dead as he quietly lowered the receiver into its cradle.

He took another look at Marienthal's photo, shook his head, and muttered, "Terrorist, my ass." He went to the bedroom, where he dressed in slacks, an open-neck shirt, a blue denim sports jacket, and loafers. Returning to the kitchen, he secured his holster beneath the jacket. Its weight felt strange; he hadn't worn it or killed anyone in four years.

He took a taxi to the Lincoln Suites Hotel on L Street and picked up a house phone in the lobby. Sasha answered on the first ring.

"Ms. Levine, this is Charlie Simmons. I'm a friend of Richard Marienthal." He generally used the fictitious first name *Charlie* because he'd decided over the years that people tended to believe people named Charlie.

"Oh, hello," she said.

"I hope I'm not calling too late," he said pleasantly.

"No, not at all. I was reading a book."

"Hope it's a good one," he said.

"A very good one."

"I've been trying to get hold of Richard all evening. I thought —"

"I have been trying to reach him, too," she said.

He laughed. "You know what writers are like," he said. "Always disappearing. Any idea where he is?"

"No."

"I know how excited he is with the book coming out and all. Boy, I have to admit that when he played some of those tapes

354

for me, my hair stood on end."

"He played the tapes for you?"

"Just some, a few selected portions. He told me all about you and Mr. Russo. I couldn't believe it when he was killed like that, right in broad daylight in Union Station with a million people around."

"You said your name was?"

"Charlie Simmons. Rich and I go back a long way."

"I'm sorry, but I don't believe he ever mentioned you."

"We kind of lost touch for a while. Any chance of buying you a drink?"

"Oh, that's very kind, but I'm afraid I'm not up to a drink. Tomorrow I must —"

"Tomorrow?"

"Nothing. Thank you for calling. If you will give me your number, I'll ask Rich to call if I hear from him."

"Sure you can't spare me even a few minutes? Not even a quick cup of coffee? Rich said so many nice things about you that I'd hate to miss the chance to at least say hello in person. I don't get to Israel very often."

There was a pause before she said, "All right. But only a quick cup."

"Great. I'm right around the corner. Be

there in five minutes. See you in the lobby. You'll recognize me. I'm the handsome one in the blue denim jacket."

Bret Mullin's experiment with going to bed sober was short-lived. The phone rang minutes after he'd turned out the light. "Mullin," he said.

"Bret? It's Rosie."

He hadn't heard from his former wife in a month; the familiar sound of her husky voice was welcome.

"How are you, Rosie?"

"All right. I hope I'm not calling too late."

"No, no, you know me. A night owl." He was aware that he sounded clearheaded, and was pleased that he did. "What's up?"

"It's Cynthia, Bret. She was in a car accident earlier tonight."

"Jesus. Is she okay?"

"Some bruises and a mild concussion. They treated her at the hospital and released her. She called me from home."

"Thank God she's okay. Not seriously hurt, I mean."

"Bret, she needs money. Her car was totaled. And she doesn't have health insurance."

"Doesn't have health insurance? How

356

can that be? Everybody needs health insurance in case something like this happens. What's wrong with her?"

He heard her sigh on the other end.

"All I mean is —"

"Bret, this isn't a time for a lecture on health insurance. She doesn't have any. That's reality. Can you send her some money?"

"Yeah, I guess I can. I've got some savings, not a lot — the divorce and all — and I can borrow against my credit union account. How much does she need?"

"She has to find a car, a secondhand one, I'm sure. I don't know how much the hospital costs, but you know how expensive hospitals can be. Five thousand?"

"Whew!" He resisted the urge to ask why his daughter hadn't called him, why she never called, why she thought she could cut him out of her life, but was comfortable taking his money.

"Will you send her the money, Bret? I'm short of funds, but I've already written a check for a thousand. Can you send four thousand?"

"Okay."

"You have her address."

"If she hasn't moved in the past year."

"She hasn't."

"Good."

"Bret."

"Yeah?"

"Don't go writing her a nasty letter with the check. She needs help, nothing more."

"Yeah, sure. Right."

"Thanks. You've been okay?"

"I'm fine. You?"

"Fine. Just fine. Thanks again. I know she'll appreciate it."

The conversation over, he went to the kitchen and poured bourbon into a water glass over a few cubes. He checked his watch; too late to call Sasha at the hotel? He decided it wasn't and dialed the hotel, was connected to her room. No answer. He didn't leave a message on her voice mail.

He was wide awake. After another tumbler of bourbon, he brushed his teeth and dressed in the suit, shirt, and tie he'd worn earlier that day. "Hey, buddy," he told Magnum, "guard the joint till Poppa gets back." The black-and-white cat rubbed against his shin, and he reached down to scratch its head. He loved that cat. He was halfway out the door when he retreated to the bedroom, rummaged through a bureau drawer, and came up with a cigarette lighter. He tried it; it worked. He pocketed the lighter and left.

It wasn't his business that Sasha wasn't in her room when he called, and he knew it, acknowledged it as he drove in the direction of the Lincoln Suites Hotel. But why *wasn't* she in her room? She'd said she was tired. She didn't know anyone in Washington except for the writer, Marienthal, and she hadn't been able to reach him. He hoped she hadn't decided to take a walk. It was dangerous for a woman to walk around alone at night, especially someone who didn't know the city and its notorious areas. How many crimes had he investigated that involved women walking alone at night? Plenty.

Had she come down for coffee or a nightcap and met someone? Women were so vulnerable to smooth-talking strangers, weirdos in sheep's clothing. This is silly, he told himself, driving faster. Chances were she'd been in the bathroom when he'd called and hadn't heard the phone. Did the hotel have a phone in the bathroom? Many did these days. Someone had broken into her apartment in Tel Aviv. Why? Did it have to do with her lover, Russo?

He pulled to the curb across from the hotel, turned off his lights, and debated what to do. Should he use his cell phone and call again? Make the call from a lobby phone? Would he look like a fool? He shouldn't have had the drinks before leaving the apartment. He should have had vodka. He didn't want to see her smelling like a distillery.

He turned off the ignition, opened the door, maneuvered his large belly past the steering wheel, planted his feet on the concrete, and straightened. He was about to close the door when he saw Sasha step through the hotel's front entrance. A man wearing a blue denim jacket was with her. Mullin's stomach churned. If she had some boyfriend in D.C., why didn't she just say so? He decided to leave, but before he could reenter the car, Sasha saw him and waved. He muttered an obscenity under his breath. How could he explain being there that time of night? What lame excuse could he come up with in front of her male friend?

He didn't have a choice. He hitched up his pants, waited for a car to pass, and slowly crossed the street.

"Hello there," she said.

"Hi," Mullin said, not looking at Stripling.

"This is a surprise," she said, suddenly aware of the awkward moment taking place. "Oh, Detective, this is Mr. Charlie Simmons. He's a friend of Richard Marienthal."

"Detective?" Stripling said, not offering his hand.

"Bret Mullin," Mullin said, extending his hand, which Stripling took. *A weak handshake,* Mullin thought. He took some pleasure in being taller and bulkier than this Charlie, whoever he was. To Sasha: "I was just in the neighborhood and —"

"Detective Mullin has been taking good care of me since I came to Washington," she said. "He's my only friend here."

As she spoke, Mullin looked more closely at Stripling's face. It was familiar.

"You're a friend of the writer who worked with Ms. Levine's — ah, former friend?" Mullin said.

"Yes," said Stripling, sounding defiant.

"Everybody seems to be looking for this writer," Mullin said. "When's the last time you saw him?"

Stripling looked at Mullin quizzically. *What is this, challenge time?* he thought. *Fat slob of a detective,* he thought. *Looks like a boozer to me. Smells like it, too.*

"I haven't seen my old buddy, Rich, in months," said Stripling.

"Any idea where he is?" Mullin asked.

"I asked Charlie the same thing," Sasha said.

"You a writer, too?" Mullin asked. He was over his embarrassment; his detective's penchant for asking questions had replaced it. There was something about this man who called himself Charlie that didn't ring right to him. He'd seen him before. He was sure of it.

"No," Stripling said. "This was really nice," he said. To Sasha: "Eight o'clock tomorrow?"

"Yes. Eight o'clock."

What's this *all about?* Mullin wondered.

"Take it easy, Detective," Stripling said.

"You, too."

It was at this moment that Mullin knew why Charlie was familiar. He'd seen him leaving Marienthal's apartment building.

"You spend much time with Marienthal at his apartment?" Mullin asked.

"What?"

"I just figured you might hang out there, know his girlfriend. That's all."

"Sorry," Stripling said. "Got to run. See you in the morning, Sasha."

Mullin watched him quickly walk away and turn the corner.

"You knew him before?" Mullin asked Sasha.

"No. He called out of the blue. We had coffee. He's very nice."

She pulled a cigarette from her purse. Mullin quickly whipped out his lighter and held the flame out to her, pleased that he could.

"Yeah, I'm sure he is," Mullin said. "Well, now that we're here, how about a drink?"

"Oh, I couldn't possibly. I almost said no to Charlie when he suggested a cup of coffee." She laughed. "Decaf coffee. I would never get to sleep if I had regular."

"Yeah, I know what you mean. Well, like I said, I just happened to be driving by and —"

"I am glad to see you again."

"Maybe I'll give you a call in the morning, you know, just to say goodbye. What time do you leave?"

"At eleven at night."

"Okay. You're having breakfast with Charlie. Right?"

"Yes. But if I don't get to bed, I will not wake up in time. Good night."

"Good night, Sasha."

He decided not to suggest walking her inside. He watched her go into the lobby, admired her legs again, returned to the car, and drove to a bodega, where he picked up a large cup of coffee to take with him to headquarters.

"Hey, pal, how's it going?" he asked the officer manning one of the computers.

"It's going, Bret. That's all I'll say. What are you doing here?"

"Run a vehicle ID for me."

"Sure."

Mullin handed the officer a scrap of paper on which he'd noted the make, model, and plate number of the car he'd seen "Charlie Simmons" get into after leaving the apartment building in which Rich Marienthal and Kathryn Jalick lived. He'd found it among a fistful of receipts he'd stuffed into his glove compartment. It took less than a minute for the information to pop up on the screen. The vehicle was registered to a Timothy Stripling.

"Charlie Simmons, huh?" Mullin mumbled.

"Huh?"

"Nothing. See what you can bring up on Mr. Stripling."

"Who's he?"

"If I knew that, I wouldn't need you," Mullin said gruffly.

The officer didn't say what he was thinking, that Bret Mullin couldn't retire soon enough. He typed in the appropriate commands, added the name Timothy Stripling to them, and hit ENTER. A picture of Stripling filled the screen. *That's Charlie,* Mullin thought.

The officer scrolled down to where available information about the subject was written. There was surprisingly little on Stripling. The MPD's central data bank, augmented by the considerably more extensive FBI data bank, had been collecting and adding information to its files for years. Dossiers on D.C. citizens, famous and not so famous, had burgeoned recently as more focus was placed on gathering information and new software had made the larger files possible. Some subjects had information on them that ran for pages. Not Stripling. Facts of his life were contained in a single paragraph.

There was his Foggy Bottom address; his Social Security number; two moving vehicle violations, one for speeding, the second for running a light; place and date of birth (Dover, Vermont — 1951); no felony arrests or convictions; credit score of 730; no bankruptcies; registered handguns — 9-millimeter Tanarmi parabellum model and snub-nosed Smith & Wesson .44 Magnum, custom; Occupation: Consultant.

"Consultant," Mullin said aloud.

"Government," said the officer.

"Sensitive job. What's he need two handguns for?" Mullin said.

The officer shrugged.

"CIA maybe. The Bureau," Mullin added.

Mullin took a printout of the listing back to his office, where he drank his cooling coffee and thought about the past few hours. This guy Stripling contacts Sasha Levine, uses a phony name, claims he's a friend of the writer, Marienthal, and gets her to spend time with him.

One thing was certain. Stripling's meeting with Sasha was no social visit. The Russo murder? Marienthal's disappearance? An hour later, after having left a message for Chief Leshin that he was taking a personal day off, and fortified with fresh coffee and a half-dozen doughnuts, Mullin was parked up the street from the Lincoln Suites Hotel.

THIRTY-FIVE

Washingtonians awoke that morning to thunderstorms that dumped torrential rain on the nation's capital. It wasn't an unwelcome event. The downpour broke the intense heat wave that had gripped the city the past week and boosted spirits, although that didn't apply to Geoff Lowe and Ellen Kelly. He sat in a chair by a window and watched the rain cascade down the panes. Ellen sat up in bed. Next to her was an advance copy of Rich Marienthal's book, which Lowe had taken from Senator Widmer's office the previous night.

It was now a little after six a.m. They'd been up since five arguing.

He turned in the chair and said to her, "Don't you get it, Ellen? How many times do I have to explain it to you?"

She bristled at his tone, but said nothing. He'd been ranting since they awoke, pacing the floor, standing over her, yelling, lowering his voice to an almost inaudible level for effect, slapping his hand on the nearest surface, chopping the air with open hands as though the gesture would cut through what he considered her denseness.

"Okay," he said in a less strident voice, sitting on the edge of the bed and taking her hand, "we have got to find Rich and the tapes. It's just that simple."

"Maybe we don't need the tapes or Rich," she offered tentatively, "now that we have the book."

"Oh, man," he said. "Don't you get it? The book only has what Rich wrote, what he claims Russo told him. But Russo saying it on tape in his own voice is something else. Come on, Ellen, get with the program. Christ!"

She wished she were back in her own apartment, away from him, away from Washington and politics and senators and hearings, all of it. "Don't you think I would do something to help if I could?" she said.

"The Dems on the committee caucused late last night," he said. "They're holding a press conference this afternoon condemning the hearings in advance. They're dismissing the charge against Parmele as nothing more than a writer's unsubstantiated claims in a book. Somehow they got their hands on a copy of his contract with Hobbes House. The contract is for a *novel*. They're using that to claim the book is fiction, made up, his imagination."

"But Rich can testify to the book being true, Geoff."

"Jesus, you still don't get it, do you?" he said, repeating what had become a mantra that early morning. "Read my lips, Ellen. The Dems will destroy Rich and his credibility. Widmer made it plain to me last night that unless we have Russo's own voice implicating Parmele in the Eliana assassination, there'll be no hearing."

"Maybe that's just as well."

"No, Ellen, Widmer's not saying he's willing to call off the hearing unless we find Rich and the tapes. What he *is* saying is that if he has to call off the hearings because I fell on my face, I can kiss my job goodbye. So can you."

Lowe wasn't aware as he uttered this threat that losing her job with Senator Widmer wasn't an unpleasant idea for Ellen at that moment. She'd considered resigning for weeks, not only from her job with the senator, but from her relationship with Lowe, too. She'd discussed quitting with her father, a former mid-level corporate executive who'd been downsized out of his job and was currently selling cars to make ends meet. His advice: "Never leave one job until you've landed another,

Ellen." His words made sense, but did the same wisdom apply to leaving boyfriends? Looking for a new job while accepting a paycheck from a current employer smacked of disloyalty, although it was done all the time. Shopping for a new boyfriend while sharing a bed with the current one didn't sound any more admirable.

What's a girl to do?

Lowe left the bed and stood in the center of the room, hands on hips, jaw jutting out, a commander about to launch his troops into battle. His pillow-disheveled hair and frayed yellow terrycloth bathrobe detracted from the image.

"Look, Ellen, here's what we do. I'm going to take another crack at Mac Smith. There's no sense in me trying to get through to Kathryn. She sounds like a broken record: 'Rich is off on a research project and I don't know how to reach him, etc., etc.' Yeah, right! I never liked her. What Rich ever saw in her is beyond me. She's dumb as hell. But maybe she'll open up to you, huh? Woman to woman. Get hold of her and tell her Rich's life is in danger. Tell her that all we want is to keep him safe and at the same time help him promote his book. She's obviously nuts about him, although why I don't know.

What a pair. You tell Kathryn that the best thing she and Rich can do is to give you the tapes and notes and whatever else he has." He stepped toward the bed, as though what he'd just said was an especially intelligent breakthrough. "That's it. Tell Kathryn that once we have the tapes and stuff, it'll be out in the open and Rich won't have to worry anymore. Who do they think they're kidding with him hiding out? He's not on any goddamn research trip. He figures if he's not available for the hearings, they'll be canceled and he's off the hook. That means you and I are *on* the hook, Ellen, big-time, strung up by Widmer and left to dry."

Ellen swung her long, shapely legs off the bed and shook her tangled mass of carrot-red hair. She wore a short pale blue nightgown. Lowe plopped down next to her and began to knead her neck. "You can do it, baby. I know you can. Get her at work or the apartment, wherever you can. Come off sweet and caring — like you are naturally." He grinned and pressed her neck harder to reinforce his words.

"Easy," she said, pulling away, standing, stretching and heading for the bathroom.

Lowe went to the window and looked out. The rain continued to fall, hard and wind-driven. He'd pull this off. He *had* to pull it off. Once it was over, maybe it was time to move on, use the leverage of his position with Widmer to land a bigger and better job on the Hill. Hell, once Parmele lost his bid for a second term and a Republican was in the White House, there might be a spot there for Geoff Lowe. The new president would know it was the Widmer hearings that brought down Parmele, and that Geoff Lowe was the brains behind it.

He'd been pursuing a dream of having political clout since high school, where he was elected senior class president, not an especially impressive victory considering the caliber of the opposition, but heady nonetheless. In college, at the University of Wisconsin, he majored in political science and became active in a small but growing student Young Republicans' Club, practicing the art of shaping the message and getting it out, proselytizing the party line, and basking in the satisfaction the wielding of power inevitably delivers. He returned home to Orange County, California, where he'd been born and raised, and worked on the campaigns of a variety of county and statewide Republican candidates, learning as he went and establishing a name for himself as a tireless, committed campaign worker with bedrock Republican beliefs. There was a time early in his life when he aspired to elected office for himself. Pragmatically, however, he soon realized that his political future lay not with running for office, but with pulling the strings behind those better suited to the more public act of asking for votes — and for money. Surprisingly — and it surprised even him — he developed a scorn for politicians and their need to straddle fences, abandon core values in order to win, and promise but only sometimes deliver on those promises. Public service? Self-service was more like it. But such occasional contradictory thoughts never dampened his fervor for the political process. It was all about power, and power was Geoff Lowe's aphrodisiac. Ask his former wife, whom he married a few days after graduating college. That marriage lasted four months; her parents managed to have it annulled.

His first job in Washington was as an aide to a right-wing California congressman. When that pol lost his reelection bid, Lowe accepted an invitation to join the staff of Alaska Senator Karl Widmer. Lowe's seeming tirelessness and commitment to the senator's agenda impressed the aging Widmer, and promotions came quickly. Lately, he wondered whether Widmer was becoming senile, so intent was he on his crusade to deny Parmele a second term to the exclusion of myriad other legislative concerns. That was all that seemed to matter these days to the silver-haired Alaskan — destroying Adam Parmele, which was okay as far as Lowe was concerned. He didn't carry a brief one way or the other about the president. What was important was that if Widmer, and by extension Geoff Lowe, succeeded in the effort, he, Lowe, would see his stock rise within Republican circles, leading to bigger things.

If there was one political operative Lowe admired, it was Parmele's political guru, Chet Fletcher, and he enjoyed projecting himself into Fletcher's role with a Republican president, the power behind the throne, the consummate insider, the one the president of the United States turned to in his darkest hours.

That was power!

He heard the shower go on and pictured a naked Ellen Kelly soaping herself. No doubt about it, she was a great-looking fox. But she was wearing thin, like Widmer and his tantrums. It would be time for a new job and a new fox, somebody with more sophistication. He smacked a fist into the palm of his other hand, stood, and nodded in self-affirmation.

THIRTY-SIX

Winard Jackson lived in a basement apartment on upper 16th Street, on the edge of Washington's so-called black Gold Coast, home to many of the city's successful African-American men and women. He'd found the apartment shortly after moving to D.C. from Boston with a degree in jazz performance from the Berklee College of Music. While most of his fellow students at the prestigious jazz school had headed upon graduation for jazz hot spots like New York, Chicago, or Los Angeles, Jackson had opted for D.C. because it was home to legendary tenor saxophonist Buck Hill.

Hill had visited Berklee as a guest lecturer and was impressed with the young Jackson's improvisational talents. He invited him to look him up after graduation and agreed to accept him as a private student. Jackson didn't hesitate to accept the offer, and Hill not only became his musical mentor but helped the young black man acclimate to the city, introduced him to a wide circle of musicians, and found him the apartment in a well-kept row house owned by a friend who rented units to young jazz performers, especially those recommended by Buck Hill. With monthly financial help from supportive parents in Texas, Jackson managed to get by with occasional jobs playing around town, anything that paid — rock bands, Latin bands, occasional studio work, wedding bands, and when the planets were properly aligned, jazz groups.

The apartment consisted of a large living room, two tiny bedrooms, a bath, and a kitchen. Photographs and posters of jazz giants idolized by the young musician covered the walls. A Yamaha electric piano sat in one corner of the living room; Jackson used this to work out new chord changes to old tunes. There was a couch and two easy chairs, a TV, a small table off the kitchen that served as a dining table, and a state-of-the-art sound system for hundreds of CDs housed in tall, free-standing racks.

It was to this basement haven that Richard Marienthal had fled.

Jackson had been playing a job when Rich arrived at the apartment; he'd left a key with the landlady. When he returned from his job at four the next morning, he found his writer friend asleep on the couch.

"The bed in that other room is yours, Rich," he said after his noisy entrance had awakened Marienthal.

"I wasn't sure which bedroom to use," Marienthal said. "I can't thank you enough for letting me crash here."

Jackson's laugh was easy and frequent. "It works out great, man," he said, pointing to a suitcase and two saxophone cases near the door. "The place is yours 'cause I won't be around for a while."

"You said when I called that you were heading out of town on a gig. What's it all about?"

"It's like a gift from heaven, man. When Charlie called me — Charlie Young, the alto player — and said Buck had recommended me for a band Charlie's taking on the road, I almost fell over. We've got seven weeks in some good clubs around the country."

"I know who Charlie Young is," Marienthal said.

"Right. We caught him together, what, a month, two months ago? He's a monster. Anyway, we've been rehearsing for the past two weeks and leave tomorrow morning for the tour, so the joint is yours, man, for as long as you want. But you've got to tell me what's going on. I catch the news on the tube and see that you're, like, at the center of a big storm."

"Afraid so," Marienthal said.

Jackson brewed herbal tea in the tiny kitchen and brought two cups to the living room, along with fresh blueberry scones. He raised his cup to Marienthal and said, "Okay, man, lay it on me."

"I don't know where to begin," Marienthal said. "You know how when you're improvising on some song and get lost?"

"*Moi?*" Jackson said, laughing, hand to his heart.

"You know what I mean. If you hadn't started in that direction, had stuck closer to the chords —"

"Uh-huh."

"That's the situation I'm in. It's like you taking gigs strictly for the money. Bad music, but the pay is good. Making a living as a writer can be as tough as being a jazz musician. I did all kinds of writing I didn't enjoy and kept thinking that if I stuck to my goals and didn't sell out — at least not in the long run — I'd make it."

"I know what you mean," said Jackson.

"So, anyway, my father — he's a big-shot lawyer, represents Mafia types, or at least he did — he represented a mobster named

Louis Russo. Russo was nailed on a drug charge and accepted a deal my father choreographed: testify against his mob friends in exchange for immunity and a new life in the witness protection program."

"Russo. The old dude who got shot in Union Station."

"One and the same. At any rate, after Russo went into the program and moved to Israel —"

"Israel?"

"Yeah. He was in Mexico for a year, then headed for the Middle East. Some sort of deal we have with the government there. My father told me stories about Russo, his days with the mob, the murders he was supposed to have committed. The more he told me, the more I wanted to meet Russo and use his life as a basis for a novel I wanted to write. The public seems to have an insatiable appetite for mob books, movies, TV series. But after I spent some time with Russo, he started talking about another aspect of his life that really got my attention. Russo claimed he was the triggerman in the assassination of the Chilean president Constantine Eliana."

"Assassination? When was that?"

"Almost twenty years ago."

"And?"

"And who headed the CIA then?"

Jackson's eyes went up. "Are you saying . . ."

"I'm not saying it, Win. Russo said it. He claimed Parmele authorized the CIA to contract with the New York Mafia to assassinate Eliana, and that he, Russo, did the deed."

"That's heavy."

"That's what I said when I heard it."

"More tea?"

"Thanks, no. I got Russo to tell me the story, and I decided that *that* would be the basis for a book, a *big* book. My shot at riches and fame." His laugh was rueful. "Know what I mean?"

"Sure I do. So you wrote the book."

"I sure did. At least I wrote a proposal based upon what Russo told me. That's when I met Geoff."

"Who's he?"

"A senior aide to Senator Karl Widmer."

"Alaska."

"Uh-huh. I met him at a party and had lunch with him a few days later. He set it up. He was all excited about the book and said he had friends at Hobbes House in New York. I agreed to let him send the proposal to them — provided I dropped the idea of a novel and turned it into non-fiction."

"And you did?"

"Yeah."

"Are they the ones publishing it?"

"Right. Hobbes House is a right-wing publisher, which turned me off at first. You know me. I guess if I had to take sides, I'd say I'm a Democrat like my father, only he's a closet liberal. I never really cared about politics. I always dismissed it as a necessary evil, a bunch of men and women out to feather their own nests, but somehow things got done and the country ran. I voted for Parmele. Believe me, I knew the book might hurt him, especially his chances for a second term. But then I figured, just how much damage could a book do? It would get some attention and hopefully sell well, maybe even become a best seller. Parmele and his people would spin it, deny what Russo claimed ever happened, and that would be it.

"But Geoff had other ideas. He convinced me — and Christ, Win, it didn't take much convincing — that if we could get Russo to testify at hearings Widmer would hold with his subcommittee on intelligence, the book would really get a lot of exposure — network TV, the cover of *Time*, all of it."

"And sink the president, huh?"

"Again, I really didn't care. I mean, I cared on some level, but those feelings were always trumped by what I'd get out of it. Geoff wanted me to testify along with Russo, and that was too seductive for me to say no. Understand? You ever been in therapy?"

"With a shrink? No."

"But you know about it. It's like what you always hear. The therapist is going to say it all comes down to your relationship with your parents. I just figure that everything I did was in competition with my father."

"And was it?"

"I don't know. Could be. He helped me, but basically he was against my doing this book, so maybe I did it to challenge his authority. Maybe I bought into Geoff Lowe's idea to use the book as a political tool to get the president, and get my father at the same time. I don't know. I'm just a writer."

Jackson laughed. "You're one of the smartest guys I know, Rich."

"Too smart for my own good."

Marienthal peered down at the rug in silent thought. When he looked up, Jackson saw that his friend's eyes were wet.

"What are you going to do?" Jackson asked.

"Stick my head in the sand, like I'm doing now. What are my choices? I could give the Russo tapes and my notes to the White House and feel like maybe I saved a presidency. I could go ahead and turn everything over to Lowe and Senator Widmer, let them hold their hearings, and watch the book take off."

"But Russo is dead. He can't testify."

"Right. But Lowe and others on Widmer's staff evidently think that by playing the tapes of Russo making these allegations, it's almost as good as having him there in the flesh."

"A question, my friend."

"What's that?"

"Do you think Russo was right, that Parmele ordered the assassination when he was head honcho at the CIA?"

"Only according to Russo. That's all I know."

Their conversation was interrupted by a phone call. At its conclusion, Jackson rejoined Marienthal, who'd gotten up and was examining the CDs in their racks.

"This is some collection," Marienthal said.

"My inspiration. So, buddy, what are you going to do?"

"Hole up here, thanks to you. Go to

sleep and hope that when I wake up, it'll all be over."

A serious cloud crossed Jackson's face. "You in real danger, Rich?"

Marienthal shrugged. "I don't know. It depends on who killed Russo."

"Had to be Mafia. Right? You think they might be after you because of what Russo told you? Making you the only, well, witness to the Parmele thing?"

"Like I said, I don't know. Maybe by dropping out for a while, I can think a little clearer."

"Look, dude, I've got to catch me some sleep," Jackson said. "You look like you could use some, too. I'll go out later and stock the fridge, at least for a couple of days. Meantime, make yourself at home. The place is yours. Use the computer, phones, put on some sounds and relax."

"Thanks," Marienthal said.

While Jackson slept in his bedroom, Marienthal put on a Cedar Walton CD at low volume and sat in the kitchen, which opened onto a small patio at the rear of the narrow row house. The first vestiges of dawn provided enough light for him to make out a small round table with four chairs and umbrella. A patch of grass was beyond, ending at a tall stockade fence separating the property from another yard and house. A pervasive sense of loneliness overcame him. He'd never felt so conflicted in his life. Kathryn had a keen sense of how to compartmentalize things, something he'd never been good at. His mind was a sticky cotton-candy mess, everything mushed into one large, confusing panorama. He stared at the kitchen wall phone and considered calling someone, anyone. Kathryn. Mackensie Smith. His father.

An urge to call Geoff Lowe and tell him he was destroying the tapes and notes came and went. Compartmentalize! Sort it out. Russo's murder was one thing. Stick it away over there. The Widmer hearings? Stash that issue in one of Al Gore's lock boxes.

The book! No matter what happened with other complications surrounding it, there were all those months of hard work to be considered and salvaged. It was being published as he sat there, and he was pleased that it was. His regret, as the hands on the kitchen clock relentlessly ticked off his life, was that he hadn't gone forward the way he'd originally intended, written it as a novel based upon Russo's tales. Geoff Lowe had been instrumental in that decision, too, and he thought back to that lunch with Lowe after having met at the party.

"I'm telling you," Lowe had said at that lunch, "you've got one hell of a best-selling nonfiction book here, Rich. A novel? Waste of time."

"But it's based on one man's word, Geoff, a former mafioso in the witness protection program. I can't corroborate what he's told me."

"You don't need corroboration," Lowe countered. "The guy has led the life, walked the walk and talked the talk. His word is as good as anyone's. It's not you attesting to the truthfulness of it. All you're doing is being a good journalist, recounting his recollection of events and filling in some blanks when necessary."

They discussed it throughout lunch. Toward the end, Lowe said, "Look, I have a good friend at Hobbes House in New York. You know who they are."

"A publisher. Conservative nonfiction."

"Exactly. I have a friend there, the top editor, Sam Greenleaf. If you change your proposal to nonfiction, I know Sam will bite."

"I thought I'd submit it to other publishers, maybe those who liked what I'd submitted to them before."

"But who didn't buy what you wrote. Right?" Marienthal had given him a thumbnail sketch of his writing career.

"Right."

"So why blow a golden opportunity?" Marienthal's expression was quizzical.

"Hobbes House. The bird in hand, Rich. Let's say I can sell it there right away. And let's say I can get old Senator Widmer *to base hearings of his subcommittee on intelligence on the book.* Let's say you can convince Mr. Russo to come and testify at those hearings, and I get Widmer to agree. Can you even imagine what publicity that would generate? Conservative books are hot these days, have been for years. Coulter —"

Marienthal's eyes rolled up into his head.

"Yeah, yeah, yeah, I know she's a loony, off the wall, but her books make all the best-seller lists. There's Bill O'Reilly. Hannity."

"Geoff," Marienthal said, "you're dredging up the wrong examples. I'm not a conservative. I don't like those people. I've been a liberal all my life."

"I'm willing to forgive that," Lowe said with a deep chuckle. "It doesn't matter what *you* are, Rich. Like I said, all you're doing in this case is being a good journalist."

"I'll have to think about it," Marienthal said.

"You do that. In the meantime, come up with a nonfiction proposal I can send to Sam Greenleaf. No obligation. You can dismiss whatever comes of it. But at least it will give you an idea of what the market will bear. You have an agent?"

"No."

"Great, then I'll be your agent, at least with Hobbes House. No commission. The truth is, Rich, I really like you — despite your being a liberal. I think we have a lot in common. I'd like to be helpful, that's all."

Lowe paid for lunch and they parted ways. A week later he called with an offer from Hobbes House. It was structured in such a way that the advance would go up as certain events fell into place, with the largest increase occurring when and if Louis Russo agreed to testify before the Widmer-chaired committee. The contract and all the other information released about the project would say it was to be a novel, a work of fiction, in order to preserve secrecy about its real form until it was time for the book to be published.

Marienthal discussed it with Kathryn.

"I'm thrilled for you," she told him, "but what about the political fallout? This will be devastating to President Parmele. You don't want to do anything to hurt him, do you?"

"That's not my concern," he replied.

"But what if what Russo says isn't true?"

"That's not my problem, either. Geoff says I'm just a journalist reporting on an eyewitness to history. Think of what happened when journalists had their say at book length with Nixon, with Clinton, with Kissinger and all. Think of the journalistic reputations and money made with such books. Geoff is right. I think I really lucked out meeting him, Kathryn. He's a terrific guy, a top aide to Senator Widmer. He got me the offer from Hobbes House and he doesn't want a cent for doing it. I'm telling you, this is the break I've been waiting for my whole life."

She realized her arguing was fruitless and not very supportive to boot. She kissed him, and they celebrated with an expensive dinner at Bistro Bis in the Hotel George, where they drank too much wine and fell into bed intending to make love, but too fatigued and elated to summon the energy.

★ ★ ★

Thinking back to that evening as he sat in Winard Jackson's kitchen, the soft sounds of *Just Friends* in the background, he realized that evening had been celebratory in every sense of the word. He had his first book contract, and judging from the enthusiasm of the publisher and his editor, Sam Greenleaf, it had best seller written all over it. The struggle was over.

But on this morning, months later in a friend's basement apartment, his mood was hardly one of celebration. He'd been so blinded by ambition that he hadn't taken a moment to step back and see what was really going on, the use he was being put to, the manipulation of him by others with their own self-serving agendas. Kathryn had seen it. His father had seen it. The only one who hadn't seen it was Richard Marienthal, and he was too wrapped up in his pursuit of glory and money to listen to them.

Louis Russo had been murdered because of him. He squeezed his eyes shut tight against that painful truth. The old mafioso had killed men in his criminal career, but didn't deserve to be gunned down to help sell a book — and maybe bring down a president in the bargain.

Had Russo told the truth when he claimed to have assassinated the Chilean dictator at the behest of the CIA, on orders from its chief, Adam Parmele? It didn't seem to matter anymore whether Russo had lied or not. His story was between the covers of a book, to be read and judged by all those who plunked down their money in bookstores or online.

His mind cleared in synchronization with the increasing brightness outside. His options narrowed to one, it seemed. The book would make its way without his help. There would be no public appearances, no signings, no interviews in which he'd have to justify what he'd written. And there would be no hearings, certainly not involving him. The tapes were his and would remain his. One day, maybe, he'd destroy them.

He looked into the living room where the large canvas shoulder bag containing the tapes and other research materials rested against a chair. Trash them now, he told himself. Burn them, or go out and find a Dumpster. Pull the tapes from their cassette cases and cut them into strips, make confetti of them. Find a big magnet and run it over them, scrambling Russo's words, true or false.

But the clarity that had made a temporary stop in the kitchen was obscured again by uncertainty. He couldn't destroy what he'd worked so hard to possess. He stood, feeling very old as he did, and walked slowly into the cramped room that would be his bedroom, at least for that day. Fully clothed, he fell on the bed, drew a deep breath, closed his eyes, and was asleep within seconds.

THIRTY-SEVEN

Mullin's head had fallen forward to his chest when a sharp tap on his window snapped him to consciousness. He looked up into the face of a uniformed police officer and rolled down the window, allowing wind-driven rain to splash against his face.

"You sick or something?" the cop asked.

"Sick? Nah."

"Then move it. This is a no-parking zone."

Mullin reached into his jacket pocket. The cop touched his holster, but Mullin quickly produced his shield.

"You on assignment?" the cop asked.

"Yeah. Thanks for stopping by."

The officer had no sooner walked away than Mullin saw Stripling pull up on the opposite side of the street, half a block down from the hotel. Stripling locked the car, ran down the street, and entered the hotel. Mullin looked around the interior of his vehicle. Why was there never an umbrella when you needed one? There were half a dozen back in the apartment. He spotted a beat-up NY Yankees baseball cap on the backseat, twisted with difficulty to grab it, slammed it on his head, and went to Stripling's car. He looked up and down the street before trying the front passenger door. Locked. He leaned close to the tinted windows and attempted to see inside, but saw only indistinguishable images. Concerned that Stripling and Sasha might leave the hotel and come to the car, he retreated to his own vehicle. He wished he'd picked up a newspaper or magazine, something to kill the time. He hadn't read a book in years.

He tuned the radio to all-news WTOP, where an announcer intoned that the stormy weather was expected to end by late afternoon, with another heat wave to push its way into the area the next day. Commercials followed. Then the day's top stories were repeated.

"This is Dave Stewart with an update on the breaking story involving the Mafia's alleged role in the assassination more than twenty years ago of Chilean dictator Constantine Eliana. A soon-to-be-published book by Washington writer Richard Marienthal claims that the assassination in 1985 was carried out under a contract given a New York Mafia family by the Central Intelligence Agency. The allegation comes from Louis Russo, the Mafia member who claims to have pulled the trigger in that assassination, and who himself was murdered in Union Station only days ago. Russo, who had traveled here to Washington from Israel, where he'd been living under the federal witness protection program, was to have testified at a hearing conducted by Alaska Senator Karl Widmer into the intelligence agency's possible role in the assassination. It's further alleged in the book that President Adam Parmele, then head of the CIA, had personally approved of the assassination. Attempts to reach Marienthal through his publisher and other sources have been unsuccessful. There has been no statement from the White House. A statement issued by Senator Widmer's press secretary says only that such hearings have been planned and that they will go forward despite Russo's death. Tapes of him recounting the story will be available, according to the statement. Stay tuned for further updates as we receive them."

Mullin spent the next forty-five minutes mulling over what he'd heard. The official MPD finding — that Russo had been murdered by organized crime in retaliation for his testimony against them — made less sense than ever to the veteran detective. Had it happened somewhere else — Mexico, Israel, New York, or Los Angeles — he might have bought it. If it had been a revenge killing, why would they have waited until Russo had reached the place where he was scheduled to tell all? And why would the mob draw attention to itself at this stage, and after all these years, by rubbing out a dying turncoat? Mobsters weren't the brightest bulbs in the drawer, but they did have a pretty good sense of self-preservation despite the decimation of the Mafia leadership.

The Parmele administration had the most to lose had Russo lived and gone before the committee. That was obvious. But the contemplation that someone in that administration might have had something to do with Russo's murder was too difficult to accept, even for the terminally cynical Bret Mullin.

Sasha had mentioned at dinner that Russo had been working with this writer guy Marienthal on a book. Now, thanks to WTOP, Mullin knew what the book was about. Even ruling out the mob, whoever killed Russo might have Marienthal in his crosshairs, too. As far as Mullin knew, Marienthal was the only one who could corroborate what Russo had said. Tapes? Did Marienthal have them? Or had he already turned them over to Senator Widmer for use at his hearings?

Who'd killed the Haitian, Leon LeClaire, Russo's assassin? Probably the same people who'd hired him as shooter. Eliminating a shooter to ensure his silence was SOP in criminal circles.

These thoughts came and went as Mullin drank cold coffee and nibbled the last doughnut, which was rapidly growing soggy in the humid air. Distracted by his thoughts, he looked across to the hotel to check that Stripling's car was still parked at the curb. It was. Stripling and Sasha were obviously having breakfast.

Ten minutes later, Stripling came out and stood beneath an overhang, casually taking in the street and the passersby. Eventually he looked up at the gray sky, held a newspaper over his head, and went to his car, got in, and drove away. Mullin started his engine, made an illegal U-turn, and fell in behind.

He didn't know why he was following Stripling, a.k.a. Charlie Simmons, or whatever other names he used. He just knew he had to. Who was this guy? What connection did he have with Russo and LeClaire and Widmer? He wasn't who he represented himself to be to Sasha. Why? Was the break-in of her apartment in Tel Aviv connected in some way?

Stripling drove slowly, which made it easy for Mullin to keep pace. He eventually found a parking space on Tenth Street and walked quickly to the corner of Constitution. He entered the Department of Justice Building. He came out minutes later, got in his car, and drove to E Street, between Ninth and Tenth Streets, parked in a garage, came back on to the street and disappeared inside the J. Edgar Hoover Building, home to the Federal Bureau of Investigation.

"He's Bureau?" Mullin asked aloud in the confines of his car. "He's official, somehow."

Why would the Bureau be involved? The Russo and LeClaire killings had been handled as local matters, with the MPD investigating. Of course, he reasoned, seeing Stripling enter the FBI building didn't necessarily mean he was an employee. But he was obviously working for somebody interested in the cases. His computer file didn't indicate that he held a private investigator's license.

He'd claimed to Sasha that he was an old

friend of Richard Marienthal. Mullin had seen him leaving Marienthal's apartment building, but he obviously hadn't been with the writer. No one was home; Mullin's attempt through the superintendent verified that.

He dialed the number for the Lincoln Suites Hotel on his cell phone and was connected with Sasha Levine's room.

"Hi. It's Detective Bret Mullin."

He couldn't see her smile at his adding his title. She knew who he was without it. "Hello," she said.

"How was your breakfast?" he asked.

"It was fine."

He sensed a reservation in her answer. "You don't sound too sure," he said.

She forced a small laugh. "No, no, it was all right. I —"

"What?"

"I don't believe Charlie Simmons is who he said he was."

"Is that so? How come?"

"He seemed to want to know so much about Richard and his interviews with Louis. It was nothing specific. I just didn't believe he was Richard's good friend as he said he was. The tapes. The tapes of the interviews. That's all he seemed to care about."

"What did you tell him?"

"Nothing. What could I tell him? I know nothing except that Richard used a tape recorder when he spoke with Louis. I was never present and never heard any of the tapes."

"Marienthal has them?" Mullin said.

"I assume he does."

"Did Mr. So-called Simmons tell you anything about himself, where he works?"

"No. I didn't ask such things."

"No, of course you didn't. Why would you? Look, he's planning to come back and see you before you head home?"

"No."

"Good. What time did you say you were leaving for the airport?"

"My plane is at eleven. Louis's remains will have been delivered to the airport. I will leave at nine, nine-thirty?"

"Better make it earlier than that, with security and all. Look, I'm not doing anything tonight. I'll drive you out there. Maybe we can have dinner at the airport. They've got some pretty good restaurants."

"That is so kind but —"

"How about I pick you up at six? Make it five-thirty. No sense being in a rush."

"Thank you."

"My pleasure. In the meantime, stay

close to your room, okay? If Simmons calls again, tell him you're busy. Same goes for the writer, Marienthal, anybody."

"Why do you say that?"

"Simmons ain't what he says he was. You picked up on that. Simmons isn't even his real name."

"It isn't?"

"Trust me. Five-thirty. I'll be on time."

After another hour of waiting for Stripling to return, Mullin drove to MPD's administrative offices, where he borrowed four thousand dollars against his credit union account. He went home, showered, heated up a slice of frozen pizza, wrote a short note to his daughter and signed it *Love, Dad*, put the check and the note in an envelope and addressed it to Cynthia in Denver. He called the hospital. Katie Accurso answered.

"It's Bret. How's the patient?"

"Doing fine, Bret. He's coming home tomorrow."

"Sorry I didn't get over to see him. Put him on."

"Can't. He's with a physical therapist planning his recuperation. It'll take a while."

"He's got nothing but time."

"How are you getting along without him?"

"I'd be doing better if Vinnie hadn't taken that bullet. These new detectives get dumber every day."

She laughed.

"How was the fruit?"

"The fruit? Oh, great. Vinnie's eaten most of it."

"Why am I not surprised? You take care, Katie. Give the Italian stallion a hug for me."

"Shall do."

He dressed in a fresh suit, shirt, and tie, talked to Magnum for a few minutes, and checked his watch. He had time to kill before picking up Sasha. Although his shoes had recently been polished, he decided a shine was in order and drove to Union Station, stopping at a mailbox to mail the check.

Bootblack Joe Jenks had just finished with a customer as Mullin approached. He climbed up into Jenks's chair and rolled up his trouser cuffs.

"Mullin, my man," Jenks said, pulling his tools from the drawer beneath the chair. "How goes it?"

"Not bad, Joe. You?"

"Business is good. Long as the AC keeps working in here, people come to cool off. Might as well get their shoes shined, is the

403

way I figure they see it. Tips've been good, too. 'Course, today's slow with the rain, but looks like it's clearing out there."

"Looks like it. Shine 'em up good, huh. I've got a heavy date tonight."

"Good for you, man. Who's the lucky lady?"

"You wouldn't know her. She's foreign. Speaks a lot of different languages."

"Uh-huh. Brainy type, huh?"

"Yup. Good-looking, too."

"Best kind, beauty and brains. I've known a few of them myself. Two. Or maybe three."

"I bet you have."

He paid Jenks and tipped well despite the bootblack's insistence that it was on the house. Mullin went to the Greenworks Flower Shop on the other side of the Amtrak ticket counter from Exclusive Shoe Shine and bought a small, colorful bouquet. "These won't wilt, will they?" he asked the shopkeeper. "I mean, they'll still look nice a couple of hours from now."

Assured they would last, he paid and went to where he'd parked in a no-parking zone, his MPD permit displayed on the sun visor. The rain had stopped, but he'd stepped in a puddle on his way to the car and wiped off his shoes with Kleenex from the glove compartment. He still had time before picking up Sasha. He found the phone number he had for Richard Marienthal and dialed it on his cell phone. The number was busy. *The hell with it,* he thought. Might as well be early at the hotel and maybe have a drink at the bar before hooking up with Sasha. After checking that he had breath mints, he drove off, the fragrance of the flowers on the passenger seat filling the car.

Mullin's attempt to call the apartment shared by Marienthal and Kathryn Jalick didn't go unnoticed by Kathryn. While he heard a busy signal, she heard through Call Waiting that someone was trying to reach her. But she opted to not put the current caller on hold in order to answer the second call. She was on the line with Rich.

She'd intended to go to work at the Library of Congress the day after she and Marienthal left the River Inn and he'd gone off to wherever he was. But she awoke on edge after a few hours of fitful sleep, and decided to stay at home. As the day progressed, she questioned that decision. Work would have taken her mind off the situation in which she'd found herself. Being in the apartment served as a reminder of recent events and made her captive to a succession of phone calls to which she had to respond — truthfully, it turned out, because Rich had refused to tell her where he'd be staying. When she told callers she didn't know where he was, she meant it.

Although she hadn't kept track of the number of calls she took that day, she later estimated it to be more than twenty, many from the media.

Rich's father had called from New York.

"Hello, Mr. Marienthal," she'd said after he'd identified himself.

"Is Rich there?" he'd asked, ignoring her greeting.

"No, not at the moment."

"I've left messages," he said. "Why hasn't Rich returned my calls?"

"Mr. Marienthal, I —"

"Look, Ms. Jalick, I don't wish to be short with you, but there's obviously something terribly wrong. Is Rich ill? Has he been in an accident?"

She tried to laugh the question away. "No, of course not," she said. "He's off researching another book. That's all I know."

Marienthal's father's silence loudly proclaimed that he didn't believe her. He said, "I'm coming down to Washington. I'm sure you have a way of reaching Richard. Tell him I'll be there and he must talk with me. This mess he's gotten himself into goes beyond him. We're getting calls here from the media, which is very stressful to his mother, who's not well."

"I —"

There was a click on the New York end.

Sam Greenleaf, Marienthal's editor at Hobbes House, called twice.

"I've got to get hold of Rich," he told Kathryn on the first call. "He's a hot topic with the media. The *Today* show, CNN, *Hannity & Colmes, Inside Edition.* Where is he?"

"I don't know," she replied, frustration in her voice.

"Come on, Ms. Jalick. His book is just coming out, the media is salivating to promote it, and he's nowhere to be found? Give me a break. What does he think, that by playing hard to get he hypes interest in the book? He's wrong. You have to —"

"I don't want to be rude, Mr. Greenleaf, but I'm going to end this call. I do not know where Richard is. Period. End of story."

He gruffly signed off and hung up. The phone rang again a few seconds later.

"Sam Greenleaf again. I'm sorry if I

sounded angry with you. Look, there's more to this than just publishing and selling a book. I'm sure you're aware of the Widmer hearings that are scheduled."

"Yes, I've heard."

"I won't go into the details, Ms. Jalick, but Rich and Louis Russo were to be a big part of those hearings."

Kathryn said nothing.

"Russo's dead, but Rich's taped interviews with him are crucial to the senator and his committee. Do you have access to those tapes?"

"Of course not."

"Rich has them?"

"Please, Mr. Greenleaf, I know nothing about tapes and hearings. You're wasting your time talking to me."

If he agreed — and probably did — he didn't state it.

"Will you call me if you hear from Rich?"

"Let me have your number."

She considered taking the phone off the hook, but was afraid she might miss a call from Rich. Later that afternoon, a call came in from Geoff Lowe's girlfriend and colleague, Ellen Kelly. She hadn't spoken with Ellen in a long time and was surprised to hear from her.

"How's it going?" Ellen asked.

"Okay. You?"

"Busy. Swamped. Excited about Rich's book coming out?"

"I — yes, very excited."

"I imagine the author is on cloud nine."

"He's — he's pleased. How's Geoff?"

"The same as always. You know Geoff."

Kathryn didn't express that she did indeed know Geoff, and didn't like what she knew. She said, "I was just about to run out, Ellen. What can I do for you?"

"I don't suppose Richard is there."

"No, he's not."

"I'm not being honest," Ellen said. "I *know* he's not there. Geoff has been frantic looking for him."

"If you're asking me where he is," Kathryn said, "you're wasting your time."

"Kathryn, I'll get to the point. Richard's life is in danger."

Kathryn felt her heart stop for a second. That his life might be in danger had been on her mind for days. But to hear someone say it, actually say it, was jolting.

"Did you hear me, Kathryn?" Ellen said. "His life is in danger."

"Why?" was all Kathryn could summon.

"The book. The tapes. Especially the tapes. Don't you see it? The tapes contain

Louis Russo's words, the same words he would have spoken had he lived and testified. It's his voice. Whoever killed him wants Rich out of the way, too."

Kathryn used a foot to pull an ottoman to where she stood and sat heavily on it. "Go on," she said.

"Kathryn," Ellen said in measured tones, like a teacher about to go through a particularly difficult lesson, "as long as Russo's tapes are floating around, there are people who will kill to get their hands on them."

"Who?" Kathryn, asked, feeling a touch of nausea.

"It doesn't matter *who.* There's only one way to protect Rich, Kathryn, and that's for him to give up those tapes. Once they're no longer with him, he's in the clear."

Kathryn's initial paralysis lifted.

Ellen Kelly worked for Geoff Lowe and Senator Karl Widmer. *They wanted the tapes for their hearings.* That's what was behind the call. Ellen and the others weren't concerned about Rich's safety. People were expendable. It was the tapes that mattered.

"You want the tapes for the hearings," she said forcefully.

Ellen responded even more forcefully: "I want Rich to be safe! Geoff may want the tapes for the hearing, but I don't give a damn about them. I'm getting ready to leave the staff, Kathryn. I've had it. Believe it or not, I've spent too long putting politics over people. I'm through."

"I didn't know."

"Kathryn, can we get together for dinner? Lunch? A drink? I'm really concerned about Rich as long as he has those tapes."

"I — I suppose so."

"Now? I can come right over."

"No. I have things to do. I'll call you."

"Kathryn, I don't think you understand the gravity of this."

"Oh, I do, I do, Ellen. I have another call coming in. Are you at your office?"

"Yes."

"I'll call you there."

She pushed Flash on the phone and heard Rich's voice. "Hold on a second," she told him, switching back to Ellen: "I have to take this, Ellen. I'll call."

She didn't wait for Ellen to say anything, simply switched back to Rich on the other line.

After waking that afternoon, Marienthal had felt a need to get out of the apartment and to walk. Wearing sunglasses and a floppy tan rain hat, he quietly left the apartment — Jackson still slept — and got a half a block away before returning to grab the canvas bag containing his tapes and notes. The bag slung over his shoulder, he wandered the neighborhood until he found himself compelled to take a cab. When he climbed into the cab, he didn't have a specific destination in mind, but the turbaned driver asked where he wished to go. "Union Station," Marienthal replied, sounding as though someone else had said it.

The station was its usual busy hub of movement when he arrived. He paid the driver, walked through the main entrance on Massachusetts Avenue, paused and, like a tourist, looked up at the towering arched skylights over the Main Hall. His eyes went to the Augustus Saint-Gaudens stone sentinels looking down at the throngs of people moving through the vast hall. The shields covering the statue's private parts had been added later to satisfy a call for modesty from some offended citizens.

He rode the escalator to the lower level, got cash from the Adams National Bank ATM machine, bought a newspaper, and took the only remaining seat in Johnny Rockets. He ordered coffee and a piece of lemon meringue pie. He looked around to see if anyone was showing interest in him. Satisfied no one was, he removed his sunglasses, and as he had never done before, read about himself in the paper. The article was illustrated with a picture of the cover of his book and a photo of Senator Karl Widmer. The statement previously released by Widmer's staff indicated that the hearings into the role of the CIA in the assassination of the Chilean dictator Eliana would move forward, and that tape recordings of the assassin, Louis Russo, could provide evidence of the agency's culpability in the murder. Adam Parmele's involvement as head of the CIA wasn't mentioned.

A leading Democrat on Widmer's committee, a firm supporter of President Parmele, issued his own statement: "The hearings proposed by Senator Widmer represent nothing more than a blatant political witch hunt, based upon the questionable word of an aging, demented former Mafia killer, who for the past twelve years has been secluded under the witness protection program, and who now claims to have taken part in the assassination. His charges, contained in a recently published book, are ludicrous at best.

Basing hearings on such absurd information makes a mockery of legitimate Senate hearings into important matters of state. I and my Democratic colleagues on the committee strenuously oppose this waste of taxpayer money in the interest of political gain."

Marienthal's name appeared near the end of the piece: "The book in which the charges are leveled, written by D.C. author Richard Marienthal, has just been published. Attempts to date to speak with Marienthal have been unsuccessful. According to his publisher, Hobbes House, the author's whereabouts are unknown."

Marienthal replaced his sunglasses and ate his pie, finished his coffee. He left the restaurant, a replica of a fifties diner, and returned to the street level. He took a circuitous route to the windows of the B. Dalton bookstore and viewed them from a distance. A pile of his books, with one perched on top to allow passersby to see the cover, occupied the window nearest the entrance. He overcame the temptation to enter the store and walked to Best Lockers, behind the Amtrak ticket counter and near Exclusive Shoe Shine. The lockers had been closed to the public after 9/11 as a security measure, but had been opened again. After taking a minute to make his decision, Marienthal located an empty locker and slid the canvas shoulder bag inside. He paused, removed the bag, and zipped it open. The tapes were bundled in plastic bags and secured with rubber bands, the notes filed in three-ring binders. He placed the bag's contents in the locker, closed the door, and pocketed the key. The shoulder bag was like a pet rock or favorite wallet to Marienthal; no sense in leaving it behind.

Before departing the station, he went to a bank of public telephones next to Best Lockers and dialed his home phone.

"Hi," he said. "How are you doing?"

"I am so happy to hear your voice," she said. "I'm all right. You?"

"Okay."

"The phone's rung off the hook all day. I took a sick day. I shouldn't have. Reporters. They're so tenacious. Your father called."

"I'm sure he did. Did Geoff call?"

"No, but Ellen did. How can I reach you?"

"You can't. It's better that way. I'd better go. I'll get back to you."

"So soon? I —"

"This'll be over soon, Kathryn. Just think about that vacation we'll be taking."

"I will," she said. "You take care."

He hung up, left the station on to Massachusetts Avenue, and took a taxi back to Winard Jackson's apartment. Had he stayed on the phone much longer or lingered by it, he would shortly have had the pleasure of meeting Timothy Stripling.

Stripling had spent most of the afternoon in the FBI's central communications room at the Hoover Building, where a series of wiretaps had been initiated, under a special order from the attorney general of the United States. His authority to authorize such invasive measures had been widely expanded in the interest of homeland security, Tim knew, and indeed, no home seemed to be safe any longer.

The first tap had been placed on the phone registered to Richard Marienthal and had become operative at the tail end of Kathryn Jalick's conversation with Ellen Kelly. Kathryn's call from Marienthal had not only been recorded but was traced to a specific bank of public phones at Union Station. Stripling left the Hoover Building before the call was over, but no one resembling Marienthal was at the station. He

416

drove the streets around the station but came up empty. Meanwhile, the agents back at the Hoover Building were placing additional taps on phones when Stripling left, and said they'd contact him twenty-four hours a day on the cell phone they'd provided if another lead developed. He'd now been given a number he could use to call directly into the com center, and used it first to report his failure to locate Marienthal.

He drove to Georgetown and had a sundae. Back in his car, he dialed a number on his cell phone.

"Jane? It's Tim Stripling."

"Hello, lover. Bad timing."

"Got a client, huh? Any time later?"

"In an hour. Make it two."

"Yeah, two. I prefer you fresh. And rested. See you then."

With any luck, his cell wouldn't ring at an inopportune time.

THIRTY-EIGHT

Mullin was at the unoccupied bar, the flowers sitting next to a vodka on the rocks, when Sasha came down from her room pulling a suitcase with wheels. She spotted him and entered the bar. *You get better looking every time I see you,* he thought.

"Right on the button," he said, indicating his watch. He wanted to kiss her.

"I try to be."

"Drink? We have time."

She seemed unsure.

"If you don't want, it's okay."

"All right. I checked out earlier."

Her eyes went to the flowers, and Mullin handed them to her, accompanied by an inexperienced grin. "Just a little something to say goodbye. They're not much."

"They're lovely, as lovely as the thought," she said, sniffing the petals and taking the stool next to him. He lighted her cigarette and said to the bartender without checking with Sasha, "A white Zinfandel for the lady."

Her mood was somber, which wasn't lost on him. "Problem?" he asked.

"I didn't know," she replied.

"Didn't know what?"

"Why Louis came to Washington. I haven't watched the news since coming here. I don't watch it at home much, either. Always sadness and sorrow on the news. In Israel. Here. But I watched this afternoon. I didn't know."

"That what, he came to testify at that Senate committee?"

"Yes."

"I just found that out, too. From the radio. How come you didn't know? He didn't tell you why he was coming here?"

She shook her head and sipped her wine. "All Louis told me was that Richard —"

"Marienthal. The writer."

"Yes. All he told me was that Richard wanted to introduce him to some politicians who were interested in his story."

"Did he also tell you that he shot people, especially that Central American dictator?"

She shuddered and reached for the flowers on the bar, brought them to her chest and closed her eyes.

"He didn't tell you that?"

"My God, no." She turned, eyes wide open, as though imploring him to understand, to believe her. "Louis told me something about his life with the Mafia, about the killing of enemies, the other crimes in which he was involved, the things that caused him shame. But to kill a man who is a leader of a country?"

Mullin was unsure of what to say. "Maybe he didn't," he said.

She said nothing.

"Maybe this writer, Marienthal, made it up. You know, to sell his book. They do that all the time."

She shook her head. "No, that is not what it says on the news. It says that Louis was to testify at the hearings in your Senate, to say under oath that he killed the man on orders from your president when he was with the CIA."

"Yeah, I know, but —"

"Louis told me that the book was about his life in New York, his days with his gang. Nothing about assassinations. I should have asked more, but I didn't." She touched the top of his hand with her fingertips. "Richard is missing. I heard that, too. Do you think —"

Mullin shrugged and downed his drink, motioned for another. "What do I think, that maybe something happened to him, too?"

Her eyes said she wanted an answer to that question.

Another shrug from the big detective. "I don't think so," he said. "I mean, who knows, huh? They say your friend was killed by his former buddies he ratted on."

"They say? Who are *they?*"

"The brass. The boys upstairs where I work."

"Do you believe that?"

"I don't know what I believe," he said, starting on his new drink. "I just hear things, like you do. I sensed earlier that they want the tapes of Louis telling his story. There's a senator here, an old guy from Alaska, who's in charge of the hearings. There's always hearings going on around here. Waste of taxpayer money. All political. Widmer — he's the senator holding the hearings — he hates Parmele. The way I see it, he wants to hold the hearings to sink Parmele's chance for another four years in the White House. That's the scuttlebutt I hear."

She cupped her glass in both hands and stared into it.

"I know what you're thinking," he said. "What I said. Yeah, sure, maybe it wasn't the mob that killed Louis. Maybe it was somebody working for Parmele's cause, in the White House itself, out to save his political rear end."

"We don't think such things happen here," she said.

He guffawed. "Think again," he said. "We had the two Kennedy brothers shot dead. Hey, next time you're over, visit Ford's Theatre, where Lincoln was hit. Yeah, it happens here, too."

He didn't continue with what he was thinking, that Louis Russo wasn't in the same league as JFK or RFK. Getting rid of an aging, sick mafioso wouldn't be a big deal to someone with political aspirations or motives. The old guy's life was meaningless in the larger scheme of things. The same with LeClaire, the Union Station shooter. You want to get away with murder, get rid of anybody who helped you pull it off. Murder 101.

"Richard has the tapes," she said to herself.

"That's what the senator wants, they say. The tapes, Russo's own voice saying what he did. Any idea where he might be?"

"Richard? No. I spoke with his girlfriend today."

"Did you? What'd she have to say?"

"She said he was away working on another book."

"No way to reach him?"

"She said there wasn't."

"Hmm. Doesn't sound kosher to me," he said. She looked puzzled. He laughed at his choice of words.

She didn't respond.

"Drink your wine," he said. "Want another?"

"No, thank you."

"Well," he said, downing the remainder of his drink, "I guess we should head for the airport, grab some dinner."

"Maybe I should take a taxi," she said.

"How come? I said I'd drive you."

"Maybe you shouldn't drive, the drinks and all."

He gave forth a reassuring laugh. "A couple a pops don't affect me. I'm fine."

She sat rigidly on the bar stool, staring at the back bar's glittering array of bottles and glassware. "Hey," he said, touching her shoulder. "If you don't want to have dinner with me, that's okay. I mean, I'll be disappointed but —"

"Who *are* you?" she asked, turning to face him.

"Huh?"

"Who are you?" she repeated.

"You know who I am."

"I don't know who anyone is," she said. "That man, Charlie Simmons, isn't who he says he is. You told me that."

"Right. I checked on him. I got his plate number and ran it. His name's Stripling. Timothy Stripling. The way I read the info on him, he's with some government agency. Hard to tell which one."

"Why would he lie to me?"

"He's looking for the writer and the tapes. You said he kept asking about them. Am I right?"

"Yes."

"So maybe he's working for the senator from Alaska. That makes sense, don't it?"

She turned her hands palms up in a gesture of confusion. "They break into my apartment," she said. "The tapes. They were looking for the tapes, copies of them?"

"Could be." The bar tab was placed in front of him and he slapped cash on it. "I'd like to know where this writer friend of yours is."

"It sounds as though many people want to know where he is," she said.

"Maybe we can get a missing person's search going," he said. "Of course, if his girlfriend says he's not missing, just away, that makes it tough, but I'll see what I can do." He didn't add that his boss's admonition to drop any search for Marienthal would make it even tougher. He stood and hitched his trousers up over his belly. "Well," he said, "if you want, I'll get you a cab. I'd still like to drive you and have dinner, but that's up to you."

She didn't reply as she slid off the stool, extended the handle of her suitcase, and looked toward the lobby. Mullin took the flowers from the bar and held them up. "Don't want these?" he asked.

She lowered her head and let out a sustained, pained sigh. "I'm sorry," she said. "Please forgive me. Louis always said it was better to distrust friends than to be deceived by them."

"And you don't trust me," he said.

She thought a moment before saying, "I don't trust myself. Yes, please, drive me to the airport." She took the flowers from him, smiled, and said, "I think you are a kind man, Detective Mr. Bret Mullin. Thank you for being kind to me."

"No problem," he said, unsure of what else to say. "Let's go. You can smoke in the car if you want."

THIRTY-NINE

The phone was ringing when Mac Smith walked through the door.

"Mac. Frank Marienthal."

"Hello, Frank. How are you?" Smith said, cradling the cordless phone to his ear as he deposited two bags of groceries on the kitchen counter of his Watergate apartment.

"I've been better. I'm in Washington."

"Oh. Business?"

"Family business. Richard. I'm staying at the Watergate. I'd like to see you."

"Want to come up to the apartment?"

"I'd appreciate it."

Mac gave directions to his building in the complex and hung up. Ten minutes later, the New York criminal attorney was seated with Smith on the terrace, glasses and a bottle of sparkling water on the table.

"Sorry to barge in on you on short notice," the elder Marienthal said. He wore a dark blue pinstripe suit, a white shirt, and a solid maroon tie. Smith had changed into loose-fitting jeans and a pale green short-sleeved polo shirt.

"I'm pleased to see you, Frank. I know why you're here, of course. Richard's disappearance has been all over the news. How much play has it gotten in New York?"

"Not as much as here, it being a Washington story. Christ, Mac, to think that Richard got himself into a situation like this is anathema to Mary and me. The potential ramifications are immense. A sitting president may be accused of authorizing the assassination of a foreign leader when he was heading the CIA. The accuser is murdered in Union Station, and his killer is also murdered. And now Richard is missing, presumably with those goddamn tapes on which Louis Russo weaves some tale about killing on orders from our government."

"Yes. You don't believe his claim?"

"It doesn't matter whether I believe it or not. I represented Russo, you know. The important thing is that whatever he told Richard for the book is being used for political gain. Do you know Senator Widmer?"

"I've met him a few times," Smith said.

"He'd do anything to derail Parmele's bid for a second term, even use the rants of a mob killer."

"Have you spoken with Kathryn?" Smith asked.

"Ms. Jalick? Yes, I have. She's lying about Richard's whereabouts. Hardly the sort of young woman Mary or I envisioned for Richard. As long as he has those tapes —"

"What can I do to help?" Smith asked.

"Help me find Richard," Marienthal said. "Before the wrong people do."

Annabel came home from her gallery and Marienthal stayed for dinner. Naturally, most of the talk at the table was a continuation of what he and Mac had discussed earlier. It was over coffee that Marienthal took something from a large manila envelope he'd carried with him to the apartment and handed it to his hosts. It was a copy of his son's book, *The Contract: The Assassination of Constantine Eliana, and the People Behind It* by Richard Marienthal.

As Annabel flipped through the pages, stopping at a photo section in which the Chilean dictator's image was featured, along with scenes from the assassination, and earlier photos of Adam Parmele as CIA chief, commingled with more recent shots, Mac sat glumly, chewing his cheek and tapping his fingertips together.

"It's obviously not a novel," Annabel said, laying the book on the table.

"That's not how the contract read when Rich asked me to review it. It's not what he told me."

Marienthal said in a low voice, "I'm sorry."

"For what?" Annabel asked.

"For Richard's dishonesty. I asked you to vet his contract, Mac, and you did, under false pretenses."

"He and his publisher obviously had their reasons for wanting it to be known as a work of fiction," Smith said. "I'm sure they tried to hide the true nature of the book for as long as possible."

"Which doesn't make it any less dishonest," said the father. "I read the book on my way here. It's filled with speculation and innuendo, vague references by Russo to contacts he had with the CIA. How absurd, this minor league thug claiming he had direct contact with CIA agents who contracted with him to shoot Eliana, on Adam Parmele's orders."

"Evidently Richard believed him," Annabel offered.

"Which doesn't surprise me," Marienthal said. "Richard's a dreamer, always has been. That's why he became a

429

writer, I suppose. I wanted him to go to law school." He looked at Mac and smiled. "If there's one thing you lose in law school, it's your sophomoric naïveté. Right, Mac?"

"Maybe to a fault," Smith said, feeling a growing need to defend his friend's son.

Annabel brought coffee to the table and returned to the kitchen to get a plate of cookies. The phone rang; she answered. A moment later, she returned to the dining room carrying the cordless phone. "It's for you, Mac," she said. To both men sotto voce: "It's Richard."

Mac glanced at Marienthal before taking the phone from her. "Richard?" he said.

"Yes, Mac. I hope I'm not disturbing your dinner."

"We've just finished. Your father is here."

"Dad's in Washington?"

"He certainly is. I'll put him on."

"No, Mac. In a minute. I need to speak with you. I need some detached advice."

"Hold on a minute." Mac placed his hand over the phone and said to Marienthal, "He wants to run something by me, Frank. Give me a few minutes with him."

Marienthal's face was gray and sunken, as though attacked by a sudden burst of

430

gravity. Large circles puffed beneath his eyes; his mouth was a tight, thin slash.

Smith walked away from the table, went to his office, and shut the door. "Before we get into advice-giving, Richard, I want you to listen to me. I understand you're under considerable pressure, and your need to become incommunicado might also be understandable. But you have a mother and father who are worried about you. I think you owe them some contact."

"I know, Mac," Marienthal said, "and I've been meaning to call. It's just that —"

"No excuses, Rich. When we're through with this conversation, I'll put your father on."

"Okay."

"Now, care to tell me where you are?"

The moment Smith said it, the possibility of his phone being tapped struck him. He was happy when Rich replied, "Not yet. Kathryn has been urging me to talk to you, Mac. I've resisted it because — well, because I suppose I'm not ready to take advice from someone else. What it comes down to is that I am very confused at this point."

"I'm glad you called. Now that the book is out — your father brought a copy with him, and the media is all over its publication — your tape-recorded interviews with Louis Russo take center stage."

"I know."

"You have them, I assume."

"Sure I do."

"And I assume you're pondering what to do with them."

"Yes."

"I don't think this is the sort of decision to be made while under pressure, Rich. If you are seeking my advice, I urge that we all meet — you, me, and your father — and that you bring the tapes. We can decide what to do with them under calmer circumstances."

Marienthal hesitated. "I know you're right, Mac. Let me give it a little more thought. But you *are* right. Kathryn said you were the one to handle this."

Handle this? Smith thought. All he wanted to do was effectuate a meeting between father and son, and let them decide what to do with the tapes.

He'd silently speculated during dinner that there were three possible options as far as the tapes were concerned: turn them over to Senator Widmer's committee; pass them on to the White House; or destroy them. But as he spoke with Richard, a fourth option emerged in his thinking. The tapes could be placed under seal at some disinterested institution such as the Library of Congress or in a school like his own George Washington University, perhaps not made available to researchers and other interested parties until a specific date, long after President Parmele was out of office.

He was acutely aware that while the immediate concern was the well-being of Rich Marienthal, the broader political ramifications were potentially huge. The book was bad enough. Although it preached to the already converted, who would wave it about as "proof" that the president was unfit to hold the nation's highest office — and his defenders would dismiss it as nothing more than braggadocio from a demented former Mafia hit man — it would do damage. But with the tapes played before a Senate committee, and played over and over on radio and TV newscasts, the hit man's actual words would provide gravamen to the charge against Parmele and throw his bid for a second term into turmoil, the need to defend himself overwhelming the presentation of more meaningful political positions. A familiar plight for modern candidates or officeholders.

"I'm going to put your father on now, Rich," Smith said. "Before I do, I suggest you not wait much longer to decide what to do with the tapes. You may end up losing your ability to determine their fate. I might have an idea for you if you'll agree to meet. Hold on."

He brought the phone to Frank Marienthal at the dining room table. "Rich wants to talk to you, Frank. Take it in my office. You can use this phone or the one on the desk." He handed the cordless to Marienthal, who slowly got up and left the room, disappearing behind the door to Smith's office.

The conversation between the elder Marienthal and his son consumed ten minutes. During it, Mac filled Annabel in. Frank Marienthal's voice was occasionally heard, the words unintelligible, the tone unmistakably angry. When he emerged, he said, "I think I finally talked some sense into him. He's promised to call again tomorrow."

"Here?"

"Yes."

"When?"

"He didn't say. I could use a drink. Scotch if you have it. Neat."

"Sure."

"If he only realized what this is doing to his mother, his name splashed all over TV and the newspapers, hiding out like some dumb kid playing a prank on his parents."

Mac brought Marienthal a tumbler of single malt. "I think Rich is genuinely afraid, Frank," he said. "I wouldn't be too judgmental at this juncture. It's not all directed at you and Mary. Maybe none of it is."

Marienthal ignored Smith's counsel and asked, "Did he tell you where he was calling from?"

"No."

The phone rang, and Annabel went to the kitchen to answer. It was a friend, an art dealer from New York confirming plans to visit Annabel at her gallery the following day. The two men sat quietly at the table, Annabel's words filling the void.

"And I'm so pleased you're coming, Karen. Your train gets in at Union Station at one? Grab a cab out front — you'll be at the gallery by one-thirty. Can't wait to see you. We'll spend time at the gallery and then find some lunch. I have some wonderful new pieces to show you. Great, see you then."

At the Com Center in the Hoover Building, two agents from the communica-

435

tions division heard *"We'll spend time at the gallery and then find some lunch. I have some wonderful new pieces to show you. Great, see you then."*

"Just a couple of ladies doing lunch," said one agent, laughing.

"Maybe it'll get juicier later on," offered the second one.

"Yeah, let's hope."

FORTY

Lights in the White House burned bright that night.

Political adviser Chet Fletcher had been at work since early morning, as had every other member of the president's most trusted senior staff. A siege mentality existed in offices manned by press secretary Robin Whitson and her aides. "We have no statement at this time" was the official party line.

"When will the president address this directly?" reporters repeatedly asked.

"We have no statement to make at this time."

"Does the president deny his involvement in the Eliana assassination?"

"We have no statement at this time."

While Whitson's staff fielded the barrage of media calls, the press secretary spent most of her day and evening conferring with other presidential handmaidens. Sides had been taken early in the day; Whitson lobbied for the president to hold a press conference and issue an official denial of the claims in the Marienthal-Russo book.

Others, led by Chet Fletcher, argued that to do so would only bestow credibility on the book's charges.

"No," Whitson said during one of a dozen meetings since the news broke — she'd lost count of how many there had been. "That's exactly what stonewalling will accomplish. The longer it festers, the more the story will be believed." She'd become uncharacteristically strident during that particular debate with Fletcher, and left the room to calm down, hopefully to formulate a more reasoned case for her position. But she was painfully aware that no matter what tack she took, she would lose out. Fletcher's power within the Parmele inner circle was unquestioned, particularly when it involved politics — and this was politics pure and simple, although a silent minority thought it might be a crime, impure and not so simple.

Robin Whitson twice met directly with the president. During those meetings, Parmele acted as though the issue was whether he wore boxer shorts or briefs, nothing more significant than that. "This is Widmer's last gasp," he told her. "He's an old fool who's grasping at straws, and I don't intend to dignify this ludicrous, blatantly political ploy." He came around the desk, his smile wide and reassuring, and placed his hand on her shoulder. "Just let it ride a while, Robin," he said in a measured voice. "Chet has had a handle on it from the beginning. We'll put out a statement when he thinks it's appropriate. In the meantime, let's not become distracted. Stay on message, Robin. Widmer wants us to lose sight of the prize, that's all. You're doing a great job. Keep at it."

His tone during one-on-one meetings with Fletcher was not quite as relaxed and heartening.

"How did we lose control of this?" he asked his political adviser.

"I don't think we have, Mr. President," Fletcher responded.

"It sure as hell sounds that way to me! I thought that when the old Italian — what's his name? Russo — Russo? What kind of name is that? I thought that when he died, it was over."

"It was, sir, at least as far as the Widmer hearings were concerned. We didn't take into consideration that there were tapes. We couldn't stop the book. Hobbes House —"

"The book isn't what concerns me, Chet. Yeah, it's bad enough, but how many people will read it? Not enough to make a difference. But those tapes the writer is

439

supposed to have are another story. They'll play them day and night on cable news channels and right-wing radio talk shows. Walt Brown tells me Widmer intends to go through with the hearings as long as he has the tapes."

"He won't have those tapes, Mr. President."

"You sound damn sure, Chet."

"He *won't* have the tapes, Mr. President!"

"Do you have them?"

"Not yet. Shortly."

Parmele's tone softened. "Good. I appreciate the way you've handled this. As unfortunate as it was, the murder of Widmer's witness in Union Station was — well, how can I put it so that it doesn't sound callous? It was fortuitous. What's the status of the murder with the police?"

"The attorney general's office is following up on that," said Fletcher. "It's my understanding that it's been ruled a revenge killing by the people he — Mr. Russo — testified against some time ago in New York. I'm also told that the man who killed Russo was in all likelihood hired by the mob for that purpose and was himself eliminated to assure his silence."

The president leaned back in his chair

and cupped his hands behind his head. "The whole Mafia notion is interesting, isn't it, Chet? What do they call it, 'my thing'? Their society is so insular, governed by its own rules. *Omertà*. Their code of silence. Judging from all the turncoats I've read about, including this guy Russo, they aren't always silent. Once the code is broken . . . I've always wondered whether there was any truth to the story about the mob being contracted to kill Castro. I know they prevented sabotage on the New York docks during World War II, and advised on the invasion of Sicily. Were they involved in JFK's assassination? Marilyn Monroe's death? Joe Kennedy didn't have any trouble dealing with them or with Hollywood moguls like Wasserman and Mayer."

"I've never put credence in any of it, Mr. President," Fletcher said. "They're just a bunch of goons trying to look legitimate and big-time."

"Like Mr. Russo."

"Exactly."

Parmele straightened in the chair. "Maybe Robin is right, Chet. Maybe I should stand up at a podium and simply dismiss the charges in the book."

"At some point that would be in order,

Mr. President. Not now."

"When?"

"After we let the press play its cards, show us what they've got."

"Nixon stonewalled and look where it got him."

Fletcher's frown wasn't lost on Parmele. "Forget I said that, Chet. I know this isn't precisely stonewalling."

Fletcher gathered papers in preparation for leaving.

"Chet," Parmele said.

"Yes, Mr. President?"

"It's important to me that you know the truth."

"Sir?"

"About the Eliana assassination."

"Mr. President, there's no need to —"

Parmele held up a hand to silence his political guru. "Hear me out, Chet," he said. "When I was over at the Company, I was aware that there were cells within the agency that preferred to follow their own agenda. It was the same with some people at NSA and the NSC. Cowboys. Have all the answers. I used to think that the toughest part of my job at the Company was figuring out who they were and corralling them, keeping them from playing out their fantasies about what was good for

America. I wasn't always successful."

A knock on the Oval Office door interrupted. An aide poked her head in, but Parmele waved her away: "Not now."

"Where was I?" he asked after the aide was gone. "The cowboys, the rogues. I knew there were people in the agency advocating assassination as a public policy tool, and I knew Eliana was high on the list. I heard all their arguments during my years there, and there were times when they seemed to make sense. It would have been a hell of a lot cheaper in money and lives to assassinate Saddam Hussein than to invade Iraq."

Fletcher listened impassively.

"But no one was going to assassinate anybody on my watch. The administration wasn't sanctioning assassinations, at least as far as I knew. Besides, all those bungled attempts on Castro's life before I got there — botulism in his cigars, which didn't work because he'd stopped smoking; depilatories in his shoes to cause his hair to fall out — made the agency the laughingstock of the intelligence world. So, no, Chet, Eliana wasn't assassinated on my orders. Maybe the buck stopped at my desk. Maybe I should have kept a tighter rein on the cowboys within the agency. But I never gave the go-ahead, never even knew that killing Eliana was in the works."

"I understand," Fletcher said.

Parmele wasn't finished.

"Congress held the obligatory hearings, and I testified. You know the result of that: 'Constantine Eliana was assassinated by unknown persons loyal to his opposition back in Chile. Case closed.' Until now."

"Yes. Until now."

Parmele ended the meeting. "You'll let me know once those tapes are no longer a problem."

"Of course, sir."

"Good. We'll ride this out, Chet. We'll leave egg on the Alaska senator's face and keep the country moving in the right direction. Your service to me is deeply appreciated."

"Thank you, Mr. President. Anything else?"

"No. Grab a nap. You look like death warmed over."

Fletcher left the Oval Office and stood just outside its door. Ordinarily, he would have gone directly to his office. He was not known within the White House as someone who mixed easily with others, who enjoyed chewing the fat or passing along the latest insider joke. But this evening he slowly walked the corridors of the nation's house, stopping to look into offices that he customarily avoided, accepting a greeting with a wan smile and flip of his hand, file folders cradled to his chest, large, thick glasses perched on his small nose, his expression that of a man sinking beneath a massive weight.

"Anything new with the chief?" Robin Whitson asked when she almost bumped into him as he turned a corner.

"No, Robin," he said. "Nothing new. But you have credibility with him."

He entered the reception area of his office, where his personal secretary and an aide conversed. "No visitors," he said.

Inside, the door closed, he settled heavily behind his desk and dropped the folders on it. The drapes were drawn; the only illumination came from a brass gooseneck lamp that spilled yellow light on the polished surface. He was overwhelmed with fatigue. His reputation with colleagues for having an unusually high level of energy was misleading. It was more a matter of will, talking himself through bouts of exhaustion that frequently threatened to consume him.

He called his wife to say he might not be home that night, told her he loved her, and settled in to review upcoming campaign plans. An aide brought him a cup of tea at nine-thirty, and a platter of small sandwiches from the White House mess. It was almost ten when a call came from Wayne Garson.

"They're drawing in the wagons, Chet?" the AG asked.

"You could say that," Fletcher replied.

"I need to talk with you, Chet."

"All right."

"Not on the phone. I'll be freed up by eleven. I'd appreciate you heading over here to Justice."

"Tonight."

"Yes, sir. I'm sure the president can spare you for an hour."

"All right. I'll be there."

He called the president to inform him he would be away for an hour.

"The president has retired for the evening," he was told by a staff member. "You'll be with the attorney general if we need you?"

"Yes," Fletcher said. He hadn't said where he'd be; his meeting with Garson was obviously known to the Oval Office.

He arrived at the Justice Department a few minutes before eleven and was told the attorney general was wrapping up a meeting and would see him shortly. Ten minutes later, Assistant Attorney General Gertrude Klaus emerged from the office and walked past Fletcher, a quick smile her greeting.

"You can go in now, Mr. Fletcher," the aide said.

Garson's white shirt was open at the collar, a colorful flowered tie pulled loose from his neck. He wore black suspenders. Fletcher felt physically consumed by the big, strapping former Louisiana attorney general as he shook Fletcher's hand and invited him to take one of two high-back red-leather chairs in a corner of the spacious office, at a glass-topped Chippendale table.

"Something to drink, Chet?" Garson, a teetotaler, kept an assortment of soft drinks on hand to offer guests.

"No, thank you, Wayne," Fletcher said, adjusting himself to the chair's contour.

"Hell of a day, huh?" said Garson, taking the other chair. His voice was deep and resonant, tinged with New Orleans.

"Yes."

"Sorry to ask you here so late, Chet."

"I understand."

"I'm sure you're aware, Chet, of how highly the president values your contributions and service to him and to the nation. I have to admit that even though I've been around politics most of my life, the subtleties escape me now and then. Good thing the president has people like you who understand what's goin' on."

Garson sounded as though he was speaking off the cuff, saying what came to mind at the moment. Fletcher doubted it. The AG had decided what he would say long before Fletcher's arrival, and had the ability to make predetermined speeches sound spontaneous, a useful talent for a politician. And Garson was a politician, regardless of claims or titles to the contrary.

"I appreciate the kind words, Wayne."

"No kindness intended. Just speakin' the truth. Look, Chet, to the chase. I'm sure you'll appreciate that."

Yes, please, Fletcher thought. His fatigue was causing his mind to wander, to think of Gail home in bed and wanting to be with her.

"Know what I could never figure, Chet?"

"What?"

"Why somebody like you — I mean, hell, let's be honest, you're a brilliant man, got your Ph.D., written books, had a nice, cushy, relaxed job at a big university, married to a real nice woman, got a fine daughter, all of it — why somebody with all that would toss it over to get in the political rat race."

Does he expect an explanation?

"None a my business, of course," Garson said. "The important thing is that the president found himself someone of your caliber to help him advance his vision for this great country of ours."

"It's my pleasure to serve him." It seemed the thing to say.

"And I want you to know, Chet, that the president and I are aware of the extraordinary steps you had to take to protect him against these scurrilous charges by this writer, Marienthal, and that liar, Russo."

"*. . . the president and I are aware . . .*"

Translation: Whatever I say here has the blessing of the head man.

"Politics are almost as exciting as war, and quite as dangerous. In war you can only be killed once, but in politics many times." Churchill's words drifted through his consciousness. *How true,* he thought.

"You ever think about goin' back to teaching, Chet?"

"Of course. One day —"

"I don't mean four or five years down the road." He laughed. "Hell, not one of us can see down that road very far, now can we? You've always struck me, Chet, as somebody who believed in sacrifice, willing to fall on the sword for the greater good. I admire that in a man."

Fletcher felt light-headed. He removed his glasses and rubbed his eyes, put them on again. He hoped the attorney general wouldn't say more. But he did.

"So much of what we have to do in government involves weighing one thing against the other, doesn't it, Chet? I get a lot of flak for beefing up security to keep the terrorists from hitting us again, for keeping prisoners of war locked up, and such, even looking at library cards, see what people are readin' or researching. They say I'm trampling on civil liberties. But what's the alternative? Let the bastards kill more Americans? The American people put us in office to make those sort of tough decisions. If we're not up to the task, we shouldn't be here. Agree?"

"Yes."

"Still, I was personally appalled to see Mr. Russo gunned down like that in our Union Station. I suppose he asked for it, ratting out his buddies the way he did and going underground or to Israel. Same thing. But when I view it in the larger scheme of things, there's only one conclusion to come to: The life of a bottom-feeder like Russo doesn't mean much when you compare it to the damage he might have done to a great president. That's what I mean by having to weigh things. That's what you had to do, Chet, and you made the right decision."

The right decision.

How many meetings had there been on that subject of Russo and the Widmer hearings once there was a whiff of information about the allegation against the president? Four? Five? They'd taken place around Washington, away from the White House or major agencies, in hotel rooms and private homes, small groups, the lid on tight, the agenda secret until those from the administration or agency representatives with unquestioned loyalty to the White House were behind secure doors.

Strategies had been offered on how to derail the Widmer hearings and Russo's testimony. They ranged from launching an aggressive public relations campaign to digging into the pasts of Republicans on the subcommittee in the hope of turning up damaging dirt on them; smearing the writer of the book and his subject, Russo, to more aggressive solutions, including buying Russo and the writer off or letting Russo's former criminal colleagues know of his plan to travel to the United States and stoking the need for revenge.

During this intense period of meetings, he'd received a call from someone at the CIA, Mark Roper, who said it was urgent that they meet. A call to Garson confirmed for Fletcher that a meeting with Roper might be useful.

They met just after dark one evening in a cutout on the Washington Memorial Parkway, across from Theodore Roosevelt Island. Clandestine after-dark meetings with members of the nation's lead intelligence agency were not something with which Fletcher was comfortable. Roper, who struck Fletcher as surprisingly young, climbed into the passenger seat of Fletcher's Oldsmobile sedan, introduced himself, and said, "I know you're busy, Mr. Fletcher, and I'll take as little of your time as possible. We've analyzed the situation with this Russo and the Widmer hearings and have come to the conclusion that extreme steps might have to be taken. We're also aware that you, above all others, are responsible for the president's political life. I'm certain you agree that a second term is vitally important for the nation."

"Extreme steps?"

"The details aren't important, but time is. We know Russo plans to travel to Washington to testify. No matter how untrustworthy his testimony might be, its impact could be, in our opinion — and after careful analysis — severely damaging."

Fletcher agreed with the CIA man's statement. The potential political fallout for the man he served in the White House had caused sleepless nights and bouts of stomach distress. He nodded.

Roper looked out his window at a car that pulled into the same cutout, and saw it contained a young couple, probably looking for a place to neck. He turned to Fletcher. "We need your permission to take whatever action we deem necessary to protect the president."

"*My* permission?"

"As the man most involved in preserving this presidency for the future."

"Yes, I understand," Fletcher said. "Yes, I — it must be stopped."

Roper looked at him intently. "Your reputation isn't exaggerated, Mr. Fletcher," he said. "The president is in good hands."

He left Fletcher's car without saying another word, got into his own, and drove off. Fletcher stayed there for a few minutes until he felt he was intruding on what was going on behind the steamed-up windows of the other vehicle. As he drove home, he was tormented by what had transpired. *Extreme steps!* Did Roper mean something as extreme as doing physical harm to Russo? The thought was wrenching; it assaulted him physically, and he feared he might not be able to continue driving. But after sitting up alone and late in his home office and sipping a brandy from a seldom opened bottle, he'd calmed down and had a less dramatic perception of what Roper had meant. More comforting was the realization that it was out of his hands.

Initial reports that Russo had been killed by mobsters seeking revenge salved any pangs of conscience he might have suffered, allowing him to focus on his responsibility of guiding Adam Parmele to a deserved second term. The meeting with the CIA's Roper had never happened.

The attorney general stood and came around behind Fletcher, placing large hands on the political adviser's shoulders and kneading them. "Russo and Widmer and his hearings will die their natural death, Chet. Business as usual, which is what the country needs to go forward." He released his grip on Fletcher and stood silently behind him. Fletcher didn't move, feet planted on the floor, waiting to hear what was inevitable.

"The best way to put this behind the president, Chet, is for us to put some distance between you and the administration. The president will accept your resignation — for personal reasons. He'll respect your wishes to spend more time with your family and to get back to the thing you love most, shaping the young minds of our future leaders. I'm sure you'll have no problem lining up a job at a top university. And there'll be the lecture circuit, Chet, after this dies down and blows away like dry seed in a gale."

"I didn't realize what would happen," Fletcher said, realizing how feeble he sounded. "When I agreed to extreme measures, I —"

Garson came around to the front of the chair and loomed over Fletcher. "You're a brave man, Chet Fletcher, and I admire brave men."

Fletcher looked up and swallowed against bile in his throat. "In the same honor are held both the coward and the brave man," he said. "The idle man and he who has done much meet death alike."

Garson's expression was quizzical. He smiled. "That's true," he said, although Fletcher doubted that the attorney general truly understood what he'd said.

Fletcher slowly got up and went to the door. He stopped, turned, and said, "The president knows?"

He was met with stony silence.

Fletcher returned to his office in the West Wing, closed the door behind him, sat behind his desk and reached into a drawer, withdrawing a sheet of paper carrying his letterhead. He uncapped a favorite Montblanc pen, and slowly, carefully, methodically wrote a letter of resignation, which he placed in an envelope, sealed, and wrote on it: *The President of the United States.* He locked the envelope in a drawer, pocketed the key, and drove home.

FORTY-ONE

Kathryn Jalick was up before the sun after lying awake in bed for what seemed an eternity, and debated going back to work. There was a ten o'clock staff meeting at the Library of Congress she knew she should attend; seventeen boxes of material left to the library by the widow of a prominent nineteenth-century Washington physician. Their contents chronicling the doctor's life in D.C.'s social circles were to be opened and catalogued.

A palpable excitement always accompanied the opening of materials from the library's vast storage areas in which more than twenty million items awaited perusal and cataloguing. The occasion marked an opportunity to peer through a window into the private lives of others, a legal voyeuristic experience that was both valuable to the understanding of history and titillating.

On the other hand, Kathryn wasn't anxious to face questions from her colleagues about Rich, his book, or his disappearance. She'd received a number of calls from fellow workers since the news broke, friendly inquiries in search of firsthand inside information to share with the curious.

A call shortly after seven made the decision for her.

"Hey," a voice said.

"Rich. I was hoping you'd call."

"I'm in a booth, can't talk long. Look, I've decided what to do."

She sighed with relief. It didn't matter what decision he'd made, as long as it resulted in some sort of action. As the shrinks say, "Any action is better than no action. At least you have a fifty-fifty chance of being right."

"I'm glad," she said. "What are you going to do?"

"I'll fill you in when I see you. You going in to work today?"

"I haven't made up my mind."

"Go. I'll contact you there this afternoon. Can you get out early?"

"I suppose so. Rich, what's going on? What have you decided?"

"I'm going to New York."

"New York? When?"

"Later today, after you and I do a few things. Look, I have to run. Call you."

He hung up.

As she showered, the FBI agent monitoring the tap on her phone cursed under his breath. He'd picked up only the last few words of the conversation, not enough to nail down the location from which the call had been placed.

When the second call came moments later, she'd emerged from the shower wrapped in a terrycloth robe, her wet hair secured with a towel. The phone tap was working fine.

"Kathryn, it's Ellen."

"Hi."

"So what are you and Rich going to do?"

"I don't know, Ellen. Rich just called and —"

"He did? Where is he?"

"I honestly don't know."

"Kathryn, for God's sake, Rich has to turn over those tapes."

"Ellen, I can't help you or Geoff. Please try and understand. Look, I just came out of the shower and have to go to work. When I talk again with Rich, I'll tell him how much you and Geoff want to speak with him and urge him to call. Okay?"

"It doesn't look like I have much of a choice, does it?" Ellen said, not sounding happy.

Tim Stripling checked in from home with the Com Center at the Hoover

Building and was told of the conversation between Kathryn and Ellen Kelly. The botched pickup between Kathryn and Marienthal wasn't mentioned. Stripling told them he'd be available all day, his cell phone on. After going through a pot of coffee, he abandoned an earlier plan to hang around the house and decided instead to get in the car and cruise the neighborhood surrounding Union Station, where the previous call from Marienthal had been made. If Marienthal called again, he wanted to be able to respond as quickly as possible to the location.

He called Mark Roper from the car.

"Where are you?" Roper asked.

"In my car."

"Make something happen, Tim. Your client is getting nervous."

"Who's my client?"

"Timothy, just resolve this as quickly as possible. There's a lot riding on it."

"If I have to go beyond simply coming up with the tapes, I'll expect the usual fee."

"We can discuss that later."

"No, we can discuss it now."

"I'm hoping it won't be necessary to go beyond that."

"So am I. But if I do —"

"Yes, the usual fee."

"More later," Stripling said.

Ellen Kelly's call to Kathryn Jalick had been prompted and monitored by Geoff Lowe, who stood next to her in their apartment.

"What did she say?" he asked.

"She heard from Rich."

"Where is he?"

"She doesn't know. She said she's going to work today."

"At the library?"

"That's where she works, isn't it?"

He walked away from her and paced the room. "Maybe he's going to meet her there," he said into the air.

Ellen picked up her briefcase and went to the door. "Coming?" she asked.

"No, you go ahead. Tell Widmer I'm running down the tapes."

She dropped the briefcase. "No, Geoff, you tell him. I'm not in the mood to be yelled at this morning."

"I'll call."

"Good."

She was out the door.

Lowe followed soon after. He climbed in a cab parked at the corner and told the driver, "The Library of Congress."

The driver's expression said it wasn't familiar to him.

"Independence and Second Street Southeast," he growled. "Christ, you never heard of the Library of Congress?"

The driver heard the tone. He slipped the aging taxi into gear and lurched from the curb, forcing Lowe against the rear seat.

Mac Smith taught his class that morning. He returned home immediately following it and called Frank Marienthal's room in the Watergate Hotel.

"Anything from Richard yet?" Marienthal asked.

"No," said Smith. "Nothing on the machine. Where will you be the rest of the day?"

"Here. I'll stay close. I could wring his neck."

Smith ignored the comment. "I'll be here at the apartment most of the day," he said. "Annabel's at the gallery but should be home early afternoon. We'll let you know the minute we hear anything."

Smith turned on the TV to CNN to catch up on the news. Rich Marienthal's book and its charges against President Parmele continued to lead the newscast

462

despite there being nothing new to report — no statement from the White House, a press release from Senator Karl Widmer's office repeating the senator's intention to hold hearings into the "Parmele matter." The anchor ended the segment reporting that reliable sources had informed CNN that the president's trusted political adviser, Chet Fletcher, was close to tendering his resignation to return to private life, in order to spend more time with his family. No confirmation from Fletcher.

Interesting, Smith thought as he turned off the set and went to his office, where a sizable pile of paperwork awaited him. He'd never met Chet Fletcher, but from what he'd heard about the man, he wasn't the sort to run from a fight, to bail out when the going got tough. *To spend more time with his family.* Where had he heard *that* before?

The large reel-to-reel tape recorder in the FBI's Com Center turned slowly and often for the next few hours. Every call to Marienthal's apartment was dutifully recorded.

Simultaneously, calls to and from Mac and Annabel Smith's Watergate apartment were taped. Intercepting calls involving an attorney was problematic, should any of the conversation involve the discussion of legal issues. The agents on duty had been warned to turn off the recorder and their earphones in the event that happened. Whether those monitoring the calls would heed that admonition was conjecture.

Tired of looking for Marienthal on the streets surrounding Union Station, Stripling dumped his car in a parking garage and entered the station, where he took a small table in the bar area of America, a street-level restaurant affording a view of the front of the station on Massachusetts Avenue. He ordered a burger, fries, and a Coke and gazed out the window at people milling about, mostly tourists from the look of them and their silly hot-weather clothing, taking pictures of each other in front of the Columbus statue or the large yellow fountain, whose dancing waters had been turned off for reasons unknown. Fountains in Washington, D.C., seem always to be off on the hottest days.

He'd just finished his lunch and ordered a triple-scoop butterscotch sundae when the cell phone on the table rang.

"Yeah?"

"We have an address for you."

He wrote down the house number on upper 16th Street and other information, pressed End, and asked for a check. Minutes later he was on his way out of Union Station and headed for the garage, the sundae just wishful thinking.

Stripling wasn't the only one with upper 16th Street as a destination.

Kathryn Jalick had just started removing materials from the first box of the physician's papers at the Library of Congress when a colleague summoned her to a phone.

"Kathryn, it's Rich. Can you leave now?"

"I — I'll just have to. Where are you?"

"At Winard's house."

"Is that where you've been all along?"

"Yeah. He left on a tour with a band. Can you come right now?"

"Yes. He's on Sixteenth, right?"

"Right. You've been here before."

"I know where it is. What are we going to do?"

"Fill you in when you arrive. Make sure nobody follows you."

"Follow me? I don't think —"

"Just be sure nobody does. See you in a few minutes."

She went into her director's office and

announced she had to leave.

"Is everything all right?" the director asked.

"Yes, I'm okay," Kathryn answered.

"Does it have to do with Richard and his book?"

Kathryn nodded. "It'll be over soon."

"I hope so. Take care, Kathryn."

"I will. And thanks for understanding."

Geoff Lowe's level of understanding of anything had reached its nadir. Upon arriving at the Library of Congress, he'd taken a seat at a table in the main reading room and looked for Kathryn Jalick to emerge from behind the scenes. He saw her a few times as she passed from one area to another, and covered his face with a magazine he'd taken from a rack. Although the air-conditioning was welcome, he was uncomfortable sitting there in the midst of a hundred people buried in books. *Weirdos,* he thought, taking in those in his immediate vicinity, some of whom looked strange — were different — in how they dressed and allowed their hair and beards to grow wild.

He made frequent trips to the men's room or outside to escape the reading room's atmosphere. He couldn't justify being there like some hotel detective hiding behind potted plants in search of straying spouses, but he didn't know what else to do. Ellen had been unsuccessful in convincing Kathryn to lead him to Rich. Senator Widmer had become irascible, even by his standards, and most of his wrath was directed at Lowe. He understood the senator's anger to some extent; the whole idea of hearings into Parmele's days as CIA director had been Lowe's, prompted by his having met Richard Marienthal. It was like handing Widmer a prized political gift, the sort of scandal that despite its origins had legs, would capture the media, and by extension sway public opinion. Was it true? It didn't matter. This was politics. Indeed, this was war, and Lowe viewed himself as a consecrated combatant.

All he wanted that day was to get lucky, to see Marienthal walk into the library to meet Kathryn, carrying a bagful of tapes. If he didn't listen to reason about handing them over — he'd use his best "It's for the good of the country" speech — he'd hit him over the head and just take the damn tapes, run back to Widmer's office and present them to the old bastard like a sacrificial offering: "Here! I offer you this young virgin! I came, I saw, I conquered! Reward me!"

He was sitting on a low concrete wall outside the library, tie pulled loose, collar open, sweat running down his face, watching people come and go, when Kathryn Jalick emerged through the main entrance after having offered her handbag for inspection by security guards inside. Keeping employees and visitors from leaving with purloined books was as pressing an issue at the Library of Congress as guarding against the unbalanced entering with guns.

Lowe turned so that his back was to her as she ran past thirty feet from him and waved down a taxi.

"Damn!" Lowe said as he got up and watched the cab with Kathryn in it pull from the curb and go to the corner, where it stopped for a red light. Another empty taxi approached from the same direction as the previous one. Lowe stepped into the street and stopped it, climbed in the back. "See that cab up there at the light?" he said to the driver. "Follow it."

The driver, a burly black man with a beard, turned and frowned. "Like in the movies?"

"Yeah, yeah, I know," said Lowe. "Just do it, okay? I'll take care of you."

Rich Marienthal anxiously awaited Kathryn's arrival at Winard Jackson's apartment. After having contacted her at the Library of Congress, he'd placed a call to the family home in Bedford, New York.

"Mom? It's Rich."

"Are you all right?"

"Yes, I'm fine."

"We've been so worried about you," she said. "You've been on the news. No one knew where you were. Your father is furious. He's in Washington looking for you. He's with Mackensie Smith."

"I know. I spoke with him there. He didn't tell you?"

"No. Richard, what is going on?"

"I'll explain it all later, Mom. Look, I'm sorry about what's happened, but it's all going to work out fine. Just fine. I'm coming to New York."

"When?"

"Today. Tonight. I'll come to the house."

"Thank God you're all right," she said, and started to cry.

"Come on, Mom," he said, "no tears. You'll make me feel guilty."

"I know," she said. "I don't mean to —"

"I have to go now," he said. "See you later."

"Be careful."

"I will."

His next call was to Greenleaf at Hobbes House in New York.

"Sam, it's Rich Marienthal."

"Jesus, where have you been?"

"Staying with a friend."

"I don't mean where you were. I mean, why did you disappear? The book's just coming out. The media's going nuts wanting to interview you. Geoff Lowe —"

"How is my buddy Geoff?"

"Rich, what about the tapes and the hearings?"

"What about them?"

"Don't get cute with me, Rich. You may be enjoying your reclusive little game, but I'm not. There's a lot riding on those Widmer hearings. The Democrats are already spinning the hell out of it, claiming the book is nothing but the figment of Russo's overactive imagination. They're saying you're afraid to face the media because you know it's all fiction. It's time to step up to the plate, Rich, get out there and use the tapes to validate the book."

"I'm not sure I want to do that, Sam."

Greenleaf's voice rose in volume. "Now,

hold on, Rich, and listen to me. You entered into a deal with us, and that included cooperating with the Widmer hearings. Russo getting killed wasn't your fault. You couldn't control that. But you can control the tapes and how they're used." He paused for breath. "I'm getting the impression that you knew all along that Russo's claims weren't valid, that you conned us."

"I didn't con anybody," Marienthal said, feeling his own ire rising. "It doesn't matter whether I believed Russo or not. All I did was write a book based on what he told me, and that's what you bought, nothing more, nothing less. You're right; Louis Russo's death was beyond my control. And you're right that I can determine what happens with the tapes. I'm sorry if things haven't turned out the way we all wanted them to. I still haven't decided what to do with the tapes, but I'm getting close."

Marienthal could almost see Greenleaf in his office chair, willing himself to become calm and to inject reason into the argument. Judging from Greenleaf's revised tone, that's exactly what he'd done.

"Okay, Rich, let's approach this in a reasonable, rational manner. There's an opportunity here to salvage the book and see it achieve the sort of success we all envisioned for it, especially you. I must admit that I don't understand why you've adopted this protective attitude toward the tapes. All they represent is what Russo told you, true or false. Playing them for the public at the hearings is the fair way to go — the American way to go, it seems to me. Let people hear what the man had to say in his own voice, and make up their own minds about his veracity."

The American way, Rich thought. A nation ruled by the political sound bite.

Senator Widmer would proclaim in stentorian tones that the American way did not include assassinating visiting foreign leaders, and that those responsible were not fit to hold high office.

The White House would disperse its cadre of talking heads to the Sunday morning talk shows to accuse Widmer and his Republican supporters of blatant political motives in an election season, and to brand Russo and Marienthal as kooky pawns of the right wing.

Either way, and no matter how the public reacted, this was not the end result Richard Marienthal intended when he set out to write a best-selling book, his breakthrough, his claim to fame, his credential

472

for a long and lucrative writing career.

"I'll get back to you no later than to-morrow," Marienthal said.

"Tomorrow?"

"Yeah, tomorrow."

He ended the conversation and waited for Kathryn to arrive.

Stripling parked across the street from the building in which Winard Jackson's apartment was located, and where Rich Marienthal had been holed up. He'd received another call on his cell phone from the Com Center in the Hoover Building, advising him that intercepted messages indicated that the subject had announced his intention to go to New York later that day, and that the subject did in fact have in his possession certain tapes.

He wasn't sure what his next step should be. He had no way of knowing how many people might be with Marienthal inside the building, and was reluctant to attempt to confront the writer there. Marienthal was going to New York — which meant he'd be coming out, hopefully soon. Better to wait for that to happen, and trust he'd be alone. He pressed his elbow against the Smith & Wesson in its holster beneath his arm, comforted by its presence, although confident he wouldn't have to use it. Marienthal was a writer, probably effete, lightweight — a lover, not a fighter. The worst that could happen was that he'd have to display the gun to show Marienthal that he meant business. "Don't be stupid, kid. Just give me the tapes and go write a poem somewhere."

A taxi arrived. Stripling slid lower in the seat, but not so low that he couldn't see the attractive young woman in a short skirt and wearing large glasses get out of the cab, pay the fare, and go to the building's front door.

A second cab came around the corner and pulled up to the curb a half block from the first. A short, stocky young man wearing a suit got out and leaned through the open front passenger window. Stripling couldn't hear the words, but it was obvious the passenger wasn't flattering the driver. He shoved his hand in the window and backed away; both cabs drove off.

The woman with glasses read names on the intercom panel, pressed a button, and spoke into the panel. There was the faint sound of a buzzer; she pushed open the door and disappeared inside.

Stripling returned his attention to the short, stocky guy standing on the sidewalk.

He'd moved behind a tree, shielding him from view of the door through which the woman had entered.

Who's he? he wondered. *Who's she?* Must be Marienthal's live-in girlfriend. Nice legs. She could do better than get involved with a writer. With so many more single women than single men in D.C., women must get desperate, he reasoned, more or less.

What's the stocky guy going to do, just keep standing there behind the tree? Is he waiting for the writer, too, or has he got the hots for the leggy gal with the big glasses? Was he the writer's buddy? That could complicate things.

Nothing to do but wait.

FORTY-TWO

"It is so good to see you," Marienthal said when Kathryn walked through the door to the apartment. They sustained their embrace and kissed until Marienthal stepped back, his hands on her shoulders, and smiled. "You look so sexy in those glasses."

"Stop it," she said. "I sure don't feel sexy. But I am relieved to see you. We're going to New York?"

"Not *us*. I'm going."

She looked at him quizzically.

He led her into the small kitchen, where they sat at the table. He took her hands in his and said, "I owe you a big apology, Kate."

"For what?"

"For being blind to reality. For being greedy. For forgetting who I really am."

She wiped away a tear that had escaped her right eye and smiled. "You were all of those things, Rich, and maybe more. But that's past tense."

"You bet it is. Here's what I want to do."

It took him only five minutes to outline his plans for her. When he was finished, he asked, "Make sense?"

"I think so," she said.

"Good. Let's get going."

He went to a small corkboard on which Winard had pinned up a typewritten list of useful phone numbers, dialed the one for a local cab company, and gave the dispatcher the address.

Five minutes later, he picked up his canvas shoulder bag from the floor, opened the front door, and locked it behind them, and they went up the narrow stairs to the front foyer. Marienthal looked through a small window. "The cab's here," he said.

They went directly to the taxi. Marienthal tapped on the front passenger window. The driver lowered it slightly, and Marienthal said in a loud voice, "Union Station."

Stripling and Lowe watched the departure of Rich and Kathryn from their respective vantage points. Stripling started his engine and fell in behind the cab. Lowe left the tree and stood helplessly on the sidewalk. He'd heard Marienthal say, "Union Station," but was without transportation.

Marienthal looked back before the cab turned the corner.

"Did you see that guy?" he asked Kathryn.

"What guy?"

"Up the block from the house. It looked like Geoff."

She, too, looked back, but by then they were off 16th Street. "Are you sure?" she asked.

"No, but I think it was."

Lowe walked south on 16th until finding a cab. "Union Station," he said. "I'm in a rush."

The driver laughed without mirth. "You guys slay me," he said. "You got to catch a train? Leave earlier! I'm not getting a ticket because you don't leave early enough." He repeated: "Slays me."

It just might, thought Lowe.

Stripling pulled into a vacant one-hour parking spot near the station, jumped out of the car, and shoved quarters into the meter. Hopefully, he'd be back before the hour was up. If not, Roper could pay for the ticket and tow charges. He ran across the plaza and reached the main entrance just as Marienthal had finished paying their driver and he and Kathryn headed inside. Told Marienthal planned to travel to New York, Stripling assumed the couple

478

would go to one of Amtrak's booths, which they did. Marienthal and Kathryn stood in a short line in front of the ticket counter and checked the departure board. The next train to New York was scheduled to leave in fifteen minutes. Stripling fell in behind them, his attention focused on the canvas shoulder bag Marienthal carried.

What now? Should he make a grab for the bag and run? Not a good idea. Too many people, including plenty of security guards patrolling the area. Besides, it wasn't his MO to play purse snatcher. His best bet, he decided, was to stay close and pick a moment when there were fewer people. He was certain the girlfriend wouldn't pose a problem, although you never knew about people. People like him. He'd been mistaken over the years for a bank clerk, an insurance salesman, and worse. He liked it that way, the faceless face in the crowd, that nondescript guy in the drab suit who was probably married to a domineering woman, a milquetoast of the first order.

He couldn't hear the transaction between Marienthal and the ticket agent, but when it was completed, Marienthal backed away from the counter and stepped on Stripling's foot.

"Sorry," said Marienthal.

"It's okay," said Stripling.

"Sir?" the agent said to Stripling.

"What? Oh, right. Round-trip to New York."

As he waited for the ticket to be issued, he kept his eye on Marienthal and Kathryn, who were walking in the direction of Amtrak's departure gates. He followed, keeping a respectful distance, until they stopped short of the gate. Marienthal reached in the pocket of his safari jacket and handed Kathryn something small, which she slipped into her purse. After a final embrace, Marienthal headed for the waiting train, leaving Kathryn standing there. Had Marienthal handed the shoulder bag to her, Stripling would have been faced with a dilemma. But he hadn't.

He followed Marienthal to the train and boarded the same car. When the writer chose a seat, he took the one directly behind him.

Marienthal had laid his canvas bag on the seat next to him; Stripling could see it through the space between seats. He tried to come up with some ruse to cause Marienthal to get up from his seat, leaving the bag behind, but couldn't conjure anything that made sense. He didn't have much time to consider it because the doors to the train closed and an announcement was made that the train to New York was now leaving.

Geoff Lowe looked like a man who'd just escaped a mugging. He was drenched with sweat, his white shirt pulled loose from his pants, his hair drooping over his ears in wet strands. He stood in the station's main hall. He went in the direction of the Amtrak ticket counter, passing President Cigars and the Swatch Watch shop, muttering under his breath and trying not to bump into the steady flow of people coming in both directions. He circumvented the ticket counter and turned left in front of Exclusive Shoe Shine.

"Shine, sir?" Joe Jenks asked.

Lowe ignored him and kept walking, causing Jenks to say to one of the other bootblacks, "Looks like the man needs a shower more than a shine."

Lowe had almost reached the gates when he spotted Kathryn Jalick coming from a public phone booth near the bank of public lockers. She carried a shopping bag she'd bought from the travel store near where she and Rich had parted.

He moved quickly to cut her off.

"Geoff?" she said, startled at his sudden appearance.

"Where is he?" he asked.

"Rich? He's — he's on his way to New York."

"New York? Why's he going there?"

"I —"

"Is he going to Hobbes House?"

"I don't know."

"He has the tapes with him?"

"I'm sorry, Geoff, but I'm late for an appointment," she said, walking away.

He stayed at her side. "He has the tapes. Right?"

"Yes. He has the tapes," she responded, picking up her pace in the direction of the Main Hall and Massachusetts Avenue.

He grabbed her arm. "Kathryn," he said, "don't play games with me. I want those tapes. I *need* those tapes."

"Get your hands off me," she snapped, shaking him loose and continuing to walk.

He kept stride with her. "Rich wouldn't have his book contract if it hadn't been for me," he said. "I set it up for him. He owes me!"

They reached Mass Avenue, where a dozen cabs awaited passengers. The dispatcher opened the door to the first taxi in line and Kathryn jumped in. So did Lowe.

"Where do you think you're going?" she asked.

"I'm sticking with you, Kathryn. You'll be in touch with Rich. He has the tapes. I want them. I'm hanging in with you until I get them."

The cabdriver, tired of the delay, turned and asked, "You want a taxi or a marriage counselor?"

Kathryn's nostrils flared as she glared at Lowe. "The Watergate Apartments," she told the driver through clenched teeth.

The train hadn't gone far when Stripling's cell phone sounded.

"Yeah?"

"Subject's female partner reported en route to Watergate apartment." The terse message ended with a sharp click.

Stripling knew the Watergate was Mackensie Smith's apartment. It occurred to him that no one knew he was on a train headed for New York, seated behind the subject of the search, Richard Marienthal — or that he was within reach of the infamous tapes at the heart of the search. Not that it mattered — except to the cop who would have his car towed. His whereabouts were otherwise irrelevant. What did matter was taking possession of the tapes and delivering them to Curly and Moe, or Mark Roper, or Gertrude Klaus, or whoever else wanted them.

He surveyed the rest of the car. No wonder Amtrak was losing money, he thought. There were only three other passengers, two women working on laptops seated at the far end of the car and a man at the opposite end who'd dozed off, his head resting against the window.

"We'll shortly be arriving at Baltimore International Airport," a voice soon announced over the PA system. "Passengers getting off at that station should be sure to gather any personal belongings."

Stripling's mind now shifted into a higher gear. How many new passengers would board this car at Baltimore? Would Marienthal decide to change his seat, perhaps move to another, more crowded car? Was there anything to be gained by waiting to arrive in New York before making his move to snatch the bag? He decided there wasn't. He'd been on this train before. The Baltimore airport stop would be a brief one, no more than a few minutes.

This was the time to act.

When the train stopped and the doors opened, he would move quickly and definitely. He would get up, step to where

Marienthal sat, press the gun to the writer's head, simultaneously grab the bag from the seat, and run from the car. It would take only seconds. He mentally timed out his moves. Two seconds to get from his seat to Marienthal, two seconds to brandish the gun and swipe the bag, three seconds to run from the seat to the door. Seven seconds in all. It would happen so fast that by the time Marienthal recovered from the initial shock of a gun at his head, Stripling would be gone, down the stairs from the platform and into the crowd. Marienthal wouldn't even see who'd taken the bag. And if he did, he'd never be able to mentally process the man he'd seen in those fleeting two seconds of face-to-face contact.

The train slowed as it neared the station, and Stripling tensed. He slipped his hand beneath his suit jacket and wrapped his fingers around the stock of the Smith & Wesson. *Just don't make a dumb move,* he silently warned Marienthal. *Don't get hurt over some silly tapes.*

Almost there.

Marienthal stood.

Stripling blinked. What was Marienthal about to do, get off at the Baltimore airport station?

Marienthal stood in the aisle next to his seat, looked down at his shoulder bag, and headed up the aisle toward the restrooms. It took Stripling a moment to shake off his surprise. He looked back and saw Marienthal disappear into one of the lavatories. The train came to a noisy stop, and Stripling heard the whoosh of doors opening. He jumped up, reached over Marienthal's seat back, grabbed the bag by its shoulder strap, walked quickly from the train, went down the steps two at a time, and hailed a waiting taxi.

"Where to?" he was asked by the driver.

"The nearest car rental agency," Stripling replied, settling back and smiling.

He was delivered to a Hertz office, where he rented a midsize sedan, drove from the garage, and headed for the highway leading back to Washington. While stopped at a light, he unzipped the bag and shoved his hand inside. What he felt was soft, cloth. He pulled two pairs of socks and shorts from the bag, followed by a black T-shirt, a handkerchief, and a leather kit containing toiletries.

"What the hell?" he muttered.

The light had turned green; drivers behind him leaned on their horns. He went through the intersection, pulled to the curb, and surveyed what he'd taken from the bag. "Son of a bitch!" he said loudly, flinging the clothing to the floor. "Son of a bitch."

FORTY-THREE

The taxi carrying Kathryn Jalick and Geoff Lowe from Union Station pulled up at the entrance to Mac and Annabel's Watergate apartment building. Kathryn had taken money from her purse prior to arriving and handed it to the driver. She opened the door on her side. Lowe opened his and grabbed the handles of the shopping bag. So did Kathryn.

"I'll carry it for you," Lowe said.

"I'll carry it myself," she responded angrily.

They entered the lobby, where Kathryn gave her name to the uniformed man behind the reception desk and said she was there to visit with the Mackensie Smiths.

"Yes, Ms. Jalick. Mr. Smith told me you'd be coming and said to send you right up." He pushed a button behind the desk that activated the lock on a set of glass doors leading to the inner lobby and elevators. Lowe headed for them with her.

"Sir," the lobby guard said sternly.

"I'm with her," Lowe said.

"No he's not," Kathryn said, pushing open the doors.

"I'm on Senator Widmer's staff," Lowe said.

"I'll call Mr. Smith," said the guard.

The doors closed behind Kathryn, and Lowe watched her enter a waiting elevator.

Mac Smith answered the internal call from the front desk.

"Mr. Smith, there's a Mr. Lowe here who accompanied Ms. Jalick. He wishes to come up."

"Have him wait," Smith said, "until Ms. Jalick arrives. I'll ask her."

A few minutes later, Smith called back. "Tell Mr. Lowe he'll have to wait until Ms. Jalick says he can join her."

"Yes, sir."

Lowe visibly fumed. "Senator Widmer won't like this," he told the guard. "Somebody's going to answer for this." He paced the outer lobby while pulling out his cell phone and calling information in New York City. A minute later he was connected with Sam Greenleaf at Hobbes House.

"Rich Marienthal is on his way to New York," Lowe told Greenleaf. "He has the tapes."

"He's coming here?" Greenleaf said.

"Where else would he be going?"

"His *parents* live in New York" was Greenleaf's reply.

"That's right. But why would he take the tapes to his parents' home?"

"This whole project is becoming nightmarish, Geoff. Pamela's on the warpath and —"

"Who's Pamela?"

"Pamela Warren. My publisher. We've gotten a couple of early notices already. They're dismissing the book as the figment of the old mobster's imagination. One reviewer is labeling it a hoax."

"Don't blame me," Lowe said. "Marienthal's the one who's screwed everything up."

Greenleaf abruptly ended the call.

Mac and Annabel Smith greeted Kathryn at their apartment door and led her to the dining room, where she placed the shopping bag on the table. "The tapes," she said.

"The tapes," Smith said, emphasizing the words. "Rich gave them to you?"

"In a sense. He'd had them in a public locker at Union Station. He gave me the key before taking the train to New York."

"He's on his way there now?" Annabel asked.

"Right. He's going to visit his mother and go to Hobbes House at some point."

"Why is Mr. Lowe with you?" Mac asked.

Kathryn explained, ending with a rueful laugh. "He thinks Rich has the tapes with him. If he only knew they were in this shopping bag that he was sitting next to in the cab."

Kathryn removed the plastic bags containing the tapes and Rich's handwritten notes from the shopping bag and laid them on the table.

"Have you heard them?" Mac asked.

"No," Kathryn said, "and I don't want to. You can listen if you'd like."

"I have no interest in hearing them," said Smith. To Annabel: "You?"

She shook her head.

"What does Rich want you to do with them?" Annabel asked.

Kathryn inhaled and blew air through pursed lips. "He told me to ask for your advice, Mac."

"He did, did he?" Smith said. "What if I don't have any advice?"

"That would be a first," Annabel said, playfully.

"Let me explain," Smith said. "These tapes — or more accurately, the use they

491

might be put to — have significant political ramifications. If they end up with Republicans like Senator Widmer, they'll be used to attack a sitting president, who, I might add, is doing a good job in my opinion. But what if the charges made by Russo on the tapes are true? What if the president *did* order the assassination of a visiting head of state while CIA director? Hardly the sort of thing a president of the United States should have on his résumé."

Annabel went into the kitchen to get something to drink and returned with a pitcher of iced tea she'd prepared earlier. She poured three glasses, handed them to her husband and to Kathryn, and raised her glass in a toast. "To the famous tapes," she said, adding, "are you interested in my opinion about what should happen to them?"

"Of course," Mac said.

"The question is whether the man on those tapes is telling the truth. Unfortunately, he's dead and can't vouch for what he told Rich. It's my understanding that Rich never came up with any corroborating evidence to support the claims about President Parmele. Am I right? Mac, you've read the book."

"Skimmed it," he said. "No, there

doesn't seem to be anything to corroborate Mr. Russo's story." He looked at Kathryn: "Do you know of anything, Kathryn? Has Rich indicated any supporting evidence he might be sitting on?"

"No," she said, sipping her cold tea. "He said a few times that he wished there were some hard facts to back up Louis Russo."

"Well, Kathryn," Smith said, "the only advice I can give you is to do with the tapes what Rich wants done with them. After all, they do belong to him."

Annabel chimed in: "Has Rich told you, Kathryn, what he wants done with them? Has he instructed you what to do with them?"

"He told me —"

"Yes?"

"He told me that if you didn't feel strongly about the tapes going to someone — to the president or Senator Widmer — that I should use my own judgment."

"I've thought recently," Smith said, "that another option would be to donate them to an institution for safekeeping, not to be opened to researchers for a specified period of time."

"But does it matter how much time passes," Kathryn asked, "if what's on the tapes isn't true?"

Neither Mac nor Annabel replied.

"I think I'd better go," Kathryn said, "but I don't want to bump into Geoff Lowe again if he's still downstairs."

"No problem," said Annabel. "We'll leave through the garage. I'll drive you."

"Oh, no, there's no need to —"

"I insist," Annabel said.

Kathryn put the tapes and notes back into the shopping bag, and Mac walked her to the door. "I wish I had some wisdom to dispense," he said, "but somehow I know you'll do the right thing without anyone's advice."

"I'll try," she said, kissing him on the cheek.

When they were gone, Smith called down to the desk. "Is Mr. Lowe still there?" he asked.

"Yes, he is, Mr. Smith."

"Send him up."

Lowe's first words upon entering the apartment were "Where's Kathryn?"

"She left," Smith said.

"Left? Where did she go?"

"I have no idea, Mr. Lowe. We haven't been formally introduced." Smith extended his hand, which Lowe took weakly. "Iced tea?" Smith asked. "My wife makes very good iced tea."

"No. Thanks anyway," Lowe said, looking past Mac into the apartment's recesses.

"I told you she's not here," Smith said. He walked to the open sliding glass doors to the terrace and looked back. "Join me, Mr. Lowe?"

They stood side by side, their hands on the terrace's railing, their attention on the Potomac River. "I'm well aware, Mr. Lowe, why you and Senator Widmer would like to have those tapes. Your hearings won't have much bite without them."

"We can do without them," Lowe said, his voice betraying his true feelings.

"Perhaps," said Smith. "Let me ask you a question. There's considerable doubt about the veracity of what Mr. Russo said on those tapes. What I don't understand is why you and the senator would want to hold a public hearing based upon allegations that can't be substantiated."

Lowe's hands in motion substituted for words. "The book, the taped voice of a dead man, the questioning. It's politics," he said finally.

"Politics," Smith repeated, not trying to keep scorn from his voice. "The *game* of politics. Well, though everybody seems to say it is, I don't consider politics a game,

Mr. Lowe. Politics are more important than that. Is winning the political game that vital to you and your boss, Mr. Lowe? Are you and the senator really willing to destroy a president of the United States in order to win what you consider a game?"

"Parmele doesn't deserve a second term," Lowe said.

"Isn't that for the voters to decide?"

"As long as they have the facts."

"The facts as you perceive them. Mr. Russo's claims don't represent facts. They might be true, but there's not a shred of evidence to back them up. I'm a lawyer, Mr. Lowe. I deal in evidence. I deal in the facts. And one fact, as far as I'm concerned, is that you and others like you don't belong in government on any level. I find you despicable. I think it's time you left. Thanks for stopping by."

"You're part of this, aren't you?" Lowe snarled. "You've been helping Marienthal hide those tapes all along. Well, Smith, you and anybody else involved in this cover-up will answer to Senator Widmer and the committee. We'll drag you in front of it and make your life miserable."

Smith left the terrace, went to the apartment door, and opened it. Lowe glared at him from the terrace, fists clenched at his sides, his face red and sweaty.

"Good day, Mr. Lowe," Smith said from the door.

Lowe stormed from the terrace and pushed past Smith, his shoulder bumping him. Smith watched him go down the hall to the elevators and disappear into one.

Smith went to his office, where he called Frank Marienthal's room at the Watergate Hotel to tell him what had transpired.

"He's gone to New York?" the father said. "What's he doing there?"

"Visiting Mary, according to Kathryn, and then having a meeting with his publisher."

"I will never understand that boy," Marienthal said. "I will never understand any of his generation."

"Well, Frank," said Mac, "I suppose they'll never understand us, either. Look, I suggest you grab a flight back home and catch up with Rich there. In the meantime, Kathryn will decide what to do with the tapes. That's the way it should be."

Kathryn Jalick entered the apartment she shared with Rich Marienthal. She changed into shorts and a Library of Congress T-shirt. She poured a glass of wine and put a Buck Hill CD on the stereo. She sat on the couch, the bag of tapes at her feet, leaned back, closed her eyes, and thought of him, of what they'd been through since he started the book. Was it all behind them now? She hoped so. She wanted things to be the way they were when they first met, easy and loving, finding the time to draw upon that love. She was deep in that reverie when the phone on the table next to the couch rang.

"Hello?"

"It's me."

"Hi. Where are you?"

"On the train. You'll never believe what happened. We were pulling into the Baltimore station. I had this sudden urge to go to the bathroom and went. I left my shoulder bag on my seat. When I came back, it was gone."

"Somebody stole it?"

"Yeah. Can you believe it?"

"What was in it?"

"Socks, shorts, a toothbrush, my overnight kit. Why would anybody want to steal stuff like that is beyond me. How are you?"

"Fine. I saw Mac and Annabel."

"And?"

"Mac said the tapes belong to you and that you'll have to make the decision about what to do with them."

"After what I've put you through, Kate, they belong to us. Like I told you before I left, if Mac didn't have any definite ideas about what to do with them, I leave it up to you. Yours is a good, clean, clear mind."

"That's a heavy burden. I know how hard you worked to get them."

"That doesn't matter anymore. Have you heard from Geoff?"

"Oh, yes, I certainly did." She told him of the confrontation at Union Station and what occurred after that.

Marienthal laughed. "He was sitting in a cab with you right next to the tapes and never knew it."

"The irony wasn't lost on me. You're breaking up."

"Batteries are low. I'll call you from Mom's."

As she twisted on the couch after hanging up, her foot caught the shopping bag, tipping it over and spilling its contents on the rug. She picked up one of the plastic bags and removed tapes from it. Rich had written on them in ink: Russo, where the interview took place, the date, and a few words to describe the contents. "Assassination" appeared on some of them.

She got up, turned the air-conditioning control on the window unit to its coolest setting, grabbed old newspapers from the kitchen, balled them up and placed them on the floor of the fireplace. She added kindling and logs left over from the previous winter that were stacked next to the fireplace, and lighted the paper. The orange flames were comforting; she and Rich had spent many nights together with the fire going, discussing their dreams — and each other.

One by one, she fed the tapes and Rich's handwritten notes into the flames. When the last tape had been consumed, she returned to the couch, raised her wineglass, and said with a satisfied smile on her lips, "To you, Louis Russo. May you finally rest in peace — wherever."

FORTY-FOUR

FOUR MONTHS LATER

"I have an announcement to make," Mackensie Smith said to the thirty guests gathered in his apartment. A blue spruce Christmas tree festooned with colorful decorations from their single days, augmented by more recent joint purchases, took up a corner of the living room. Other judiciously selected and placed representations of the Christmas season that was only a week away added to the party's festive spirit. Annabel had arranged an array of food on the dining room table.

"I don't have permission to make this announcement, but somehow I don't think the subjects of it will mind," Mac said. He raised his champagne glass: "To Rich and Kathryn, who informed me only today that they've decided to tie the knot, tie one to the other for life. Here's to them and to many blissful years together — close together."

There was applause and "Here! Here!" and a few inevitable but funny comments about the perils of married life. A man raised his glass and said, "I have a toast to propose, too. To another four years with President Adam Parmele."

Smith said, "I know this is Washington, but there'll be no politics spoken in this house, not at this time of year."

"What else is there to talk about in Washington?" someone quipped.

"The Redskins, the new season at the Washington Opera and Kennedy Center, anything but politics," Annabel proclaimed with enough force to indicate she meant it.

Rich and Kathryn were the last to leave.

"A wonderful party," Kathryn said. "I feel as though it was to celebrate us."

"It was," said Smith. "You deserve it. Set a date yet?"

"The spring," Rich said. "In Kansas. I called Mom and Dad this morning to break the news. Actually, I put Kathryn on the phone and she made the announcement."

"His mom cried," Kathryn said, shedding her own tears. "She sounded really happy."

"And your dad?" Mac asked.

"He congratulated me and said they'd come out to Kansas for the wedding. For him to volunteer to go to Kansas is the coup of the year."

"As it should be," said Annabel.

"How's the new job?" Mac asked Marienthal.

"Good. I mean, grinding out press releases for the Department of Agriculture doesn't represent my life's goal, but it'll do until I finish the new book I'm working on and it gets published. By the way, it *is* a novel."

The call to fill a position in the agriculture department's public information office had come out of the blue from one of the president's appointees. Had destroying tapes that might have thwarted the president's quest for a second term played a role in the job offer? Follow-up articles about Rich's book mentioned that he'd destroyed the tapes because, as he'd been quoted, "I seriously question whether what Louis Russo claimed in my book actually happened. That's why the tapes are gone." He added with a chuckle, "But I still think it makes for a good read."

Unfortunately, the negative publicity surrounding the book seriously eroded its sales. Of the 30,000 copies in the initial printing, more than half would be returned to Hobbes House for full credit or end up on remainder tables at the sale price of a dollar.

"Whatever happened to your buddy, Mr. Lowe?" Smith asked as the young couple prepared to leave.

"Last I heard, he left Senator Widmer's staff and was going to work for some Texas congressman."

"His choice to leave?" Annabel asked, "or was he asked to leave?"

"We don't know," Kathryn said. "His girlfriend, Ellen Kelly, broke up with him and left town. I've lost touch with her. And with Senator Widmer announcing his retirement after canceling the hearings, there wouldn't be a job for Geoff anyway."

"As shrewd as old Senator Widmer is, he put too much faith in Lowe where the tapes were concerned," Smith said, helping Kathryn on with her coat. "If the subcommittee had subpoenaed the tapes, putting a torch to them like you did would have landed you in some legal hot water."

"That's all in your past," Annabel offered, kissing them on the cheek as they went through the door, a paper plate of Christmas cookies nestled in Marienthal's arms. "It's all future for you now."

There were many holiday parties going on in Washington on that day, including one in full swing at an Irish pub near

504

MPD's First District headquarters. A large banner strung across the back bar read: HAPPY RETIREMENT, BRET.

Two dozen of Bret's colleagues and a smattering of their wives and girlfriends had joined the big, beefy detective to celebrate his leaving the force. Many of his buddies had taken full advantage of the free drinks and were on their way to a serious headache the next morning.

Mullin held a glass of ginger ale in his hand as he accepted their congratulations and a stream of wisecracks from fellow cops. Vinnie Accurso stood next to him, his arm around his former partner's shoulder.

"Where's Leshin?" Mullin asked. "He didn't come."

"He'll be here, Bret," Accurso said, punching Mullin on the arm. "You think the chief would miss the chance to celebrate getting rid of you?"

"I wasn't that bad," said Mullin, sipping his drink.

"What are you gonna do retired?" someone asked.

"I thought I'd do some traveling," Mullin replied. "You know, see the world. My daughter wants me to come out to Colorado and spend some time with her." He pulled a letter from his pocket that he'd received the previous week in which she suggested they spend some time together — now that he no longer drank.

"I also figured I'd go overseas," he said. "I've been reading a lot about the problem in the Middle East. You know, Israelis and Palestinians killing each other. I thought maybe I'd go over and see for myself what's going on."

"What are you going to do, Bret, solve their problems all by yourself?"

"Yeah, maybe I will. I'll go over there and bust heads and get them to start getting along."

There were hoots and hollers at that, which caused him to laugh and order another ginger ale from the redheaded, freckle-faced barmaid.

"It wouldn't have anything to do with that lady you squired around town, would it?" Accurso said into Mullin's ear.

"What? Who? Sasha? Don't be stupid, Vinnie, I mean, maybe I'll look her up when I'm there, have her show me around or something. I don't speak Jewish and —"

Heads turned as Chief of Detectives Phil Leshin came through the door. He went directly to Mullin, placed both hands on his shoulders, and said, "You won't believe this, Bret, but I am going to miss you."

"Come on," Mullin said. "You don't have to say that."

"No, I mean it," Leshin said. "But you have to answer one question for me."

"Shoot."

"What got you to finally go to AA?"

"I don't know. I guess I wanted to get sober. It's like, I didn't mind being drunk on the job, but I sure as hell don't want to be drunk in my retirement."

There would be no party this holiday season at one home.

A jogger running through Rock Creek Park on the first day of December stumbled upon a lifeless body, which was partially obscured by brush and low bushes. Chet Fletcher had died of a single gunshot to his right temple. The remaining bullets in the revolver gripped in his right hand matched the shot that had taken his life. His were the only fingerprints on the weapon.

The police thoroughly searched the area surrounding his body and found little in the way of useful evidence — a discarded jogger's shoe, a hiker's map of the park, a ballpoint pen, a discarded fresh Good Humor toasted almond ice cream wrapper, a used condom, an earring of the costume jewelry variety, and a Washington Redskins

T-shirt that had obviously been there for a very long time.

His wife, Gail, told the police that her husband had become increasingly depressed since resigning from his White House position, particularly after rumors found their way into second-tier media that he'd resigned after having ordered the murder of Louis Russo and the killing of Russo's assailant, Leon LeClaire.

"The people circulating these vicious rumors, and the irresponsible media that reported them, killed my husband," Mrs. Fletcher said in the only press conference she gave before packing up their home and moving away. She characterized the city she left behind as "a place where the only thing that matters is personal gain and greed, winning and losing, and where the lives of decent people like my husband mean nothing. He was driven to take his life, and those who drove him to it should rot in hell."

The president called Chet Fletcher a brilliant man, whose contributions to the political process and to the nation were incalculable. "He was my friend," said the president, now about to begin a second term. "I shall miss him, and so shall this wonderful nation. God bless America!"

About the Author

Margaret Truman has won faithful readers with her works of biography and fiction, particularly her ongoing series of Capital Crimes mysteries. Her novels let us into the corridors of power and privilege, poverty and pageantry, in the nation's capital. Her new work of nonfiction is *The President's House*. She lives in Manhattan.

The employees of Thorndike Press hope you have enjoyed this Large Print book. All our Large Print titles are designed for easy reading, and all our books are made to last. Other Thorndike Press Large Print books are available at your library, through selected bookstores, or directly from us.

For information about titles, please call:

(800) 223-1244

or visit our Web site at:

www.gale.com/thorndike

To share your comments, please write:

Publisher
Thorndike Press
295 Kennedy Memorial Drive
Waterville, ME 04901